From the producer of *Wagons West*
and *The Kent Family Chronicles*

A THRILLING NEW ADVENTURE
SET IN THE LANDS AND
TIMES OF LONG AGO . . .

CHILDREN
OF THE LION

A STIRRING SAGA OF
EPIC QUESTS, LEGENDARY LOVERS AND
A DREAM OF POWER AND GLORY!

Enter the world of
The Children of the Lion . . .

THE STORYTELLER
Keeper of the legend of the
Children of the Lion.

ABRAHAM
Born to lead his people to greatness,
ever following the haunting vision of land.

HAGAR
Dark-eyed slavegirl not free to
give her heart; mother of Abraham's
first son, yet an outcast.

SHEPSET
Taken by the pagans of Sodom, she will
sink to the depths of depravity against
her will, until redeemed by one man's love.

BELSUNU
A Babylonian skilled in the arts of
weapon-making who seeks his lost son.

SNEFERU
Hagar's one true love, a war-wise soldier
doomed to share her tragic anguish.

ZAKIR
An artist who loses his art but finds himself.

AHUNI
Lost son of the armorer Belsunu
and marked from birth with the sign
of the Children of the Lion.

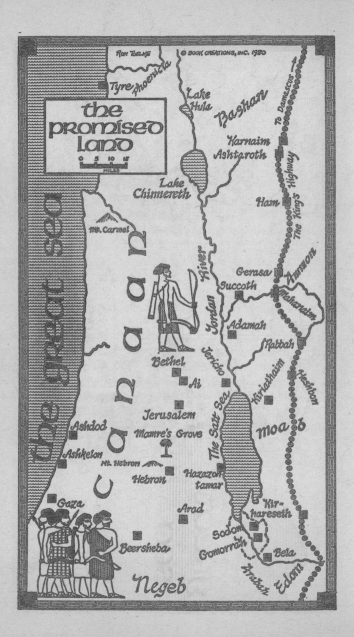

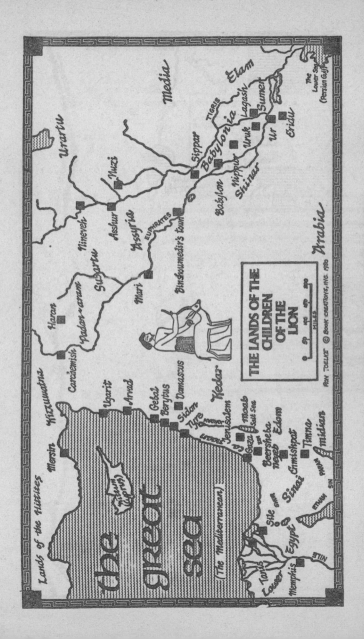

Lands of the Hittites

Media

Urartu

Mersin

Kizzuwatna

Nuzi

Haran

Carchemish

Padan-aram

Subartu

Nineveh

Ashur

Yssyria

TIGRIS

Elam

Lagash

Sumer

Uruk

Nippur

Ur

Eridu

The Lower Sea
(Persian Gulf)

Sippar

Babylonia

Babylon

Shinar

EUPHRATES

Binshumedir's town

Mari

Ugarit

Arvad

Gebal
Berytus

Damascus

Kedar

Sidon

Tyre

Jerusalem

Gaza

Moab

Edom

Beersheba

Negeb

Timna

Salt Sea

Arabia

THE LANDS OF THE
CHILDREN
OF THE
LION

RON TOELKE © BOOK CREATIONS, INC. 1980

0   50   100   150   200

MILES

the
great
sea

(The Mediterranean)

Cyprus
(Alashiya)

Sinai

Ammishpat

Midian

SIN

ETHAM

Sile

Egypt

Memphis

Tanis

Lower

NILE

BOOK I

CHILDREN OF THE LION

PETER DANIELSON

Created by the producers of
Wagons West, White Indian,
Saga of the Southwest, and
The Kent Family Chronicles.

Chairman of the Board: Lyle Kenyon Engel

BANTAM BOOKS
NEW YORK · TORONTO · LONDON · SYDNEY · AUCKLAND

CHILDREN OF THE LION

A Bantam Book / December 1980

Produced by Book Creations, Inc.
Chairman of the Board: Lyle Kenyon Engel

Illustrations by Louis Glanzman

DOMAIN and the portrayal of a boxed "d" are trademarks of Bantam Books,
a division of Bantam Doubleday Dell Publishing Group, Inc.

ISBN 0-553-24448-5

Published simultaneously in the United States and Canada

Bantam Books are published by Bantam Books, a division of Bantam Doubleday Dell
Publishing Group, Inc. Its trademark, consisting of the words "Bantam Books" and the
portrayal of a rooster, is Registered in U.S. Patent and Trademark Office and in other
countries. Marca Registrada. Bantam Books, 666 Fifth Avenue, New York, New York 10103.

PRINTED IN THE UNITED STATES OF AMERICA

RAD   15   14   13   12   11   10   9   8

PROLOGUE

"In the name of God, the merciful, the compassionate . . ."

The Teller of Tales turned and scanned the crowd, his gaze sharp-eyed and piercing, his expression alert as he brought his listeners to attention with the ancient invocation. His first words rang forth in a strong and mellifluous voice that silenced the last murmurs of the crowd. An expectant hush fell upon the audience.

With an enigmatic smile and a wave of his hand, he silenced the last stragglers. His voice pealed forth once again:

"Draw near . . . draw near, O my beloved," he began. "Hear now the tales of old, as your fathers heard them before you and their fathers before them. Gather around me, my children. . . ."

Everyone listened, hanging on each word and every gesture. His hawklike eyes searched their faces one by one. There was a hypnotic, fiery quality to his words.

"Hear now the tales of the Children of the Lion, the men of no nation, and of their ceaseless wanderings among the tribes of men. . . ."

The hush was broken by a low murmur of approval. This was a favorite tale, perhaps the more so for being less frequently told than some others. The Teller of Tales lifted his hands for silence. "Hear of how they met, and joined forces with, the caravans of Abram, the father of nations and the Friend of God, as he came forth from the Land of Goshen into Canaan, to

I

make covenant for his seed forever with El–Shaddai, the One True God. . . ."

His voice quickened, gathering power. "Hear now of Belsunu the Babylonian, the man without a tribe, and of his long search for his lost child. Hear now of Ahuni, the slave, and of his great journey from the Land of the Two Rivers. Hear of Hagar the Egyptian, whose beauty was as the moon's, and of her great love and great loss. Hear of the son she bore unto the Friend of God. . . ."

The rapport between storyteller and listeners was now an unbreakable bond. The words rolled forth easily. It was a new story, an old story; it was all stories in one, perhaps. A tale of hunger and loss and of love sought, lost, and won again. A tale that began as all tales must begin.

Once upon a time, in a land far away . . .

BOOK
ONE

CHAPTER ONE

I

Above, in the cloudless blue sky, the blazing disk of the midafternoon sun beamed malevolently down on the sweating, helmeted forehead of Senmut, governor of the Egyptian king's eastern domains and commander of the frontier fortress of Sile. For perhaps the twentieth time since the great review of troops had begun at his command, he glanced nervously from the corner of one wary eye at the envoy from the royal residence at Lisht, stifling the urge to wipe his steaming face. But, as before, it was in vain, for there was no sign of emotion in that impassive, hawklike profile.

The parade of the border troops was a solemn ceremony. It had been called by the governor to honor the visit of the king's emissary to the easternmost bastion of the Egyptian empire. As such, it could not be interrupted. Even the great Pharaoh Sesostris himself, the Lord of Two Lands, while visiting the frontier outpost a year before, had chosen to watch the entire ritual through, honoring with his presence the brave officers and men who guarded his domain from the attacks of the savage Bedouin of the eastern desert. He had remained in place, striking a decorous pose, until the last soldier had paraded past him. Nor would his minister, Nakhtminou, do less than his king had done.

Senmut breathed a prayer to Horus, guardian of the Sile outpost. The visit had been unheralded; there had barely been time to organize the present ceremony to

5

honor the king's ranking minister in lower Egypt. Why had he come? Why had the purpose of his visit been kept secret throughout the long afternoon's festivities under the scorching heat of the sun? And why, every time he glanced at it, did that flinty face seem even colder and harder than ever?

Biting his lip, Senmut watched as his soldiers, in the court below, celebrated the ritual of receiving arms from the House of Weapons. Twenty archers, just now, were doing the war dance of the Maaziou Bedouins as their comrades marked their jerky, repetitive movements by clapping their hands or striking two throwing sticks together. The archers sprang high as they went through the motions of brandishing their bows, placing them on the ground, and picking them up again. Each of these actions was punctuated with shrill cries.

Then came the chariots: Their frames of wood and leather poised on six-spoked wheels that rotated around acacia wood axles, sparsely ornamented with bronze and light enough to be carried on a single man's shoulders or drawn with lightning swiftness across a battlefield behind two wild-eyed stallions. After these came the light infantry, each soldier bareheaded, with neither apron nor shield, bearing his bow in his left hand and in his right either an axe, throwing sticks, or guidon, according to his rank. The unit's officer paraded proudly past, carrying only a commander's baton.

"You are wondering why I am here," uttered the rasping voice of Nakhtminou.

Senmut, taken completely by surprise, turned and gaped at the emissary standing beside him. "My lord?" he said hoarsely.

"Eyes front," the minister said dryly. "We owe the rabble decorum. It is expected. It is small enough a price to pay for the honor of commanding so . . . ah . . . prestigious a station." The irony in his speech was a cubit thick. Sile, a command whose military complement was filled out with lop-nosed convicts, the dregs of the empire, was one of the least desirable posts in the Civil Service. "The punishment of the Two Lands," an earlier overseer had called it, and indeed it was a place where one's only company was the gnat at sunset and the midge at noon.

Senmut came back to attention. "My lord?" he said again, a feigned confidence in his voice.

"You are wondering why I came," Nakhtminou said. "You do well to wonder. You would also do well to have your affairs in order."

Senmut's heart skipped a beat or two. "M-my affairs in . . . ?" he said, his words trailing off tremulously.

"Oh, well," Nakhtminou said in a voice heavy with sarcasm. "I could of course read you the proclamation, or have it read to you. 'Horus, life of births, lord of the crowns, king of Upper and Lower Egypt, Sesostris, son of the Sun, Amenemhet, ever-living unto eternity. Order for the follower Senmut. Behold, this order of the king is sent to thee to instruct thee of his will. . . .'" The speaker's words, which had been delivered in a singsong voice, suddenly stopped. His eyes were still absently trained on the marching troops below. Senmut, by now very frightened, swallowed hard and listened as the king's minister resumed. "Well, you know the format. I don't have to recite it to you. But let me tell you, my friend, the important thing is that your career is hanging by a single thread—and perhaps your life as well."

Senmut's hands gripped the railing before him. His head was swimming. He felt faint. "M-my life, my lord? But . . ."

"Oh?" Nakhtminou's tone had turned supercilious. "Surely you know what you've done?" he said incredulously. "By the gods, man! Let us not insult one another's intelligence."

"Is it . . . is it something about the renegade Sanehat? The one who lived abroad and then came back asking for repatriation? I . . . I'm sure I did everything I could. I even uncovered treason by my questioning of him. As a result, a ranking official of my court is under house arrest, under suspicion of having had illegal correspondence with dissident forces beyond the frontier."

Nakhtminou's answer was a snort of derision. "Foolery!" he said. "Do me a favor of not wasting my time with nonsense." His brown fingers tapped on the railing impatiently. "Surely you . . ."

But then something occurred to him, and now for the first time he broke his iron decorum, looking with incredulity at Senmut. "Can it be? Can it be that you *don't* know?" The thin lips turned down at the corners in disbelief. "Your hide is all but skinned and tanned. You are one step ahead of the bastinado or worse. Yet you mean to tell me . . . ?" The frown turned into a lopsided, unpleasant grin.

Senmut, not daring to look away from the parade below, said in a broken voice, "I . . . I have no idea. I have done nothing wrong. I . . ." He swallowed hard. "Please," he said. "Please tell me."

Nakhtminou's laugh was short and harsh. "By the gods," he said again. "By the gods, what a nurseling babe." He looked back at the scene below the reviewing stand. "Look here, you'd better pay attention. The parade's over. Here come the officers to salute us. Here, look sharp." His own spine stiffened; he stood erect and alert, nodding his head in approval as he received the homage of the garrison's officers and standard-bearers. Senmut followed suit, hiding as best he could the misery that was in his heart.

When the call to disperse had been relayed to the troops, Nakhtminou turned to Senmut, his powerful arms folded over his naked chest, his hawk's eyes boring into the garrison commander's very soul. "Look," he said, a touch of solicitude creeping into his voice. "That rich Mesopotamian herdsman of yours. The one you had working over at Tanis with his tribe and his retainers during the famine?"

"Y-yes," Senmut said, not understanding. "I know the one. His name is Abram, I believe. He and his people are living near Tanis now."

"Send a runner for him in a hurry, man, if you value your life. Send him with orders to bring the Mesopotamian back here, alive and well, in all possible haste. But for the love of all the gods, man, handle him with care!"

"Why, of course. Of course. But . . . why?"

Nakhtminou let his breath out in a disgusted sigh. "Because you've offended him, curse you for a fool! Haven't you learned by now to find out something about a stranger before taking the chance of offending him?"

"I . . . I don't understand," Senmut said, terrified. "What . . . who is he, anyhow?"

Nakhtminou, his eyes narrowed to slits in his brown face, leaned forward. "Fool! Worse than fool!" he said. "The man's a sorcerer, that's what! And here you've sent one of his wives to Lisht to take her place in the royal harem, and . . ."

"W-wives?" Senmut said, stunned. "But . . . I was told she was his sister. I had no idea . . ."

"Fool! Thrice fool! Don't you know 'sister' means 'cousin' among these people? Don't you know they marry their cousins? Don't you realize what you have done? Without inquiring, without thinking, you sent your retainers in the dead of night to haul the woman away and ship her upstream to share a dishonored bed with the Lord of Two Lands?"

Senmut trembled with fear. His superior was clearly beside himself with rage. Worst of all, the fierce dressing-down he was taking was being witnessed by half the officers in his own personal guard. "I . . . how could I have known?" he said weakly.

"Bah!" Nakhtminou said. "Well, it can't be undone. But we have to minimize our losses, whatever happens. The woman is being brought back. The important thing now is to get that Mesopotamian bumpkin down here in a hurry and see what we can do to placate him—and get him to lift the spell."

"Spell?" Senmut said. "What spell?"

Nakhtminou had half-turned as if to go. Now he faced his subordinate once again, and his words came out in a rasping monotone. "The one on your master and mine, you idiot," he said. "The Lord of Two Lands . . . this Mesopotamian sorcerer has struck him blind."

II

The moment Hagar entered the garden her spirits began to rise again. It had that effect on her, usually, and now she did not regret having come this way. The heat was dry and blistering in the afternoon; only in the garden, with its shallow rectangular lotus pool, could a spot of cool shade be found. Her eyes, previously somber, brightened at the sight of the reflecting pool bordered by oleander, jasmine, mandrake, and dwarf crysanthemums. Its tranquil depths mirrored the blue sky. She paused in the shade of a spreading fig tree to look at the reflections of the gaily colored flowers.

It was a lovely sight, but it was not enough to quell the dream that had haunted her throughout that long day of work and preparation. The mournful expression returned to her large brown eyes.

It was a festival day, but she did not feel in the least festive. Instead, she felt a sense of foreboding, almost of approaching doom.

Was it in fact a prophetic dream that she had had? That horrid dream of loss, of disinheritance, of being driven out into the desert to die? The fearful images had remained in her mind long after she had awakened—the vultures, the endless salt flat vistas, and with them the sudden and certain knowledge that she had been abandoned to her death.

Suddenly feeling chilled in the shade, Hagar hugged her bare arms to her body. What, after all, did it mean? The thought of seeing a soothsayer in the village, of asking his opinion, went swiftly through her head and was as swiftly banished. She had no wish to provoke answers to questions that were more than she could fathom.

Why should she have had this dream that seemed to

betoken beggary, loss, and death? For of all the household retainers in Sile and its domains, who enjoyed a more secure position than she? To be sure, she was technically a slave—but she was the slave of Psarou, a rich scribe and a man of uncommon kindness and generosity. She enjoyed a status that was more privileged in some respects than that of many a wife. As head of Psarou's household in all but title, she wielded considerable power. Psarou leaned on her, depended on her. If it had not been for his age—which precluded his using her or the other women of the harem for sexual gratification—she was sure he would have freed her and taken her as principal wife some years before.

Her present position was far more than anything she had dreamed of as a child, and her future prospects were secure. Psarou had hinted on many occasions that she would not only be freed upon his death but well provided for. He would instruct his executors to take a hand in arranging a decent marriage for her and providing her with a small dowry.

So why did she now dream of disinheritance, dispersal, poverty, death?

She shivered again and, turning, saw on the stone wall behind her the girl, Shepset, standing and staring at her, too shy for the moment to speak.

Hagar smiled in spite of herself. The child was so inexpressibly lovely! "Shepset," she said. "Come and join me by the pool."

The girl's mouth opened in a tentative smile. "I . . . yes . . . thank you, my lady." And she tripped lightly down the stairs on tiny bare feet.

Hagar watched her come. Shepset, slim as a reed, her little breasts hardly more than buds, had drawn the duty of servant girl for the evening's festival gathering of Psarou's household. She was exquisitely coiffed for the event, and her fresh young face was carefully, if lightly, made up. She wore a necklace of tubes of colored faience and a single strand of beads that hung low on her slim hips. Otherwise she wore nothing at all.

Hagar's eyes ran up and down the girl's narrow

brown body, pausing at the flat belly with its patch of soft black hair. "Ah," she said aloud. "To be so young and slim! How many years has it been since I could venture forth naked at a festival without worrying about a blemish here, a touch of fat there."

Shepset smiled again, blushing. "My lady is too kind," she said. "I . . . has my lady work for me to do? If . . ."

"No, no," Hagar said. "I was just admiring you, child. Once I looked much as you do. Not too many years ago, either! Hagar was twenty-four—twice Shepset's age—and although very beautiful, no longer young by Egyptian standards. "Here," she said. "Let me straighten your hair." And with nimble hands, she rearranged the girl's blue-dyed and heavily oiled hair until it hung in fine tresses that reached almost to the ground. "There. You look a positive delight. My lord will be pleased."

"Thank you, my lady. Is . . . is there something wrong? I mean . . . you look . . ."

"I look sad," Hagar said. She straightened the faience collar and stepped back to look the girl over. "I had a bad dream, no more. It has been bothering me all day. I am perhaps foolish to think of it."

"My lady is not foolish," the girl said. "May I do my lady some service?" Hagar looked at the delicate face with its clear green eyes, ringed, as hers were, with black. There was such obvious sincerity in the girl's concern that she reached out and put one reassuring hand on the child's bare shoulder.

"No," Hagar said in a weary voice. "No, thank you. It is just that . . . I do not dream much. And for my dream to be so . . . so specific . . ." Her words broke off short.

"Ramisou, the astrologer, speaks of an unfavorable conjunction," the girl said helpfully. "If . . ."

Hagar shook her head and looked down at the shallow water before her, at their two pairs of feet, hers sandaled, the girl's bare, standing at the water's edge. "Shepset," she said, hugging her arms again. "I was not born into a noble house like this one. I was a workman's child, the daughter of a sandalmaker, a poor one. I helped my father in his shop. I ..." She held out her brown hands now, smiling humorlessly down at them. "These hands held the sole while my father cut its pattern. I pulled the thong tight with my baby teeth." She extended a brown foot in its expensive leather, turning it this way and that. "As a girl I could not afford my own father's shoes. I walked on reed soles even on festival days. Psarou saw me in the marketplace and bought me from my father. I was ... oh, your age, perhaps."

"Yes, my lady?" The girl kept her answers neutral, not wishing to interrupt the train of thought. "Surely you were far more beautiful than I could ever—"

"I was beautiful," Hagar said. Her tone was soft, vulnerable, reminiscent. "Else Psarou would not have seen me, noticed me, taken me away to live with him, to join his household. Oh, mind you, he was old even then. I think that he seldom visited the women's rooms for love. And never did he visit me. Can you believe it, child, I am now as virginal as you?" She brushed away the girl's reply. "Yet it has been a good life. I could not have asked for more. I am happy, comfortable, respected ..." She let her words trail away, the mournful expression returning to her eyes. "If I were to lose that now—"

"My lady?"

Hagar turned to look at the girl again. The eyes were wide-set, compassionate. And suddenly she found herself telling the child her dream, in broken, halting phrases: the loss, the rags, the banishment ... the harsh, forbidding desert before her, the ugly red skulls of the vultures, the shimmering wastes sloping off into the horizon. She found herself weeping beyond all control, hugging the girl's bare body to her own for comfort. "I ... I tried to go back to sleep. But every time I closed my eyes, I would see it again ... trackless desert, a burning sun, just rocks and sand and low shrubs with sharp spines."

Then suddenly she felt the cold chill inside her heart, and she stepped back out of the girl's slim, comforting arms, holding her at arm's length. "I ... I'm sorry, child. By the gods, I must look a mess." She tried to smile, blinking back the hot tears. "Here," she said. "Come and help me repair my face. Will you? I can use some company just now. Here, your legs are dusty. I'll sponge you off . . . and I have a bracelet which should look lovely against that wonderful skin of yours. You can wear it tonight, at the gathering."

Shepset smiled, not quite sure what to make of the familiarity of her mistress. "As my lady wishes," the girl said. Her eyes sought out Hagar's tearstained face, with its smeared eye makeup, and her brown hand reached out to wipe a tear from her cheek. "Now, will my lady come inside to the women's rooms? Here, now." Her eyes on Hagar's stricken face, the girl gently guided her up the stone stairs into the main house of Psarou's villa. Outside, the sun had begun to sink, and a late afternoon breeze stirred the air.

III

"In the name of the gods, stop fidgeting," Nakhtminou said, nimbly sidestepping a puddle of slops in the gutter. Senmut, hurrying to keep pace with the king's minister, followed him miserably through the narrow streets of Sile. Why, he was thinking, why did they have to go through the poorer quarter just now? It was bad enough that Nakhtminou's surprise visit had caught him just before the scheduled biennial white-washing of the city walls and the public buildings. Even in the best of times, though, no administrator could cut much of a figure showing off the native quarter of an impecunious backwater town like Sile.

No wonder, then, that he was nervous. The terrible news Nakhtminou had brought down from Lisht was guaranteed to spoil any man's innards. There was nothing in the world he needed so much just now as a strong drink, but how could he indulge this impulse under the eye of the king's terrible minister, who hardly opened his mouth other than to chide him for something?

But Nakhtminou was pushing forward again, faster than ever, leaving the slums behind, passing a confectioner's stall, a leatherworker's shop . . . gods! He was actually heading for a tavern! A beer-house! His heart pounding, Senmut hurried after him, praying to the gods to let his choice fall upon one of the more decorous establishments.

But there! He was entering Motour's shop, the Star of Horus, named after the fine premium wine Motour imported from upriver for the upper classes of Sile. That was a good sign; little need happen in the Star of Horus to embarrass him. And . . . and what was this? Nakhtminou and Motour were embracing each other like brothers! Puzzled, Senmut hurried through the door into the reception room, with its mats, stools, and armchairs and its rows of large amphorae stacked against the walls.

". . . Motour, you old devil," Nakhtminou was saying, an unaccustomed smile on his hawklike face. "You've grown fat as an ox! I'll bet you're your own best customer." He clapped the heavyset innkeeper affectionately on the bicep and sat down in one of the chairs in the middle of the room. Already the other drinkers had begun to make room for this obviously important personage; their haste to seek the far corners of the room increased as the more familiar Senmut came through the door. "Senmut," the king's emissary said. "This is my old orderly, from the days of the Nubian campaigns." He looked up with great regard at the beaming proprietor. "Here, what do we . . . oh, sit down, Senmut! What do we have to drink, now?"

"Well, Captain," Motour said. "We have wines of Syena, of the Oasis, wine of Bouto—"

"Wine? What need have we of wine?" Nakhtminou bellowed. Senmut stared at him open-mouthed. He was a changed man. "Bring us beer! Beer is a soldier's drink."

"Splendid, Captain. What kind? Sparkling beer? Lupine beer? Spiced beer?"

"Hmmm. Do you remember that thick, strong millet

beer the blacks make, up above the fourth cataract?"

"Yes, sir! And it just so happens——"

"Well, don't stand there, man! Bring us a couple of jars of that! And quickly, too! I have a thirst!"

Senmut sat back in his chair, speechless. Nakhtminou was a man of surprises, all right! Maybe things wouldn't go so badly after all.

Dusk came and went. So did three jars apiece of the thick, sticky Nubian beer. Senmut, rising to relieve himself, found his legs shaking beneath him and decided to put the matter off for a few minutes. He shook his head, trying to clear it. Nakhtminou was talking as familiarly to Motour, who had joined them at the table, as to an equal.

So far it had been mostly soldier chitchat, centering on old campaigns, old hardships, old whores. Suddenly he found himself listening more attentively: ". . . this damned fool here lets his overseer kidnap the wife of a sorcerer from . . . oh, wherever the devil it is, over on the Euphrates, half the way to the end of the world. And what happens? I'm sent down by the court to take away the spell. . . ."

"Look here," Senmut found himself saying. "That was no fault of mine. I've sent men out in chariots to bring the Mesopotamian back as fast as possible. What else can I do? I mean, I ask you. . . ." He stopped. His words were coming out slurred. He sounded like a drunken fool.

Nakhtminou, however, was feeling mellow and tolerant. He almost smiled as he spoke. "Well," he said, "since you asked, I'll tell you what I'd do if I were in your place. I'd start casting about me for some nice rich bribes for the Mesopotamian. I'd think long and hard about that—but I'd think fast. And mind you, I'd make sure I didn't bribe him with land—or with anything that would give him reason to stay around in the emperor's territories! Not if he can bewitch a man a dozen days' march away from him." He examined his cup and found it empty. "Here, Motour! We're dry and thirsty again."

Senmut sat back and regarded him. "I'm listening," he said. "Bribes?"

"Yes. Oh, yes, in the name of the gods! Cattle, asses, chattels, movables, slaves. Women. Lots of women. Anything in the world but land." He frowned. "Unless . . ."

"Yes?" Senmut leaned forward, suddenly sober.

"You said sometime back that the Mesopotamian passed through the northern territories we administer? The land south of the Hittites' domain? The . . . what's the name? Canaan?"

"Yes. He had some story about this god of his telling him the land would be given to him and his descendants." He laughed derisively. "Frankly, I didn't take the man seriously. He's no young man, for all his vigor. And they say he has no children. Yet here he was, talking about his 'seed,' his descendants."

"Yes. But fool or no, he has a certain power which we must neutralize and remove from the delta lands forever."

"And . . . without violence. Without offending him."

"Yes. For the love of all the gods . . . he may not be the only sorcerer of his party." Nakhtminou frowned again. "I forgot to ask. How big is his party, anyhow?"

"I told you. He's an uncommonly rich sort of Bedouin. He has——"

"He's no Bedouin for all his nomadic habits. But go on."

"Well . . . I can show you the reckoning. But I remember there were over three hundred in his party, all of his kin or servants of his kin."

"And, I suppose, herds to match? All that sort of thing?"

"Yes. He is, in a word, consuming all that is in our storehouses."

"All the more reason to . . ." Nakhtminou looked up at the tray Motour was handing down to them. "Ah, thank you! Thank you, my friend . . . although, in the best of worlds, I *should* stop right here, shouldn't I? What is the proverb? 'He that abandons himself to drink is like an oar broken from its fastening, which no longer obeys on either side. . . .' How does the rest of that go, now?"

" 'He is like a chapel without its god, like a house without bread, in which the wall is wavering and the beam shaking,' " completed Senmut. "You were saying . . . about the Mesopotamian. . . ."

"Oh, yes." Nakhtminou drank deep and wiped his mouth with the back of his hand. "Give him the land. The land."

"But I thought you said *not* to give him any land. I mean, after all we're trying to get him to leave, once he has taken this spell off our lord and master."

"Not *our* land, you fool! Land in Canaan! Land far to the north of here. Land which he will then be eager to occupy, the more so since this provincial god of his has promised it to him already. Him and his 'seed.' " He belched and chuckled appreciatively.

"By all the gods!" Senmut said, taken aback. "Now I see why I am the small-time administrator and you are the Great King's personal emissary. I—"

"Never mind the flattery," Nakhtminou said. He belched again. "No, go ahead. Flatter me all you wish. One never gets quite enough flattery. Let me tell you, you get precious little of it at all at Lisht or Memphis."

"It's brilliant!" Senmut said. "Load him down with chattels, asses, oxen, whatever. Slaves, women, everything portable. Then give him this wretched land of his up north. Tell him it's his. And then let him head up there and try to pry it loose from the Canaanites. By the gods! They'll pick him clean."

"I have no doubt. Unless he can cast a spell on them."

"It's brilliant." Senmut reached for the new jar, filled his cup, and drank deeply.

"Well, that's what I'm paid for," Nakhtminou said. "To *be* brilliant. To bail the Lord of Two Lands out of the trouble you minor functionaries land him in. No offense, now; don't get your back up like a house cat. You know what I mean. There is a problem, after all. There's no denying that. God knows, the poor man is miserable. You'd be, too. He's—"

"Is he really blind?"

"Completely and totally. Can't see the hand in front of his face. Can't tell whether it's night or day. Can't—"

"And you're sure it's witchcraft?"

"I . . . let me put it another way. I don't believe in spells and such things. But what the Lord of Two Lands believes in, I have learned I'd better believe in. And he believes fervently that this man has bewitched him. Perhaps the woman told him so. What's her name again?"

"Sarai."

"That's right. Anyhow, as long as he believes this man has struck him blind—"

"You mean the surgeons can't find anything wrong?"

"Exactly. Suggestion, I say. The power of suggestion. The woman has told him her husband is a powerful sorcerer who has put a spell upon him. Well, she seems to be something out of the ordinary herself. His cousin, you know, and he's the son of one of these Mesopotamian patriarchs, a man named Terah.

"For some reason they'd all been living in Haran, up north. It appears this dismal god of theirs spoke to the old man too. Made him leave Ur with all his quite considerable entourage."

Nakhtminou nodded and drank again. "Well. I told you I don't believe in spells, and that's true most of the time. But, as I say, I spent my time up the river with the Nubian campaign for a while, and . . . well, I've seen some things I can't account for. Magic. That sort of thing. The blacks up there, they have some tricks that can drive a man crazy. Eh, Motour?"

The innkeeper, at his elbow, nodded. "My friend Ani, a sutler with the fourth troop, cheated one of the blacks at barter. He died horribly, and no one laid a finger on him. I can swear to that. He strangled to death. Swore up and down that there was a cord around his neck, choking him. Nobody could find a thing. But he died all the same, sir."

"There. You see? Best to get rid of the man and all of his tribe. Bribe him. Bribe him first with what you have, then with what you don't have. Give him a freehold in Canaan, in the name of the Lord of Two Lands. And then let him go up and try to grab it—and get butchered."

"Brilliant. I congratulate you." Senmut drank, then frowned. "Chattels and movables, eh? I wonder what I can find in a hurry?"

Nakhtminou drained his cup and put it down carefully. "I'm sure you'll think of something," he said.

IV

As the last rays of sunshine faded in the west over the delta marshland, Ennana, courier to the king's overseer, found the deep ruts in the baked road harder and harder to negotiate. He pulled gently on the leather reins and slowed the twin stallions to a brisk trot.

Suddenly, as the road left the levee and wound its way down to the protected lowlands, the ground underfoot grew softer. Solicitous of the horses, Ennana checked their speed again, bringing them down to a walk. The road, no longer rutted, wound underneath overarching palms below the level of the high breakwater where fog had already begun to gather. The courier shivered, feeling the goose bumps breaking out on his bare chest. This damned delta weather! One minute burning you black with its pitiless sun, the next freezing your behind.

The dark came quickly. Dusk lasted no more than a few minutes, the time it took to count to a thousand. For a while, the sky retained a vestige of its luminosity; then, as suddenly as if someone had blown out the last candle in a dark room, the fog swept over everything, making it impossible to see. Halting the horses, Ennana dismounted to hold the near horse by its harness and painstakingly search the ground ahead of him for signs of the trail.

Another, much deeper, shiver ran through him. He

was thoroughly lost in this gloom—and even if he were to retrace his steps and regain the high ground, up above the fog, there was little chance that he could find his destination.

He sighed. "Horse," he said to the tall steed beside him, "I hope you have some idea how to get there. Because, by all the gods, I don't."

It was a problem, all right. Just going back to Senmut, frightened and nervous as he was, and explaining that you hadn't made it to the Mesopotamian's camp by nightfall because you'd stopped at a tavern for a quick bracer and a couple of moments' conversation with a serving wench who . . .

He shuddered again. No, that wouldn't do. That wouldn't do at all.

And now even the dense, thick-as-Nile-water fog seemed to lose its semiluminosity, and it was pitch darkness all around him. He stepped out before the lead horse and peered into the dark.

There! What was that?

Far in the distance a fire seemed to be glowing. No; not one. Several. Several dim patches of color.

As he watched, they fanned out around him. He swiveled, watching the dim fires ring him round until he stood in the middle of a broad circle of fog-blurred lights, each stationed well back from him, the person or persons who manned each light still quite invisible.

Suddenly he felt a sharp pain in his ribs!

His hand flew to his chest. He stepped back, reaching out with his other hand to grasp the long-shafted pike that had pinked him so neatly. His hand slipped down the long blade as it pulled away from him. Ah . . . a Babylonian pike? His hand felt the thin trickle of blood on his chest. A flesh wound, nothing serious—but it certainly had frightened him.

"W-who's there?" he managed to ask, wishing he hadn't unbuckled his short sword and hung it over the frame of the chariot on the way over from Sile.

A deep voice came back at him from inside the ring of fires. The owner of the voice was quite invisible. How far away, though? Eight paces, perhaps ten?

"Who is *there?*" the voice said in passable, but heavily accented, Egyptian. "It is for us to ask, you to answer." And to make things a bit clearer, another of the pikes poked painfully at his naked back.

"I . . . I am the messenger of the lord Senmut, overseer of the fortress at Sile. I . . ." He let the words trail off. His eyes peered through the gloom at the ring of lights. There! Some vague form had passed in front of one of the torches. He could dimly, and for no more than the blinking of an eye, make out a human form, perhaps halfway back to the row of lights.

"Yes?" the patient voice said. "You have been observed for quite some time now, since before you left the high road that runs along the canal." The voice hesitated for a moment, as if its owner were thinking.

"Well? I am waiting to hear your business."

Ennana tried to speak and found his throat was dry. He coughed, swallowed, and tried again. "I . . . I have a message for . . ." Damn it! What was the tribal leader's name anyhow? This was no time to go forgetting it! ". . . for the Mesopotamian . . . Abram."

There! Now if only . . .

"What manner of message?" the voice barked out. "Give me the message. I will deliver it." The tone was harsh and abrupt.

Ennana swallowed again and screwed up his courage. Here, now! He had to put a good face on things. And if they thought he was going to deliver a message this way, a message from the personally appointed overseer of the Lord of Two Lands . . . "I . . . my message is for the ears of the Mesopotamian, Abram, alone." He hoped he'd pronounced the name properly. "From . . . from the Lord of Two Lands."

The pike poked him in the back again; it was all he could do not to cry out this time. "There is only one land, Egyptian," the voice said, "and there is only one Lord of it. And that Lord is not some spindly-legged, ill-bred dog of a Pharaoh who mates with his sisters and besmirches the good name of women who—"

The man's voice broke off so sharply that Ennana strained to hear more. Then, just as he was about to speak out, the voice came up again. This time there was a softer note in it. "My lord Abram will meet with you and hear your message."

"I am grateful," Ennana said. "If—"

"My lord Abram asks whether you have eaten. If you have not, he will be pleased to have you join him in his tent." The voice, this time, was thoroughly cordial.

"I . . . I will be honored," said Ennana, remembering the gravity of his commission, the necessity for observing the rules of protocol.

"My lord is pleased," the voice said, drawing nearer. "Come with me."

V

The music had a delicate clangor; soft, insistent, and soothing at one and the same time. The six girls stood a little bit apart from the guests who had been assembled to share the hospitality of Psarou and his household. They were barefoot with long white robes that left one breast exposed. Four played on lyre, lute, harp, and double reed pipe while the remaining two banged tiny tambourines and alternately danced and sang. Conversation rose up against the soft background of the instruments and from the warm pools of light below the torches.

Shepset, happy and enthusiastic, circulated among the guests and her fellow servants with a little bowl of ripe figs, offering it to whomever she passed, smiling silently. The tiles of the floor were cool against her bare soles, and the soft night air was a balm to her naked body. She wore only a string of multicolored beads and the beautiful bracelet that Hagar had given her. The air was so cool that the tiny cone of perfumed fat she wore atop her elaborate headdress had not yet melted to spread its delicate scent down her tanned young body.

For virtually the first time in her young life, Shepset felt acutely aware of her nakedness. Raised like the daughter of a noble family by the protective Psarou, she had never felt herself a slave, never felt anything demeaning in having others choose what she was to wear. And nudity, in her childhood, had always been a matter of simple comfort, a totally natural state in good weather.

But now it seemed different, somehow. For one thing, she had been chosen to play the role of a serving girl at Psarou's festive gathering because of her extraordinary, though still unripe, beauty. The other girls, those now circulating at the far sides of the room, were used to the attention they received. They had come into their growth some time ago, and their bodies had long been on display. But this was the first time that Shepset had been selected for such an honor in Psarou's household. It filled her with pride and made her all the more radiant—so that when the eyes of the guests ran up and down her body casually, they always returned to her face, and the smiles their own faces bore showed their delight and appreciation.

There was one pair of eyes that lingered on her young frame for a longer period of time and that looked into her own with a smile that was less simple than those of the other guests. Ankh-ren, son of the rich merchant Senbef, stared penetratingly into her eyes when she offered him the fruits from her bowl. His eyes locked into her own and would not let them go for the space of several long breaths. His smile was not a neutral one; and when his eyes ran over her breasts and her belly, her face grew flushed. It was unsettling. She resented it. And yet . . .

What was this? Did it have something to do with what the older girls had told her of the way men and women were when they . . . ? The thought made her purse her lips and knit her unlined young brow. And a soft shudder of . . . of something new, whatever it was . . . ran through her body, and her skin broke out in goose pimples.

"Figs, my lord? Fresh figs, my lady?" *Keep busy,* she told herself. *Don't think too hard about it! . . .*

When the bowl was empty, she went back to replenish her supply. Katsenut, the fat household cook, took the vessel from her and refilled it. "Here," she said. "Stay a moment." And, going to the large table behind her, she came back with a heavy, jeweled metal cup. Into this she poured red wine from an amphora.

"Here, child," she said. "Your first glass of wine. You're an adult now. Drink it."

Shepset lifted the glass but did not bring it to her lips at first. She looked thoughtfully, perhaps a little sadly, at Katsenut. "Adult," she said. "I . . . I don't know what I think about that. It's a little frightening, perhaps."

Katsenut smiled understandingly. "Ah, yes. I can remember that feeling all right. You're not sure where you stand, and not sure if what you're losing is equal to what you may be gaining. You have all the disadvantages of adulthood, and you don't yet know what the advantages are. Drink up, my dear."

Shepset remained holding the cup. "A man . . . a young man . . . he looked at me just now. He . . . looked at me. It was . . . different. I mean, he . . ."

"Ah," Katsenut said. "So that's the way it is, is it?" She leaned back against the edge of the cold stove. "Well, it's about time. Relax and enjoy it, my dear. You won't look like that forever. The time to worry is when they stop looking at you like that."

"It was as if . . . as if he owned me, possessed me. I felt . . . I don't know what it was that I felt. But I suddenly felt as though . . . well, I wanted to go put on my long dress and cover myself up. Especially . . ." She looked down at the wine but did not drink it. Unconsciously one young hand cupped one of the little breasts. "But on the other hand it felt . . . well, good. But frightening, too."

"Ah," Katsenut said. "Well, the other girls have

things in hand, I suppose. Look, take a few moments off. Take your wine out on the porch and drink it. Come back when you're done . . . and don't misplace the cup, for the love of all the gods! But go. Drink the wine. And good health to you. . . ."

On the porch the air was deliciously cool. Shepset looked out over the pool where a pale moon lay reflected in the shallow water. And she took the first sip of her wine, letting it roll around in her mouth before swallowing it cautiously. There! It wasn't bad. It was . . . She took another sip and liked it even better.

Suddenly soft voices cut into her consciousness; voices coming closer. A man . . . a woman. Psarou! And here she was drinking wine when she should be . . .

Clutching the cup close between her young breasts, she flattened herself against the wall behind a column. Oh, if only they wouldn't come this way! If only . . .

". . . wanted to come talk with you," Psarou's aged, quivering voice said, "because there are plans I have made which I must tell you about."

"My lord?" the woman's voice said, low and husky. It was Hagar's voice.

"Yes, my dear. You know . . . I've had a long and in many ways a very happy life. You know, of course, that I began as you are, as a slave."

"Yes, my lord. But . . . if it please my lord, I do not feel a slave. You have never made me feel a slave."

"Ah," the old man's voice said. "That was something I learned from my second master. The first was . . . well, better leave him to the gods of the underworld. He's passed on, poor man, for all his faults. But my second master was . . . ah, Hagar, my child, he was like a father to me. Like a god too, in some ways, for all that I fear blasphemy. He taught me much, I mean even beyond the business of raising me and giving me an education as a scribe, to which I owe everything I have. He taught me to value people, large and small. He taught me that the slave who feels a slave will not work as hard for you as the one who feels himself a respected and valued servant."

"My lord," Hagar said with obvious affection, "you have seldom if ever allowed me to feel myself a servant."

"Thank you, child." The old man's voice softened. "My master wrote up the manumission documents for me himself. Things were simpler then. You didn't have to register the matter with the government before it was valid. Now, with everything in the hands of functionaries who give the profession of scribe a bad name . . ." He chuckled. "But I digress. I was going to announce tonight, at the end of the party, that I have given orders that documents of emancipation be drawn up at the beginning of next week. All of you, all the members of my household, are to be freed."

"My lord!"

Behind them, in the darkness, Shepset's sharp intake of breath echoed Hagar's surprise. She almost dropped the cup. All of them! *Why . . . why, that means me! Me, too!* she thought.

"Yes, my dear," the old man went on patiently. "All of you. I think everyone will be pleased when I announce it. Perhaps the women as much as anyone. I have . . . well, I will likely be able to arrange marriages for some of them. The merchant Senbef, for instance. He's looking for a woman for his son, to settle him down. Perhaps you could advise me in this. There are several young women his age. I noticed him looking with favor on one of the serving girls tonight."

"Shepset, I think," Hagar said. "But . . . this is so sudden."

"Yes, it is," Psarou said. "But you know, my dear, I haven't been feeling well lately, and I'm getting old. I'm ten summers older than my master was when he died. And . . . well, there have been accusations bandied about by certain persons. . . . Senmut has placed me under the equivalent of house arrest. I must get his permission to travel anywhere, even up the river to the court to defend myself against my accusers. Under the circumstances, it seemed imperative for me to make some provision for you, my household, in case . . . in case things go badly with me as a result of these accusations."

"My lord! But who would accuse you?"

"It doesn't matter. Disgruntled business associates whom I've bested in trade, perhaps. The main thing is that I protect myself—and, more importantly, that I protect the lot of you. And . . . Hagar, my child, I took you aside separately to tell you what plans I have made for you."

"For me, my lord?"

"Yes, my dear." The old man's tone was as strong and fatherly as his voice was weak. "You have in many ways been a model administrator of my household. If I had been younger, I would have felt the greatest honor in unhesitatingly taking you to wife. As it is, I should have freed you years ago. You would have held an enviable status in our community by now if I had. But I was a fool, and kept putting things off."

"Oh, my lord. I am honored. But do not call yourself a fool."

"I am only saying of myself what I would say of another who did the same things. It is a deserved epithet. But I can rectify my oversight in part. Hagar, my dear, I am not only freeing you, I am making you the mistress of my villa at Tanis and deeding over to you the rents on the rich delta lands two days' ride in width. A week or so from today you will be one of the richest women in Lower Egypt." His voice took on a humorous, half-bantering tone. "I thought of finding you a husband myself . . . but if I make you a rich woman with a fabulous dowry, you can take your time and make your own choice. Because with your beauty, and with the money I'm bestowing on you, you can be sure you'll have every eligible male north of Memphis itself down here besieging you." His voice changed its tone again. "Here, what's all this? I thought I was making you happy."

Shepset, her hand over her wildly beating heart, listened as Hagar sobbed softly. "I . . . my lord . . . I had no idea . . . I had no thoughts of ever . . ."

"No, no," the old man said, his voice rich and kind. "I understand. When my master freed me and paid my way through the scribes' examinations, I could not believe it either. And when he made me, whom he had previously owned, first his overseer and then his partner . . . well, I understand. But you'd better get used to the idea, my dear. Ah, look. You've spoiled your eye makeup. Better go fix things up a bit. We have to get back inside to our guests. And"—his tone changed yet one more time, and suddenly the voice sounded young and strong again for a moment—"I have an announcement to make. A very happy sort of announcement."

VI

Shepset hardly dared to breathe until Psarou had stepped inside the great door of the house. For a moment afterward, catching her breath, she stood leaning against the cool marble of the building, her face flushed with excitement and anxiety.

Freed! And with . . . with plans for marriage being made.

She could hardly believe it. It was almost more than she could take in at one time. Freed! And in no more than a matter of days.

Then, however, she looked up and saw Hagar standing in front of her, her face in the dim moonlight obscured by her headdress but her form unmistakable in its regal bearing. "Shepset? I thought it was you."

"My lady," Shepset began. "I—"

"Oh, it's all right. I'm sure you didn't mean to eavesdrop. But . . . but did you hear it all?"

"Oh, yes," the girl said, moving away from the wall. "Is it really . . . ?"

"He means it," Hagar said. "Here, come with me. Help me with my makeup, will you? I'm as excited as you. I knew he had provided for me in his will, but I expected to wait for many years."

Shepset felt Hagar take her arm and guide her inside to the women's rooms. When they had reached her mistress's room and seated themselves at her dressing table, Shepset wanted to stay forever and talk over the wonderful future now stretching out before them both. Hagar stopped her: there would be plenty of time for that later. For now they must hurry and return to the feast.

After the guests had departed, Psarou gathered all of his retainers together in the great hall of the villa. Seated on a low platform, in the crosslegged manner habitual to scribes, he began to speak in a calm voice, his elderly face lit with a beatific smile. "I have labored many years in the happy service of two great kings. It has been a pleasurable and profitable life, and as I grow old and prepare for the last great journey, I can look about me and see on every side faces I have come to love and cherish. Indeed, I have so much that it will be hard to distribute it all—even taking into account what I can take with me into the next world."

"My lord!" a servant said, alarmed at the talk of death. Psarou, however, raised his hand. "There, now. It is a time which must come to every man. One must embrace death with the same joy with which one embraced life. I have determined to die as I have lived, as a happy man. And what happier choice might I make in my latter days than to share my happiness with those I love? Therefore . . ."

He paused for a moment and looked at the intent faces around him. "Therefore," he said unhurriedly, "I would like to announce that I have given the order that within the week all of my slaves will be freed. I—"

The uproar that broke loose was quickly silenced when Psarou raised his hand once more. "There, now," he said. "Time enough for reacting to the news when I have told it all to you. As I said, I am manumitting my entire household. Moreover, I am making a disposition of my property that will amply provide for all of those who have earned my confidence so richly in the past. I have already told Hagar, the head of my household, of the settlement which awaits her as soon as the royal scribes can arrange transfer of title to the property which is soon to be hers. Now in the case of Rekhmira, overseer of my lands at Sile, I know that he has long wished to return to the lands of his birth, on Lake Menzalah near the Tanitic mouth of the great river. Well, my estates at Matariyah have long been poorly tended for lack of an astute overseer. This will no longer be the case. Rekhmira will be their new lord and owner."

Hagar, her heart pounding, turned to get a quick look at Rekhmira's thunderstruck expression. How wonderful for him! she thought. At last he had found his heart's desire. And yet, when she turned back to Psarou, she found herself troubled by the same anxiety she had experienced earlier in the day.

"My lady?" whispered Shepset, who sat close beside her. "Is something wrong?"

"No, no," Hagar said in a low voice that the murmurs of the crowd made almost inaudible. "It's just that . . . it's all coming upon me so suddenly." She bit her lip. "Shepset. I had that terrible dream. I thought . . . but the dream lied. It was a false omen. I know that. I know it now. But . . . it's all so perplexing. Everything is happening so fast . . . and I can't seem to erase the bad dream from my mind."

"Oh, my lady," Shepset said. "Don't worry. The dream meant nothing. Really! Look, you'll have forgotten about it in a day or so. Why not—"

There was a sudden loud knock on the door of the great hall. Psarou looked up, cutting off his words in mid-sentence. Then he continued in the surprised hush that had come over the room as a result of the knock. "And as for Paheri, keeper of my livestock," he said, smiling, "there is a section of land on the southern shores of Lake Balah."

The knock sounded again, this time more insistently.

"Here," Psarou said. "Will someone see to that?" His voice carried only the smallest hint of petulance. "As I was saying, for Paheri there will be a whole section of land. Rich bottom land it is, too, for all that foreigners have been working it for some years now and paying me a share of the crop. I can safely say, I think, that under Paheri's much more skilled hands—"

There was a commotion in the outer hall. Psarou stopped, looking up. His face wore a puzzled expression. "Here," he said. "What's going on, please? Will somebody . . . ?"

Several manservants had gone to investigate. Now they were shoved brusquely aside, and into the broad hall stepped a tall, commanding figure in the uniform of a captain of the royal guard. He was flanked by two gigantic Shairetana of the guard: fierce, black-bearded men they were, bearing long double-edged swords and leather shields. They wore the distinctive round helmet of their tribe, which was horned and crowned with a round ball.

Psarou uncrossed his bony legs and stood up slowly. "I beg your pardon, sir," he said. "What service may I do for you in my house? Which," he added, an edge of asperity in his voice, "you seem to have invaded without invitation."

The officer looked him in the eye, unsmiling. "Psarou?" he said. "That is your name? Psarou the scribe?"

"Yes," Psarou said. "But by what right do you . . . ?"

"I have here an order for you to appear at the *divan* of the lord Senmut, governor of the eastern domains of the Lord of Two Lands and commander of the Sile fortress, on the morrow." He waved an unopened papyrus scroll. "Would you like me to read the order to you?"

Psarou remained unruffled. "Ah," he said. "A captain of the guards, but a man with an education. A man who can read. You'll go far in the king's service, my friend. That is, if you can learn to show respect to trusted servants of the Lord of Two Lands who have earned the right to such respect by years of long and faithful dedication."

"I know little of this," the officer said. "The charge is treason. Whatever your rank may have been, it is all one now. I ask you: shall I read the scroll? Or . . ."

Psarou, his face dark with suppressed rage, snatched the scroll from the officer's hand. "Treason!" he said, his voice heavy with scorn. "I've never heard of such nonsense. When the Lord of Two Lands hears of this . . ."

But when he had read the scroll, his face fell. His voice, when he spoke again, was weak with fear. "I . . . I don't understand . . . this is an order for . . . for . . ."

"For confiscation of all your assets," the officer said, ignoring the massed intake of breath from the other people in the room. "Lands, chattels, movables, slaves . . . all are forfeit to the crown. By this time tomorrow night there will be military administrators on all your lands. The keeper of your records is already in prison, which is where you will likely be before the sun has risen twice."

"But . . . this is highly irregular. . . ."

"Not in a treason case," the officer said. His voice was thick with scorn. "You should have thought of the consequences before you conspired with enemy forces against our garrison."

The officer waved one hand, and one of the Shairetana moved forward to take Psarou's arm. The other moved to the doorway to stand guard. The captain of the guards nodded to someone out of sight beyond the hall door. "Surround the villa," he said. "Make sure that no one enters or leaves until we have a full accounting of all names. No member of this household is to leave at all." He turned to the guardsman beside him. "Deliver him to Setna, chief of the guard. Then report back to me."

Shepset, shocked beyond words, watched from the rear of the room, her little body suddenly chilled to the bone. She hugged herself miserably as her eyes scanned the crowd, searching for Hagar. When she located her mistress, it was hard to recognize her. She seemed to have aged ten summers in a matter of moments. "My lady," she said.

"I dreamed it," Hagar said dully. "I knew what

Psarou promised was too good to be true. I
knew. . . ."

VII

Nakhtminou sat up, stretched, and yawned. The
light coverlet fell away from his broad, battle-scarred
chest. He shivered once in the dawn chill and scowled.

The girl beside him moaned in her sleep and turned
over on her side. He blinked and lifted a corner of the
coverlet away from her body to look at her, at the
graceful brown back and the strong, firm little buttocks. He yawned, let the cover drop, and stretched
again.

Suddenly he sat upright, listening.

Drums?—war drums?—here at Sile?

He stood up and looked about him for his clothing.
He smiled ruefully at the disorder in the room and
looked once again at the graceful curve of the girl's
rump beneath the silken cover. Well, they had had
quite a tussle of it the night before. He would have to
remind himself to reward the wench handsomely when
he left. But where could he have left his sandals?

At length he managed to find his loincloth—the
plain white one he wore under his *shenti*. He wound
this around his waist and, barefooted, stepped out of
his room into the corridor.

A guard nodded at him in silent salute, his big body
stiffening slightly to indicate attention. "Sir?" he said.

"Stand easy," Nakhtminou said. "I was just going
to inquire what that damnable din was outside."

"The drums, sir? I don't know, sir. If you'd like, I
can inquire of my superior."

"Yes, do that, would you?" Nakhtminou said. "I'll
mind your post for you. And . . . oh, yes. Is there
anything to eat around here, perhaps?"

"Yes, sir. Uh . . . there is a bowl of dates behind the screen. One of the cooks was so kind . . ."

"I understand. And you have a little understanding with her, eh? Good soldiering, my friend. A soldier always takes care of the essentials first. Now run along with you." He grinned at the guard's retreating back; then he found the bowl and scooped up a handful of dates, tossing one into his mouth.

Well, he thought. The Mesopotamian and his people will be coming in for the lord commander's morning *divan,* and it will be damned interesting to see how Senmut handles him. Not only interesting. For Senmut it will be a most crucial day indeed. How he handled the barbarian in the present situation would largely determine his future status in the empire. The Lord of Two Lands would allow one mistake—not two. And if Senmut handled things adroitly—if the God-King's sight were restored, if the barbarian were adeptly shuffled out of the lands of the Two Kingdoms, never to return—Senmut might well find himself in line for promotion. Otherwise . . .

He grinned, munching on a date. *Well,* he told himself, *isn't it nice not to be in his place any more? You've surely had your own share of bad duty, working off blunders . . .*

Thinking this, he suddenly scowled. Of course, it was his own duty, now, to make sure that Senmut either made the right decision or was replaced on the spot. Well, he'd just have to watch the fellow closely. If he . . .

He stopped, listening to the drums.

They seemed to be closer now. Putting down the bowl, Nakhtminou strode to the door. The guard was bustling back up the stairs, puffing. "Here," Nakhtminou said. "What *is* that noise anyhow?"

"Beg leave to report, sir. The . . . the Mesopotamian . . . he's moving on the fortress with his . . . his whole entourage!"

"Catch your breath," Nakhtminou said. " I take that back about being a good soldier. You're out of condition. Or has that 'cook' you were talking about . . . ?"

He snorted. "No matter. The Mesopotamian, eh? Well, does the lord Senmut know of this?"

"Yes, sir. He's ordered an escort to meet them and bring their leaders to the fortress. The others are ordered to wait outside the gates."

"Good," Nakhtminou said. So the barbarian wouldn't come without his guard, eh? Well, good for him. "Here," he said. "You mind the premises. I'm going to get dressed and look over this country bumpkin and his . . . ah . . . entourage." He nodded at the guard's salute and strode back to his quarters, his mind alert and his mood anticipatory. It should indeed be an unusual day, he was thinking.

By the time he joined Senmut atop the wall, the caravan was already in sight. "By the gods!" said Nakhtminou. "Just look at them, will you? Certainly enough of them, I'd say. I'd forgotten the barbarian . . . well, I'd assumed he traveled light."

Senmut looked down, biting his lip. "No, no . . . there's something like three hundred of them. Men, that is. I don't know how many women. And he brought them down all the way from Haran, through that tricky little nest of warring tribesmen up Canaan way."

"They seem to be well enough armed. And look at the way they're deployed. By the gods, my friend, the man's a soldier like us! Yes—a damned good one, too! I'll have to make note of that formation. It's ingenious. I could have used that a few years ago, about forty days' march up the Nile."

"I'm trying to pick him out," Senmut said, "but I can't so far. I wonder if . . ."

"Well, if you can't, it's an opportunity to save face. Don't let him see you looking down at him, waiting for him to come in. Get back to your quarters and prepare to put on some show as the high and mighty representative of the Lord of Two Lands. Don't worry about all this theatricality out here. He hasn't any intention of fighting. This is just the usual swagger one chieftain puts on when he meets another for . . . let's see, it is the first time? Am I right?"

"Well, yes. The first time he came through, one of my lieutenants . . ."

"Hmmm," Nakhtminou said, frowning. "Look, I won't report that this time. But . . . don't ever let a subordinate handle an affair of state, no matter how damned petty it is. If the subordinate fouls up, it'll be your head on the block."

"Right," Senmut said. He glanced in Nakhtminou's direction and then turned back to the advancing formation, a worried look in his eyes.

Senmut had had two choices. One was to receive the barbarian in state, surrounded by a gathering of the most notable men of Sile—a gathering, he reflected, that would now be distinguished by the conspicuous absence of Psarou, the richest man in the region. The other was to make the reception a sort of private ceremony. He had chosen the latter unhesitatingly; there was enough pressure on him right now without adding to it.

Sitting on the high seat flanked by his guards and with Nakhtminou at his left elbow, Senmut found himself fidgeting. Where was the damned Mesopotamian anyhow? If he thought . . .

The herald stepped into the middle of the long aisle of armed men. "The lord Abram, of Ur."

He stepped back.

From the far door three men approached.

The one in front was a man of mature years, gray-bearded but tall and athletic-looking, with a straight back and large, powerful shoulders. He walked forward with a no-nonsense, purposeful soldier's stride, wearing the single wraparound fringed garment of the Valley of the Two Rivers. His long right arm bared to the shoulder was long-muscled, hard, baked deep brown by the sun. He was a man accustomed to hard work and to leadership.

But it was his eyes that were most striking. Dark, piercing, with an owl's unblinking glare, they stared out from beneath beetling brows that were as yet untouched by the gray that his beard displayed. Were they the eyes of a madman? a sorcerer? a . . .

"You summoned me?" the man said in heavily accented Egyptian.

Here now, Senmut thought. *This is outright insolence. If the damned bumpkin thinks that* . . . But he looked into those sorcerer's eyes again and found himself swallowing hard. "I . . ." He swallowed and tried again. "Yes," he said. "I am Senmut, governor of the eastern . . ."

"I know who you are," the man said. "I am Abram, son of Terah. Your men abducted my wife."

"Look," Senmut said. "That was a terrible mistake. I . . . I accept full responsibility for it. My . . . my heartfelt apologies. Your wife is being returned to Sile. It . . . it should be no more than a day or so. The Lord of Two Lands sends his respects and asks your pardon for the . . . the offense."

"Here now," Nakhtminou whispered behind him. "Don't carry on so."

"Good," the barbarian said. "My men and I will remain encamped outside the gates until she is returned to us. And . . ."

"Uh, that's another thing," Senmut said. "There was a . . . how do I say it? The matter of a spell." Damn it, how did one bring it up? "If you would be so kind . . ."

"There was no spell," the barbarian said. "I know what it is that you speak of. Your master has felt the wrath of the One True God, whose servant I am. When your master has made good the wrong done his servant, my wife Sarai, and purified himself, he will no longer feel the heavy hand of the God upon him."

"Purified? But . . ." This was getting out of hand. Senmut sighed. "Look, my friend. I have been told that you assert some . . . ah . . . claims to land in Canaan."

"Claims?" Abram said in that penetrating voice of his. "The land is mine. I care not for title, patents, grants. The God spoke with me and told me the land was to be forever mine, the land of my people."

"Uh, yes. That's what I was going to talk to you about. The Lord of Two Lands agrees. And while these lands fall under the hegemony of my master and pay tribute to him, he has decided to give you the right to settle there with your people, and—"

"The right is not his to give. But tell him I thank him. You were saying?"

"Yes, I ..." Damn it, the man was infuriating! Senmut bit off a tart reply and went on. "The Lord of Two Lands respectfully grants to you the land you choose to settle in the northern territories. And as a further token of his friendship, he has ordered to be transferred to you certain properties." He swallowed again, miserable, embarrassed. *Thank all the gods,* he told himself, *you had the good sense not to do this in front of witnesses!*

"Thank your master and tell him that I have no need of properties. I go north, as soon as my wife is returned to me, to take possession of the land that is mine. You may thank him for his assurance that he will not interfere with my claims."

"No, no," Senmut said. "Not real properties, land, whatever. There has been a recent confiscation of ... of chattels, from a man of property here who has been found guilty of treason. The Lord of Two Lands has authorized me to offer you his flocks, his slaves."

"Flocks? Slaves? That's another matter," the man said, his eyes lighting up. "I'll need strong bodies, all I can get. I'll have to fight for the land the God has given me. And livestock will help me clothe and feed them. Tell your master I accept his gift. You said flocks?"

"Yes. Sheep. Asses. Oxen. I don't know how much. The estate is being audited. It was considerable. The former owner was a man of means."

"All the better. My nephew here, Lot"—he indicated the shorter of the two men who flanked him—"will act for me in receiving these properties."

"Then ... then you intend to leave soon?"

"As soon as my wife is restored to me, and your gifts counted and merged into my own holdings. We march north in a matter of days. We have been ready to march for a month now."

"Splendid. You, sir? Lot, I think the name was? If you could remain behind ..."

The patriarch gestured to his nephew, who gave a short, curt nod of approval. "Good," he said to Senmut. "Then our business is at an end. Until my wife is returned . . ."

Then, without additional formalities, he turned on one sandaled heel and strode out through the ranks of guards.

An overseer was dispatched to go with Lot to the villa of Psarou. Senmut sat slumped in the big seat, looking down the hall at the dispersing guards.

"Well," Nakhtminou said. "He's quite a fellow, this barbarian of yours. And when he says he's going to fight for his land, I bet he means every word of it."

"I don't care," Senmut said. "All I want is to be rid of him. That was one of the most unpleasant incidents in my whole life."

"I understand. He had you outflanked at every turn. We didn't scare him a bit. Let me tell you, I wouldn't be surprised if he *did* take that land he wants. And at the point of a sword, too." Nakhtminou grinned, shaking his head. "And I'll tell you this, too—I'm glad it's not me he's going to be fighting for it. He's a soldier, whatever he may have been in Haran, or wherever it was he came from. I can tell the signs. He'd be a real problem. You wouldn't win any decorations fighting *him*."

"You're damned right you wouldn't," Senmut said ruefully, forgetting protocol in his distress. "I feel as if I were lucky to get away with a whole skin." He pounded suddenly with his fist on the marble seat. "Damn him! *Damn* him!"

Nakhtminou nodded and turned away. "Don't worry," he said. "I'll tell the Lord of Two Lands you handled him quite well. I suppose it's more or less true anyhow. It was sticky business. I'll be glad to see him go myself."

"Damn him!" said Senmut.

VIII

It was three days, however, before the palanquins of
the Great King reached Sile, bearing the wife of the
barbarian Abram. She had first been ferried down the
Nile to the delta lakes, then borne across the marsh
country in a carrying chair on the stout shoulders of
four towering Nubians to the frontier fortress. She was
accompanied by a unit of the royal guards, one of a
size befitting the conveying of a woman of high rank in
the government.

Nakhtminou, a captain of guards at his side, rode
out to meet them in a chariot—and was delighted to
find that the commander of the escort was his old
friend and comrade in arms from the Upper Nile
campaigns, Kha-emhet. "Greetings!" he bellowed unin-
hibitedly, dismounting.

The pair embraced. Kha-emhet handed the escort
over to a subordinate and took his old friend to one
side, ignoring the cloud of dust in the distance that had
been stirred up by the wagons of Abram. "Nakhtminou!" the messenger said. "I'd hoped to find you here—
but expected you to have gone back upriver by now.
How do you stand it here?"

"Oh, it's not so bad," the old soldier said. "Actually
it's been rather amusing in some ways. The garrison
commander has been in a terrible predicament, and it's
been fun watching him squirm. But what of the Lord
of Two Lands? Has he . . . ?"

"Much better," Kha-emhet said, rolling his eyes
skyward. "Thanks to all the gods for that. The royal
doctors are calling it heat stroke. Our lord and master,
however, thinks differently. He and his astrologers will
be quite interested to know the exact time you promised the barbarian his wife back and heard him accept

whatever bribes you offered him." His face changed slightly. "I trust you loaded him down with booty, eh?"

"He'll be a rich man," Nakhtminou said. "Frankly, I'm impressed with him. You should have seen him with Senmut. He accepted everything as his due and didn't even thank us. We offered him unofficial title to some land up north, in that worthless buffer country between the delta and the Hittite country. North of the desert. He didn't think much of our gift at all. He was prepared to take the land at sword's point anyhow."

"He'll have some stiff fighting over its ownership, all right, for all the royal blessing. But come to think of it, that crowd with him looks tough and seasoned."

"We added considerably to his entourage at that. We made him the present of a rich merchant's estate here. Everything the fellow owned that walked on two legs or four."

"Good," said Kha-emhet. "That'll look good in your report. Well, my lieutenant seems to have managed the transfer all right. Do I have to report to the garrison commander now?"

"I'll take care of that. I'll have this fellow who came out with me take a message to him. Meanwhile, you and I can cool our thirst at a tavern run by an old orderly of mine from the Nubian days."

"Yes," said Kha-emhet. "A draught of strong beer would be just the thing. But what about this rich gentlemen you've robbed to pay the barbarian? What's going to happen to him? And what was his crime?"

"Crime?" Nakhtminou said, taking his friend's arm. "Oh, I'm sure it was a frame-up pure and simple. It doesn't matter. He collapsed and died shortly after we brought him in. The charge was treason, but I don't believe for a moment he was guilty."

"Ah, the perils of political life. Me for being a soldier."

"I'll drink to that," said the king's emissary.

Back at the tents, Abram was barking orders right and left. "Form the caravans! We're moving out in the morning, at dawn. Mass the columns according to plan—and tell Lot to put the best man he has up ahead, to be alert and watchful." Turning suddenly, he took note of a man and a woman who were wearing the simple loincloths of slaves. "Here," he said. "I don't recognize either of you."

"Paheri," the man said. He was dark, sharp-eyed, and had an air of competence about him. "Paheri, sir. Recently keeper of the herds of the lord . . ."

"Ah, fine," Abram said. "There's going to be plenty of work for the likes of you, my friend. Go with the man I just sent away and tell him I said to put you to work. And you, woman?"

He looked her over as she spoke. She was quite beautiful, actually, with dark eyes and graceful proportions. Her breasts jutted up proudly above the brief skirt. There was a somber expression on her face as she recited her name and her duties in her former household. "Hagar, eh?" he said. "And you were a household administrator? Well, there won't be much use for that here. You'll have to learn a few new chores." He looked at the long-lashed, downcast eyes, the once-proud neck bent in an attitude of bitter submission. "Here—look to my wife, will you? Help her wash that Egyptian muck out of her hair and scrub that red stuff from her palms and soles. If she . . ."

"Don't go blaming me for that," said Sarai from inside their tent. "It wasn't my idea to go upriver to those heathen." She stepped outside the tent, her dark hair still tatted in the court style. "Well," she said. "You, girl . . . come here. I *can* use some help, you know." Her sharp eyes took in the girl's nakedness and attitude of submission. They also missed nothing of her softly feminine beauty. Her eyes rose to engage Abram's. A sudden flash of understanding passed between them. "Well, come along, girl," she said, her thin lips curving in a mirthless smile. "What are you waiting for?"

The drums awoke Shepset in the first moments of dawn. Low, insistent, rhythmic, their beat was geared to the deliberate pace of the nomad, accustomed to the slow meandering of the herds of sheep and cattle.

Shepset yawned and sat up. The goatskin fell away from her fresh young breasts as she rose to stand.

"Up yet?" said the overseer Enosh, passing by. "There's a good girl. Now go to the food wagon for your bread and goat's milk. You'll need all the sustenance you can get in the days to come." His eyes ran up and down the young body in its skimpy apron. There was a look of hunger in them for a moment; then it softened. "Don't worry," he said. "You're young and strong. You'll do all right."

"I hope so," she said. She smiled shyly. "I . . . sir, could you tell me something? Please?"

"Surely child," the overseer said.

"Sir . . . where is it that we are going?"

"Ah," he said. "Canaan. It is far to the north of here. No more than half the way to Haran, mind you, but still a long way." He looked down at her slim legs, and scratched his head. Poor child, she'd have a hard time of it for a while, with soft feet used to Nile bottomland, and many days of marching across hard rocks and salt desert ahead of her. "Don't worry, daughter. You'll make it. The main thing is to develop stamina. Don't drink too much water at a time, now."

"Yes, sir. But sir . . . what kind of a country is it? Is it like this?"

Enosh sighed and looked at her with compassion. He realized that it was no use lying to her—she would learn the truth soon enough. And for some reason he could not divine, Enosh wanted to keep her respect. The eyes were so clear, so trusting. They made him remember that he too had been exiled from the land where he was born and raised.

"I won't lie to you, my dear," he said. "It's not going to be easy. By the time you're done, those little feet of yours will be as tough as leather. You'll be as dark from the sun as any Nubian. Skinny as you are, you'll be lighter by a measure of rice or two. We've all gotten fat and out of condition in this lush bottomland of yours, but the trip will take all that softness out of us. And a good thing, too, because when we arrive in

Canaan, we're going to spend at least the first three moons fighting for our lives just for the right to stay there."

"Fighting?" said Shepset. "But someone told me that the land had been given to our . . . our master by the Lord of Two Lands himself."

"No matter, my dear. The Lord of Two Lands collects tribute, when he bothers to send someone up that way. But he doesn't exercise much control over those barbarian tribes up there. No, we're going to have a tough fight on our hands. And you women will have to mend us when we're hurt and worry about us when we're gone."

Shepset sighed, and Enosh regretted that he had been so candid. Poor child, she had enough burdens to bear without his adding to them by making her worry. "Here," he said. "Don't fret. It'll be all right. Really it will."

But he would give anything he'd ever owned, back when he'd owned things, to have called back his words, or to be able to erase the film of tears that clouded those clear young eyes just then.

The command to move, sounded by the ram's horn, was picked up by one captain of the march after another as it echoed across the entire encampment. And slowly the drums began beating again, with their broad, hollow timbre.

Hagar, half-naked, marched barefoot behind Abram's asses, unprotected against the morning sun. From the pit of her stomach, a dull ache of foreboding throbbed with the hateful drumbeats. She did her best to pay it no mind but it continued to haunt her. . . .

Words of farewell formed on her lips. Farewell to Egypt, to the land of soft morning mist, gentle evenings, and sweet-smelling air. Farewell to the river lands, with their soft alluvial soil made fertile by the cyclic overflowing of the Nile. Farewell to the land whose gods, embodied in the person of the God-King himself, protected owner and slave alike against want and hunger. Farewell to life as the household administrator of a gentle and fatherly master whose yoke lay as heavy on the shoulders as a parent's kind and forgiving hand. Farewell to . . .

And now the first voice sang out, in rhythm with the slow beat of the drum to which all their footfalls were attuned. It sang a joyous song of hope, of longing for the promised land to come, of thanksgiving for the blessings promised by the god—the incomprehensible, nameless god—of Abram's people. And as the strong young voice boomed out far up the line, Hagar, her eyes brimming now with tears, heard other voices joining in—strong young voices that sang of victories to come, of conquest, of the seizing of power, of the handing down of Abram's promised earth to one's children and one's children's children. . . .

It was a song of hope, falling on the ear of one who had dared to hope for a single brief joyous moment, and who had then seen that hope dashed forever. In Hagar's ear it rang poignant, bitter, false. There was no song in her heart as she marched behind the animals, her eyes streaming now, her slim brown hands over her ears as she tried vainly to blot out the sound of the songs of thanksgiving, the songs of praise, and above all, beyond all, the bitterly hateful songs of hope. Those, of all songs, were the worst. Because for her all hope was gone, and forever. Biting her full lower lip, she wept uncontrollably and vowed to herself that she would never entertain so much as the ghost of a hope again. Never! Never!

CHAPTER TWO

I

The reputation of Zakir, the metalsmith, was well known in the bazaars that lined the west bank of the Euphrates within the walls of the great city of Babylon. He was, as a friend had put it some time before, a simple man, but one who contained many contradictions. A sensual, comfort-loving man, he nevertheless lived alone and modestly in a commercial quarter of the town. Strong as a bullock, he was also the gentlest of men. Sober and industrious during market hours, he led a roistering life after dark in the taverns and brothels and was known to every seller of wine or women in the commercial quarter.

His life was apportioned into a series of routine activities, which, taken together, bridged the separate aspects of his existence. This dependence on routine was by now so well established that any deviation from it was a source of concern to Zakir's associates and friends. It usually meant that something was amiss.

So when he failed to show up at his forge one morning in late spring, the shopkeepers who occupied cubicles near his own delegated one of their number to look for him. Perhaps he was drunk or lying abed with some wench from the taverns? Or perhaps ... perhaps the poor fellow was ill? This last possibility, however, was not very likely: Zakir hadn't missed a day's work due to ill health in years and normally had the constitution of an ox.

Iddina, the wine merchant, handed over his business for an hour to an assistant and wound his way through the narrow streets that lay below the vast unfinished area of the Tower of the Planets, heading for the crowded complex of houses where Zakir made his home.

On the rooftops, he could hear the women already at their work, washing linen or kneading dough and chatting to one another. The richest, with slaves to do this work for them, used the time instead to recline upon cushions and embroider as they gossiped; but still it was the rooftops of the city that drew them on these cool mornings, and they would not forsake this exalted forum. There they remained until the noonday sun drove them indoors.

Iddina stopped and called up to a plump housewife who stood at the edge of the roof scouring a pot. "You! Woman!" he called. "I'm looking for the smith Zakir!"

"Ah," she said, smiling wryly down at him, her hands still working. "And for what might you want him? Are you perhaps collecting a gambling debt?"

"No," he laughed. "But I see you know our Zakir well. I'm a neighbor of his in the bazaar. He wasn't at the forge today, and we wondered if anything had happened to him."

"My husband met Zakir last night," answered the woman. "He said he'd just collected a fat purse from a customer and was off to the slave markets this morning to buy a helper for his forge."

Iddina thanked the woman and continued on his way. Well, he thought. It must have been a fat purse indeed; a grown slave in good health could cost thirty-five shekels—the price of three or four bullocks. More, if the slave came from Subartu or Lullu or if one were purchased in Babylon itself.

Business, then, must indeed be picking up for the smith. Well, no surprise. With some of his work on display in the Temple of Bel and in the palace of the king, he had the custom of the wealthy and powerful in the city. Even foreigners from upriver—from as far as Mari on one occasion—had come to order samples from Zakir. He was beginning to be compared to the master smiths of Ur, where the art had originated.

Well! He'd congratulate the smith on his good fortune. Perhaps the two could repair to a tavern for food and drink in the middle of the day. Zakir was generous and open-handed when a newly earned purse was in his belt. Iddina smiled as he turned west, steering his course closer to the great river.

When he reached the market of Nebo, the slave merchant, he spotted Zakir standing among a group of men waiting for the bidding to begin. "Zakir!" he said in a loud whisper. "I heard you were here."

"Greetings," said the smith, his smile broad and warm. "Are you here to bid?"

"No, only to watch." He let his eyes scan the array on the stand. Two comely Lullu women were already on the block, naked, their slaves' robes cast carelessly at their feet. Iddina's brow rose in appreciation. If only . . . but no. He was already overextended as it was. As he watched, Nebo sold the girls to a hawk-eyed old merchant with an atrocious Mari accent. "I take it you're not in the market for female help," he said.

"What?" Zakir answered. "Oh, no, not that. No, I need a helper for the forge. Work's beginning to come in almost faster than I can handle it."

"Why not buy an apprentice?" Iddina said. "If—"

"Oh, that's some months ahead, I think. What I need right now is just . . . oh, someone to keep the forge stoked and hot. A boy, perhaps. I lost time at the forge myself doing these menial tasks."

"Well, there's one now," Iddina said. "But he doesn't look like much."

Zakir looked where his friend pointed. Nebo was leading an underfed-looking boy to the stand. "Huh," he said. "As you say, he's no prize. Of course, feed him regularly and he might come into his strength in a year or two. How old would you say he is? Ten?"

"No," said Iddina. "Twelve at least. Look, he's already hung like a man."

Zakir looked the boy up and down. Nebo had pulled off the boy's sole garment and was turning him around now. Zakir saw the red stripes of recent beatings and winced. "By the gods," he said. "There ought to be some sort of law against mistreating a boy that way."

"There is," Iddina said, "but it's not enforced much. Sullen little devil, isn't he?"

"I'd be myself in his place," Zakir said, frowning. "He's an odd type. Not from around here—and not from Lullu or . . . no, not from Subartu either. I wonder how he came here. Captured in a raid, no doubt. But you'd think they could feed him."

"Well, he may not look like much to us, but he seems to have attracted one buyer's attention. Look over there. The one with the prissy beard. He's just offered ten shekels."

"Too rich for my blood," Zakir said. "He can have him—although from the looks of that fellow with the curls, I pity the lad if he falls into *those* soft little hands."

"You don't think much of men who . . . ah . . . like boys, eh?"

"Well, a man's tastes are his own. But that one's effete. Unmanly. There's something ill-looking about him. I don't think I'd like being a male slave of his. Iddina . . . what's that mark on the boy's back?"

"I didn't see it. Where?"

"Look, Nebo's turning him around again. There it is, just above the hip."

Iddina looked. "Why . . . it's like the paw print of an animal, isn't it? That's odd. I've never seen that before."

"An animal—a cat, perhaps. A lion . . ."

"It looks as though nobody else is going to bid. Well, the gods help the boy. He'll have a lively time of it tonight, I'll wager."

Zakir bit his thick underlip. Then, to his own surprise as much as anyone's, he found himself holding up his own hand and bellowing out in his strong baritone voice, "Twelve shekels!"

"Twelve it is," Nebo said from the stand. "I have twelve shekels for this strong healthy boy. Who'll say fifteen?"

"Good heavens, Zakir," Iddina said. "I thought you didn't want the boy. He looks sickly. He—"

"I don't know," Zakir said. "It's just that . . . well, there used to be some sort of old legend about the paw print of a lion . . . something they told me when I was apprenticed. The story . . . I can't remember. It was something about a lion. I think it meant good luck or something. Good luck for a smith, anyhow."

"You're not going to throw away twelve shekels because of a legend, are you? And look, the sissy with the beard. He's going to outbid you. Yes, thirteen shekels. And did you see the look he gave you? Well, I never!"

"Fourteen!" yelled Zakir. Then, in a loud whisper, to Iddina, "Call it what you will. But . . . oh, I just had a sudden feeling. A feeling that good fortune might attend this purchase."

The bidding rose. The androgynous-looking bidder across the square from Zakir grew ever more petulant, and his voice rose with every bid. The sum passed twenty shekels . . . thirty. . . . "By the gods," Iddina said. "This is getting expensive. How big was that purse you picked up yesterday, anyhow?"

"Big enough," Zakir said. "You know, I'm just being stubborn now, but . . . I have the feeling that if I let this boy fall into the hands of that simpering fool over there . . . well, I just can't let it happen."

"Look. He's coming over here to see you."

"Yes. What's the bid now? Thirty-two?" He pursed his lips and bellowed out, "Thirty-three!"

"You!" The man with the curly beard said. "You offend me. If you know what's good for you, you'll let it go right there."

Standing with his legs apart and his hands on his hips, Zakir grinned and looked him up and down. "You know the rules," he said. "The highest bidder gets the merchandise. And don't you think threats are . . . well, in bad taste, for one thing?"

"I have thirty-three," Nebo was saying. "Thirty-three shekels."

"Thirty-four!" cried the fop in his shrill high-pitched

voice. "Thirty-four!" he stated in anger at Zakir, his small hands clenched into fists. "Bahe," he said, turning to a slave. "How much have I with me?"

"Thirty-six shekels, master," the slave said. "If . . ."

Zakir grinned devilishly. "Thanks, friend," he said. "Thirty-seven!"

"You'll pay for this," said the fop. "In more ways than one. Just remember. You can be sure I won't forget."

"I'm already beginning to forget," Zakir said, chuckling. "And in your case it'll be a pleasure forgetting. But just for the record, who *are* you, that I should tremble in my shoes before you?"

"Soulai," the popinjay said, a tiny glint of triumph in his malevolent gray eyes. "Soulai, the son of Habasle, assistant to the chief magistrate of the city. Remember that, if you remember nothing else." Then he turned on one heel and walked mincingly away.

"Thirty-seven shekels it is," Nebo called out behind Zakir. "Sold to Zakir the smith."

Zakir and Iddina stopped at a riverside tavern for lunch and feasted on freshly caught fish and palm wine from jugs chilled in the waters of the Euphrates. The attendant took the boy below stairs with orders to fix him a plate of something hearty. Zakir and Iddina had drunk several rounds of palm wine and were enjoying the noisy chatter of the Babylonian stews when a commotion past the open door to the kitchen drew their attention.

"Huh," said Zakir. "Sounds like the boy. Maybe he's got into some kind of trouble. Come on." The two went down the stairs to the cool cellar where their food had been prepared.

At the foot of the stairs the cook was mopping up what remained of the boy's lunch. The boy was on his knees, retching miserably. He looked up once at Zakir, his eyes glazed with pain. "Here," Zakir said. "What in the devil have you been feeding him? Can't I trust you to . . . ?" Then he stopped. A look of sudden understanding came over his face. "My apologies," he said. "I'll pay for the mess. Here, son, come along."

He helped the boy to his feet, his face suddenly clouded over with concern as he felt the weak, stringy muscles of the child's shoulders.

"What's the matter?" Iddina said as they stepped out onto the terrace above the river. "Did he have something that wasn't good for him?"

"Not really," Zakir said. "Here, boy. Can you walk now? There. Sit down on the retaining wall for a moment. Catch your breath. Have the cramps gone away? No, that's all right. Just sit there until you feel better."

Iddina took note of the look the boy flashed Zakir. It was full of pain, fear, apprehension—and something else. Confusion. By the gods, hadn't anyone ever treated the boy humanely at all? "It looks like you have a case against Nebo," he said. "The boy's ill. And all sales are predicated on the soundness of the merchandise."

"No, he'll be all right," Zakir said. "Won't you, son? It's just that I didn't get the message at first. He can't take good hearty fare yet. I'll take him home and feed him a little gruel, mixed with goat's milk. A little at a time, that's the trick."

"But what's the matter?"

"Gods, look at him," Zakir said with a sigh. "Lean as a crane. I tell you, it just makes you sick sometimes, thinking of the things people are capable of. Boy," he said. "When was the last time you had anything to eat?"

The boy looked at both of them, his eyes darting to and fro. A muscle twitched spasmodically in his bony cheek. "I . . . I don't remember," he said. "Two days, three."

"Gods!" Zakir said disgustedly. His big first balled convulsively. "That Nebo . . . did he beat you too, boy?"

"Beat me?" the boy said. "No . . . it was the other one. When I tried to escape. He said . . ." But he couldn't finish. He barely got his head out over the Euphrates in time to heave up the last of the meager dinner he'd wolfed down at the tavern. When the spasms stopped he said, "I . . . I'm sorry, sir."

"It's all right, boy," Zakir said, flashing Iddina a look that was half compassion, half anger. "Come on, now. We're going home."

"Home?" the boy said.

II

The boy's name was Ahuni, and his accent was a curious one indeed. It had traces of the accents of cities upriver, downriver, even of the Valley of the Tigris many miles away across the hills. It was the strangest accent Zakir had ever heard. As the boy, seated at a low table in Zakir's house, slowly ate the gruel his new master had made for him, Zakir looked at Ahuni's narrow back, with its bruises and stripes, and pondered.

"Easy there," he said. "Take it slowly. When you've finished that bowl you'd better lie down for a bit. The less churning up your guts take right now, the better." The boy turned, looked at him through eyes that still held traces of fear and distrust; then, his thin lips still moving, chewing the lumpy gruel, he turned back to his supper.

"Don't trust me, eh?" Zakir said. "Well, time enough for that. I gather from your speech that you've had a lot of masters—what? Five? Six? And they may not have treated you too well."

"Sir?" the boy said, craning his head on that skinny neck.

"Huh? Oh, you want to know how I guessed about the masters. What was it? Six?"

"Yes, sir. Six that I remember. But—"

"Your speech. I counted that many strains. Look, I'm an old Babylonian, for all that I apprenticed down-river. Everybody comes to my forge, everybody. I can tell where a man came from by his words before he's

finished placing his order. No, no, finish your dinner.
You'll need a good night's rest. I'm going to work you
nice and hard tomorrow, believe me. I've got some
samples to finish. But first I'm going to visit some . . .
ah . . . ladies of my acquaintance down at the Sign of
the Crescent Moon." He had a sudden thought. "You
wouldn't try to run away, now?"

"No, sir," the boy said, flashing him that look again.
Zakir, looking him in the eye, couldn't tell whether he
was telling the truth or not. He shrugged his heavy
shoulders and yawned. Then he rose and changed into
his robes, after washing carefully at the basin.

"Remember," he told the boy as he went out the
door into the darkening street. "Allow no one to enter.
But when the moon is low in the western skies, well on
toward morning, you may hear a bunch of loudmouths
outside, singing bawdy songs and trying to lug something toward the house. That'll be me. They'll probably
need some help carrying me in. You might give them a
hand. I weigh a bit, you know. And tonight I've
decided to close down no less than three taverns."

"Yes, sir," the boy said solemnly.

When Zakir had gone, Ahuni sat on his narrow bed
looking at the closed door. The pain in his innards had
gone away for the time being, but he was sure it would
be back. He felt a bit dizzy. Perhaps if he were to lie
down for a moment.

But instead of lying down, he found himself standing
and looking about him. Zakir lived simply, with no
frills or frippery. The only indulgence he allowed himself was that of sleeping on a raised bed rather than on
the floor—and apparently this privilege was to be
granted his slave as well. The house was plain but well
lighted. Everywhere, the small flat lamps, consecrated
to Nusku, the god of fire, burned brightly. Zakir did
not skimp on oil—or on food, drink, or women, for
that matter.

What kind of master would he be? Ahuni thought
about this. So far things had gone well . . . but that had
happened before, and then things had gone wrong little

by little. Or they had gone wrong overnight, when the master married and his new wife suddenly decided the slaves were having too easy a time of it. No, it would be better to stay on one's guard.

Ahuni looked at the door again. It was easily opened, after all. One might slip out into the street, make his way to the river, to the quarter of commerce ... stow away on a boat headed downstream to the delta lands.

He put his hand on the latch, then hesitated.

Look, he told himself. *You don't really know he's going to change. You just know all the others did—all the others who started out nice, anyway. It could be all right. This one could be different.*

He opened the door.

There would be no leaving by any of the city gates tonight, anyhow. They were closed for the night, and the fortifications of Babylon were impregnable. Beyond the walls a broad moat circled the city. The only break was the broad river itself, which cut through the city and divided Old Town from New Town. And no ships ever left the docks at night. He could slip down to the wharves and wriggle his way under the covering of a boat loaded for debarkation on the morning tides.

Yes, and what then? He still bore the slave-mark, which had been branded onto his arm when he was so young that he could not even remember the pain of it. His hair, shaven for the auction, could grow back eventually, but the slave-brand was indelible—and the penalty for effacing the brand of a slave was having your hand cut off at the wrist. Local law was rough on slaves who tried to pass as freemen.

And if you fell into the hands of someone new? What then? The new "owner," however false, could well be worse than anything Zakir could turn out to be. He could be a bugger, for instance, or the sort of person who got his pleasure from hurting people. He could ...

A soft breeze stirred the evening air. Ahuni, standing in the doorway, could smell the tempting odors of dinner from a dozen household fires. There was a deliciously cool balm in the air. If one were only free—free to roam the streets at will, to follow one's own desires . . .

Yes,—and what would those desires be? What do you want, Ahuni? What would you go looking for, if you were free to go wherever you chose and do whatever you wanted? Ahuni bit his lip and hated himself. His hand trembled on the door. *Coward!* he told himself bitterly. *Coward!*

Zakir and his companion in drink Irsisi had sampled the wares of three taverns by the time Iddina caught up to them. By then Zakir was bleary-eyed and somewhat incoherent. When Iddina entered the door of the Crescent Moon, Zakir was bellowing in his strong unmelodious voice the song the legends ascribed to Siduri, the alewife, who sang to Gilgamesh:

> Gilgamesh, where are you going?
> You'll never find that life you're looking for;
> When the gods created all beings,
> They set aside a mortal life for man
> And kept immortality for themselves.
> You, Gilgamesh, fill your belly,
> And make merry both day and night. . . .

Iddina pushed his way through the crowd. "Zakir!" he yelled. He tripped over the outthrust leg of a drunken seaman and sprawled on the floor. "Zakir!" he cried again, picking himself up and dusting off his soiled robe with his hands.

"Iddina!" Zakir said. "Come and have a drink on me, my friend. We are celebrating. . . . By all the gods, I can't remember what it is that we're celebrating. Irsisi? What are we . . . ?" But Irsisi, a wench on his knee, was otherwise occupied, waving a bowl of strong palm wine in the air and singing a coarse song of the waterfront. "Iddina, sit down and—"

"Zakir, I have to talk to you," Iddina said. "It's important. Judge for yourself. Anything that could drag me away from my good Humerelli and the children this late at night—"

"Oh! What a sobersides. Iddina, you don't know

how to enjoy yourself. But that's all right, you're a good fellow for all that. Here! A drink for my friend! Tavernkeeper, a drink."

Iddina sat down in a chair across from Zakir and put a hand on his thick knee. "Zakir, I have to tell you something. This morning, at the market—"

"Market?" Zakir said, grinning stupidly. "But I did not go to the market today, my friend. I took the day off. Bought myself a helper, and then I went to the taverns and . . ."

"Please. Listen to me. That fellow you offended there . . . the effeminate one . . . I heard something about him."

"Oh, don't bother me with *that*. They are all the same. They never amount to anything. He'll stamp his foot and mince about, and it'll all be over."

"Zakir, for the sake of all the gods put together, listen to me, will you? You may be in danger. That fellow is—"

"Danger? From that popinjay? Don't be—"

"Zakir, listen." Iddina, his face dark with worry, put a hand on each of his friend's burly shoulders and tried to catch his eye. "This Soulai character . . . I did some asking about him. He has a bad reputation for throwing his weight around. . . . No, damn it, don't make any stupid jokes about his not having any weight to throw around. Listen. *Listen,* confound you! He draws a lot of water around here, let me tell you. His father—"

"His father's a judge," Zakir said, his grin fading a bit. "I heard that much. But—"

"His father's the acting magistrate of the city, you fool! His father's Habasle, of all people, and from all accounts he's a mean bastard like his son. And with the chief magistrate of the city out of town on business, Habasle is the most powerful man outside of the court of the king himself! And if you've offended his—"

"Iddina," Zakir said, suddenly reasonable if not quite sober yet, "Babylon is a city of law. And if I may have offended a citizen, it has not been the sort of offense one is called before a magistrate for. I'm an upstanding citizen, am I not? Don't I pay my taxes like the next man? And rather more than most, I dare say, what with business picking up this way. And if it's a matter of influence, for goodness' sake, isn't my work on display at the Temple of Bel? At the Palace itself? Who'd want to haul a master metalworker into court, unless he'd really done something bad? Now, I ask you."

Iddina sighed. "I'd hoped to get you to listen to me. Look, its not too late. You can send a messenger to make your peace with the fellow. You know, with a bribe or something. Write him a nice flowery greeting in which you say, oh, that it was the heat and you weren't feeling well."

"On the contrary. I was feeling better pulling his nose than I've felt in days. Best medicine in the world. I wish I felt that well right now. Frankly, I think I've had too much to drink. This palm wine must have been fermenting for a week. Take the top of your head off. Here, as a matter of fact I could use a bit of fresh air right now. Could you help me up? There's a good fellow."

Iddina managed to get him erect and walk him to the patio outside. "Look, Zakir," he said. "You probably have a long day's work ahead of you. Why not go home now?" Then, propping his friend up and gently nudging him toward the outer gate of the tavern, Iddina steered Zakir to the street.

In the alleys Zakir began singing again in his off-pitch, drunken voice. He sang the song of Enkidu, the wild man, when the temple prostitute taught him to drink hard liquor:

> Enkidu ate the food she gave him,
> Ate until he was bloated and sated;
> Seven goblets of liquor he drank,
> Growing more cheerful with each one. . . .

At length they found themselves in front of Zakir's house. Zakir leaned his back against the wall and bellowed: "Ahuni! Help put me to bed. I'm too heavy for Iddina." There was no answer. "He must be sleeping," said Zakir, "after all he's gone through. Ahuni! Wake up, my boy! We need your help!"

But there was no answer: and when they searched the house, Ahuni was nowhere to be found. The boy was gone.

III

In the morning Zakir rose with more than the usual difficulty. *Some day,* he told himself. *Some day you're going to learn.* Really, he'd have to give up palm wine one of these days—or at least stick to new wine and stop drinking the highly fermented stuff they sold at the Crescent Moon.

He stretched and yawned again. The morning sun was already strong in the sky and its glare hurt his red eyes. *By the gods!* thought Zakir. *It's late and I'm overdue at the forge.* Scowling, he stumbled toward the entrance. Then, just as he was about to step out into the street, he tripped over something and fell sprawling.

Zakir cursed as he picked himself up, wondering what had caused him to fall, and then suddenly gasped. The boy Ahuni lay collapsed on the brick platform at the entrance. He was not moving. His face was smeared with blood and his body was covered with welts and bruises.

Suddenly alert, Zakir bent over the boy. "Ahuni!" he said. "Ahuni . . . are you . . . ?" For a second, there was no response, and then one of the swollen, black-and-blue eyes opened almost imperceptibly and then shut again. "Ah," Zakir said. "Alive. Here, boy. Let me help you up. Can you stand up? No? Ah, here. Let me . . . let me help you. . . . Now your arm over my shoulder. Does that hurt? Sorry. Now . . . take it slowly! . . ."

Iddina turned up a little while later. By this time Zakir had put the boy to bed and washed his wounds.

Ahuni had slipped off into a fitful sleep broken by little cries of pain and fear. Iddina looked him over and came back with Zakir to the table by the door. "What happened to him?" Iddina said, sitting down opposite his friend.

"He ran away," Zakir said. "Believe me, I'd likely try to do the same myself in his shoes. But . . . well, he made his way down to the water, hoping to stow away in a boat headed for the delta. You can imagine the rest. He fell into the hands of a boat crew. It appears they had their way with him. He won't be able to sit down comfortably for a week. But he fought them pretty hard before they got to him, from the looks of the beating they had to give him. Good boy; he didn't make it easy for them. Did you see that arm?"

"Yes. What happened?"

"He was trying to obliterate the slave-brand. I'll have to give him a bracelet for his arm, to cover that up for a while. You know what the penalty is for that. Poor child. You know, Iddina . . . this slavery business—I . . ."

He stopped, sighed, frowned.

"It's a good way to get a helper cheap."

"Yes, but—"

"Gods. For a pittance I'd have a horoscope drawn on you. You're too softhearted to survive."

"Wait a season or so and we'll compare our holdings. I'll be as rich as you within the year if business holds up. I may be softhearted, but I'm doing pretty well, let me tell you. As well as you, or—"

"I know, I know. For one thing you have the advantage of me in that most of your sales are right here. You don't have to bribe officials to get past customs. You don't have robbers attacking your caravans."

"Come now. There's perfect security all the way from Nineveh to Arbela, from Arbela to Kalakh."

"You're changing the subject. You know what I'm talking about. You're thinking of manumitting the boy."

"No, I'm not. Well, maybe. Later. Much later. What I am thinking of doing is apprenticing him. I mean, if it turns out that he has any dexterity. There'll always be work for a smith. And there's word coming up the river lately about a new smelting process."

"Well, at least you'll wind up getting your money out of him that way. But why are you getting so softhearted all of a sudden?"

Zakir looked at the bright light streaming in the doorway. His expression was thoughtful. "I don't know. There's something about the boy that I rather like. And . . . well . . . there's some sort of legend connected with that funny birthmark of his . . . something to do with my profession. I've been wracking my brains trying to remember. It must have been something I picked up back when I was an apprentice myself."

"Nonsense. You're just thinking up excuses to do what you've already decided to do. A birthmark is a birthmark. What significance can it have? Here," he said, standing up. "Are you coming in to work today? Or are you going to be a nursemaid for the boy?" His expression was gently chiding.

"Oh . . ." Zakir frowned, pursed his lips, and blew out. He looked over at the bed where the boy slept restlessly. "Huh. There are a couple of commissions I ought to be getting to. But damn it all, Iddina. Living alone the way I do, there's nobody to care for him, you know."

"How about one of the women you know so well?"

"Who? Banatsaggil, for instance? Let her in this door, and she'll never come out again. She wants me to marry her. And if I marry her, what am I to do with the rest? No, no. I'd better tend to him myself." He looked up at Iddina sheepishly. "For today, anyhow."

It was a week before Ahuni was ready to come to work at the forge. Business was business, however, and Zakir was back at work three days before that. Friends, passing his forge, found him singing a bawdy song of the stews, punctuating his words with stout wallops from his hammer. "You're looking cheerful today," one man said in passing. Zakir only grinned at him and hammered all the harder, beating a chased design into the copper pot on his anvil. And he thought: *With an apprentice to mind the fire and keep it blazing hot, the metal will liquefy better. With a boy standing by, manning the blowpipes, I'll have both hands free.*

Two commissions came in on the morning that Ahuni, a copper armlet covering the scar on his arm, came to work. Zakir put him to stacking the shipment of charcoal the merchant Madie had delivered so carelessly the day before.

After lunch he handed Ahuni the blowpipe and told him where to direct the flow of air as he himself picked up a copper fitting with his forceps and beat it into shape with a tiny hammer. "And for the love of all the gods, don't breathe in. Take a breath through your nose—so—and blow out, slowly, steadily. You'll get the rhythm of it in a while."

They worked well together from the first. The boy was alert and eager. Zakir liked him more and more. As the days passed, it even became evident that the boy had a craftsman's fist. His hands were quick and deft and his eye sure and true. Zakir found himself showing him more tricks. And when friends from other markets in the city dropped by to talk shop, Zakir found himself no longer pointing to Ahuni and referring to him as a slave. Instead, directing their attention away from the armlet on the boy's bicep, he found himself saying proudly, "This is Ahuni, my new apprentice."

Soulai, the magistrate's son, stopped by the quarters of Nebo, the merchant of slaves, a month later. A visit from Soulai was an occasion of sorts. He swept in with an escort of up to a dozen retainers—the boon companions or favorite catamites of the moment. Nebo looked the painted faces over, maintaining an expression that was deferential to the point of being obsequious.

"Nebo?" Soulai was saying petulantly. "Have you nothing better than these?" I've never seen such a lot of starvelings in my life." He felt the naked thigh of a young male slave from the high mountains, pinching it so hard the boy winced. Then, disdainfully, he moved to a second stand where two Nubians, a male and a female, stood with vacant expressions on their faces. "Hmm," he said. "I could use a black or two if they were tame enough. Strip me that one."

"The woman?" Nebo asked ingenuously.

"Oh, come now," Soulai said in a simpering tone. "You know me better than that. Here." He performed the job himself, unwinding the giant black man's loincloth. He looked the bared body up and down, and with a smile on his epicene face, reached out to touch the black's genitals. The slave's body jerked spasmodically and the black hands clenched themselves inadvertently into powerful fists. Soulai looked up through fluttering eyelashes at the black face struggling to control its rage. "Oh, pooh," he said. "Well, he'll learn. There are ways. Yes, this one. Have it sent to my house tonight. Send the bill to my father, will you?"

"Are you sure?" Nebo said. "Your father . . . the honorable Habasle rebuked me mightily the last time I sold you a slave of spirit, the kind that had to be . . . uh, tamed, a bit first."

"Leave it to me," Soulai said. "I'll have him tamed, don't you worry." He smiled his sweetest, most patently false smile at the anxious-looking black. "I have an infallible formula. It involves a red-hot coal decorating the navel of a rebellious slave." The smile grew ever sweeter as he looked the giant slave in the eye. Then he dismissed his new property with a shrug. "What I *really* wanted here," he continued, "was a boy. A nice fresh boy, about twelve or so. Something like the one that burly lout outbid me for at auction a month or so ago."

Gods, Nebo thought, *I was hoping you wouldn't bring that up.* "Oh, yes," he said. "Well, there *is* a new shipment due in any day now, sir. I'll be sure you have the first selection, sir, a good customer like you."

Soulai's pale face, however, had settled into a frown. "Tell me," he said. "This lower-class boor who bought the child. What's his name? I owe him an ill turn sometime."

"Oh, sir, please," Nebo said. "I'm not allowed to give out that sort of information."

"Not allowed? Nebo, my friend, you aren't very realistic. With the chief magistrate out of the city for awhile, who is the law in the quarter? Who decides what is to be at every level of the city below the palace of the king? I'll tell you: my father, Habasle, that's who. And if he learns that my will has been thwarted by a merchant of slaves, a man whose license to buy and sell has to come up for review every so often . . ." A quick smile of triumph flitted over Soulai's face. "Ah, that one struck home, didn't it? You do have a renewal examination coming up, don't you? Well, I'd watch my step if I were you."

"Please, sir," Nebo said. "If—"

"The name. The name, and right now, or—"

"Oh, sir. It's . . . it's Zakir. He . . . he is a metalsmith in the Bazaar of the Three Palms. But sir, I wouldn't—"

"Never mind," said Soulai, smiling again. "Now: a new shipment, you said? And due soon?"

Now it was Zakir manning the pipe and Ahuni—a very nervous Ahuni, feeling very clumsy and out of place—holding the hammer. "Now!" Zakir said between puffs. "Strike! Strike while it's hot! There . . . right there." And, his eyes bulging, he went back to puffing. The piece of metal in Ahuni's forceps glowed white-hot. He struck a timid blow, recoiled from the glare in Zakir's eyes, then struck again, harder this time. Zakir nodded vigorously, still puffing. Ahuni struck again. The metal flattened, taking shape with each blow.

That evening Zakir took the boy with him on a visit to a better quarter of town. He led Ahuni through the streets until the two stood before a broad, imposing house. "There!" Zakir said. "How would you like to live in that one, boy?"

"Sir?" Ahuni said. "But—"

"I haven't told anybody in the market. But . . . well, I've been talking to the brokers. I've even consulted an astrologer about it. My numerologist is picking me out a proper date for making a contract. It's time I lived at a better address. I'm getting up in the world, you know." He beamed down at the boy, one hand on Ahuni's shoulder, taking note of the newly hardened muscle on the boy's deltoids. "What do you think, son?"

Ahuni's face changed at the word *son*. He looked Zakir in the eye, an expression almost of fear in his unbelieving eyes. He hesitated. Then he said, "It looks wonderful, sir." He blushed. What else could he say? Anything else would be presumption in a slave. But Zakir so clearly wanted him to say more that he gulped and tried again. "I . . . I think I'd like it," he said. "Sir."

"Like it?" Zakir said, beaming. "Of course you will. And—see up there? That little window at the top? That'll be your room. The one below it, the one with the balcony . . . that's mine. And the kitchen will be over there, and there's a room for the cook, and—"

"Cook, sir?" Ahuni said. He looked at Zakir, thunderstruck. "But—"

"Oh, yes. About time I started putting some sort of household together. I'm not getting any younger, you know. And—gods, I can afford it, son. Business has never been better." He turned away and started talking about his plans for the house. They went right over Ahuni's head. He was thinking—or trying to. His head was swimming. A room of his own? A master who called him "son"? Life in a big house, with a staff? Apprenticeship to a paying trade, rather than the usual dull chores that had no future? Apprenticeship, with its built-in chance of eventual freedom once his indentured years were over? It was hard to believe all this was happening, no matter how hard he tried to accept it.

IV

The progress Ahuni had made at the forge continued to amaze Zakir. His neighbors in the bazaar marveled not only at the quick mind and ready hands of the boy but at the change that had come over Zakir as well. Previously, when things were not going well, Zakir would hurl curses at the forge, at the red-hot metal that stubbornly refused to assume the shape he had in mind for it, or at anyone or anything that happened to cross his path.

But he seemed always to be smiling. When a customer entered his shop, he greeted him with a pleasant courtesy that had been foreign to his nature before. "The boy's good for him," whispered the merchants in the bazaar, scratching their heads in wonder. No one could explain why the metalsmith's relationship with his young slave had wrought such a drastic change in him. Perhaps the most plausible answer was provided by the wife of Iddina, who, visiting her husband at the bazaar one day, was heard to exclaim: "For heaven's sake, hasn't it ever occurred to any of you that the man might have been *lonely?* I mean, for someone to talk to? Well, after all . . ."

This made more sense than anything else. Little by little, most of Zakir's friends came to accept Ahuni: they even began to accept the fiction that Zakir had put out about the boy's status: that he was in fact an apprentice rather than a slave. After all, if the boy made the smith happy, what did it matter?

One day Zakir left Ahuni at the forge for a morning to go across town, ostensibly to purchase ore for a commission. Ahuni said good-bye to him and then squatted down intently at the little forge to shape a copper shinplate for the ceremonial use of a leader of the royal guards. Halfway across the bazaar, Zakir waved at the boy before disappearing behind the wall of a building.

Iddina came by the forge when the sun was not yet high, looking for his friend. "Here, boy," he said. "When does Zakir return?"

Ahuni smiled up at him from the forge, skipping a beat or two. "After the midday meal," he said. "Shall I tell him you called, sir?" His manner was deferential. He liked Iddina, and there was a touch of affection in his voice as he answered the wine merchant.

"No, boy. I'll come back when . . ." He looked up, and Ahuni, catching the look in his eye—a look compounded of shock and surprise, with perhaps an undercurrent of fear—followed with his eyes where the vintner was looking. "Ahuni," Iddina said. "Go about your business. Let me handle this."

Ahuni's face reflected his own apprehension. Soulai, the son of the magistrate, Habasle, was walking through the bazaar with a retinue of perhaps half a dozen satellites. He stopped before the forge. "You!" he cried. "Don't I know you from somewhere?"

"I beg your pardon," Iddina said, stiffening.

Soulai drew closer. "Yes," he said. "You accompanied . . . what's his name? Zakir the smith. You accompanied him when he outbid me—humiliated me—in the market. And . . . and this?" His eye lit on Ahuni, squatting before the banked fire. "This is the slave he won from me." He looked the boy up and down, his eyes virtually caressing the boy's mostly naked body.

"Now," he said, looking first at the boy and then at Iddina. "Now there's something odd. I see no slavemark. Yet I would wager a year's earnings that this was the same boy." He frowned; then a cunning smile came over his face. "Here, boy," he said. "Let me see that armband you wear."

Ahuni looked up at Soulai and then, his face falling, at Iddina. "Sir?" he said tentatively. "Must I . . . ?"

"I'm afraid so," said Iddina unhappily. A slave was always open to challenge. He could perhaps bluff it out—once. But if he were caught at it, or if the person who had first braced him were later to learn . . .

Ahuni slid the bracelet down his now hard young

bicep. Iddina watched Soulai's eyes ... and then his heart sank. "What's this?" said Soulai. "Has somebody been trying to obliterate the marking on this slave's arm?"

Attracted by the furor, Zikha, the cobbler who occupied an adjoining cubicle, blurted out: "Slave? But this is Zakir's apprentice. He told me so. He said that ..." And then, realizing his mistake, he tried to backtrack. "No, I meant that ..."

But Soulai interrupted him coldly. "I know what you meant," he said. "So the smith has been conspiring with the boy to remove the badge of his slavery from his arm? Doesn't he know what the penalty is for this? Well, now. This is most interesting. That's all right, boy. You can cover it back up again. It isn't very pretty, is it? I'll wager it hurt putting it on. Didn't it? Eh? Speak up, there. I can't hear you. It hurt, didn't it? The white-hot brand cutting into your flesh ... burning ..."

"Ohhh!" Ahuni screamed in pain, dropping the pincers into the flames. His thin shoulders contracted in pain as he hugged his hand to his body. His eyes stared at the magistrate's son through a film of tears. He made a low moan and rocked back and forth in pain.

"Look now," Iddina said angrily. "You've made him hurt himself. Here. I don't care who you are. I'm going to have to ask you to leave. If you don't, and right away, I'll have to call the ..."

Soulai looked the merchant in the eye and sneered. "Yes," he said. "And who will you call? The guards? Who are under my father's command in this quarter? To throw me out of the bazaar?" His eyes shifted to the boy, glancing at his stricken face and then down his thin body. "I am sorry, boy," he said. "I do hope you understand." The smile on his face held neither remorse nor pity. "Come," he said to the gaggle of retainers who had accompanied him. "We have business elsewhere. Urgent business." His eyes searched Iddina's; then, with a small, high-pitched laugh, he swept away in a swirl of softly tinted robes, leaving a faint smell of perfume behind him in the late morning air.

Zakir wound his way through the tangle of streets east of the great Processional Way that led northward to the Ishtar Gate of Babylon. Walking, with nothing else on his mind, he found himself thinking—as he had done in recent weeks—of Ahuni. Who was the boy? What sort of people could he have come from? He did not have the look of any of the traditional tribes from whom the empire usually drew its human chattels. And he had been made a slave so early in life that he had no memory either of the action or of the parents from whom he had been taken.

It would be interesting, he was thinking now, to trace the boy's background if it could be done. At the moment he had scarcely a clue. A boy could become a slave by so many routes, after all. He could be born a slave, into a family of slaves. He could be captured in war. Indeed, there were those in the bazaars who cynically asserted that half the reason for the many small wars the king started against the outlying areas was the need to find new, and cheap, manpower for the many construction projects he had initiated or taken over—the unfinished Tower of the Planets among them.

Driven to extremes a father might also wind up selling his wife, his children, or even himself into slavery if he were unable to repay a debt he had contracted. An adopted child, too, could be sold as a slave if he renounced his adoptive father. Any of these paths could have led Ahuni to the slave block. Well, some day he would find out. A boy had a right to know who his father was.

Thinking these thoughts, Zakir found himself in the merchant quarter. Just before reaching the bazaar, he was approached by a seller of songs who boldly tugged at his sleeve. "Songs, sir? Rhymes? A fit song for a special occasion?"

"Sorry, no," Zakir said, shaking himself loose. "I seek a man named Kannounai. An old man. He was once a member of my caste—which is that of the smiths."

"But for a single song, sir, one might . . . listen, sir. I

wrote this for the captain of the king's guards. It goes, *In the street I met two harlots . . .*"

Zakir interrupted him, dismissing the song with a wave of his hand. "Yes, and in the street *I* met one nuisance. If you cannot direct me to the house of Kannounai, you are wasting my time."

The song-seller stepped back, abashed. "Right over there, sir," he said. "He lives above the seller of sesame oil."

"Thank you," Zakir said. He made his way across the square without looking back.

Meeting with a former master of the craft involved a complex protocol. Zakir presented his credentials, said the right things, deferred constantly to the old man—and listened. Catering to the vanity of the old was a bother, but sometimes it was necessary.

Finally, cutting through the old man's chatter, he saw his chance. "Kannounai," he said. "I came to you because you have traveled far and know a great many things. There is a story—perhaps it's no more than an old wives' tale—that I heard when I was a boy, and I've been trying to remember it. I was wondering if perhaps your memory might be better than mine."

"It might well be," said the old man. He settled back against the cushions of his raised bed. "I find now that I can remember with great clarity things that happened when I was a boy, sixty or seventy summers ago . . . but I can't remember where I put my crutch an hour ago. What is on your mind?"

"The story, sir . . . there was something about a birthmark. A birthmark that looked like the paw print of a lion. It had something to do with the caste of smiths, as I remember it. There was an old story, and I only heard it once, in passing . . . and then I forgot."

"Birthmark, you say? And like the paw print of a lion? No, I can't say I know that one. It must be a tale from some other region. Perhaps downriver, in Ur. That's where our craft began, you know. When the city was destroyed, many secrets of the forge died with it . . . although there are tales of the metalwork done in Egypt, far across the great desert, and in the lands on the shores of the Great Sea."

"Well, perhaps . . . could you direct me to someone who might know about this?" Zakir steered the conversation back to the subject. Old men had a tendency to ramble.

"Well, since you ask . . ." Kannounai's old hands, long palsied, closed around the small purse Zakir pressed into his palm. "I will have a visit from an old friend from Uruk. It will not be this week or the next, but soon. He is coming to the city to sell golden fixtures to the court of the king. I have had a letter from him. . . . Let's see, it was around here somewhere. . . ."

On the way back to the Bazaar of the Three Palms, Zakir kept trying to drive away a feeling of malaise. Something—he could not say what—was eating at him now, and he didn't feel well. What was the matter with him? There had been nothing in the conversation with Kannounai to upset him. And things were going well, all in all, better than they had gone in many, many months.

As he threaded his way through the warren of streets and crossed the Processional Way, once more his apprehension intensified. Had someone cast a spell upon him? Was it time to visit the barber and be bled? The magician? He shook his head and tried to master the depression that gripped him.

When he entered the Bazaar of the Three Palms, he was too preoccupied to take note of the frantic signals that Iddina, across the square in his shop window, was trying to send him. Then suddenly he found himself confronted by two burly soldiers of the city's guard. "You are Zakir the smith?" one of them asked in an up-country accent.

"Yes," said Zakir in a hoarse voice. He tried to continue forward, but the guard blocked his way. "I beg your pardon," Zakir said. "I'm not feeling well, and I'm going over there to—"

"You'll have to come with us," the guard said. "There has been a complaint."

Zakir looked up into the guard's brown eyes. "Complaint?" he said, suddenly wary. "Complaint? Complaint of what? And by whom?" There was no answer to be found in the impassive faces of the soldiers. "Iddina!" he called over the guard's shoulder. "Take care of the boy, please! I'll come back . . . but look out for him, will you?"

"Zakir!" Iddina said over the rising noise of the crowd. "The boy is gone! I haven't seen him!"

The guards each took an arm. Zakir struggled only once, trying to look back. Then, his strength and resolve sapped by the sick feeling in his stomach, he allowed himself to be led from the square.

The trial, before a hastily convened assembly, was swift and devastatingly to the point. Witnesses were paraded before Habasle's court to assert again and again that they had seen the telltale signs on Ahuni's arm of an attempt—allegedly incited by Zakir—to remove the boy's slave-mark. Zakir's bellows of denial were in vain. Even in the absence of Ahuni the multiple denunciations were enough to convict Zakir. Waiting miserably for sentence, he thanked all the gods that Ahuni had had the good sense to run for it before the guards appeared. There was a penalty for slave and master alike in such cases; caught, the boy would be mutilated. Zakir's heart was empty. He knew the penalty usually prescribed by law for his alleged offense: death.

He scarcely heard the sentence. He allowed himself to be led away meekly, and spent the next six hours in solitary confinement trying to prepare his mind for death.

But when they led him forth, it was not to the square where criminals were commonly executed, but to an underground room deep inside the palace. And it was not his neck that went on the block to be chopped off with one crushing blow of the executioner's axe. It was his right hand.

CHAPTER THREE

I

A heavily armed guard of Shairetana marched alongside the great caravan of Abram all the way to the
edge of the great desert. There, the captain of the
guards halted the column and sought an audience with
Abram.

He was a handsome sight in his Shairetana uniform,
with its long skirt and striped jerkin, the metal-studded
leather buckler on one brawny arm, and the big
double-edged sword hanging by his side. Hagar busied
herself with securing the harness on the ass that had
borne Sarai thus far and watched as the captain spoke
with her master, trying not to think of the pain in her
sunburned back and breasts and the constant ache in
her bare feet.

"I leave you here," the captain said. "The escort
must go back to Sile."

"That is good," Abram said. His eyes sought the
younger man's and liked what they saw there. His tone
did not take on the slightly exaggerated dignity it had
borne in the audience with Senmut; this, after all, was
a soldier, a leader of men like himself, and they need
not stand on ceremony. "We will have no further need
of armed force. Other than our own," he smiled.

The Shairetana captain smiled ruefully, looking at
the caravan. "You have the manpower," he said. "You
want arms."

"You have my thought exactly," Abram said. "Well,

thanks to the bad conscience of your master and the bribe he has offered me to ease it, I am rich enough to pay any reasonable price for arming my people. The problem is finding the men to arm me. Have you any suggestions?"

"Yes. If you follow the direct route through the Wilderness of Shur, it should, if I remember right, take you very near Timna. This is our best mine for copper ore. The smelting operation is right there. You can purchase metal right at the site. And I'm sure you'll find someone who can be hired to arm—yes, and perhaps train—your people for the fight ahead."

"Wonderful. I thank you for your help . . . and for your escort."

The captain smiled, his teeth white in the dark face. "I accept thanks for the advice. The escort wasn't my idea. I was ordered to escort you to the nearest border. I gathered that the idea was to make sure you left and didn't come back."

Abram's expression was guileless. "No fear of that. If we never see the delta again, it will be too soon. Well, Captain. Good luck to you." He handed over a purse. "Use this to treat your men to something."

"I'll do that, sir. And good fortune! You'll need it up north, I think."

"The hand of the God is upon us. But I appreciate your good wishes. Farewell!"

Hagar watched Abram turn and walk slowly over to the wagons. The captain of Shairetana looked briefly at her, turned away, then looked back at her again. And he walked over to her. "You," he said. "You look familiar from somewhere. Have I . . . ?"

Hagar bit her lip and turned her face away, suddenly ashamed of the quick burst of tears in her eyes. "I . . . I don't know, sir," she said.

"Yes, you do." His tone was suddenly gentle. So was the dark-skinned hand he put under her chin to lift her face so that he could look into her eyes. "Ah, yes. You were of the household of . . . was it Psarou, the merchant?"

"Yes, sir," Hagar said. She tried to blink the tears away.

"Ah," he said, his brow suddenly knitting. "I'm sorry. I see ... when he died his goods were given away. And you—"

"I was among those 'goods.' " Her tone struggled to cover bitterness with dignity, but in vain. "Now? Well ..."

"Ah," the captain said. "A great pity. Fortune smiles upon us today and curses us the next. And you ... you will march across that wilderness? Behind the wagons? Dressed so?"

"I do as I am told."

"Look. Ask for a ... a hood of sorts. Cover up in this heat and glare. Tell the other women to do so. Hmmm. I see you're barefoot. I know you won't believe me just now, but actually that's better than sandals. The quicker your feet get toughened up, the better. South of Beersheba you'll cross a couple of mountain ranges. By then your soles will be tough as leather, and you'll be able to negotiate the climb with ease. Make sure any children in the party get plenty of water, even between stops. They tend to dry out quicker than we do. And drink a goodly amount yourself."

"Yes, sir," she said, her head bowed again. "Thank you, sir." But when she raised her head, she found him meeting her gaze, a look of empathy and compassion on his dark face.

"Luck go with you," he said, squeezing her hand once. "I have stood where you stand. This is how I became a soldier. Only I left my home in somewhat a different manner. I watched my home in flames, my parents flayed in the streets. Let me tell you, girl. Don't let it reach you, all the way. And don't ever accept your fate. Know that you are above it. Keep up your pride. If you do these things you will survive. You will prevail." He smiled, the look of something better than pity still in his dark eyes. Then he nodded curtly, turned, and left.

Above, the relentless sun beat down. . . .

Abram's party did not reach the first well until they had marched three days across the barren lands east of Succoth. During this period, some of the cattle succumbed. A mother lost a newborn child to a fever, but on the second night of the march, an Egyptian slave named Eben gave birth to a strapping boy-child.

Hagar delivered the child herself, as she had been trained to do in Psarou's household. Not trusting the help offered her by attendants in Abram's entourage, she called for Shepset and coached the girl through the woman's labor. The baby was born in the small hours of the morning, just as dawn was breaking over the pink-tinged mountains in the east.

Hagar and Shepset stole an hour's rest on a pair of bare pallets as the other women prepared meal for the morning repast, grinding the grain on portable millstones and refining the flour with crude mortars and pestles. But neither could sleep. The waking noises of the camp, added to the excitement of the woman's labor, had made them too tense to slip off into dreams.

Hagar rose on one elbow. "Shepset," she said bitterly. "I could weep. Why did we help give Eben's child life, only to see it born a slave?"

"Oh, my lady," Shepset began, but broke off her words.

" 'My lady,' " Hagar said, a great grief in her soft voice. "And now I'm nobody. Why didn't I kill the child and have done with it?" Then she caught the hurt and reproach in the girl's eyes and took hold of herself. "I'm sorry," she said. "It's just that—"

"I know," Shepset said. "We came so close to being free, to being the equals of the people around us. And now . . . " She sighed.

"Who are you working for?" Hagar said. "I didn't know. I just sent for you. They didn't say where they found you."

"I am working for the wife of Abram's nephew, Lot. I . . . I wish I were with you."

"Does it have something to do with Lot? Or his wife?"

"No . . . well, not anything I can put my hand on.

They don't treat me too badly, I guess. They work me hard—but I'm used to that by now. It's just that . . . "

"Oh. Lot is interested in you." Hagar sighed. There was nothing to be done for it. If Lot were to choose to have the girl, and if Abram did not object . . . "I wonder. Perhaps if I please the lord Abram and his lady Sarai, I can ask to have you brought here."

"Would you, please? I mean . . . I didn't expect this to be easy, but—"

"Yes, I know. I have seen Lot. I cannot believe that he and the lord Abram are of the same family—but they are. From all I can tell, Abram is hardly more impressed with him than we are. But if they are of the same blood, after all . . ." She sighed again. "Just try to stay away from him if you can. That's all I can say. All of the protections we used to know are gone now. We'll have to use our wits if we're to survive."

The girl sat up, hugging her little bare breasts, which by now were as ruddy as Hagar's. "I also seem to have drawn the notice of Ah-mose, who used to keep some properties of the lord Psarou's down near Pithom. I had never seen him before the night the guards came. He was in Sile on the lord Psarou's business when the order came."

"Poor man. I remember him. Well, he is young and doesn't look too bad. If you . . . but of course he's a slave now too, and what does it matter? We will all be mated to whomever the lord Abram has chosen. Or we will become concubines of his poor relations. Or we will be bred like cattle. Or sold. Or traded away for better land in Canaan." She shook her dark head.

No. She would not let herself sink into despair. You had to keep some part of you, deep down inside, unspoiled and unbroken. You had to remain above it, to keep yourself apart from it so that it could not hurt you. The more you whined, nursing your hurt, the worse it would be in the long run.

"I'm sorry," she said now. "I won't let myself go that way again. Shepset, my dear. Keep in touch with me as much as you can. I want to hear from you whenever you've got a free moment and can sneak away without arousing someone's displeasure. I need a friend here, and so do you, I think. Let's remain friends. We must not be broken by our misfortunes or dragged down to the level of pack animals or breeding stock. We're equal now; I'm not 'my lady' any more." She took the girl's thin hands in hers, hands that were already calloused by toil.

"Come," she said. "From now on we're sisters, and nobody can tear us apart."

Shepset smiled through her tears. "Sisters," she repeated.

II

Ka-Nakht, overseer of the Great King's mines at Timna, came out of his tent smiling. His smile grew broader as he recognized the burly figure who stood watching him at a respectable distance beyond the circle of tents, his arms crossed over his broad chest. "Sneferu!" shouted the overseer.

His countryman perfunctorily made the ritual signs of obeisance, but the broad grin on his face belied all formality. "So I see a soldier is not yet quite forgotten by old friends in the trade," he said.

"How could I forget a man who still owes me an *outnou* from a past wager?" Ka-Nakht said. But his quick theatrical frown fooled neither of the two. They stepped toward each other and embraced warmly. Then, holding his friend's biceps and looking him in the eye, the overseer said, "Forget the *outnou*. The race was crooked anyway. What brings you to Timna so late into the season?"

"What brings a mercenary soldier anywhere?" Sneferu said. His expression turned wry, and the strong hook nose above the comically downturned lips sniffed in chagrin. "I'm between jobs, of course. I just finished negotiating a peace between two warring tribes east of the Jordan, only to find that my services were no longer needed."

"You did too good a job," Ka-Nakht said. "Always leave a little undone. Always leave one avenue for dispute. Make sure the atmosphere of menace remains. Haven't we had this drilled into us enough times in our youth?"

Sneferu shrugged. "I get bored with that. I keep wanting to finish what I've started. I've put myself out of more jobs that way. And I can't carry on that deceit anyway, lying to the prince and telling him all about that hostile army that's out there waiting to pounce. Not when I've just finished beating hell out of the bastards until everyone with an eye can see that they're licked."

"You'll never learn," Ka-Nakht said. "Here. Will you join me for a draught of beer? I took pains to bring half a dozen women brewers out with me this time."

"Not quite yet," Sneferu said. "I've adopted a regimen. No strong waters before dusk. Meanwhile, what's happening here? Any tribal princes dropping by to buy ore or arms? Somebody I can talk into hiring me to show him how to use them?"

"Not at the moment," Ka-Nakht said. "But you're welcome to stay around for a bit at the Great King's expense. There's a fund for that sort of thing. Stay around for a week or two. I can use the company. This is dull duty."

"Well . . . until something turns up. What's happening now?" He looked up around him at the deeply gouged cliffs, and at the loinclothed men digging away at the hillsides with stone-headed hammers. Near them other workers hacked away at the malachite the miners had dug out of the hill, breaking it into smaller pieces for smelting. "Quite a lot of them working here now. Midianites, I'd say, from the look of them."

"Oh, yes," Ka-Nakht said, looking up at the carved hills. "Good workers. Summer's a bad season for them. I'll have them until fall, when the birds fly away. Look, down there in the valley; that's where they grind the ore. And the smelting furnace is down there. Oh, yes.

There's someone you might like to meet. I remember you always liked to watch a good craftsman at work."

"Ah. A metalsmith?"

"Yes, and one of the best. Belsunu. Comes from Ur, across the desert. He's here on a job for the commander at Sile, in the delta, who needs a pair of bronze doors for his palace. Well, he'll get them, and I hope he appreciates them. They're really quite good. This fellow has a new way of smelting. He's been introducing changes. It's a matter of raising the temperature. That's always the problem with this stuff anyhow."

"Interesting. And he made up the way of doing this himself?"

"Well, maybe. Maybe not. He claims it's just a refinement of the way they did it in Ur before the city fell. He's about our age."

"I see. A doddering graybeard." The irony was heavy. Sneferu was forty. "Well, no matter. Any man who can improve the process of metalsmithing is all right with me. What kind of fellow is he?"

"Well, don't mention it to him . . . but he's a sick man. Very sick. I'd be surprised to find him alive by this time next year. I came by his tent the other morning to wake him and found him drenched in sweat. And it was a chilly morning too."

"Oh." Sneferu's face registered understanding. "And he's skinny? Can't put on weight no matter how much he eats?"

"Yes. I see we understand each other. That cough . . . it used to come only in the morning, but it's an all-day business now, and getting worse."

"Coughing up blood?"

"Yes. Poor devil. And he's not a bad chap at all, Sneferu. Not at all. He's not even bad company, sick as he is, when he's able to stop coughing and talk. He's been a lot of places. The life's much like yours, much like my old life before I got tired of moving about so."

"Yes. A metalsmith, a good one, is always welcome anywhere. He can cross any border any time except in the middle of a really desperate war, and sometimes even then, if they need him badly enough. Yes, I think

I'd like to meet him. Maybe I can barter something to him for a new sword. The handle of my old one has gone loose on me."

"Ah. Mucked it up in a battle?"

"Gods, no. A barrel of wine fell on it in a tavern in Damascus. You know how it is. These things never happen to us in heroic circumstances. Of course, one lies about them shamelessly. You tell everyone you broke your arm in hand-to-hand combat—and another soldier, listening, will take you aside when you're done and ask you if it didn't really get busted by the owner of a whorehouse somewhere . . . and the hell of it is, he'll be right."

Ka-Nakht laughed. "Look, you'll stay a week or two, or I'll hobble you myself and make you. It's been lonely here. Nobody to talk to . . . except the smith, and he's fading fast. Sick men make melancholy company, however pleasant they may have been when they were well."

"Perhaps," Sneferu said. "Still, I'd like to meet this fellow. I'd like to talk to him."

They stood on a rise looking down at the smith and his assistants, at work casting the great door. To one side a small smelting furnace, fed from a charcoal mound nearby, lay half-buried in the ground. There were holes in the sides of it, and on either side a worker trod a pair of ingeniously formed bellows. First they inflated one bladder by yanking on a string that let it expand; then they trod down on the other, forcing air into the cauldron under pressure. Inside, a crucible of molten bronze bubbled sluggishly on white-hot coals.

"Clever," Sneferu said. "But that process is largely Egyptian, not Mesopotamian."

"Oh, yes," Ka-Nakht nodded. "But Belsunu is working on ways of further refining the process. If he succeeds, we will be able to smelt a great deal more copper for bronze. He's applying the process to other stages as well. Look over there now: there's the door mold. They're doing it by stages—by layers, you might say. See, they're pouring the molten bronze through those vents into the mold. The gases escape over there."

"Ah, yes. It ought to be quite handsome." But Sneferu's eye was not on the clay mold; he was watching the smith. "Gods," he said. "This is Belsunu? But no, it couldn't be anyone else, given your description."

"Yes. Poor devil. His skin grows grayer every day."

"From the span of those shoulders I'd say he used to be a real ox before the weight started falling off him." Sneferu, pursing his lips, scowled compassionately down at the big man. "It's terrible to see a strong man struck down this way."

"As you say," Ka-Nakht observed, "He was a powerful man once. I met a man who had known him earlier: he said Belsunu at one time could lift an ass with each arm and stand up. He won a lot of wagers that way."

"I wouldn't be surprised. Tell me, my friend: is he as sad as he looks?"

Ka-Nakht looked at his companion, his face full of mixed emotions. "I'd say he was," he said. "Only it's not what you think. I believe he regards his illness mainly as an annoyance, as a thing which gets in his way. He has other burdens to bear: burdens I'm glad I don't have to carry. But make friends with him. He'll tell you sooner or later. Approach him. It'll be worth your while. He's a thoughtful man and has much to say, if you can get him to say it."

Sneferu watched the big man supervising the pouring of the molten bronze; watched him interrupted in the giving of an order by a fierce burst of desperate coughing: deep, racking, painful coughs that sounded as though he were going to spit up his guts. "I think I'll wait awhile," he said quietly. Then he turned and his manner changed. "Meanwhile, my friend, what does one do for women around here?"

The overseer and the itinerant soldier celebrated their reunion that evening before a big fire with beer and roasted game. A hasty call to the camp of the

Midianites brought singers, musicians, and dancers to their campfire. The brown limbs of the girls flashed in the firelight. Sneferu, whose travels had taught him many tongues, sang lustily the bawdy Midianite song about a wronged husband and his erring wife. Ka-Nakht bellowed with laughter, calling for more beer for all.

The group had brought a handful of children with them; these capered happily back and forth in a counterpoint to the stately dances of their elders. And now a dark-eyed Midianite beauty defied the catcalls of her friends to step up to Sneferu and drag him by the hands into the dance. "All right, all right," Sneferu said with a tipsy laugh. "I'm not sure I remember this dance, but ... here I go." The barrel-chested soldier had a natural grace about him and had kept his wits despite the number of drinks he'd downed. Sneferu fell easily into the complicated steps and soon looked perfectly at home in the ring of dancers. Ka-Nakht, with a slim pubescent girl on his knee, watched him enviously until he passed on the other side of the fire; then he turned his mind to the more urgent business at hand. The girl giggled, cuddled closer to him, and put up her thin face for his kiss.

Then he looked up and there was Belsunu standing by the fire, looking around at the people from the Midianite camp. Sneferu danced past him ... and then stopped, looking sheepish. The music faltered and stopped.

Belsunu looked around him, embarrassed. "I'm sorry," he said. "Please continue. Someone told me ... there was a boy here, about so high ... but I see everyone here is either too young or too old." He raised one of his broad hands imploringly: "Please. Start the music again. I didn't mean to spoil your entertainment." Then, his great shoulders slumping, he fell into a fit of coughing and moved out of the circle of firelight. The music struck up again.

Sneferu moved over to Ka-Nakht, his arm still around the girl's slim waist. "What was all that about? I mean, the business about the *boy?*" He shook his head incredulously. "To look at him you wouldn't have thought his tastes lay in that direction."

"Pardon?" said Ka-Nakht. "Oh, I see what you . . . no, no. It isn't that at all. No, you have him wrong. Come, sit here. Give the girl a rest on your knee. But bring the jug of beer with you, will you? And pour into my bowl . . . so . . ."

Sneferu, joining him on top of the quarried stone platform, lifted the girl and perched her in his lap. Then he poured beer from the big jug into both bowls, put the jug down, and gave the girl a sip from his own bowl. He took a mighty draught, belched appreciatively, and turned to his friend again. "You were saying," he said, his tongue suddenly thick. "About the smith."

"Oh, yes. I was telling you . . . well, he's no boy-lover. As a matter of fact, he doesn't have too much to do with women either these days. He's pretty sick, you know. He doesn't get too close to anyone, male or female."

"Oh. Then why?"

"He's looking for someone. Someone he lost. It's a long story, and I was going to let him tell it when you got to know him, but . . ."

Sneferu pinched the girl playfully. She let out a tiny scream and wriggled—but wriggled closer to him. "You tell me," Sneferu said hoarsely.

"Well," Ka-Nakht said, shifting the girl to his other knee and handing her the bowl of beer, "it seems he was living near Mari, in the Valley of the Euphrates. He had a job working for the Palace. Then one day the astrologers told him, just as he was leaving to accompany the king's party on a scouting mission upriver, that it would be bad luck to go with them. He laughed it off and said farewell to his wife and children. He had a little boy and an older daughter, as I remember. He was very fond of them."

"Your story is taking too long," Sneferu said, nuzzling the girl.

"There's not much more of it. He went away with the king's party . . . and while they were gone there was a raid on the city. When he got back he found his wife and daughter dead, with their throats cut. They had been raped—" he sighed half in pity, half in disgust at human cruelty "—and then impaled. Poor bastard. Having *that* on his conscience."

"Oh. But . . . you said he had how many children? Wasn't it two?"

"Oh, yes. Well, one of the neighbors had witnessed it all and had managed to escape. He said that the boy had been hauled away crying—he was just a small child, maybe four—with a rope around his neck. For the slave market, obviously."

"By the gods, that's a terrible story. But the smith? You mean . . . you mean he's still looking for the boy? After all these years?" Sneferu shook his head incredulously. "In the name of . . . how would he recognize him? I mean, isn't that sort of . . . ?"

"Watch him at the forge. There's a mark on his side. A red birthmark, one he says breeds true in the male side of his family. If the boy's still alive, he bears it."

"Well, I'll be damned," Sneferu said. He took another drink, spilling the beer on the ground. When he spoke again, it was in a cracked voice. "By the gods," he said. "I'm getting tipsy. Here, sweetheart, you finish this. And . . . and . . . what was I talking about? Oh, the smith. You said a birthmark? What kind of birthmark? The raised kind?"

"No, it's just a red pattern. It looks like the print of a lion's paw."

III

Sneferu liked the smith from the moment he met him. This came as a surprise to him as he had expected a monument of gloom. He had the soldier's aversion to sick or wounded men who had the pall of death upon them.

Nevertheless, though the flesh had fallen away from Belsunu's face in recent days, there was something in the man's eyes that belied his decrepit state. He had the air of good-humored tolerance, of ready sympathy, of fearlessness that was usually found in only the strongest men. Sneferu, whose intuitions about people had rarely failed him, felt drawn to the smith immediately.

As he approached, Belsunu was examining a sword he had just made. It gleamed in the morning sun as he tested blade and shaft, swinging it at the end of a long, still powerful arm. Then he looked at Sneferu, an immensely likable grin on his bony face. "Ah," he said. "You'd be the Egyptian our host was telling me about. Here, try this out, will you?"

Sneferu nodded, accepting the weapon Belsunu offered hilt-first. And it was almost as if a small shock ran through his whole arm. He grasped the handle hard; it felt utterly at home in his hand. And the balance . . . "By the Gods!" he said in an awed voice. "What a weapon! I've never felt its like before. My friend, you shouldn't have put this in my hand. Now you'll have to kill me and pry it out of my palm. It's grown to my hand." He swung it once, twice. It felt better each time.

"No, I won't," the smith laughed quietly. "Ka-Nakht has told me about you. He says you're an honorable man. That's why I handed it to you. Go ahead; test it out. It's yours."

"Mine?" Sneferu said. "I don't understand. I'm between jobs; I don't have two coins to rub together."

"I know. Precisely why I want you to test it for me. It's a new design. The sort of thing you couldn't fob off on a regular, who has to have everything just so, the way he's had it for years. The only person to test a new variety of weapon on is someone like yourself, an unemployed captain of irregulars. Besides, a soldier between jobs is . . . is more open-minded." His speech faded off into a fit of coughing. The smith bent over, racked by painful spasms that came from the inmost reaches of his huge chest, his hand on the cold anvil supporting him. Sneferu started to reach out to him, but the smith, seeing him out of the corner of one eye, held up a cautionary hand. "It's . . . it's all right. . . . I'm . . ." The coughing again drowned his words, and Sneferu, looking down, saw him spit up blood that was tinged with green bile. Wincing, he looked away.

"I'm sorry," the smith said, straightening. "I've not been well lately. Too much idleness, no doubt. Well, apparently that won't last long. It appears I may be working for Arioch, the king of Ellasar, and perhaps for some of his allies over in the Valley of the Salt Sea. It's no secret that there's a war brewing there. The battle lines are all drawn up."

"That's interesting," Sneferu said, still hefting the magical weapon, unwilling to let it go. "I'm thinking of working for him myself. We may well find ourselves in harness"—he made another series of practice moves with the sword—"a prospect which pleases me no end, friend. If you can arm a troop I command with such weapons, you'll make me a wealthy man."

"Use it in good health," the smith said, smiling again. "An armorer depends on the strong and skillful arm of a master soldier to spread his good name about. Win me many victories."

Sneferu felt a sudden rush of warmth for the big man and found himself acting on impulse, for perhaps the first time in years. "Look, smith . . . I'm sorry, I don't remember the name. I'm Sneferu of Luxor, and here's my hand in friendship."

The smith extended his big paw. "Belsunu. I was born in Ur, but I've kept on the move pretty much since." The cough caught up with him again; he shielded his mouth with one long-fingered hand.

"Well," Sneferu said. "Belsunu, I think you've made a friend. I feel strangely attracted to you. I think we'll work together over there in the Sink. And . . . well, one needs a friend, someone who speaks the same language, on one of these jobs, working for border princelings fighting over beggarly little kingdoms that smell of sheep manure. I realize this is rather presumptuous of me . . . but I'd like to propose a sort of . . . well, partnership."

"Well, now . . ." the smith began. But again he was seized by a furious fit of coughing that left him weak, gasping for breath. "I'm sorry. . . . I . . ."

Sneferu, suddenly taken aback by his own apparent haste, felt callow and foolish. "I realize," he said lamely, "that—"

"No, no," the smith said between racking coughs. "I . . . I wasn't saying no to you. . . . It's just this confounded . . . illness of mine. . . . I'd be . . . I'd be happy to travel with you. . . . Ka-Nakht . . . he says you're the best soldier . . . he ever served with." Finally the coughing spell ended. Belsunu leaned back against the anvil on its stone platform, trying vainly to catch his breath. Finally he turned to Sneferu and said, with a wan smile, "I'm sorry. I can't seem to get rid of this illness. And the physicians don't seem to know what to do. Spells. Bleeding. All nonsense." He gasped for breath between phrases. "All nonsense. Travel the world over, the less you believe in any specific little set of gods, or the specific little bits of mumbo jumbo you're supposed to use to invoke them."

"A man after my own heart," Sneferu said. "I don't know how long it's been since I met an old soldier who believed in anything at all other than, perhaps, the skills of a lifetime. Well, friend, I believe in mine. And I believe in yours." He hefted the wonderful sword again and, pulling his old one out of its scabbard, replaced it with the new one. "Here," he said. "Take the old one. Melt it down. Make it new."

Belsunu took it, but put it down carelessly. "Thank you. I prefer to make weapons out of bronze I make myself."

"Admirable," Sneferu said. "When are you supposed to talk with this fellow from the Salt Sea?"

"Tomorrow morning."

"Fine. I'll go with you."

They rode out shortly after dawn on asses Ka-Nakht had loaned them. On the way Sneferu found himself humming a tune learned among the Midianites some campaigns before. It was a curious tune, not the usual sort of Midianite song. The melody was lilting, almost doleful, but the words were bawdy. As usual, they dealt with an unfaithful wife's insatiable hungers.

Belsunu waited until the end of the verse, and then he began to sing the same song in a tongue Sneferu did not know. Its meaning was totally different—one could hear that without understanding a syllable. The comedy had been replaced by one of melancholy and longing. Sneferu listened to the end and looked at Belsunu, his eyes questioning.

"A Sumerian song," Belsunu said. "One of the saddest songs ever sung. The young man laments that his god has forsaken him and has chosen him alone among his fellows for suffering and death. He prays for a reversal of the terrible fate that has overtaken him:

> O God, the sun shines bright over the land, but for me the day is black as pitch,
> The demon of fate clutches me in its hand, carrying off my breath of life,
> The malignant sickness-demon bathes in my body. . . .
> My father, you who begot me, I lift my face to you:
> How long will you withhold the hand of protection from me?

"Poor fool," Belsunu said, coughing. "Toss your prayers in the air and watch them scatter to the four winds like chaff." He smiled, but the smile was a sad one. Sneferu wondered at the memory that had retained that particular song, learned during childhood many years before.

They reached the tents of the Ellasarites an hour or so out of the valley. The expected audience was not to be, however. Dismounting, the smith fell into another wild fit of coughing. Doubled up in pain, he hacked and spat. He could not catch his breath. Sneferu rushed to his side and held him, feeling the great shivering sobs shake the big man's wasted body as the coughing shook him like a brown leaf in the first bitter winds of late autumn.

Sneferu was forced to bring the smith back to Timna

in a wagon. Upon their return, Ka-Nakht set two of the Midianite women to caring for the smith in a tent pitched deliberately next to his own. He joined Sneferu at the campfire that night, handing the mercenary a brimming bowl of beer. "I had a look at him," he said. "It looks pretty bad this time. I'm not sure he'll make it all the way back from this one."

"Damn it," Sneferu said, sipping his beer thoughtfully. "What a waste. He . . . did I show you the sword he gave me?"

"He showed it to me before he gave it to you. I envy you the gift. He may well be the greatest armorer of them all." The overseer shook his grizzled head sadly. "And a good man too. The best."

"Just before he had the attack I'd suggested partnership with him. Hiring out together from now on. I suppose I hadn't realized how sick he was."

"It was a good thought," Ka-Nakht said. "If he recovers, you've got yourself the makings of the kind of fortune that will allow you to retire on a patch of land you can't measure the perimeters of in four days' ride. But alas . . ." He sighed, long and deeply.

"By the gods," Sneferu said, angrily. "Look, I'm not going to take that Canaanite job. Do you suppose I could live off the Lord of Two Lands another month or so? Long enough to either nurse our friend here back to health . . . or, the gods pity the poor devil, bury him? There'll be other jobs along eventually. There's real trouble brewing over in the Valley of Siddim, the way I understand it. Multiple alliances on both sides. The other side'll be down here to buy metal stock soon, too, and the overseer of the Lord of Two Lands will be prosperous and busy selling metal to both sides at a handy profit."

"Of course," Ka-Nakht laughed. "That's part of the job. Keep the border princelings at one another's throats. That keeps them from getting any ambitions about lands under the direct hegemony of the God-King." He raised both hands palms high, in a gesture that said it. "But for the rest of your question: take all the time you like. I'll provide for you. I like the smith myself. And . . . well, I want to be able to send some samples of his work to Sile one of these days. If His Majesty's smiths can be taught the process . . . well, I could wind up with a villa myself before I'm much older and fatter."

"Thank you," Sneferu said. His eyes were thoughtful.

CHAPTER FOUR

I

The tavernkeeper stopped by their table, looked down, made a face. "I don't care what you say," he said disgustedly. "It looks like he's done for the night." He looked at the sodden figure slumping forward in the seat, immobile, unseeing, uncaring. "For the love of all the gods, he's passed out. That does it. Get him out of here."

Irsisi nodded, smiling his servile smile. "I've tried to get him up," he said. "He's too heavy. Look, let me send one of your people after a friend of ours. Maybe between us we can get him home."

"You'd better do that." The innkeeper signaled for a servant. "Meanwhile, you're taking up space in my tavern. Ordinarily I get paid for that."

"Yes, I understand." Irsisi pulled the leather purse out from under Zakir's inert left hand. It had bulged with coins when they arrived; now it held three or four coins at most. "Here," he said. "Bring me another bowl while I wait. And . . . you." He looked up at the menial the innkeeper had summoned. "Do you know the house of Iddina, the wine merchant, in the Street of the Two Lanterns?"

"Yes, sir," the servant said. "He sells to my master."

"Well, go get him, and on the double. There's a small gratuity for you if you hurry. Tell him . . . well, tell him Zakir's in trouble. Zakir the smith. Can you remember that? Tell him to come right here, as quickly as he can. Have you got that?"

"Yes, sir." The servant turned and went out the door.

Irsisi accepted the bowl of palm wine the tavern-keeper handed him, drank slowly and reflectively, and stared disapprovingly at the great bulk of Zakir slumped beside him and snoring drunkenly. He looked around, a small smile on his ferret face. Then his hand closed around the purse again and jingled the few remaining coins. With a shrug, he slipped the leather bag into his own garment.

Well, he thought, this is about the end of it. Time to move on . . . and perhaps to change taverns for a month or two. The life of a boon companion—a professional boon companion like himself—necessitated many changes of locale, as patrons and wealthy "friends" changed character or lost their money. Zakir, here, had come to about the end of the line. In a week, a month, he'd be a pauper, back in the streets where, rumor had it, he had started. Time to find a new friend, one whose source of income was more secure. Income? He snorted. Zakir had no income. As a matter of fact, crippled and unable to complete several expensive commissions on which he had already received advance payments, he was in danger of being sued for the advances. That almost certainly meant seizure of his house and shop.

Well, he thought, sipping the palm wine, anyone who bought the forge at auction would get no more than the bare shell of a building now. Someone, three nights before, had burglarized the place and stolen all of Zakir's samples—and all his tools as well. Irsisi shook his head ruefully; someone had got there first on that one. He had had eyes himself for that lovely collection of gold samples—that delicate little image of Ishtar, for instance.

It had been a month now, a month since Zakir had come stumbling glassy-eyed out of prison, dragging that useless stump of a right arm. Gods! How a man could go downhill in a month. Look at him now: bloated, his once fine features indistinct, his nose still unhealed from the brawl in which it had been broken a week or so after his release. His hair uncombed, his face unshaven, his clothing as filthy as a drover's, his limbs reeking of sweat and vomit.

Irsisi patted the slim purse inside his garment. He'd been milking Zakir for days, a coin or two at a time, accepting money to pay their tavern bills and then pocketing the change. Now . . . well, the old cow's udders had gone dry. Too bad.

Irsisi found himself wondering about Zakir's household goods. If only he could get inside Zakir's place, and . . . But no. The neighborhood women, shrews all, were keeping too good an eye on the place. They'd report you to the guards the moment they saw you trying to haul anything out of there.

No. Better leave well enough alone. He drank the last of the palm wine, wiped his thin lips, and stood up, smiling insincerely as he looked around him. Now was the time; now, when no one was looking. Leave the drunken fool here for his friends to find . . . yes, and for his friends to pay that little "gratuity" he'd promised the servant sent to fetch him. They could well afford it, particularly Iddina, who was easily worth a fortune.

He paused at the door, looked back for a moment, then vanished into the night.

Perched on the wall of the house of the priests of Marduk, Ahuni watched the "tick-bird," as the street children contemptuously called Irsisi, thread his way through the narrow streets. He was on his way to another quarter, perhaps never to return. Ahuni watched for a moment in disgust; and then, after glancing once more at the tavern, he ended his own vigil for the evening.

A few moments earlier, he had seen the messenger leave, headed on some errand in the general direction of the bazaar. Well, no doubt he was going after Iddina, or . . . but no. Iddina was out of town with his family, burying a close relative of his wife's. No. The messenger had been sent for some other friend of Zakir's. Well, they could take care of him. It would not pay for Ahuni to involve himself. For him to reappear in the market would be to court the same treatment Zakir had received at the hands of the city's magistrate and guards. . . .

He scurried down the wall and leaped across six feet of darkness to land on the roof of a beehive house. For a moment he was close to falling to the street below; but his strong young fingers caught a projecting timber and held. He dangled helplessly for an instant; then his toes found a hold and he managed to right himself and continue his descent.

Before leaving, though, he found himself looking back for a moment, and suddenly a wave of feeling swept over him. Quick tears came to his eyes.

Zakir . . .

If only it had never happened. If only . . .

The future had seemed so fine—for the first and only time in his young life. Zakir, a man on the verge of great success in the community, had wanted to manumit him and train him in the secrets of his craft. The smith had been kind to him; and thinking of him now evoked that other memory—or was it a dream?— that came to him from time to time, its outlines blurred and indistinct. *A soft-bosomed woman with brown hair . . . a girl-child a little older than himself? A black-haired giant with big gentle hands and a deep voice?* But no. Probing that area raised too much pain. It was better to forget entirely.

Well, it was all one. None of his dreams would ever be realized. All he could hope for now was to stay out of sight of the authorities for a little while longer, grubbing for scraps in the streets when no one was looking. Maybe the chance would come to escape downriver where nobody knew him.

He glanced at the tavern once again. Zakir . . .

The smith had come to grief on his account—there was no denying that. Through kindness to him, Ahuni, the smith had been mutilated, deprived of his vocation, and transformed from a happy, jovial man to a drunken derelict. If Ahuni had not entered his life . . .

No! No! Ahuni gritted his teeth. What good did it do to think that way? It did not help the smith—and it made him vulnerable to the same fate. He thought of the freezing cold dungeon, the quick flash of the axe, the red-hot cauterizing iron searing flesh that had been multilated only a moment before! . . .

No! No!

Biting his lip, Ahuni blinked the tears from his eyes and made off down the dark street at a dead run. He did not look back.

The messenger came back with the news of Iddina's absence, and cursed Irsisi for having absconded without leaving him the promised coin. The tavernkeeper looked at the bloated body of Zakir and scowled. "Well, we've got to get him out of here. It's closing time. Here, give me a hand."

Quickly he checked Zakir's garments. "Ah. Just as I thought. That little river rat who came in with him has lifted his purse. Gods! This big ox leads a star-crossed life. If I were he, I'd just give up, I think I would."

The messenger said nothing, but the thought ran through his head that this was exactly what Zakir was doing . . . one night at a time.

"Here," said the innkeeper. "You take his legs."

Zakir came out of his stupor as they were attempting to wrestle his bulky frame down the stairs. "Here," he said. "I can . . . stand up for . . . self. . . ."

"Sure you can," the innkeeper grunted. "Look out, there! Damn it, you almost dropped him! For all I know . . . the big ox . . . still has a friend or two . . . who can . . . bring suit . . . look what you're doing! . . . bring suit if he's hurt . . . on the premises. Now . . . now easy does it."

"Just get feet under me . . ." Zakir said.

"My friend, you couldn't . . . get home now . . . on hands and knees. Better wait until your head clears."

"Hands and knees," Zakir sang drunkenly to himself. "Hands and knees." He held up the stump of his right hand, his body a dead weight. He regarded them, blinking in the moon. *"Hand* and knees," he corrected himself. "Fi-five fingers. Used to have . . . how many?" He chuckled humorlessly. "I forget. So long ago.

Month at least. Hold . . . work in fire, boy . . . now hit it just so, not too hard . . . takes two hands."

Sweating and cursing, the pair managed to get Zakir down to street level. They tried to stand him up, but his knees buckled and they settled for propping him up against a building across the street from the tavern. He watched them go, bleary-eyed; then, his huge head nodding, he slipped into a fitful sleep.

The dogs woke him at dawn, sniffing at his filthy clothes. "Get out of here, curse you," he shouted, flailing away at them with both hands. The stump of his right hand struck one of them, causing Zakir to cry out in pain. The fingers of the other hand closed around a rock. He heaved it at one of the dogs. It struck the animal over one ear—a lucky hit. The dog yelped and beat a hasty retreat; the others followed after it in full cry.

Zakir looked up. *Time to get up,* he thought. The guards would be along in a few minutes, and they would have little sympathy for anyone they found hanging about in the streets. Recently, the king had issued an edict that the streets of the city be cleared of derelicts and beggars. And here he was, with a recently amputated hand, the sure sign of a felon in the first place, and with . . . he checked his garments. . . . Oh yes. To be sure. That little rodent Irsisi had taken his purse with him.

Well, time to raise some new money, he said to himself, standing up. Back to the forge. He could always sell the samples and the tools. He staggered to a public fountain and sloshed water over his face. Then he headed for the Bazaar of the Three Palms.

Moments later he was standing before the wreckage of his forge, marveling at the extent of the damage. The burglars had struck first, then the vandals. Between them they had left him nothing, nothing but the shell of his formerly thriving little business.

Well, that was it, wasn't it? His creditors had a lien on his house, so he couldn't sell that either. To be sure, he could sell the property in the bazaar. But not for much. And it would be a matter of hours before his creditors petitioned the city to make sure he couldn't sell even that.

He sighed. Somehow it all seemed so simple. If he had had his hand, there would have been a way out. But now? Now, with all means of working out his problems gone, everything suddenly grew clear. He walked out of the bazaar, heading for the Ishtar Gate. He'd just go out of the city an hour's walk or two, up north past all the settlements. He'd take himself a walk up the Euphrates, in the soft morning sun. He'd make his private peace with the gods, and then he'd simply complete the job.

His backbone was straight and his step firm as he walked north along the quays. But the expression on his face was as blank as the whitewashed wall of the Temple of Bel, and his dark eyes registered nothing, nothing at all.

II

Iddina's barge passed the watchtower and entered the outer walls of Babylon under the noses of the guards high above the water. It was a busy morning. The river was thick with lateen-rigged sails, and small boats were heading upriver for the fishing. His barge was the only one carrying passengers; the rest bore downriver cargo for sale or trade.

Humerelli, her still handsome face half visible inside the veil she wore in public, caught his arm as they passed the mouth of the peripheral canal. "Iddina," she said, "isn't that Zakir? Over there walking along the quay?"

"Where?" Iddina said. "God! If it weren't for the hand, I'd hardly have recognized him. Poor devil! He looks like he's slept in that robe every day for a week."

"Slept in the gutter, most likely. Iddina, can't

we ... can't we and our friends in the bazaar do something for the poor man? I mean, take up a collection? Something?" Her tone was gently insistent; she had always liked Zakir. He had always had a compliment ready for her when he had visited Iddina's household, and Humerelli had often tried to pair him off with various of her female relatives—but to no avail.

"Oh, we could raise money for him, all right," said Iddina. "The trouble is, we all know what he'd do with it. He has no mind for anything but the taverns anymore. Not that he enjoys himself there. He drinks to attain oblivion, that's all."

"How sad. Look at him. I wonder where he's going?"

"Looking for a place to sleep, I'll wager. I hear the magistrates have posted a guard on his house. Humerelli, I've talked to him again and again. He points to the stump of his right hand and says, 'What good is a one-armed smith? I'd rather they'd made a capon of me.' And then he laughs—bitterly, with no humor in it at all—and he says, 'Well, as a matter of fact they have, haven't they? Just as well as if they'd cut off my ...' Well, you know."

Humerelli sighed. "Iddina, if only—"

"Yes. Yes. But ... a man's destiny changes. The gods turn away from him, and ..." His palms-up gesture told it all. There was a great hurt in his eyes.

Iddina left the servants to escort Humerelli and the children home. He had news for the merchants of his bazaar, news from upriver, and it wouldn't wait. He hurried through the narrow streets surrounding the Esagila, the area bordering the Tower of Bel and the Temple of Marduk, trying to blot out the sorrow in his mind.

Dodging an oxcart, he stepped back into an alley. As he did, he heard a loud whisper behind him. "Sssst! Iddina!" He turned, blinking in the gloom of the shadowed street. The head of the boy Ahuni peeked out from behind an abutment. "Iddina ..." the boy said. "Please. I have to speak to you. Don't betray me to the guards. Please."

Iddina shook his head, chiding himself; but he followed the boy into a dark cul-de-sac around the corner. "Yes?" he said. "What do you want with me, boy? You realize I'm legally under obligation to report having seen you."

"I know. Give me a moment's lead, maybe two, and report me all you want." The boy's gaze was clear-eyed and fearless. "But I have to ask. You were a friend of Zakir's, perhaps his best friend."

Iddina looked him up and down. He was dirty and ragged, but he had grown since Iddina had seen him last. "You know I won't report you," he said. "Go on. You were telling me about Zakir."

"Yes. I saw his shop last night. Someone's stolen all his samples. I managed to get his tools out. The place is a wreck. The tools are hidden. I want to get them to him. How do I find him?"

"What do you care?" Iddina said, looking the boy hard in the eye. "Look, stay away from him. He has enough trouble already. If he finds you, he will try to help you. And it will only land him in worse trouble, poor man, than he's in now. You're wanted by the guards, you know. And any accomplice in keeping you away from them . . ."

"I know, I know. But . . . Iddina . . . Zakir was good to me." The boy's eyes filled with tears. "Iddina . . . it's gnawing away at my guts. If it were not for me, Zakir would never have had any of this happen to him. It's all my fault. What can I do? What can I . . . ?"

Iddina thought a moment. "Me too, boy," he said sadly. "Zakir had friends . . . but there's nothing we can do for a man who has given up on life. You should see him now. We spotted him a few moments ago, walking on the riverfront—dirty, bleary-eyed, shambling."

"You've seen him?" the boy asked, suddenly alert. "Where? On the river, you say? Upriver? Down? Where? Along the quay? Please! I have to know."

"On the quay, as you say. Up above the Ishtar Gate, but inside the other wall. Near the place where the bridge passes the peripheral canal."

"Maybe I have time to catch him! But . . . where

was he going? What could he be doing up there? So far out of town?"

Iddina pondered the question, not liking what his mind suddenly caught hold of. "Now that I think of it, boy—"

"Yes? Yes?"

"His head was high, and his step was lively. It was as though he had an appointment." He looked at the boy and said no more.

"An appointment? Who could he have an appointment with?" Ahuni's eyes narrowed. "I can't understand. If he . . ." Then he looked up. "Oh, no!" he said. "You don't mean . . ." His face lost expression altogether. "You *do* mean it. Gods! Gods! I . . . thank you, Iddina." He turned on his heel and headed toward the boulevard. At the corner, he waved once and then took off at a dead run.

Ahuni ran at top speed, threading his way through the streets which, by now, no one knew better, bowling over beggar and tradesman alike. He skirted the grounds of the great Temple and of the Tower as well, wary of the ever-present guardsmen who patrolled the area. Nevertheless, he came close to running into a party of guards on the fringe of a bazaar and only escaped by ducking into a side street and climbing over a low wall.

At the great quay that lined the eastern bank of the Euphrates, he stopped to inquire of several boatmen. Had they seen a black-bearded man with one hand? But at the mention of a man with one hand they tended to turn away. No one wanted anything to do with a man bearing the universal badge of dishonor. Cursing them to himself, he fell once again into a trot and headed upriver along the quay.

He paused to catch his breath at the Gate of Ishtar. It would not do to attract attention in a place that was so central to the life of the city. He sat down on a stone railing and looked up at the massive and heavily fortified gate. Each of its ramparts stood taller than many tall men together and each was heavily reinforced, inside and outside, by a curtain of mud bricks.

Connecting the ramparts was a passage that was open to the sky at certain intervals where archers were posted. An attacker attempting to penetrate the city could be stopped for questioning and detained here or at a half dozen other places.

Ahuni frowned. If he tried to pass through by himself, he would almost certainly be stopped. The only chance was to attach himself, as unobtrusively as possible, to a party on its way through the gates. In that case . . . how about that one over there? No, too small. The people would notice him and shoo him away. But that larger group ahead . . . perhaps, just perhaps . . .

Taking a deep breath, he slipped in at the end of a procession of well-dressed men who trailed a retinue of servants behind them. Ahuni pressed in among them, hoping not to be noticed because of his ragged garments.

He passed the first inner gate.

At the first checkpoint, a guardsman gave him an odd look, but, frowning in disapproval, waved the entire group through.

The procession passed into a tunnel. Ahuni felt a hand stroke his thigh and instinctively recoiled. In the semi-darkness, he took a look at the man on his right—the only one who could have touched him. His face was fat, soft, epicene; its smile was coy and suggestive. "Oh, don't be so standoffish, darling," the man said. "If you kick up a fuss, the guards may take notice of you. And I think you wouldn't like that." There was a cold glint in the green eyes, and the voice held the smallest touch of malice.

Gods! Ahuni thought. *I've blundered into a nest of boy-lovers off on an outing.* He gritted his teeth and tried to smile back. "If you'd just wait until we're outside the gates . . ." He tried to say the rest with his eyebrows, hating himself all the while for it.

As the procession emerged into the late morning sunshine, his companion of the inner gates sidled up to Ahuni. "Well," he said, grabbing the boy's hand with his own hairy paw. "I'm so glad you decided to join us."

Looking around for guards, Ahuni yanked his hand

loose. But at this movement, the rest of the group began to take note of him. Ahuni backed away, scanning the group, warily, and bumped into a slave attached to the party.

"Bahe!" a high-pitched voice screamed out from the center of the group. "Stop him! Hold him! That's the one . . . the one with the red birthmark. Remember? Soulai! Soulai! Come see what we've found."

Ahuni struggled in the tight grasp of the slave. "Let me go!" he growled.

The crowd parted to make way for its leader. Soulai's face was a mask of malicious pleasure. "Ah!" he shrilled. "Hold him, Bahe! He's wanted for criminal offenses by the king's guard." He turned and fluttered his eyes at his entourage, shrugging his shoulders and lifting his eyes heavenward in mock sympathy. "And of course we'll be glad to do our civic duty and turn him over, won't we? After, of course, we're through with him."

There was a round of appreciative laughter. Ahuni relaxed his body for a second; then he tensed his young muscles and tried to twist away. *Zakir!* he thought. *I've got to get free and find Zakir, before . . . before . . .* But the slave's grip was too strong.

"There, there," Soulai said. "We, of course, intend to enjoy the next hour or two with you, my dear. Whether *you* choose to enjoy it or not is entirely up to you. We've a little outing in the country planned, and we've decided to have you along as our guest. And," he said, rolling his eyes again for his friends' benefit, "we *won't* take no for an answer."

Ahuni took a deep breath. "Well," he said. "Your man scared me. And he's hurting my arm. I don't know what to think. If you'll promise me nobody will hurt me, maybe . . . please. My arm's all bruised."

"Ah," Soulai said, stepping forward almost to arm's length, looking Ahuni in the eye and smiling sweetly. "No, we don't want that, now, do we? Bahe, let him go, my dear." And he extended a soft hand to caress Ahuni's cheek.

Suddenly, Ahuni bent down almost into a ball. Then

he uncoiled, driving his fist into Soulai's groin with every bit of strength he possessed. The blow slammed into the young nobleman's pubic bone, jarring Ahuni's arm all the way to the elbow. Soulai sank to his knees, moaning with pain.

Ahuni took off at a desperate run toward the Euphrates, dodging an ass-drawn cart and almost pushing a gray-bearded old man into the water.

"Stop that boy!" voices called out behind him. He heard feet pounding on the stone wall of the circumferential moat and redoubled his efforts. "You! Guards! Stop that boy there!"

Ahuni, running at top speed, looked right and left. Down the quay a bit, between the moat and the city wall, two armed men in uniform looked up. Drawing a murderous-looking short sword, the nearer of the two set out at a light jog, heading upriver, his eyes on Ahuni. *Please,* Ahuni prayed to himself, *let me make it to the corner before they do.*

The second guard fell in step with the first. Ahuni gauged the distance to the quay, straining to increase his speed. "You!" the guard in front yelled. "Halt, in the name of the king!"

Ahuni ran to the corner where the moat wall joined the quay. He tried to change direction and lost his footing on the slippery stones. The guards were almost upon him as he got up from one knee. He looked quickly back down the moat wall at the running men. "Zakir," he sobbed despairingly, and bounded to the quay's edge to look down at the river far below. He teetered on the rim and then dove forward, far out from the stone wall. His arms flailed awkwardly just as he hit the brown waters of the Euphrates with a wild splash.

III

He came up gasping for air and choking on the filthy, silt-rich Euphrates water. Flailing about miserably, he was finally able to roll over on his back where, holding his chin high against the choppy water, he concentrated on getting his breath.

He could hear the shouting now from atop the wall. "You! Boatman! Man overboard! There on the right!" He looked up, blinked the water out of his eyes, and saw the men and guards on the wall above him, pointing. He rolled over again and, treading water unsteadily, tried to look around. Some distance away a lateen-rigged fishing boat was tacking his way and trying to shorten sail. He could see the boatman standing erect, his naked body burned black by the sun, his white teeth gleaming.

"Here, my friend," a rough voice said in a vile upriver accent. "Grab onto this." Ahuni held fast with one hand to the proffered gaff and reached for the hull of the boat. As he did, a calloused hand grasped his arm and pulled. "Easy, now . . . now up she goes . . . all right, all right." And in a moment Ahuni was sitting up, dripping wet, spewing water, and clawing the wet hair out of his eyes.

Up above the voices bellowed all the louder. "You! Boatman! Bring him to the dock! In the name of the . . ."

The boatman grinned. "Listen to the bastards," he said. "As if a river man would give up his salvage." He stood up, sunburned, bare as an egg and lean as a crane, and, arm raised high, flashed the sign of the fig at the guards on the wall. "Yes, yes," he chuckled, "curse away for all the good it'll do you. I'm headed back upriver, and the back of my hand to you." He turned back to Ahuni. "You, son. These people mean anything to you?"

"Me?" Ahuni said. "Oh, no. No. They're a lot of boy-lovers. They grabbed me as I came out of the Ishtar Gate and wanted to . . . well, I ran, and then the guards . . ."

"Oh, yes. I see. Well, there are a lot of their kind down along the water. The rich ones come around to proposition the sailors. Usually they have the good sense to bring along a few bodyguards. Otherwise they wind up in an alley somewhere with a nice new smile cut in 'em, about two fingers' span south of the old one." He nodded appreciatively at the thought, as if cutting a man's throat were part of the day's work. "And now," he said. "You, my little fish. Now that I've caught you, what shall I do with you? I can't eat you. Should I salt you and hang you up to dry?" He chuckled, but there was no malice in his laughter. "Or . . ." He saw the slave-brand now. "Will your master be looking for you? With a nice reward, perhaps?"

"The only reward you're likely to get," Ahuni said, slipping out of his single garment and wringing it out to dry, "is from the guards on the wall. And you know what *that* reward's likely to be."

"Oh, yes," the dark man said. "That I do. 'Look here, you, why didn't you bring him to shore sooner? Ten days! Next!' " He sat down and took the tiller in hand again. "Well, then. You're on the run, I take it?" The words came out very matter-of-factly. "Watch your head!" he said sharply as the yard shifted.

Ahuni ducked. "Well," he said, shaking his wet hair. "I was thinking up a story to tell you. But . . ." He looked at the man at the tiller. The face was battered, but friendly and carefree. "You saved my life. Why?"

"By the gods!" the other man said. "I follow my nose. I do as I please. I'm no friend of the king's guards, if that's what you mean. And when I see a lad like yourself being chased by the bastards in full armor . . ." He grinned. "Look, you don't have to worry about telling me anything. I'm headed home with a full purse after selling a catch. I had a mate aboard but he jumped ship in the city. I could use a hand for now if you do what I tell you."

"Wonderful," Ahuni said. "I think I'd be safer on the river than I'd be on dry land right now. But . . ." He hesitated, looking into those friendly brown eyes. Then, somehow, he found himself blurting it all out: Zakir, the false charges, the mutilation, and the sad decline; Iddina's fears that Zakir meant to do away with himself. "I . . . I have to find him," he said. "I feel as if it's all my fault. And . . ." He swallowed hard and found he couldn't go on for a moment.

The dark man's expression had turned thoughtful. Then the smile came back again, and it was not the gaily mocking smile of before. "And you're willing to risk your neck for this smith with one flipper missing, eh? Although you know what sort of penalty you're courting?" He shook his head. "I'll bet you're not from the city but from up-country, aren't you?"

"I don't know," Ahuni said. "I can't remember a time when I didn't live in the city. I don't even know if I was born free or not."

The dark man sighed. "Well . . . look, boy. If you like, we'll keep near the east bank. All right? If you see your friend down by the shore . . ."

"Oh!" Ahuni said. "Thank you! I . . . I was going to call you something, and I remembered I didn't know your name. I'm named Ahuni."

"I'm Binshoumedir," the dark man said grinning. "Welcome aboard."

They had passed the outer wall, with its high watchtower, and now they were sailing through open country. The banks of the great river were lined with palms. In the distance, beyond the row of trees, lay farmland, and at intervals they could see paths that led down to the water's edge where women washed clothes or filled their jugs to take water back to the farmhouses. Binshoumedir grinned and waved gaily at the women.

There was, even this far up, an enormous variety of craft on the river today. They passed men in crescent-shaped canoes being towed upstream by men on shore.

A swift galley went by, its mighty oars dipping in rhythm to the beat of a drum amidship. The sun was high, the winds propitious; they made good time.

Ahuni had thought of putting his garment back on once it had dried, but Binshoumedir cautioned him against it. "You'll draw too much attention. Fishermen like me work in our skins. Nothing to wash, nothing to dry off. Put on that raggedy robe of yours, you'll look like a stranger. In your bare ass, boy, you'll look just like what you seem to be: a new helper I'm breaking in. Relax, boy, enjoy the nice weather. It's summer. The gods are good to fishermen in the summertime. Look there." Ahuni looked where he pointed. A great bird dived down, its beak skimming the water. Soon it came up with a fish, beating the air furiously with its strong wings to compensate for the extra weight as it soared away.

At floodtide that spring the river had undercut a good section of the bank, leaving an overhang whose soil was held together by the roots of the palms. Zakir, lost in thought, sat on the bank's edge, dangling his feet over the side.

Out here things appeared so much more peaceful than they had back in the city—or even in the farm country that lay between the inner and outer walls. The broad brownish-green river moved sluggishly between the remote banks; the white birds soared and swooped; the three-cornered sails out on the water billowed and flapped.

Zakir smiled bitterly. *Well,* he told himself, *you've been looking for the right time and place.* And here was peace and calm. A better time could hardly be imagined. A better place . . .

Curiously, he found himself abandoning the idea of prayer to the gods, of purification. The gods seemed as remote out here in the countryside as the problems against which one invoked them in the city. *Peace,* he thought.

But then on the far bank he saw a young woman approach the water, set down her jug, and, with a glance around her, slip out of her garment and stand

nude at the water's edge. Her body was young and
slender—that much he could make out even at this
distance. She stepped ankle-deep into the shallows and
bent to splash water over herself. Her movements were
naturally graceful; he almost laughed with pleasure at
her little shudder when the cold water touched her
body. But the pleasure soon left him. His days with
women were over. He had been impotent ever since
he'd lost his hand. He could not look at his own
mutilated body without disgust; how could he expect a
woman to look at him any differently? Besides, a
woman wanted a man with money, possessions, a profession.

He sighed. He felt empty, alone. He wondered idly
about his old friends: Iddina, the innkeepers, the
whoremasters, the wenches themselves. But the emptiness in his heart was too great, too complete, and it
could no longer be filled by thoughts of the people he
had known. A void it was and void it would remain.

And Ahuni? Zakir's brow knit for a moment; then
his mind dismissed the boy. He'd taken off, and a good
thing too. If he had stuck around, the guards would
have nabbed him within a day or two. Well, good
fortune to him, and a better master than his last. For
after all, what good was a master who could no longer
either feed or house you?

He watched the girl across the way turn, her full
young buttocks moving with liquid grace, and walk
back out of the shallows to slip on her garment again.
She filled her jug and walked slowly, carefully, up the
path.

Zakir sighed ... and felt emptier than ever. No,
what good would it do, propitiating the gods? The gods
were cruel, without compassion. They gave a man his
life and then took it away. They dealt out bitterness,
destruction, and death with a terrible impartiality. A
man's destiny was defeat and despair. All the rest were
palliatives of no more than temporary usefulness. Love
and friendship were no more than toys, and toys could
be broken.

The sky was blue above, and the sun warm. White
clouds gathered low over the mountains far away to

the east. Zakir stood up, feeling very empty, and walked slowly down to the towpath beside the river. He thought of removing his filthy garment, but it didn't seem to make much difference now. Indifferent to the chill of the water, he walked forward steadily until the river came up to his chest. Then he lay face down and began swimming slowly and deliberately in the direction of the main channel.

When they caught sight of him, they tacked hard to meet him. "Zakir!" cried the boy, standing in the bow. "Zakir! Over here! Please . . . faster . . . faster . . ."

Zakir looked up once, but his mind had already abandoned itself to thoughts of death; and when the current hit him for the first time—the full current, out in the deeper water—he simply stopped paddling with his arms, rolled over, and let himself sink.

As soon as he saw him go down, Ahuni vaulted over the side and, struggling against the powerful midriver current, dived after Zakir. Finding nothing, he surfaced. At this, Binshoumedir brought the boat about making the sail go slack. Then, hurriedly, he heaved his anchor over the side and joined Ahuni in the water. On the second dive they grabbed Zakir and struggled to bring him to the surface. Wrestling with one heavy arm, Ahuni went down again; but when he came up once more, he saw that Binshoumedir had one hand firmly on the stern of the boat while the other arm encircled Zakir's neck, holding his thick head free of the water.

They pounded on his back until he had vomited up all of the water he had swallowed. Then Binshoumedir hauled anchor and turned the little vessel back into the wind. Sitting at the tiller, he smiled as he watched the boy squatting at the man's side. "It's all right now, my boy," he said. "He'll make it."

Zakir stirred and raised his head. Then he pushed himself up off the planking. "Ahuni," he said, "I . . . I know you meant well, and . . . and did what you did out of concern. But . . . you should have let me die."

"Zakir!" the boy sobbed suddenly, hugging the big

man to his skinny chest. "Zakir, I had to look for you."

Zakir sighed and held the boy as he wept. "What good am I to you, son? I . . . I've lost everything."

Binshoumedir caught his eye just then, and the expression on his bony face softened. "Ah, you damned fool," he said. "You haven't lost anything. You've found something—something more precious than anything you could ever have lost." He shook his head and, turning away, spat into the spume behind him. "May the gods give you the good sense to keep the thing you've found," he said. "Both of you."

Then all was quiet for a time, except for the high-pitched cries of the seabirds soaring above them.

CHAPTER FIVE

I

Eastward marched the great caravan across the desert, eastward into the morning sun. But now the distance between wells was not as great, and there were slashes of greenery that ran down the sides of the bare slopes. Abram's hunters, ranging out ahead of the party, came back one night with a remarkable kill: three gazelles. Another hunter reported seeing a lion on the slopes above, beyond the reach of his arrows.

Scouts of a Canaanite war party stopped them at one mountain pass. Abram sent word that the caravan was only passing through, and after some consultation, the guards let them pass without hindrance.

Flat wasteland became rolling country dotted by small mountain ranges. Hagar felt the strength beginning to flow back into her. As the Shairetana captain had told her would happen, her feet had toughened, and by now she could negotiate any climb a man could make. The softness had gone from her body, and the muscles of her long legs rippled when she walked. Nevertheless, the hard exercise had made her look years younger and more lovely than ever.

This did not escape the notice of Sarai, Abram's aging wife, who lost no opportunity to remind her of who was mistress and who slave. As Hagar attended to her daily chores, robed only in the slave's loincloth, the eyes of the male members of the caravan followed her wherever she went. As a result, the petty complaints and sarcasm issuing from Sarai became an almost ceaseless flow. However, Abram, singleminded as ever, was completely absorbed in the problems of the march and took hardly any notice of her at all.

Her master remained an enigma to her. She wondered why he took such pains to be so accommodating to some members of the caravan who appeared to waste his time. With her discerning eye, she noticed that he paid special attention to the behavior of Eliezer of Damascus, commander of the advance guard, who, it was said, would be Abram's heir if Sarai remained childless.

Hagar, whose duties included the provision of food and drink at important audiences, missed few nuances in Abram's behavior toward his subordinates, despite his customary undemonstrativeness. She saw, for instance, that Abram was unimpressed with Eliezer of Damascus as a leader of men. He never reproved Eliezer directly, but he took pains to place limits on what the younger man could do without asking his permission. Hagar sometimes fancied that she could see a hint of irritation in Abram's eyes after a lengthy audience with Eliezer.

Among Abram's people, blood ties counted for much. This was the only explanation Hagar could come up with for Abram's tolerance and patience in dealing with his brother's son Lot. Alone among the men of the party, Lot rode on an ass's back across the desert, pleading a lameness which he sometimes forgot to feign in Abram's camp at nightfall. Yet Abram remained patient and courteous when dealing with his nephew. Hagar marveled at his forbearance.

The encounter with the guards at the pass marked their first real entrance into Canaanite country. Abram doubled the size of the scouting party at front and on each flank of the caravan. The scouting units had orders to send a runner back to Abram whenever a Canaanite party was spotted, whether it was friendly or hostile. Like any good commander, Abram knew when to delegate authority; but he also had the wisdom to keep himself informed of virtually everything under his jurisdiction.

The second night after the encounter, Hagar was awakened in the middle of the night by the sound of groaning coming from Abram's tent. She rushed to the open flap of the tent. "My lady?" she said. "Is anything wrong? May I help?"

"No, no," Sarai said irritably. "Go back to sleep. The lord Abram is just having another one of his . . . his *visions*." There was a sharp edge of irony in her tone. Hagar crept back to her tent, but the groaning went on and she got little sleep that night.

In the morning, while making preparations for departure, she overheard sharp words between Abram and Sarai. She kept apart from them, not wanting to be within range of Sarai's scolding tongue, but managed to catch bits of the conversation here and there:

". . . going to have an heir, are you? By whom? Not by me, that's a sure thing. What makes you think—"

"It was in my dream," Abram said in a calm voice. "And the voice told me my heirs would live in the lands north of here, and have dominion over them. They would found a great nation, a nation of kings."

"Nonsense!" Sarai's voice was sharper than ever. "Tell it to some soothsayer. Don't try to convince me. I won't listen. You talk like an old fool, and little wonder, too. If you would—"

"Sarai!" The voice did not get any louder, but there was an undertone in it which no one in the caravan, having once heard it, would wish to hear a second time. But Hagar knew her mistress would bring the subject up again, the moment Abram's mood softened.

The well near which they had camped was a modest one, hardly more than an opening in the rocks through which a small underground stream found its way to the surface. Hagar took her jug to the spring to fill it and met Shepset there. The two embraced; then, holding the girl at arm's length, Hagar looked into her eyes. "Shepset," she said affectionately. "I've seen little of you lately, my dear. Is everything all right?"

Shepset's eyes suddenly would not meet hers. "Oh, I . . . I've been busy. Work, and . . . well, you know."

Hagar put her hands on the girl's bare shoulders.

"Shepset," she said. "Look me in the eye. Is something wrong? I have to know. Is Lot treating you badly? Have you—"

"No, no," Shepset said, trying to pull away. "It's just that . . . oh, Hagar. I don't know what to say. I wish I understood what to do—"

"Is it a man?" Hagar asked. The moment she spoke, she knew that she had found the problem. "Is it Ah-Mose? Has he—"

"No, no," Shepset said. "Ah-Mose is interested, but . . . when the lord Eliezer found out about his interest, he assigned him all the way to the other end of the caravan. I never see him any more."

"Eliezer?" Hagar said, suddenly wary. "What has he to do with . . . ?" She saw the girl's eyes fall again and shook the thin shoulders. "Shepset, look at me. Has the lord Eliezer . . . ?"

"No, no, Hagar, it's just that . . . he seeks me out at the end of each day. I can't escape him. And he talks to me . . . he tells me that if I'm 'nice' to him, he'll—"

"Shepset, you stay away from him. Please. He's a cruel and vain man, and a terrible liar. He doesn't mean a word of what he says. If you let him . . . well, you'll be sorrier than you've ever been. Really. Listen to me."

"I'm listening," Shepset said miserably. "But what can I do? He's the heir of the lord Abram. Can I forever manage to say no to him? He keeps at me . . . battering me down . . . and Hagar, I don't know how to handle men. You know. No man has ever . . . if someone could only show me how to keep him away."

"Please," Hagar said. "Tell the lord Abram. No, I'll try to tell him for you. And don't let him get you alone. There's always a way to stall them. Even if you're a slave, with no rights, you're not *his* slave." She had a sudden horrible thought. "He hasn't asked the lord Abram for you, has he?"

"N-no. That's the problem. He says he's going to. And . . . Hagar. I'm not sure it wouldn't be a good idea. There's a worse alternative, and he says he's going to ask for me to keep that from happening."

"A worse alternative? What could that be?" But the moment she said it she knew exactly what the girl meant. "Oh, no. You don't mean—"

"Yes. Lot intends to ask his uncle for me, the moment the caravan reaches the place in Canaan where we're to settle. Hagar, I . . . I wouldn't like that. Lot's slaves . . . there is talk about him. Both the men *and* the women, you know. And his wife's the same way. If the lord Abram knew—"

"Oh, no. Shepset, no."

"What can I do? If Eliezer can get me out of that—"

"Shepset. Oh, my darling."

The two women hugged each other. Hagar's heart was empty of anything in the world but heartache.

The land they marched through grew perceptibly more green. Shrubs dotted the hills, and acacias grew in many places. The trees were in bud and would bloom within the month. Perhaps, Hagar thought, as she marched with an easy stride behind the wagons, perhaps Canaan would not be so bad after all. The lord Abram had said it was a green and pleasant land, a fine land for grazing animals, watered by a great river that flowed through a long and beautiful valley. The river, barred by the very terrain they were passing through, ended in a great fissure in the earth, far below beetling cliffs.

Abram's runner came back from the point around noon. "My lord," he said, "the lord Eliezer wishes to report that he has reached the Egyptian mines we were told of. He recommends this as a good place to make camp tonight. There is good water and forage."

"Excellent," Abram said. "I was told to look up the overseer there if I wanted help in arming us against future trouble. Tell Eliezer we'll camp there, at Timna. And thank him for me, will you?"

That night, after dinner, Shepset, troubled, wandered away from the fire to walk down by the water. They had camped at a beautiful spring fringed with spreading acacias and date palms; the water, by daylight, was crystal-clear all the way to the sand-covered bottom, and its taste was fresh and clean.

Now, in the moonlight, it shone with a shimmering beauty. Standing beside the pond, she tossed a small pebble into the water and watched the little circular waves spread outward, the moonlight touching each one. Idly she stretched out a bare toe and stirred the cool water at the bank's edge.

She thought, *if only* . . .

"Shepset," a voice said behind her. She wheeled, and saw Eliezer standing in fresh robes, his arms crossed across his strong young chest. "I was hoping I'd find you here," he said. "I'm pleased." He stretched out his arms to her. She could not see his face. It was in shadow.

Shepset stepped backward, suddenly frightened, and felt her bare heel sink into soft sand at the water's edge. "Please, my lord," she said. "I . . . I have to get back."

"No, you don't," he said. "I passed Lot's tent a moment ago and told him I needed you for an errand. He won't miss you anyhow. A Midianite trader passed through camp at dusk and Lot purchased a goatskin bag of strong wine from him."

"But . . . please . . ."

His hands touched her arms and pulled her to him. "Now, don't be frightened," he said. "I won't hurt you. Ah . . . that's nice. You're a delightful armful, you know that? Sweet as honey." She turned her head this way and that, avoiding his lips. "Now, now," he said. "Don't be coy. You're not going to tell me this is your first time, now."

Afterward she wandered back to the big campfire. She walked dejectedly, brokenly, her head down, unable to look any of her friends in the eye. Somehow she knew, now, that there would be no more talk of his asking Abram for her. She was soiled, spoiled, and he would no longer care for her. Worse: he would tell Lot of this. She knew that. She had heard the two of them exchanging salty stories. She knew that a slave's feelings meant nothing to them; they would joke about her in front of her, and Lot would ask embarrassing questions in that coarse voice of his.

Someone passed close to her ... but drew away. She looked up into the eyes of Ah-Mose, wincing at the scorn she could see clearly there in the firelight. He shook his head once at her but did not speak; then turned away from her and walked into the darkness outside the circle of light. And somehow, in her dejection, she could not find it in her heart to blame him.

II

One morning when Sneferu came to visit the smith, he found his friend haggard-looking but bright-eyed, squatting on his heels before his forge, building a fire. "Here!" he said. "Back to work so soon? Don't you think ... ?"

The smith grinned good-naturedly. "Sneferu, my friend," he said. "Haven't I told you this thing has tried to kill me before? And failed? Well, it'll fail again. I'm more robust than you think. Give me a day or so and I'll arm-wrestle you to a turn. Come, play 'prentice for me for a moment. Take this thing here, blow on the flames. And remember, don't breathe in." Although his face was gaunt, his grin was as always.

"There," he said. "That's one way of silencing a man when he's trying to lecture you. Put him to blowing on the fire. Yes ... right there. The heat has to be very high and very even." He winked at Sneferu and reached for his hammer, talking between blows as he removed the sword blade in his forceps to the anvil and beat it slowly, carefully, into shape. "Besides ... you slept late this morning ... and missed the news. There's a big caravan camped ... outside the valley ... a countryman of mine, I gather. And he may need a couple of old campaigners ... like you and me."

Sneferu lowered the blowpipe. "A countryman of yours? From Babylon, you mean?"

"Stop talking and keep blowing. It was hard enough getting that fire started without . . . now look what you've done. If you were my apprentice, I'd beat your backside black and blue. No, not Babylon. According to Ka-Nakht's pickets, he's an old man who remembers Ur, before the Fall. He and his family went away to live up north somewhere and missed being in at the end. He's been in Egypt—and gotten rich, somehow, while he was there—and is coming to Canaan to carve out a place for himself."

Sneferu lowered the blowpipe again. "Mighty ambitious for an old man. Well, he'll have his work cut out for him. When did he come in? Yesterday, while I was gone?"

"Yes. I had a chat with the picket who stopped him after supper last night. Damn it, keep blowing there! Here, let's heat this thing up again. Yes, he's ambitious. But that's the way people are, back in the Valley of the Two Rivers. Anyhow, he's got the manpower, it appears, to make some sort of a dent in Canaan, but they're untrained in arms for the most part. And . . . he's going to need weapons. Lots of them." Belsunu watched the Egyptian's eyebrows rise. "I see you begin to get the picture. Keep blowing . . . anyhow, he's got the money to pay for anything he wants."

That afternoon, after the midday heat had eased, Sneferu rode out with Ka-Nakht and a small escort to meet the rich Bedouin and bring him to the overseer's camp for a modest ceremonial feast—and, incidentally, to meet Belsunu, who, though he denied it, was not yet ready to travel. Sneferu knew that he would find work with the Bedouin, but he also wanted the smith to be hired, since he felt their destinies to be linked. It was not just a matter of liking the armorer, although by now the bond between the two was as strong and deep as between blood kinsmen. There was also the fact that the smith's weapons were far and away the best Sneferu had ever seen in any campaign in his twenty-five years of service. Indeed, several times on the ride out he found himself drawing the marvelous sword from its scabbard and testing it.

Once he found Ka-Nakht looking at him and smiling tolerantly. "Caught," Sneferu said, red-faced; but he did not reholster the weapon. Instead he swung it to and fro, hacking imaginary necks. "By the gods! Isn't it a beauty?"

"You don't have to tell me," Ka-Nakht said. "You should see the one he made for me, for my retirement parade. I don't take it out much; I'm saving it for the big day. But I'll be the envy of the court." He sighed. "Pity I can't take the smith back to show him off. Feather in my cap."

"I see you aren't fooled by his sudden recovery."

"Not at all. Poor devil. But you'll get a few weeks' work out of him, perhaps. That is, if we can convince the fellow we're going to visit now that he's well enough to hire."

"The lord Abram," as his second-in-command presented him to the two Egyptians, turned out to be a man's man for all his age, tall and straight and still strong as a bull, Sneferu would have wagered. His eye looked right into yours and his voice was powerful and forthright. He even spoke a decent, if accented, Egyptian. The three of them passed the usual formalities back and forth; then, without further ado, Abram turned to Sneferu. "Someone praised you to me as a soldier," he said, "an experienced leader of troops. I gather you're at liberty. Can you train this band of mine for war?"

Sneferu smiled. "How fast do you need them?" he said.

"In the best of worlds they would have been ready now. But . . ." He shrugged.

"I see. Well, I can't say until I've seen them. If I had the choice, a couple of months would—"

"I don't have that long."

"All right. I'm sorry. I can't work for you. I have no intention of training anyone to lose a battle."

"The problem will be that bad?"

"By the gods! Have your people ever had to fight? I mean, seriously? To attack?"

"No. We repulsed a few bandit attacks on the way to Egypt. But the losses were heavy."

"You don't want any of that any more. You'll have to give me time to teach them hand-to-hand combat. There's no way I can train archers in a hurry . . . unless . . . are there any hunters in your party?"

"We have archers. A few. Good ones. But my people don't know the sword, by and large. And we need weapons as well."

"All right. We know where we stand." Sneferu caught Ka-Nakht's eyes, saw his slight nod of the head: *Keep it up, you're doing fine.* "It so happens there's an excellent armorer here—one of the best. With your permission I'd like to take you into camp, you and a few of your people—to a little feast we've prepared. You can meet the smith. He's a compatriot of yours, I understand, from the Land of the Two Rivers. He's been ill, but he's recovering now. I could have him producing arms for your people, full time, in a matter of days."

"I don't know," Abram said. "I hadn't intended to leave camp just now."

Sneferu impulsively reached into his belt for the marvelous sword. The movement wasn't particularly threatening, but several of Abram's retainers started; more than one hand went to a weapon's hilt. "No, no," Sneferu said. "I mean no harm. But Abram . . . have a look at this." And he handed his sword to the old chieftain hilt-first.

Abram didn't speak at first, hefting the sword. And whatever the combat readiness of Abram's following, Sneferu would immediately have bet that their leader had seen some warfare before, during his long life. His movement, holding up the sword, feeling the exquisite balance, bared a forearm that might have been carved of oak. And the chieftain's smile was slow to come, but appreciative. "Ah," he said, looking Sneferu in the eye. "Now *this* is another matter, isn't it? I see. You've made your point. Weapons like these would be worth waiting for, if I had to camp outside Canaan for a full season." He handed the sword back, and when he spoke, his voice had another tone instead, one with fewer reservations. "And you? Are you as good a soldier as this man is a smith?"

Ka-Nakht started to speak up, but Sneferu, his eyes on Abram's, held up his hand. "Sir, it may well be that nobody, anywhere, is as good a soldier as this man is an armorer. But if I have as long to train your men as it takes for him to arm them, and if you and I can come to an understanding, I will win any war for you that you propose."

"What kind of understanding are you proposing?" There was no particular asperity in his tone; he just wanted the facts.

"I will be subordinate, in all matters pertaining to warfare, to nobody but yourself. I can do wonders with one master; I can do nothing with two."

"Fair enough. All right, done. Here's my hand on it. I want to meet this smith of yours. Eliezer! See that riding stock is ready. Gentlemen, my camp is yours. I'll be with you in a matter of moments. Now if you'll excuse me."

Sneferu, seeing Ka-Nakht in conversation with Abram's Syrian assistant, turned away and wandered through the nest of tents toward the oasis. The little pond was fringed with date palms; the wind stirred the surface of the water. He bent to drink out of one cupped hand and suddenly saw a woman's figure reflected in the water across the pond from him.

He looked up and slowly got to his feet.

She gave him a piercing glance, from large, limpid dark eyes. Then she cast her eyes down and bent to fill the jug in her hands. Even this was not enough; he saw her glance at his reflection in the pond.

She stood, the jug balanced in her hands, and looked at him with a regal and dignified air. Her back was straight, her neck slim, her head held high. Her naked breasts were round and firm. But above all else it was her eyes that fettered him to the spot where he stood. They looked into his soul, it seemed, and knew him. And there was a great sadness in them, a sadness that seemed to be intensified by the small smile that played on her full lips.

"I ... I'm Sneferu of Luxor," he said. "You're Egyptian. I can tell." He spoke in the language of the Two Lands.

"My lord is correct," she said. "I am Hagar, slave to the lord Abram, formerly slave to the lord Psarou of Sile." The words identified but did not define her. Her head remained high. "My lord wishes ... ?"

"I'm not anybody's lord," he said. "I'm a soldier." His voice was suddenly husky. "I'm ... I've just been hired by Abram to arm and train his people for war." He felt like a fool—he, who had just faced down a rich Bedouin leader and driven a hard bargain. Now he could think of almost nothing to say. He wanted to look her up and down, to revel in the beauty her brief garment bared so fetchingly; but he could look nowhere but into those dark eyes. "Then ... then we'll see each other again, I suppose," he said lamely.

"As my lord wishes," she said. "Now ... my lady Sarai calls for me. If my lord will excuse me?"

And she turned and left, the jug now balanced on one shapely bare shoulder. Her back was as lovely as her front. He watched her until she disappeared around a tent.

Gods! he told himself. You've been out there too long. Shove a pretty girl in front of you, and ...

But no. If it had only been a pretty girl he would have reacted quite differently. He would have given her the once-over, and ... But no. If someone were to ask him now what the woman who had stood before him a moment before looked like, what would he say? Was she tall or short? Were her breasts large or small? Were her hands, her feet, graceful? Was her voice melodious? Who could say? He had looked at her, but had not gotten past her eyes: those big, melting, dark Egyptian eyes of hers—eyes that said more with a single glance than any five women he had ever known could have said with their voices, their bodies, anything.

Now? All he remembered was that message in the

eyes. How had life hurt her so? Was there anything that he, Sneferu, could do about it? Because if there were, he would not refuse to help.

Sneferu shivered. His thoughts were a hopeless tangle. *Hagar* . . .

III

Sneferu introduced the smith to his new employer; from that point the two began to converse in a language the Egyptian did not know. The interview seemed to be going well, and the smith's eyes were bright as he showed his visitor the forge and the projects he was engaged in finishing. Abram examined each metal artifact carefully, showing interest and even enthusiasm; from time to time a sword blade, a buckler, would draw from him a slow smile.

After a time Belsunu turned to him and to Ka-Nakht. "Pardon me," he said. "It is so long since I've heard the language of my original homeland . . . I couldn't resist the opportunity to speak it again. Let me explain. The lord Abram is the son of a great man among my people, a leader named Terah. Terah often warned of the impending fall of Ur, and nobody would listen. So he took all his people and possessions and migrated north to Haran, in a time when there was peace between the people there and the Hittites."

"My father had a vision," Abram explained. "Before he died he told me about it. I think the God spoke to him, as He has since spoken to me many times. At any rate the vision was of Ur in flames and the enemy in the streets, killing and looting."

"This was a terrible time," Belsunu said. "Abram has relatives who would not listen to Terah. Word came to Haran that they had lost everything. Myself, I was 'prenticed at the time and was on a trip with my master. When we heard the news of the Fall, we never returned." He turned to Abram with a smile. "I guess we've both been pretty much on the move ever since. Isn't that right, sir?"

"Well, we had a period of some years in Haran," the old man said. "But I began having the same visions myself, on the death of my father. Only these told me of a destiny my tribe would find far to the south, in Canaan. And, after a rather roundabout sort of journey, here I am, entering Canaan at last." One gray eyebrow lifted at the Egyptians. "And now, seeing our friend's weaponry here, I finally begin to believe that we will, in fact, take our rightful place here—and keep it.

"So," Abram said, smiling at both of them. "It appears that we have made a bargain, my friends. Several of them. I've made a deal with our friend the overseer of the king for ore—whatever our smith friend here needs for his work. I've hired myself an armorer and an officer. All that remains is to mark the matter with a feast—and our friend the king's steward tells me his people are preparing one for us."

"A modest one," Ka-Nakht said, "in no way worthy of the occasion."

Abram waved him away. "It is not the size of the ceremony that matters, but the quality of the bargain. And in spite of the fact that we have yet to talk wages, friends Sneferu and Belsunu, I consider that I am striking a good bargain."

"Pay me what you like," the smith said. "The son of Terah will not underpay me if I have given him good value."

"Good," Abram said, his deep voice full of affection. "We will discuss the matter further. And you, Captain? What will you have of me?"

"I won't need anything but my keep, sir, until we've fought your war for you. After that, nothing—if we lose. If we win . . ." He turned one palm to the sky.

"Good. And let me tell you that if we win, Captain, you have only to ask. The pick of my chattels. A herd? Slaves? You may even find yourself a wife among our women. She will come to you with a rich dower." Abram approached his two new liegemen and put a big hand on the shoulder of each. "My friends, you are no longer young. There comes a time when soldier and smith alike must settle down. Make a place for yourselves among my people, and we will grow old together. My people have come to Canaan to stay—forever. We will be few and our enemies will be many. We will always need stout friends." His smile was warm and fatherly, his tone open and all-embracing. Sneferu looked into his eyes and felt the better for it. It seemed that Abram, too, had the gift of friendship in his own way.

And suddenly his mind went back to Abram's camp, to the oasis, to the girl at the pond's edge. And he was thinking the sort of thought that hadn't crossed his mind more than twice since his youth: a woman, children, property of his own. *If we win, Captain, you have only to ask. The pick of my chattels . . .*

It was, all in all, a different sort of a feast. By nightfall another contingent of Abram's people rode in to join in the festivities, and among them were some women, Sarai and others. Sneferu looked about the camp for Hagar but could not find her, although an attendant claimed to have seen her among the party.

There was dancing around the campfire—but it was a far cry from the wild dances of the Midianites. The dances of the tribe of Abram were slower, more stately, so that even the smith, weakened as he was, found himself being drawn irresistibly into the ring of dancers. His warm smile, coming out of that craggy face with the deep-set, cavernous eyes, was reassuring. He stopped, though, when the exertion brought on a fit of coughing. He joined Abram and Sneferu at the places of honor before the fire.

"I was noticing," Abram said in that slow voice of his. "There is a certain mark you bear on your body."

The smith's eyes went to his, quickly. "Yes," he said. "A birthmark . . . it runs in the family, on the male side. Why? Have you seen another bearer of it? Perhaps . . . a young boy . . . I'd say around puberty now?" The eagerness drew the words out of him in rapid order, out of breath though he was.

"No, no . . . I'm afraid I can't help you there. But . . . this birthmark. It is like the paw print of a lion, am I right?"

"Yes. See? Back here."

"Ah." The sigh escaped him a little at a time. "Lot? Eliezer? Did you see? This is something to tell your grandchildren about. You have seen with your own eyes the mark of Cain."

"Mark of Cain?" Belsunu said. "I don't understand. It's just a family thing. I—"

"Was your father a smith?" Abram said, his old eyes bright.

"No. Well . . . yes. My father was an armorer of Ur. He died. My mother married again, and my new father was a merchant of cloth. In accordance with my mother's wishes he apprenticed me to a smith when I was still a child."

"Ah. And your father bore the mark?"

"As my mother told me. Why?"

"Well. There is an old legend having to do with the creation of the world and of the first man and woman, the first parents of us all. They had two sons. The elder was a farmer, who, for his pleasure, liked to work with metal. The younger was a herdsman. . . ."

Sneferu listened with interest, watching the faces of Abram and Belsunu as the story progressed. It was a fit tale for a campfire and a feast, a story of jealousy, injustice, and murder. The God, as Abram called him, refused the sacrifice of the older brother, Cain, whose name meant smith in a dialect of the low country of the Tigris-Euphrates, and accepted that of his younger brother, Abel. In a rage Cain killed his brother. The God forbade him to settle among men—but put a curse on any man who dared to harm him. To identify him instantly to all men and warn them not to lay hands on him, the God put a mark on Cain's body. The mark would enable him to pass all borders with impunity, but would discourage any tribe he visited from keeping him around too long. So Cain became an eternal wanderer, knowing no permanent home, his craft available to all men, who learned from the first murderer in the world the skills and weapons of killing.

"Of course," said Abram, "it's only a story, the sort of thing a mother in Ur, before the Fall, would tell her child at night, after dinner. But . . . there you are. The tale does have a kind of ring of truth about it, doesn't it? After all, the smith's trade is a lonely one; for he alone can cross all borders, even in time of war, because his services are always needed."

"Yes, sir," Belsunu said, his voice thoughtful. "And after the war he's usually sent packing pretty quickly."

"Quite so," Abram said, his voice kindly and understanding. "That is why I repeat my earlier statement. You are growing no younger, and, unless I mistake myself, you are not in robust health these days. Think about what I say. You cannot wander forever, rootless like this. Consider my offer. Find yourself a bride among our women. Live with us. Grow old in a place of honor among us."

Belsunu caught his breath suddenly, and Abram's eyes went to his gaunt face. The smith's eyes were abrim with tears. "My lord," he said. "I . . ." He stopped, gulped, stammered out his apologies; but Abram found himself drawing the smith out, little by little—and Belsunu found himself pouring out, as if with total recall, the tale of his own lost family, the murdered wife and daughter, the lost baby boy. "And . . . as I travel," he said in a hollow voice, "I find myself looking among the younger slaves of the peoples I meet. Wondering . . . always wondering. Will I find my son among them? There is always the initial hope . . . and always the hope is for naught. I think that's why I stay on the road. That . . . and the fact that the moment I start thinking about a woman, a family . . . I remember . . ."

"Ah," Abram said. "And . . . the mark of Cain. The boy, if he lives, bears it?"

"Yes. Low on the back, near where mine is. I . . . I know it's most likely he's dead. But I can't give up hope, not while I'm alive."

"I see. Well, I'll tell you what, my friend. When

we're settled in Canaan, I'll send someone east along the trade routes, to our birthplace—yours and mine. My relatives are still there. I'll have my messenger ask about the matter. Will that help? I realize it's not much of a chance . . . but until you're ready to travel all that distance yourself once again . . ."

Belsunu looked up now, into Abram's eyes. "I . . . I thought of making that journey myself, a while back. But . . . as you say, it's unlikely I'd survive such a trip." Now, little by little, the cough began to return. He held his hand over his mouth, shaking his head. "I . . . I thank you, sir . . . if . . ." But now another ferocious burst of coughing stopped him, and he could not continue. He rose, apologized between bouts of coughing, and left the campfire.

"A terrible story," Abram said, looking at Sneferu. "And you? You have been his friend—how long?"

"A month, perhaps. I found myself drawn to him. And that's surprising. Unlike yourself, sir, I don't have the gift of friendship. I don't make friends easily. Never have. I suppose Ka-Nakht and I . . . well, I've known him longer than anyone else who's left alive."

"I see. Your profession discourages you from becoming too deeply attached to a comrade, knowing you may lose him at any moment. Am I right?"

"Yes, sir. But the smith . . . Belsunu . . . he's different."

"That he is," Abram said. "And, like yourself, I find myself drawn to him somehow. There is a quality there . . . well, I grow old, you know. And I have no son . . . although El-Shaddai, the God who speaks with me, has promised me a son in my old age, a son through whom my seed will prevail in Canaan and found a great nation. I know," he said, holding up one hand. "It sounds foolish of me as I say it. Sometimes I cannot believe it myself. But—the visions persist. The God continues to speak to me, although I have not sought Him out. Somehow it will all come true. I do not know how." He looked around him; Eliezer and Lot and their relatives had joined the dancers around the circle. "And now? Now I have no real heir, no one

I can trust who is close to me. Eliezer has been a disappointment. He is shallow, unreliable. And Lot, my brother's son . . . anyone can look at him and see what he is." His gesture dismissed them utterly. "My son . . . my heir . . . I know what I would want him to be. I would want him to be a man among men, a person of judgment and substance. A man like the smith . . . or like yourself, my friend."

"My lord." Sneferu bowed his head, raised his eyes again to Abram's. "I am only . . ."

"You are a soldier, a competent man. Ka-Nakht has told me about you. And . . . there is that in you which goes beyond the usual character of your trade. You turned down a rich job recently, working for a king in the Valley of Siddim. Why? You didn't want to leave a friend to die." Again he held up his hand. "No, no, don't lie to me about it. I have not grown this old without seeing men sicken and die of the same malady, many times over. I know the signs. The hand of death is on the smith. But, as you say, he is an unusual man, one a person feels drawn to. And . . . one doesn't want to see him die alone, among strangers who don't care about him. One wants to see him die among people who value and love him—to see him buried properly, mourned properly. And, along the way to death, it's better for a man to feel useful, to work a trade he loves and at which he excels." Abram let a small smile of understanding play on his lips. "Have my thoughts any affinity with yours, my friend?"

"Yes," Sneferu said. All of a sudden his throat was dry, hoarse. "I . . . I am in your debt, sir."

"Well," Abram said, smiling broadly again. "Then pay your debt in the coin of your trade, by making me mighty. From today you are my strong right arm. That arm will have to carve me out a place in Canaan." The voice gathered strength without getting any louder. "And this phantom child of mine, this son who has yet to be conceived? Believe in him, my friend, and keep him in mind as you train my people for war. As you make them strong, you will make him strong. In time you will make him a king."

IV

The moon was huge in the desert sky. The stars were out in wonderful profusion. There was a delicious, cool balm about the night air as the asses, surefooted as goats, picked their way across the rocky track back to Abram's camp.

Sneferu, at the head of the token guard Ka-Nakht had ordered for Abram, sat silent and thoughtful on his mount's back, his mind turning over and over again the events of the last day and night. *Gods!* He hadn't felt such enthusiasm in years. He'd thought, as a matter of fact, that he was beyond such enthusiasm. But no . . .

It was curious how Abram had gotten to him, with his talk of a hypothetical son as yet unconceived, a son for whom the three of them—Abram, Sneferu, Belsunu—would create a mighty kingdom. If anyone had told him a week before that he, Sneferu, an old and seasoned soldier, would be listening raptly to such talk . . . Yet there you were. Abram had, even at his present age, the gift of inspiring his listeners, of building a fire inside their hearts.

It was a trait he had seldom run into in a lifetime of hiring out to one alleged leader after another. More often than not, his task had been to shore up the crumbling throne of a weakling or give focus to a fool's desire for self-aggrandizement. In most cases, it had been he, Sneferu, who had provided what leadership there was. And in every case, as soon as the prize was won or the throne successfully defended, he had been all too glad to get away, knowing how the continued presence of a strong personality like himself could arouse the jealousy of a king who knew himself to be weaker than his commanding officer.

This, he was thinking now, was not the case with

Abram. Here, for one thing, was a man who had brought his people intact all the way from the Land Between the Rivers to Egypt and back again. Moreover, he had not been weakened in the process but had actually prospered. There was evidence enough already of his strength and authority, and it was powerful evidence indeed.

But no such evidence was needed. One had only to look into his clear eyes or hear his strong voice ring out orders to know that this was a man. Gods, the man was a spellbinder—and more so in informal circumstances, sitting around a campfire speaking in an everyday voice, than most men could be while inciting a drunken mob to riot. And—this was rare indeed—he had the gift of making the listener feel important in the enterprise at hand: important, needed, valuable.

He also had the priceless gift of imparting a sense of hope—of confidence, even—that a given course of action could be successful. He had the gift of faith.

The old man sat tall and straight, his head held high. The look on his face, so far as the moonlight allowed it to be seen, was tranquil and confident. How was it, Sneferu was thinking, that a man could be so full of strength that he could give you a gift of it without even trying—and without in any way diminishing his own?

Here he was, thought Sneferu, an old man, dreaming not of a slow decline but of the destiny of an entire people. The more he thought about it, the stranger it seemed. And now, with his heart full to bursting, he found himself feeling younger than he had in many years.

Abram's farewell was warm, effusive. The old man embraced Sneferu as he might have embraced a blood relative, with a word or two of caution about "not letting our friend Belsunu strain or overwork himself." Sneferu agreed, promising to talk to Belsunu about taking on a number of apprentices from Abram's camp and delegating the less essential work; and his own tone as warm as Abram's, he took his leave of the old man.

Sneferu walked his ass down to the pond to drink

before heading back. As the animal bent its shaggy head to drink, he looked down at the reflected moon in the pond's still water . . . and once again saw a figure mirrored in it, moving before the silver face of the moon.

He knew who it was, somehow, even before he raised his eyes to her. "Hagar," he said.

"Yes, my lord," the husky, gentle voice said. "I . . . I heard you were here. I beg your pardon. The Egyptians in our party are clustered far behind me in the column. I get so little chance to hear the language now."

"You're homesick," he said. He was almost afraid to move toward her, afraid she might bolt like a startled animal.

"Yes." Somehow she caught his thought, and with her empty jug in one graceful hand, took a step or two closer, turning her face toward his. "I . . . I have never left my homeland before. I am among strangers."

"Ah," he said gently. "I can remember the first time that happened to me. I can remember it as if it were yesterday. On the march, as a young soldier who stood shorter than the spear I carried, I struggled to look strong and unperturbed and grown-up. But in the night I would creep out into the desert and weep my eyes out."

"Oh," she said. "Do soldiers weep?"

"Do women weep?" he said. "A soldier is only human. And I was many years a slave in the ranks until I won my freedom by my valor in a raid."

"I . . . " Her voice broke, and Sneferu suddenly found himself stepping forward to put one gentle hand under her chin and tip her face up into the moonlight. Her soft cheeks were wet with tears. "I'm sorry," she said. "Forgive me."

And then something inside him changed. A door in his heart opened and let her inside. And he found himself holding her close, close, feeling her small, warm body firm but soft against his, and something like a shiver against the winds of winter went through him. "Hagar," he said in a voice grown suddenly husky. "I came back to see you. I had to see you again. If only to see what you looked like. I could remember only your eyes, and I could think of nothing else."

"Please," she said, struggling to get free—but not too hard. Then, with a sob, she stopped resisting, and clung to him with something very like desperation. "I'm the lord Abram's property . . . his slave."

"Yes," Sneferu said, a hard confidence coming into him now. "Yes, and I'm his second in command, as of tonight. The smith Belsunu and I have joined the caravan. I will train the men of Abram's party to fight. The smith will arm them. When we have won the war that will surely follow Abram's entry into Canaan, he tells me I have my choice of all his chattels."

"You . . ."

"Please. Please. I have to say this. There is something about you . . . I have never felt anything like this, not in my most distant youth. There is a feeling inside me for you that I cannot describe. If I spent money for a soothsayer, he would pocket my coins, look at the moon-struck expression on my face, wink at his assistant, and find some pattern in the stars, real or imagined, that would tell me the gods had destined you to be my woman for the rest of my life, and perhaps for whatever life lies out there beyond death. Hagar, hear me. The lord Abram owes me nothing now. In a month, two months, he will owe me much. I am a mighty soldier, a man experienced in many wars. Believe that, even if I don't have the fancy speech to make it sound any better. In a while the lord Abram will be in my debt. I . . . I want to ask him for you."

Her eyes sought his; there was an expression closer to pain than to pleasure on her beautiful upturned face. "Oh," she said in a broken little voice. "My lord . . . I had told myself never to hope again. . . . Hope hurts too much."

"I am not your lord," he said, his arms tight about her. "Not in that sense. I am plain Sneferu of Luxor, a man without lands or cattle or possessions. But I grow old. There comes a time for finding a place to stop and stay, and make children and a home. My hand on a sword is still quick and sure; but this will not be for long. I stand a chance of growing secure and prosperous here. Abram is an honorable man and no weakling who will send assassins after me the moment the battle is won. I suddenly find myself a man with a future of sorts. I . . . I suddenly find I want you to spend it with me. Your eyes have been before me with every step I took since I saw you."

"Oh," she said. She laid her face against his chest. He could feel her heart beating beneath the soft, naked breasts pressed against his flat belly. She sighed, almost a sob. "Please," she said in a small voice. "Don't say these things and then forget you have said them. Don't say things you don't mean. I couldn't bear it. I just couldn't bear it."

Her hands met behind his broad back. He took his arms away from her and placed one broad palm on each side of her face and turned her eyes up to his. "If I fail you," he said, "may I die when I least expect it, when the hope shines brightest in my own heart. May I die on the doorstep to happiness, with everything I ever wanted in plain view of me."

"Hush," she said. "Hush. Don't say that." And suddenly he felt her small bare feet atop his own insteps, and she was holding him tight, pulling his face down to hers, pulling it down with her eyes, which looked deep into his soul. Her lips were warm and demanding.

CHAPTER SIX

I

Between cruises a fisherman's work was mainly a matter of maintenance: caulking the bottoms of boats grown old and creaky from constant service, sewing sail, mending nets, braiding rope. There was no time to be idle, ever, and a slacker in camp would have been turned out to starve within the first cycle of the moon.

In the fishing camp of Binshoumedir, no exceptions were made. Within two days of landing, Ahuni, using the clumsy methods he had learned so far at Zakir's forge, had fashioned a crude hook of scrap metal, and Binshoumedir had worked it into a wood frame and lashed it to Zakir's handless arm. While there was little a man could do aboard ship in the height of the fishing season with one arm and a hook, there were plenty of uses to which Zakir could be put between cruises.

Now, on the first day of the third week since they had landed, Zakir found himself being shaken awake at a frightful hour in the morning. He groaned and turned over, throwing a curse at the person or persons who dared to waken him. "Go away," he said. Instead, he found himself bellowing in sudden pain as the handle end of a fish gaff slammed against his bare soles. He awoke in a black rage, remembering the bastinado from the dungeons of Babylon. "You—!" he said. "Touch me again and I'll kill you."

Then he looked up to see Binshoumedir's taunting grin. "No you won't," the fisherman said lightly. "You might *try*. Others have tried before you. But I lead a charmed life. You are looking at a man who has wrestled a shark, down in delta waters, and lived to tell about it. After that nothing anyone could possibly do to me could throw a scare into me. Many men have tried, on the Babylon docks. A net in the face and a gaff in the rear end, friend. It's stopped bigger men than you."

"Damn you," Zakir said, sitting up. "I . . . say, is the boy back yet? Ahuni?"

"Not that I know of. Come; rise and get to work. We've rope to braid today. Come, Zakir. We've done just as you said: we've cleared a space, straight as an arrow's flight, for many *gar* in length. The women are already at work braiding the rope."

"Then what in the name of fifty demons do you need me for?" Zakir said, shaking his shaggy head. "The whole point of the ropewalk is to put the non-productive people to work." He scowled and stopped dead. "Oh. Of course. I'm one of those nonproductive people, am I not? Right you are. I'd better get to work, hadn't I?" His tone was bitter as gall. "That's about what I'm good for now, isn't it? Thinking up work for the women to do."

"Oh, for the sake of all the gods, you damned fool, get up and stop feeling sorry for yourself. You did quite enough of that last night before you passed out. You've got quite a head on your shoulders, don't you know that? Here we've been braiding rope in the off season for many years, and we've always run out halfway through the season because the braiding time was never adequate. Now you've revolutionized our whole setup in a matter of days, putting the women and the old men to work like this."

"Yes," Zakir said bitterly. "The women and the old men and the children and the cripples and the one-armed indigents, and all the people who aren't worth a damn at doing a man's work."

"Oh, be quiet," Binshoumedir said, a little less patiently this time. "Frankly, I'm tired to death of your damned self-pity. You've been whining like a eunuch for days now. Isn't it about time you started sounding like a man for a change? Come on, get up. There's work to be done."

True enough, the villagers had cleared a long path all the way along the waterfront and moved all the stalls to one side to make way for it. At one end someone had placed one of the big wooden platforms used to hang fish on while gutting them; on the back of this were several bronze rings ordinarily used for hanging netting. The women, following Zakir's suggestion, had run hemp fiber through these rings and were slowly backing their way down the improvised street as they wove the fibers into rope. Anchoring the material at one end this way allowed one woman to handle the whole braiding process by herself, one woman per rope, and it allowed her to keep the rope taut as she braided. Already the fishermen could see the advantages, which included stronger, more tightly braided line.

Zakir met smiles virtually everywhere in the little marketplace (they were already beginning to call the little street the Ropewalk). He nodded back; smiles came hard to him now.

He and Binshoumedir walked on until they reached the river. Suddenly the fisherman grasped Zakir's arm and pointed downstream. "Look there," Binshoumedir said. "What's this? Has Mousidnou picked himself up a new apprentice in the markets with that fat purse he's bringing back from the Babylon waterfront? Or . . . look, he's waving to us. Well, I'll be damned."

Zakir looked at the little boat tacking across the current toward them, and his puffy face lit up for the first time in days. He raised his good arm and waved back at the boy in the bow. "Ahuni!" he bellowed in a voice Binshoumedir could hardly recognize: strong, lusty, masculine.

"Well, now," the fisherman said. "You *can* smile, after all. I'd been wondering if you were perhaps born without the right muscles for it."

Ahuni was first off the boat and tied it up expertly as Mousidnou dropped anchor. Binshoumedir looked with approval at the boy's sun-darkened body, at the hard muscles that were beginning to develop around the shoulders and under the arms. He'd worked his way back upstream after meeting Mousidnou on the waterfront in Babylon, and the days spent crewing for the fisherman had burned his hard young body as dark as a professional boatman's, from crown to toes. The boy's white-toothed grin seemed all the brighter for it as Zakir stepped out onto the dock to embrace him. "Binshoumedir!" the boy called happily over Zakir's shoulder. The fisherman grinned back at him.

"Where have you been?" Zakir said. "Oh, I know —you've been in Babylon. That's obvious. But . . . why did you go away like that, without telling me?"

"I had to get something. Something I'd buried before I left the city. Binshoumedir! Could you help me with something? It's too heavy for me to lift. Maybe too heavy for two of us."

Stooping to unlash a tarp amidships, Mousidnou said, "Yes, come on board. Give us a hand, Binshoumedir. I almost pulled my back out getting the damned thing on board. Three of us, though, ought to be able to lug it ashore without anyone getting ruptured."

Zakir stood, open-mouthed, and watched as the three of them groaned and swore over the long coffin-like object under the tarp. And as they wrestled it up onto the dock, he knelt beside it, his good hand grasping a piling, and got his hook into the canvas to help pull it up onto the planks. The hook caught on the tarp and pulled it free, baring the wooden chest underneath. Zakir's expression was at first incredulous, then despairing, then almost angry, then resigned. "Of all the things to . . ." he began. But then the resignation entered his voice, and some of the old petulance. "Well, all right. I suppose it was a smart thing to do. But you could have sold the stuff in Babylon for more than you'll get upriver. But no: of course you couldn't. Except to the waterfront thieves, and then only at a loss—and then somebody would have cut your throat for the money. I understand, but . . ."

"Well, *I* don't understand," Binshoumedir said, looking down at the closed chest. "What is it? It feels like you've got a whole live ox in there."

"It's his tools," the boy said proudly. "I got them out of the shop before anyone could steal them. I knew he'd need them. And we're not going to sell them. We're going to keep them."

"Keep them?" Zakir said bitterly. "What for? I can't use them." He held up the arm with the hook on it. "Can I hold a hammer in this?"

"No," the boy said, beaming. "But I can in these." He held up his own tanned young hands. "You're going to teach me to be a smith. You're going to teach me everything you know." He turned to Binshoumedir, grinning broadly. "Zakir was the greatest metalworker in Babylon. Everyone said so. He had work on display in the temples, in the palace." He turned back to the ex-smith. "He can be the greatest metalsmith again," he said with enthusiasm, his eyes sparkling. "But this time he'll be using a different pair of hands—mine!"

Binshoumedir, on impulse, turned to the ex-smith, scanning the puffy face. For the first time it seemed to bear a thoughtful look. Cautious, and afraid to hope, perhaps; but thoughtful.

II

Binshoumedir's boat had been careened and scraped and reconditioned, and when it was ready to put in the water again, he went on another fishing cruise. This one took him all the way downriver to the environs of Nippur, and when he came in to Babylon to sell the huge catch, he found that the price of fish was running high, and he made more money than he had ever made before in a single cruise. He gave thanks to the gods, just in case, and even made a small contribution at one of the temples. Then, leaving the bulk of his hoard with a friend from his own village, he went on a carouse.

Three days of drunkenness and wenching left him exhausted and queasy; but when he made his way back to his boat and started working his way upstream, he had a certain amount of new information he had been at pains to pick up in the stews of the city. When he docked he went looking for Ahuni and Zakir.

He found them busily at work at a small forge they'd built of stones. Master and pupil had reversed positions, and now it was Zakir pumping the bellows and Ahuni, his dark eyes bright with enthusiasm, deftly if inexpertly working a copper blade into shape. "Here," Binshoumedir said. "What's this?"

"I'd show you but I can't stop pumping," Zakir said. "Look over there. The piece cooling in the sun." He nodded toward a number of burnished implements gleaming in the sunlight.

"Huh," Binshoumedir said. "If I didn't know better, I'd think it was some newfangled kind of gaff. Ingenious. But you'd never get a fisherman to . . ."

"Your brains have been addled by that damned reek aboard your boat, fish-killer. Look again." Zakir scowled at him. "What's the main problem with the gaffs you've been using since the beginning of the world? Eh? It's the fact that it's easy enough to get the damned fish onto the thing, but a pain in the rear end trying to get him off. Now look at that thing in your hand, will you?"

"Huh." Binshoumedir turned it this way, that. "It might work a trifle better at that. But . . ."

"But you're so damned conservative one couldn't get you to try a new net the fish were guaranteed to swim into." Zakir snorted. "You . . . no, Ahuni. The other side now, while it's hot. Get the point into the fire now. Right. Right." He looked back at the fisherman. "Look, you damned fool. We may have saved you a lot of bother. If this thing does what I think it'll do, we have another item to export to Babylon. And this village may turn into another Uruk or Nippur."

"Huh," Binshoumedir said again. He turned the point back and forth. "Oh, that reminds me. I spent some time in your old quarter You can't go back to Babylon, either of you. That fellow you insulted—his father'll hang you if he can, the moment you enter the gates." He grinned at the boy, working so hard at the forge. "Ahuni, it may please you to know that Soulai has been walking with a cane for a month now. I think you may have put him out of business for a while."

"I wish I'd killed him," Ahuni grunted, wrestling the blade into position for another hammer blow.

"No you don't," Zakir said. "Killing a man solves nothing. Look," he said. "Let's take a rest. Go down to Noubta's and pick up a couple of loaves of bread. We'll have lunch down by the docks. And tell Noubta we'll mend her pot tomorrow. No, now, let's don't get hasty. Lay your work out in the sun, just so. A good smith keeps a neat forge. That way you always know where to look for things when you need them. Now, run along."

Binshoumedir watched the boy go, his young back straight and strong in a smith's rough tunic. "I gather he's doing all right," he said.

"He's doing fine. Making faster progress than I ever did. The apprenticeship process is ordinarily damnably slow. The whole process is based on getting as much beastly hard labor out of a boy for as many years as you can without really teaching him anything until the end of the indenture. That way he never knows enough about anything to leave you—until, of course, you actually have to let him go. I've often wondered how fast a boy could move in the process if you left out all the deliberate delay. Well, now I'm learning."

"Good. I was going to tell you what I learned. It *is* true: you can't return. Trumped-up charges. And I think you won't be able to send your better work— once Ahuni is capable of it—to Babylon for sale. Not if there's the smallest chance of anyone's recognizing patterns people associate with you."

"That's no problem. One can always think up new patterns. But we do have a problem: how the devil do I get new ore? What do I trade for it? I'd better find a new market source. And I'd better find it upriver. Hadn't I?"

"Well, yes. You can't stay here forever. There's not going to be much of a market for your work. Nobody in the world but fishermen come through here."

"Well, I guess that settles it. It's Mari. Even though the town is many days upriver, I can't think of anywhere else. In virtually any other trade you can find work in obscurity in small towns. But a metalsmith needs to be on a trade route, or in a city or a seaport or wherever. Besides, there's other business I'd like to transact, business that requires access to a court of law."

"Court? I'd have thought you'd had your fill of courts."

"In that sense, yes. But . . . well, my friend, I'd like to free Ahuni. Adopt him. Make him my rightful son and heir."

"Ah! That's good news. And I think the better of you for it. Does he know about this?"

"I've never mentioned it, if that's what you mean. But . . . you know, he's never known anything but slavery. And . . . well, now, he's slave *and* felon. If he were to be recaptured, it'd go hard with him."

"True."

"The little devil. He took quite a chance going back to the city for my tools."

"Yes." Binshoumedir grinned back at him. "You know, my friend, we'll miss him here. He's made a friend of every man, woman, child, and dog in the entire village. And people from other villages, people who've stopped here on the way up or downriver, ask about him next time they come by." The fisherman frowned, scratching his shaggy head. "I suppose we'll miss you too, smith—for all that I'd never have predicted it."

"You've made me at home here," Zakir said. "I'm in your debt. This gaff—I worked it up in an attempt to pay off some of what we owe you."

"Owe? Eventually you'll have made us rich, exporting rope. But I know what you mean. I thought, when the boy and I first pulled you out of the water, that . . ."

"I know what you thought: that I was over the hill.

Well, maybe I was." He shrugged. "I owe you and Ahuni most for the fact that I'm not. It's discouraging that you can never quite pay people back for the favors they've done you."

"I know. All the people I owe the most to are dead and gone. All you can do is pass the favor along, next time you see somebody who needs one."

"Right." Zakir held up the hook on his mutilated arm. "You know, I thought I'd never get over the shame of this. But now . . . I'm thinking of coaching Ahuni through the making of a . . . well, you know. A *dress* hook. Something that doesn't look quite so—"

"Yes." Binshoumedir grinned. "You know, smith, I have a rule: never drink in camp. But this evening I think I might break the rule. And I've brought back some choice stuff from the city, mellow as a dove's breath. Send the boy to bed early, and we'll go down on the docks and kill a jug or two."

"Thank you, my friend," Zakir said. "A month ago I'd have shared it with you, and gladly. A month before that I wouldn't have waited for the invitation: I'd have stolen it from you. But now . . . well, would you be offended if I said no? If I said that I thought I'd drunk enough palm wine this year? Enough palm wine to last me another couple of years, as a matter of fact?" He put his good hand on the fisherman's bronzed skinny shoulder. "I appreciate the sentiment."

"Sentiment my eye," the fisherman snorted at him. "I was testing you—and you passed the test. I'm glad for you." He grinned that old lopsided, half-mocking grin again. "By the gods! Did you think I really meant it? Share the best palm wine Babylon has to offer with a toper who—"

"I understand. Better than you think. And thank you."

"Huh. When do you plan to leave?"

"Well, if this were back in the city, I'd consult an astrologer, and then I'd have a numerologist work out a proper date, and . . . well, you know. But I think I'll just pick up and go. The track follows the river, right?"

"All the way. Within a couple of hours' walk at

most. But if you'll wait a week I think I can arrange a ride for you upriver on one of the boats. Part of the way, anyhow."

"That would help. And . . . Binshoumedir?"

"Yes? Oh, that. Damn it, don't go getting sentimental on me, now."

"I won't forget it. Ever."

Binshoumedir looked him once in the eye, and all his usual jocularity was gone now. "Make sure you don't. Make sure you don't forget any of it, my friend. You've got a choice now, you know. A choice whether to wallow in despair or make something out of yourself again. You figure out for yourself which feels best, despair or hope. If it turns out you like pain best, go ahead and heap the dirt on your head. But if you don't . . . well, you know what to do. And I won't remind you again that you have more than just yourself to live for, now."

"Your words are like a cold bath," Zakir said. "But you make sense. As I said, I won't forget."

Mari was many days upriver, a separate kingdom which had managed to escape the revolutions and wars that had kept the city-states of the south in constant unrest for generations. It was also sufficiently distant from the constantly warring city-kingdoms of the upper Tigris to have retained its independence. Yet it was on a major trade route connecting the Valley of the Two Rivers with the Hittite and Amorite cities and ultimately with Damascus, Egypt, and the Great Sea.

It would, everyone agreed, be a good place for a smith to set up shop, starting small and working his way up as his expertise and his reputation developed. One could start with easier jobs and gradually work his way up to better-paying projects. And in a city that lay across the route of major caravans plying the avenues of trade in an important area there would always be work for a smith, whether it be the fashioning of golden ornaments by lost-wax casting or a simple matter of hammering a bent sword blade straight after a skirmish on the frontier.

Zakir had explained this all to Ahuni and had been

more than a little surprised to find the boy well ahead of him. "Yes," he had said. "It was what I was hoping you'd say. I think we've got a better chance of making a new start. I talked with Iddina once, when I was sneaking into the city to get your tools out. Did I tell you? He helped me, loaned me pack animals to get the box to the docks. But, Zakir, he said even if we could return to Babylon, you'd always be haunted by the past, by what you'd been there. He said the only thing was to start anew."

"My friend Iddina was a wise man," Zakir had said. And now, waiting on board for Kiddinou, master of the boat that would take them upstream, he found himself suddenly thinking of Iddina, and of his old neighbors and friends in the Bazaar of the Three Palms, of the aimless life he'd led there, spending the increasingly greater sums he earned as fast as he could earn them—and then winding up in the end with nothing to show for any of it. "Iddina," he found himself saying aloud now, "was right."

"Sir?" the boy said beside him.

"Iddina," Zakir said. "He said one must go forward. Remember? You told me."

"Yes, sir," Ahuni grinned. "Isn't it exciting?"

Zakir reached over the boy's broadening shoulders and hugged him with his good arm. Kiddinou had finished loading and was preparing to cast off. Now, as the final moments neared, Binshoumedir appeared at dockside and impulsively leaped aboard. He embraced Ahuni with affection and clapped Zakir on the bicep with his strong, skinny hand. "Ah," he said. "I remember leaving my own village to go be an apprentice to a fisherman. My mother wept and wept. Me, all I could think about was the wonderful future that lay ahead. Is that what's running through your mind, boy?"

"Yes, sir," Ahuni said. "Although ... I'll miss the village, sir. And Noubta, and all my friends here."

"Nonsense," Binshoumedir said with that strange one-sided smile. "Village? It's a cluster of hovels built around a dock. The only street is the Ropewalk, and we owe that to you and Zakir. It might amount to something some day. You never know what's going to happen. But ..." He shrugged. "Will you miss me, boy? I'll miss you. Damn it, it seems life keeps dumping new friends in my lap and then taking them away."

"What are friends, Binshoumedir?" Zakir said. "They're no better than this little village of yours. They're walking chunks of meat and bone, mostly without a thought in their heads. They're eminently replaceable. And yet we wind up caring for some of them so disproportionately that it's hard to account for it if you go on the facts alone. Whatever the reason, you emaciated, sun-blackened devil, you stink of fish and carrion and you have a terrible sense of humor, but we've come to value you more than you know. It's hard saying good-bye to you. I think we will carry a part of you with us for most of our lives."

"And I you, smith. You too, son. Be good to each other. Prosper. Be happy. Live long. Farewell!" And, with that devilish, infectious grin splitting his dark-brown face, he turned and leaped onto the dock and walked briskly away, not looking back, a stringy-muscled, long-legged scarecrow of a man clad in no more than a rag around his loins, his hair dark and shaggy, his gait carefree and confident.

Behind them Kiddinou hauled anchor. The sail began to fill. Zakir and Ahuni looked back at where the women of the town were working their way slowly backwards down the little thoroughfare, the unbraided ends of rope stretched tight in their hands. The morning sun shone brightly on the thatched roofs. A town? A cluster of hovels. It didn't even have a name.

Suddenly Ahuni found himself weeping. Zakir, his own eyes moist, held the boy tightly to his broad chest with both arms, the able one and the crippled one alike.

CHAPTER SEVEN

I

Abram's voice woke Sneferu around dawn. The Egyptian, shaken awake by the commotion, sprang to his feet, his new sword in his hand. Blinking away the sleep, he peered about him into the dim light.

At first he'd thought: *An attack*. But now he could see it was only Abram, kneeling in an attitude of prayer and facing the east. The old man's lips were moving, and the words were in the same language he had spoken with Belsunu. Sneferu, shaking his head, put the sword back in its scabbard. And now, watching the old man, he saw Abram fall silent and bow his head in reverence.

He sat on a rock and watched the dawn rise over the hills that lay above the Salt Sea. His expression was one of the mildest distaste. Abram was an easy man to admire most of the time—a decent administrator, fair and just; a lordly man with a lot of inner strength that could be drawn upon in adversity. He was in many ways an almost ideal employer.

It was only at times like this that Sneferu's admiration for the old man began to wane. Sneferu, in his years of service on many borders, in many wars, had come around gradually to the old soldier's all but implacable hostility to all religions. It was curious, he thought: the only military men he'd ever met—barring the most primitive tribesmen, of course, and even some of them shared his point of view—who believed in the

deities were military men who had lost their nerve for
one reason or another. It seemed to be something that
occurred to a man only after he'd been butchered and
lost both legs, or an arm, or whatever. It was, most of
the time, only when you lost faith in the strength of
your own good right arm that you began looking for
some god to lean on.

Given this set of facts, it was curious that he now
had to find himself making excuses for Abram. Look
at it any way you might, though, Abram was no
weakling, for all his age, for all the fact that his much
younger wife tended to ride roughshod over him, to his
own tolerant amusement. Yet here he was, totally in
thrall to this as yet unnamed god of his: praying on his
bony old knees as devoutly as any coward.

Abram had approached him once about his own
religious feelings; he'd stated his case matter-of-factly
and Abram, unlike your average sort of zealot or
fanatic, had nodded understandingly and even smiled
at him without the smallest trace of the usual sort of
superciliousness you found in the average Believer.
And he'd never brought up the subject again, which
most of the time made for a situation that Sneferu
found to his own taste.

Now, however, he found himself wondering. Just
what was it that the old man got out of this god of his?
Out of the ritual and fuss that were slowly beginning to
develop around his attachment to this will-o'-the-wisp
he prayed to? Perhaps he'd have to ask Abram one of
these days.

Well, he thought, yawning and stretching, now—today—was as good a time as any. Yesterday the old
man had told him to get ready a couple of the riding
stock and the two of them would take a little trip up
north. Where to? Sneferu had asked. *Oh, up north . . .
Bethel, Ai, places like that.* Past Jerusalem, then?
Shouldn't they be taking a troop of warriors with
them? *No, no . . . the God's hand is upon me. We will
find no enemies along the way.* Not even in Jerusalem
—perhaps the strongest of the city-states nearby, the
only one that none of the little border wars ever dared
draw into battle? *No. Least of all Jerusalem. The king*

there is a priest of the One True God. Abram's tone had been confident, reassuring.

That had been another thing. The arm of Melchizedek, king of Jerusalem, was a long one. His guards would surely take note of anyone passing through their domain, and perhaps stop them for questioning; Jerusalem and its approaches lay solidly in the way between Timna and Bethel. How did Abram, who claimed never to have met the High King of Jerusalem, speak with such confidence about his reception there?

Curious. This business about Melchizedek being a priest-king of the same god Abram invoked so constantly . . . this was the first sign Sneferu had had that this nameless "God"—the old man always spoke as if there were no other, as if the entire Egyptian pantheon had never existed, as if the Chaldean gods were so much moonshine—had another worshiper in the world than Abram. For it was an observable phenomenon around Abram's camp that virtually nobody, least of all his own family, seemed really to share his belief or his piety. And now to hear that this Melchizedek fellow was a co-believer . . . Well, it'd make for another question or two. They'd have plenty to talk about on the road, in those places, down on the flat, where the asses could proceed two abreast.

"Good morning." He looked around, startled. Abram, his morning prayers complete, stood smiling at him. "Have you been up long?"

"Not very, sir." He stretched again. "Did you sleep well?"

"Sleep? I don't know. I had another vision in the night. I couldn't tell you whether I was awake or sleeping at the time. But it was wonderful. I feel as if I had slept and rested for days. I feel twenty years younger."

"A vision, sir?" Sneferu said, half dreading what was yet to come.

"Yes. The God spoke to me. He told me to go up into the hills, to the temple I built when we were here before between Ai and Bethel, and look upon the lands that would be mine and my descendants'." The old man's sharp eye did not miss Sneferu's slight frown.

"Ah," he said. "Like all the rest, you doubt this talk of mine about 'descendants.'" His smile was tolerant, forgiving. "My wife doesn't believe me either. But she is concerned enough about my sanity that she is thinking of bringing me to my senses. She wants to give me a concubine."

"A concubine, sir?"

"Sarai thinks herself barren. Now, that isn't what she says, but it's what she thinks down inside. She's terribly touchy about that. She covers it up by telling me that there is something wrong with me, that at my age I simply cannot father a child."

"What do you think, sir?"

"I think that when the God wants us to have a child we will have a child. I think the God wants to settle us on the land that will be ours, and make a safe place to bear children in. Then, and then only, will he allow me to make a child in Sarai's womb. And there is something else. When He spoke with me last night, in my dream . . . there was talk of a covenant. A covenant between the God and me and mine forever."

"What kind of covenant?"

"I don't know. That will be revealed when the time comes. I'm confident of that." He held up one hand. "Getting back to your question. Sarai thinks that if she gives me a concubine to sleep with me in my . . . my dotage, one of two things will happen: either I will come to the conclusion that my loins are indeed exhausted and I will cease this 'prattle' of mine—"

"Oh, no, sir, I don't think—"

"Now, now. This is what she thinks. And the other possibility will be that the concubine will in fact conceive, and I will have my heir, which Sarai will then raise as her own. And I will be content and will stop bothering her."

"Ah," Sneferu snorted. "Women." He looked up quickly. "Sorry, sir. I didn't mean that, not the way it sounded. I meant no offense to the lady Sarai."

"No offense taken, my son. Look," he said, changing the subject. "What's this I've heard about fights between my herdsmen and my nephew Lot's?"

"It's true, sir. I've had to discipline several people on either side. I'm afraid I've had to enforce the discipline a little harder on the side of your own herdsmen, as a matter of fact. There are more of them, and if we were to have a full-scale riot . . ."

"I understand. Something about grazing rights?"

"Yes, sir. There's really not quite enough graze to go around. Lot should settle elsewhere through the winter, sir."

"Yes. He has been bothering me about that. He wants to settle in the Valley of the Salt Sea for the winter. The seasons, with the exception of summer, are milder there."

"Would I be out of line if I offered advice, sir?"

"No, no. Not at all." The old man began breaking camp, covering up the ashes from the night's fire. "You are going to tell me I should let Lot go."

"You see inside my mind, sir."

"Not at all. We think alike. I am thinking as you are: Lot's men are not fighters. They are soft and weak. He wouldn't be much use to you, would he? I mean, in a battle?"

"Totally underfoot. I think his continued presence here is actually slowing down the process of arming."

"Good. I'll let him have his head. I'll have to keep an eye on him, of course."

"More than just an eye, sir. I mean, if he's going to settle in Siddim Valley . . ."

"I get your meaning. That's a volatile area. He could get in over his head. And there's word of some sort of revolt brewing. Several of the cities of Siddim are beginning to balk at paying double tribute to Egypt *and* Elam and getting no protection for it."

"It's been stable for years, sir."

"Yes, I know. But you don't believe that stability will last the year out, and neither do I. Nevertheless, Lot has sent feelers out and has received tentative permission from Bera, king of Sodom, to settle there. There's good graze for the stock; Bera's people aren't pastoralists, for the most part, and he'd just be occupying land which they regard as worthless since you can't grow crops on it. The proposal has some advantages. He'd be out of *my* hair, for one thing." Abram winked solemnly at his lieutenant.

"Yes, sir." Sneferu unhobbled the asses. "And now? Where do we go today?"

"We should find the altar I built, I think. I will give sacrifice to the God. Then ... well, I think I have something to show you."

They found Abram's altar late in the afternoon, and Sneferu watched respectfully as the old man prayed and communed with the unseen Presence he claimed was there. Then, as dusk's deep shadows grew, he led Sneferu to the top of a pass that led over the hills to wind its way down to the Jordan Valley.

The land below, spread out beneath them like a map, was lush, cultivated, dotted with patches of green —forests, olive groves, orchards. The shadows were long on the land, and wisps of evening fog dotted the wadis, spreading out at the far end of the valley to blot out the bottoms entirely. It was one of the loveliest sights Sneferu had ever seen.

Abram didn't speak for a moment, looking down, a look of wonder on his old face. Then he spoke, and his voice was not wistful or supplicatory at all. It was calm and collected: the voice of a ruler, gentle with the gentleness that could come only from the knowledge of great power.

"The God spoke to me in the night," he said, "and bade me come up here. 'Then,' He told me, 'raise your eyes and look out in all directions—north, south, east, and west. And all the land you can see in any direction I will give to you and yours forever. And I will make your descendants as numerous as motes of dust, so that they will cover the earth.' "

The smile on his face was exultant; his voice rose. " 'Rise!' the voice told me then. 'Go forth and ride the length and breadth of the land. Explore the land I give to you. . . .' "

And suddenly Sneferu found himself inexplicably moved by the sight and by the sound of the old man's words. *Yes!* he thought. *I* will *make your son a king.*

And . . . yes, I'll settle here, Hagar and I, and grow old in peace. . . .

It was only much later, as they made camp, that he reflected on this moment again. And, looking sidelong at Abram as he made the evening's cooking fire, he thought: *Amazing man! He's done something I've never seen anyone do before. He's sold me a piece of his dream.*

II

Shepset rose while the first pink tinge lay on the eastern sky. She quickly built the morning cooking fire and began making bread for the Egyptians in Lot's party. She scattered several handfuls of grain on an oblong stone and ground them with a second, slightly rougher stone. She dampened the rough flour from time to time from a jar of water she had drawn at the pond the night before. Then, after passing her flour several times over the mortar and leavening it with starter from the day before, she kneaded it into thumb-sized cakes.

By this time the fire had produced a certain amount of hot ash; after she had laid the raw cakes on a flat stone she heaped hot ashes on top of them and left them to bake. Then, washing her hands and forearms with water from the same jug, she went to wake Rekhmira.

The former overseer of the lord Psarou's lands at Sile was now a lowly herdsman tending Lot's flocks; under Abram, men said, he would already have risen to a foreman's job after the long march across the Sinai desert and the Negeb. Lot, unlike his uncle, tended to pay little attention to his herds, taking note of the administration of his budding empire only when things went wrong. Thus Rekhmira, who had heroically brought his portion of the herd across the desert with minimal losses, remained in a position of equally minimal responsibility. A slave most of his life, he accepted the fact philosophically. It was the only way to deal with it; Lot would, in the years that remained to him, change only for the worse.

Now Rekhmira rose at the first touch of Shepset's narrow hand. "Ah," he said, blinking twice but instantly awake. "It's early. Is there some reason?"

"No, no," the girl said in a loud whisper. "I . . . I want to go see Hagar. I can only do this if I get up very early."

"I see. Hmmm. I smell bread cooking. Egyptian bread." His smile was cordial.

"Yes. I made the cakes for your work day. Yours and that of the other Eygptians here. If the lord Lot or his wife send for me . . . could you make excuses for me? Please? Tell them I am cooking breakfast or something?"

"Certainly. And thank you for the food." He looked her in the eye now. "Shepset," he said. "There's been a change in you, child. What's the matter? Has the lord Eliezer . . . ?" But she turned her face away from him. "Gods! If one were free . . ."

"No, no," she said. "If it were only that simple . . ."

"I don't understand." Rekhmira put his hands on her shoulders and made her turn her face to him. "Shepset? Tell me, child. Please."

"Please, don't. Don't make me. I can't tell."

"I won't let you go until you do. Is it . . . well, is it one of the herdsmen? One of the guards? Because I—"

"No, no," she sobbed. "It's worse than that. Much worse. I . . . the lord Lot called me to his tent last night."

"Lot?" he said. His face changed. And suddenly she could not look at him, could not face him at all. She felt the pressure on her shoulders ease. His hands stiffened. "Shepset, he didn't . . . tell me he didn't."

"I can't," she said, barely able to speak. "He did, and—and his wife did. And . . . if there'd been anyone else to give me to . . ."

"His wife?" Rekhmira said. "His *wife?*" He shook

his head, clearly beyond his depth. "But—you're the property of the lord Abram—"

"Yes!" she said in a strangled voice. "Yes. That's why I have to talk to Hagar. She'll know what to do. She'll be able to intercede for me with the lord Abram, or—or his wife, or somebody."

"I don't know," Rekhmira said.

"Well, maybe . . . maybe there's that soldier she's so taken with. . . . Rekhmira, I've no one else to turn to. She has to be able to help. She has to."

"Sneferu? I know him. He's a good man. No fancy airs. But my dear, he's away for a couple of days with the lord Abram. Up north somewhere."

"Rekhmira. I have to ask. I have to talk to her. Please, please don't let them know where I've gone."

"Oh! Of course, of course. It's just that . . . my dear, I don't know what Hagar can do. I don't know what any of us can do." His face lost all animation, went dead. "It's a different world we're living in," he sighed. "If only . . . but no. It's no use speculating about what things would have been like. Go, child. But hurry back."

Hagar heard her out, hands to her brown cheeks, her dark eyes wide with horror. "Oh, my darling," she said, stretching her hands out to the girl. "Oh, my poor darling." Shepset came into her arms and wept in great shuddering sobs. "Look, my dear. I can't do anything about what's already happened. Nobody can. But . . . look, maybe I can do something about seeing that that sort of thing doesn't happen in the future. Surely the lord Abram won't allow that sort of thing here. He's very proper, you know, and won't have anything out of line in his camp."

"B-but . . . that's just it. Lot's leaving the camp. And . . . he thinks I'm going with him."

"Leaving? But I don't understand."

"He—he's going to ask Abram . . . when he returns . . ."

"Well, I don't know anything about that." Her hands rubbed the girl's thin back. "But . . . look, my dear. You go back to camp before anyone misses you, and . . . well, keep out of their sight. There's always some sort of way to do that."

"No there isn't. Not after dinnertime. Hagar, I've tried. For days."

Hagar stepped back and looked the girl in the eye. "I forget," she said. "I'm not the older person, with the experience, whom you can come to for advice any more. Poor darling, you've picked up some experience I've been spared so far. Well, all I can do is try." The two women embraced again.

Shepset turned to leave . . . and then stopped and turned toward her friend. "Hagar. I'm so stupid and self-centered. How is it with you? I didn't even ask."

"Shepset . . . he's going to ask Abram for me. I'm almost afraid to breathe for fear something will ruin it. And . . . oh, my dear. I'm so much in love I can't see straight. I've never felt like this before in my life. If only I could share it with you."

"Hagar. Has he . . . ?"

Hagar found herself blushing, to her surprise. "No," she said, embarrassed. "But . . . I think when he returns from up north, tomorrow, perhaps even tonight." Her expression was torn between pity and eager anticipation. "I feel like a child. I don't know what to—"

"Good fortune to you," Shepset said in a tight little voice, her face desolate. She turned and fled before she could come completely apart.

Enosh, sitting on the back of one of Abram's choicest asses, rode to the top of the rise and waited for Belsunu to catch up with him. When the smith pulled even with him he pointed down toward the west. "Ashkelon," he said proudly. "And . . . the Great Sea. Isn't that a sight worth a day's ride?"

Belsunu smiled his cadaverous smile. It made his gaunt face look even sadder than before. "Splendid," he said. "In my impressionable youth I'd have written a poem about it, or perhaps a song for the lyre. But now, my friend, all I feel is tired. Ashkelon, viewed in that sort of context, looks like any other medium-sized seaport to me. And while the Great Sea remains as impressive as ever, all I can think of is getting off this animal's back and having a good stretch."

"Ah, yes," Enosh said. "And perhaps a little something to take away the pain, eh? A draught of something wet?"

"Maybe at some other age. But these days that sort of thing doesn't agree with me. My problem isn't that of killing the pain. It's that of getting the strength to feel anything any more." He coughed shortly. "Sorry. I didn't mean to burden you with my troubles. It's altogether too easy to let this damned ailment turn you into a bird of doom."

"Never mind, sir," Enosh said. "There. I've got to get back to calling you 'sir' again, sir. You're spoiling me. Wait until I get back in camp and forget to call the lord Eliezer 'sir,' just because you've got me used to not standing on ceremony."

"It's all one," Belsunu said. "Slave, freeman, peasant, king. . . ." He coughed again, longer this time. "But I'll go back to the proper protocol if you like. I don't want to get you in trouble with your master. Although, just between you and me, my friend, I've seen some worthless, useless young popinjays in my time, but Eliezer——"

"Uh, you said that, sir. I didn't. Although . . ."

The two men dismounted and slowly led their animals down the incline. "I understand," Belsunu said. "I don't imagine he's too pleasant a master to work for."

"They're mostly all the same, sir."

"You don't mean that. Not for so much as a moment."

"No, sir, I don't. But I had to say something."

"Ah. Don't trust me much, do you? Well, I understand. I wouldn't trust me either. A man with one foot in the grave, what's to keep him from saying things at the wrong time just because he doesn't give a damn whether he lives or dies? He might just up and say something because he wanted somebody to kill him quick and have it all over with. Like spitting in a lion's eye."

"Oh, no, sir. I wouldn't look at it that way, sir."

"As you please."

In the market they visited twice at metalworkers' forges to talk shop. At the second one Belsunu suddenly stopped and held up a crude axe. "Ah," he said appreciatively. "You didn't make *this*, my friend. I'd wager a year's income on that." He held it up to the light, noting the dull gray glint of the metal.

"No, I didn't, as a matter of fact," the smith said. "I swapped a Hittite trader a surpassingly fine bronze sword for it. I got the best of the deal, too."

Belsunu handed it to Enosh. "Heft *that*," he said. "That thing has bashed a great number of heads in its day, I'll wager. No work of mine could stand up to it." He grinned his death's-head grin at the smith. "Or yours either," he said. "I don't care how good a metalworker you are. Not unless you had a supply of this ore. And it doesn't grow on trees, let me tell you that."

"The story is that it falls from the sky, hot as if you'd picked it right out of a white-hot fire," the smith said. "And you're quite right, however much I'd like to deny it. Bronze hasn't a chance against this. But it's so rare. If anyone were ever to find an ore like this in the earth somewhere, in some quarry . . ." He spread his hands, palms high. "But there I go, dreaming again. Friend," he changed the subject, "you're no merchant. You're a smith yourself. Welcome."

Belsunu exchanged greetings with his fellow craftsman. "You can tell by the calluses, can't you? And the burns. Well, I'm guilty, all right. I'm Belsunu, sometime of Babylon. I apprenticed in Ur as a lad. Someday that's going to be a badge of pride, I think—if I live that long. Metalworkers who 'prenticed in Ur are getting scarce."

"You're the first one I've ever met," the smith said. "Glad to meet you. What kind of items do they make there?" Belsunu handed over his sword. The smith did not say anything at all for a moment. "Gods!" he said. "Why didn't someone tell me I was bandying words with a master of the craft? Friend, you're out of my league. But this is an occasion. Here, I'll close up shop and buy you a drink."

"No, no," Belsunu said. "I'm here to look at slaves. I take it there's an auction block nearby."

"In the next street. Ask for Zimri. But look, my friend. You're an event in a small town like this. Where are you working now? I hope you don't move to Ashkelon: you'll put me out of business."

"No, no, I'm working for a countryman of mine named Abram, over near Timna. Although we'll be moving up north of Jerusalem, way I hear it, before long."

"Ah. Good thing you're not moving into the area around the Valley of the Salt Sea. Bad things are brewing there, word has it." The smith's tone was confidential, almost conspiratorial. "There's a rebellion in progress there. Chedorlaomer, King of Elam, for a dozen years or so has been extracting absentee-landlord tribute from all the cities of Siddim. After a while he let things get lax, and several of the kings of the valley cities banded together to throw off the yoke. They thought that just because he'd let the tax-gathering get out of hand, he'd grown soft. But they've got some surprises coming."

"What do you mean?" Belsunu said, smothering a cough behind one big hand.

"What they didn't foresee is that he's put together a punitive expedition to Canaan. And he's gathered a few rather formidable allies around him. People like Arioch of Ellasar—"

"Ah. I almost went to work for him. Please go on."

"Ah. Then you'll understand me better. A friend of mine took the job you apparently turned down. He says the plan is for Chedorlaomer's troops to swoop down and quash the revolt before it can get anywhere. My friend said that if he can accomplish it, Elamite control of the area will be stronger than ever—and there'll be a number of cities in flames around the Salt Sea, and a lot of brand-new widows in Siddim."

"Interesting," said Belsunu. In some haste he bade farewell to his fellow smith. When he and Enosh were alone again, he took the overseer aside. "Look, this is important. I want you to ride back to the lord Abram and tell him just what you heard here. Every word of it. You'll have to go alone; I can't keep up with you these days. Don't worry. I'll be all right. I still want to attend the auction. But Abram has to hear about this. And fast. You understand?"

"But sir—"

"No excuses, no nothing. Ride! Ride like the wind!"

Belsunu stayed another day, scouring the slave marts of the port city. But none of the boys on the block bore the red birthmark. *I'm a fool,* he thought. *Wasting my time like this after all these years . . . it's about time to give up. The boy has to be dead by now.* But he knew he couldn't stop looking. It was a habit by now, like any other. A habit as ingrained as breathing.

III

From a hilltop Abram and Sneferu looked down on Abram's camp. Sneferu, noting the changed layout of tents, herds, and pickets, frowned. "Something's different," he said. "Very different. And I'd better get down there and find out, fast, what it is."

"Hold," Abram said. His long-fingered hand waved his captain to stillness. "I think I know what it is that is different. Lot has gone already—and taken his herds with him. See?" His hands pointed to the undefended opening of a box canyon across the great encampment. "Lot's herdsman Rekhmira had the bulk of Lot's flocks worked into there. There was good forage, enough for another month or so. Rekhmira is an able man. He would not have moved the animals unless—"

"Unless he'd been told to. Why, the damned fool. What a time to move."

"He couldn't face me," Abram said. "I knew he'd

want to leave soon. There is something about Siddim that attracts him. But he is a weak man and could not look me in the eye and ask me. Well, no use going down there. You might as well take your time. I know what you'll find."

"Nevertheless," Sneferu said. "With your permission, sir, I'll go down and look to the disposition of our own herds. And I'll have the animals on the left wing of the camp moved up into the canyon. If you . . . hmmm. What's this? A runner from the camp?"

They watched the slave make his way up the hill toward them. "My lord," he said, bowing to Abram. "Captain? I was sent to find you. Enosh the slave has returned from Ashkelon with a message from the smith Belsunu."

"Message?" Sneferu said. "Out with it, man."

The messenger passed on Belsunu's warning about the rumors surrounding Chedorlaomer of Elam: the Great King, in league with Amraphel of Shinar, Arioch of Ellasar, and one other whose name the messenger had not understood, were planning a preemptive raid on the rebel cities in Siddim. Five small city-states were to be put to the sword: Bela, Zeboiim, Gomorrah, Admah, and Sodom. At the name of the last city Sneferu shot a quick glance at Abram. "Yes," Abram said. "As you observed, Lot's timing is as bad as ever. Well, let's hope the cities of Siddim are well defended."

"Yes, sir." Sneferu turned again to the messenger. "You said 'a message from Belsunu.' Didn't he return with Enosh?"

"No, sir. He'll be along later. He thought the news too important to wait, and he wasn't up to a forced march across the desert. He'll be about a day behind."

"Hmm. And his work at the forge?"

"He has a dozen apprentices in training. He has a curious way of working, sir. The apprentices are making nothing but rough blades."

Sneferu looked thoughtful. When he turned to Abram he saw the patriarch nodding interestedly. "Yes," Abram said. "I can see how there might be advantages that way. He knows how much of a hurry we're in to arm."

"Even more so now," Sneferu said. "This rebellion and the counterstroke against it will likely force our hand. I'd better get to work and speed up the training, even if it means training some of our people with wooden swords for now."

"Yes," Abram said. "A good idea. Go then: move the animals into the canyon. Set up a training schedule. You are in charge of getting our people ready for battle." He sighed resignedly. "I had hoped to have more time."

"I too, sir. But we'll make the best of what time we have. And—just in case, I'll double the pickets around the camp, and keep scouts on the move around the perimeter."

"Go with the God."

Hagar moved into Abram's path as the old man made his way toward his tents. "My lord..." she began.

Abram, preoccupied, looked down at her. His eyes seemed far away. "Yes?" he said.

The matter-of-fact tone of his voice almost tied Hagar's tongue. She began to speak once and found her throat dry. She swallowed and tried again. "My lord, the lord Lot has left the camp, and he has..."

"Ah, yes," Abram said. "I'd already heard. Well, it's his privilege if he chooses. I won't detain him. Thank you for telling me, though." He turned to go.

"But...my lord...he has taken some of your slaves with him. My friend Shep—"

"Please," Abram said. His mind was evidently elsewhere. "I'm hot and tired, my dear, and I've been on the road since early this morning. Could you perhaps be so kind as to bring me a jug of fresh water from the spring? Nice and cool right from the well? There, thank you."

Hagar, her heart in her stomach, watched him pass. And as she looked beyond him to his tent, she saw Sarai emerge from her quarters. Abram's wife looked at her husband, then at Hagar, then at her husband again. When, a second time, she looked at Hagar, there was visible, even at this distance, a look of cold resentment and loathing on her thin face.

Tired as he was, Enosh made haste to answer the call Sneferu put out for him as soon as Abram's captain had rejoined the camp. He found the soldier mustering the herdsmen of the left flank and barking a series of orders, swiftly and efficiently. Only when the last herdsman had been sent on his way did Enosh step forward. "You called for me, sir?" he said.

"Oh, yes. You're Enosh?" Sneferu paused a moment to survey the sturdily handsome young slave. "Good work. You did well to ride ahead. Your information has proven most valuable. But . . . the smith, Belsunu? How was he when you left him? Do you think he can make it across the desert from the shores of the Great Sea alone? Or should I send someone after him?"

"It might not be a bad idea, sir. He's weak. He has a great heart and won't let on how travel tires him. But the trip has taken a lot out of him. I think sending someone after him would be a smart thing to do."

"Good. If you'd be so good as to have someone sent . . ."

"Sir. If I could volunteer?"

"You? But you've just finished half killing one of the lord Abram's animals getting here. You must be half dead yourself."

"Nevertheless, sir . . . the smith is a good man. I'd consider it an honor, sir."

Sneferu looked the man in the eye and smiled. "All right," he said. "You may go. I like your spirit. Take a couple of men with you. He may have exhausted himself entirely." He held up a hand, halting the slave's retreat. "I think I sent you on a scouting trip a week ago, didn't I? The face is familiar."

"Yes, sir. Scouting a new site for our training. Someplace less vulnerable than this, more out of the way."

"And you recommended an oasis near Hebron, I think."

"Yes, sir. At Mamre's Grove. There's a fine grove of oaks and terebinths, and the place is a lot more easily defended than this. The animals will winter better there, too, sir . . . and so will we."

"You know this area, then."

"Yes, sir. I was with the lord Abram's party when it came through here before, on the way to the delta and the black lands. The lord Abram used me as a scout then, sir. And I have a sort of gift for languages, sir. I pick up information where another man might not."

"Good. I like that. Keep up the good work. I may ask Abram for the loan of you, if that's all right with you." He waved away the slave's eager reply. "All right, then. Go bring in our friend the smith, and take the best care of him. I'll admit I like him too, and I'm glad to be able to think he'll be in good hands. And Enosh?"

"Yes, sir?"

"Report to me when you return. I can use a good man at my right hand. Maybe you're the one."

"I hope so, sir."

Sarai's strong hands worked on the taut muscles at the back of Abram's neck. Her eyes roved around the tent, focusing on nothing. "Is that better?" she asked. Her voice was softer than usual.

"Yes, yes," Abram said in a tired voice. "Thank you . . . now, perhaps farther down, over the shoulder blades . . . yes, yes. That's good. Oh, yes."

"There is a rumor going around," she said. "I hear that we may leave Timna."

"I am thinking of it," Abram said. "For one thing, my nephew has left us, with his usual haste, and may be moving into a bad situation. He's gone off to Siddim, and the word we have is that there's a war brewing there. We may have to keep an eye on him. No, no," he said, holding up a hand in warning, "don't chide me about that. Blood is blood. And I made a promise to his father—my brother."

"But . . . oh, well. There's to be no arguing with you, I suppose. But where are we moving to?"

"My man Sneferu has had the area scouted. It appears the best and safest place to winter is off to the northwest, near Hebron. You'll like it better than here in Timna, I think. The weather's nicer. The area's well watered, and the camp would center around a thick grove of trees."

"Ah," she said. Her hands were gentle now, soothing. "That's an improvement. But how permanent is this? Are we always to continue moving?"

"No, no," Abram said. At times like this, when peace reigned between the two, his voice took on something of an old man's gentle singsong. "We're here to settle permanently, for the first time since our long stay in Haran. But the God has not spoken to me of where. Never fear, the time will come. I have not come this far to raise my son as a nomadic chief, a Bedouin herdsman. Before the fall of Ur my people were city people. We will be again."

"Your son," she said wryly. "Abram, when will you face the facts? If we were ever going to have a child . . ."

"Patience, my dear," he said. "There'll be a proper time for everything. It is all in the hands of . . ."

"I know," she said exasperatedly. "Don't tell me about it again; I've heard it all a thousand times at least."

Her hands roved over his old but still powerful back, working on his taut muscles. But now they were less gentle and reflected the sudden hard feeling that had come into her heart. Her eyes blazed; her lips drew into a straight, humorless line. *There's no use arguing with him,* she told herself. *You know what you have to do. Go ahead and do it.*

Enosh's party found Belsunu shortly before nightfall. He had fallen off his mount and the beast, startled by the sudden loss of the heavy burden on its back, had bolted—but had remained within the smith's view, grazing on dry grass that grew along a wadi. The smith had tried to reach it but had failed. He was weak from exposure and much dehydrated, but he was still alive. His dark eyes in their deep sockets burned up at Enosh; his smile was wan but appreciative. "Enosh," he said. "I knew you'd come for me."

"Yes, indeed, sir," Enosh said. "I'll have the men

work up a sling. You're in no condition to ride right now, sir. What you need is rest. We'll have you home in no time, sir. We'll have the prettiest of our women waiting on you hand and foot. Nothing but the best, says the lord Sneferu, for my friend the smith. Just take it easy there, sir. . . . That's right, boy, bring up the water . . . right here, now. . . . And drink slowly, slowly. . . ."

Sneferu rode out to meet them and accompanied the improvised sling in which they'd put Belsunu. Sneferu walked on foot beside them, holding the smith's big hand in his own. Their talk was gentle raillery, the kind men always used with sick friends.

At camp's edge Sneferu sent a runner ahead. "Find the slave Hagar," he said. "Send her to me. I'll need someone reliable to tend to our friend here. Then have someone tell the lord Abram she's over here; I don't want her to get into trouble. *Enosh!* Oh, there you are. Look, the more I think about it the more I think we'd do well to move, to break camp and make that move we were talking about. If the word about this uprising is already over in Ashkelon, well . . ."

"Exactly my thought," Belsunu said, trying to rise. "We're always the last to hear. Better to get out of the line of fire until we're ready."

"Lie back down, damn it. But you're right. And from what Enosh tells me, we may even find allies there. The fellow the grove's named after, for one. He's no friend of Chedorlaomer, from what I hear."

"No, sir," Enosh said. "The Amorites have been delinquent in their tribute-paying for quite a little while, and not by accident. Mamre has two brothers, too—Aner and Eshcol—and they're just as feisty and stubborn as he is. I've met Eshcol. I think you'd like him, sir."

"All right. I'll bring it up to Abram tomorrow morning. Meanwhile, we've got to get our friend here to bed." He grinned down at the recumbent smith. "I heard about the new methods you're introducing at the forge. Ingenious."

"Not . . . ingenious . . . at all," the smith said in his

husky voice, stifling a cough. "The quality of the weaponry will suffer terribly. My weapons won't be any better than ... than anyone else's. But the situation seems to call for haste, for quantity rather than quality, and although I'd prefer it otherwise ..." The cough finally broke through his defenses, and although he tried twice to speak, the words wouldn't come. Sneferu patted his broad chest reassuringly. They marched slowly into Abram's encampment in the lengthening shadows, the asses' heels kicking up little puffs of dust in the otherwise clear air.

Hagar came to the smith's tent shortly after dark. Sneferu stepped out of the shadows and embraced her. "Thank you," he said, "thank you for coming." He was more than a little surprised at the hunger in his own voice; he fought it for a moment and then abandoned himself to the feeling, holding her tight, feeling his own heart beating as fast as hers.

When he finally released her, it was to look down at her in the dim light. He could make out nothing but those huge, expressive eyes. "Hagar," he said. "I sent a man to tell Abram I needed you. To tend the smith." He sighed. "It *is* true; I need you for that. But ..." His voice broke.

"He's your friend," she said in a calm voice. "I'll tend him as if he were your family." She squeezed his big hands in her small ones. "Sneferu," she said. "I've been afraid of you. Afraid to give you my heart. I've lost so much. I was afraid of allowing myself to have anything again, for fear of losing it. But that's an empty way to live. I cannot live with that. I'd rather be dead." He could almost make out her face now, with its soft, full lips and white teeth. "I'm a slave and have no right to love. But I love you."

Then—it was inexplicable, and beyond all his earlier experience—Sneferu, gathering her to him, felt something like a great tremor run through him. It shook him to the soul, and for the first time the icy wind of fear ran through his own heart. It was a fear he hadn't felt since he was a child, but he remembered it, recognized it immediately. And in his heart he found himself making evil-eye signs against it. It was the worst, the most painful fear of all, just as she'd said. Because now he, too, had something to lose. Everything.

IV

Sneferu and Hagar saw each other only fleetingly in the next few days, occupied as both of them were with the move to Mamre's Grove, just north of the trade route that connected Hebron with the coast city of Ashdod on the west and with the overland route to Hazazon-tamar on the Salt Sea on the east. Hagar's duties were mostly involved with minding Belsunu, and she took seriously what Sneferu had told her: "This man is not only my friend, he also means the difference between our being able to stay here in Canaan in peace and being driven away from it at sword's point. Remember this, my dear. As far as our future safety is concerned, there is no more important man in the camp of Abram. Not even me. Tend to him as you would to me or to the lord Abram."

Tending to Belsunu was not at all unpleasant. The smith possessed a natural charm and, quick to see the bond that had developed between his friend and the beautiful Egyptian slave, treated her with a gallantry and gentleness her station did not merit. Ill as he was—and Hagar, no stranger to sickness and death by now, could see that the armorer's strength was waning with every passing week—he retained a ready wit and an almost unceasing good humor. The men had rigged him up a hammocklike sling between two pack donkeys, and, on the march, Hagar's job was to walk alongside the animals and keep them well separated, prodding them with a stick when they moved too closely together. This put her close enough to Belsunu to talk with him, and the talk helped to while away a long, punishing forced march as Abram and his captains, in some haste, moved the herds and flocks to the plain of Mamre's Grove.

At the end of the first day's march Sneferu managed to drop by their tents before riding out to check the pickets around the camp. He greeted Belsunu warmly—and his powerful embrace, as he swept her into his arms, was the warmest reassurance Hagar could remember receiving.

"Here," he said, squatting beside Belsunu's bed, propped up before the roaring fire. "I've only a few moments. I wanted to tell you, both of you, what's been happening, though. Belsunu, that war we've been expecting. The one you sent warning about."

"Ah, yes. I take it it's started."

"Yes. The Four Kings—Chedorlaomer, Tidal, Amraphel, and Arioch—they've decided to make an example of some of the smaller towns that turned away the tax-gatherer last year. Instead of simply subjugating them and looting them, they've put them to the torch. The slaughter has been pretty terrible."

"Ah," the armorer said. "That's bad. Which towns?"

"Ashtaroth-karnaim, for one. And Ham; and they butchered the Emim, over in the plain of Kiriathim. Wiped them out, every man, woman, and child. Our scout came across the scene a day later. He said it was the worst sight he'd ever seen." He turned to Hagar. "I'm sorry you have to hear this, my dear. But Belsunu and I . . . this is our business. It's what we do for a living. And . . . well, that could happen to the lord Abram's camp too, if we relax our guard for so much as a moment."

"I don't understand," Hagar said. "I thought this was a matter of punishing tribes who refused to pay tribute."

"Yes," Belsunu said patiently. "That's how it started out. But once an army gets used to slaughter it's hard to stop them." He turned to Sneferu. "Where are they headed now?"

"There's a report of a battle at Mount Seir. The Horites there have been driven back as far as El-Paran, at the edge of the wilderness. They're terribly outnumbered. As far as the rest is concerned, all I can say is that if I were their commander, and Enmishpat lay in my path as it does in theirs—their path toward the Salt Sea—I'd hit it from both flanks and wipe it out. It's almost indefensible as it is. And Enmishpat was one of the towns that refused tribute, you'll remember."

"Ah, yes. But that's to the southeast of here."

"Exactly. And the cities of the Plain of Siddim are well fortified from attacks from the south. That's the only direction they'll be expecting an attack from."

"Oh?" Belsunu sat up. The motion drew a cough out of him, and Hagar tried in vain to get him to lie back again. "I see. The trade route goes over the hills to Hazazon-tamar, on the shores of the Salt Sea. Well to the north of the Five Cities of the league."

"That's right. And once again, if I were commanding the army coming over from Enmishpat, I'd strike right through the mountains and take Hazazon-tamar by surprise. And then—mind you, the moon will be full in a week—I'd take the army down the west bank of the Salt Sea by moonlight, and I'd fall on Sodom around dawn and—"

"Ah. Sodom. Yes."

"But . . . that's where Lot's party went," Hagar said. "Lot! And . . . Shepset!"

"That's right, my dear." Sneferu reached out and took her hand; the touch of him was like static electricity running through her. "And there's more to it than that. The way to Hazazon-tamar runs just south of here." His brow rose as he looked at the armorer. "On the one hand, it'll give us a look at them. I'll be able to size them up."

But the look on his face wasn't an enthusiastic one. It was troubled. He fell silent for a moment. "I don't understand," Hagar said. "What's the matter?"

"The matter?" Belsunu said. "Nothing. Except that we're in their way. Just as Enmishpat is. And we're underarmed, partly thanks to my own damnable illness, and undertrained, which is a matter over which our friend Sneferu has little control. He's had every male member of the caravan doing sword drill every night after making camp. But—" here he shrugged and sighed "—he hasn't had them doing it for very long."

"Nowhere long enough," Sneferu said. "And we're outnumbered three or four to one, depending on whoever it is that you're talking to. All I can hope for is that we can find allies at Mamre's Grove, or perhaps in Hebron itself. Otherwise . . ."

"Otherwise?" Hagar said, taking his big hand in both her own.

"Otherwise," Sneferu said with a sheepish grin, "I'm going to have to get going and start living up to this inflated reputation of mine."

Hagar, ignoring the self-mockery in his tone, looked quickly at Belsunu; but his dark eyes held little reassurance, and his expression was serious to the point of solemnity.

V

The caravan halted at some distance from Mamre's Grove. Abram conferred briefly with Sneferu and at length decided to ride in with his captain to meet Mamre and his brothers. As they clattered across the stones in an ass-drawn wagon of vaguely Mesopotamian design, Sneferu took note of the pickets posted above them on the heights. "Look," he said, pointing to left and right. "Our arrival hasn't escaped their attention."

"All the better," Abram said. "If they prove friendly to our notion of settling here for a while, we can use all the sharp-eyed scouts we can get. I think the more of them for being vigilant. And look: this must be Mamre and his brothers coming out to meet us."

"Something like them," Sneferu said, instinctively patting the full scabbard at his side. "Ah," he said. "Horses. You didn't tell me they were Bedouins."

"I asked around. Mamre's people were once desert

people, from down in Paran. An ancestor was driven out for some sort of offense, and settled here."

"Splendid animals. And the men ride like Egyptians."

"I'll pass the compliment on to them," Abram said. "But I'm not sure how they'll appreciate it. The Bedouins of Sinai aren't too fond of the Egyptians."

"I'm aware of that," Sneferu said ruefully. "I bear perhaps a dozen scars, large and small, bought in fighting them. They're tough people. Look at the way the middle one rides. He looks like quite a fighter himself."

Abram held up his hand in greeting as the three pulled up in a rough semicircle around their wagon. "Greetings," he said. "I am Abram, once of Ur. I seek graze for my stock."

"Mamre," said the thickset man in the middle. He looked once at Sneferu and then turned his eyes back to Abram. "These are my brothers, Eshcol"—his head inclined to his left, indicating a tall, thin-faced man— "and Aner. I think my brother has met one of your men, who told him of you."

"A man named Enosh," Eshcol said. "A slave, but an able one."

"Ah, yes," Abram said. "He will have told you we come in peace."

"Hmmm, yes," Mamre said, lifting one dark brow. "With an Egyptian soldier at your side." His tone was rough and bordered on the sarcastic. "Well, never mind. We can get along with an Egyptian, so long as he does not come with the notion of collecting tribute in mind."

"Who, me?" grinned Sneferu. "I'm no tax-collector. I'm a mercenary, friend, in the service of my friend Abram, here. It's been ten years since I worked for the Lord of Two Lands. If you're looking for collectors of tribute, the armies of the Four Kings are headed this way."

"Scouts have reached me with this news," the heavy-set man said. "This Enosh, he tells us your people are no friends of Chedorlaomer."

Abram started to speak, but Sneferu caught his eye and went on. "We're no friends of anyone who levies taxes on land he neither owns nor works upon," he said. "It's true, we're not exactly anxious to fight a war over it just now. Our people are herdsmen and are only beginning to learn about fighting. But if a fight comes —if the Four Kings decide they'd like a tithe of our sheep and slaves—well, they'll find them . . . uh . . . expensive." He grinned his conspiratorial grin at the three of them. "And how about you? What if they send the collector to the grove, friend? Will you give in or . . . ?"

"They will collect nothing but lumps," Eshcol said. "Mamre . . . is your thought running together with mine?"

"Huh," Mamre said. "We did not join the open rebellion against the Elamite claims last year. We simply turned the tribute-gatherer away empty-handed, without blustering. Chedorlaomer may have some notion of striking a blow here . . . but if he finds our numbers augmented by . . ." He fell silent for a moment and then addressed Sneferu. "How many able-bodied fighting men have you? Trained or no?"

"Hmm. My figure isn't exact. We've recently had part of our caravan split off and settle elsewhere. But we ought to be able to muster . . . oh, say three hundred and twenty or so."

"Three hundred eighteen," Abram said.

"Thank you, sir. Anyhow, the Four Kings really have designs on Siddim, the way I understand it. They've been doing a lot of slaughtering of small, undefended towns along the way . . . but it's mainly been easy targets they've chosen. I haven't noticed them trying to burn Beersheba, now . . . and it'd surprise me if they attacked Hebron."

"They wouldn't dare," Mamre agreed. "They want a full-muster army to take down into the valley. They'd lose a third of their men trying to attack Hebron."

"My point exactly," Sneferu said. "Pooling our people and yours, we could put together a complement they'd also be well advised to leave alone on the way through." He suddenly thought of something. "I'm a little behind on my scouting reports," he said. "Have they hit Enmishpat yet?"

"Burned it to the ground," the quiet brother, Aner, said in a bitter voice. "Killed all the civilians. Bastards! I had friends there."

"Ah. Too bad. I expected it, though. Well, Mamre? Are we allies or not? I think they'd be damned fools indeed, attacking us if we stand together."

"Hmm. You look like a man who's seen a battle or two. And three hundred men . . . that'd be very helpful." He turned to Abram. "All right. Camp just beyond the grove. Pasture your stock in the valley beyond it, and augment my pickets with your own. We'll work together until they've passed. Oh, I forgot. This Enosh . . . I think he is supposed to have said your caravan has its own armorer. Is this right?"

"The best," Sneferu said. "He's been ill, but he's supervising the arming of our camp. He makes a blade you could use one moment to behead an ox and the next to shave your beard off with." He reached into his scabbard with a grin and tossed his sword casually to Mamre. Perfectly balanced, it made a single lazy turn in the air to land in Mamre's outstretched palm.

"Ah!" Mamre said. He hefted the sword, swung it back and forth. "Ah, now that is something! Friend, consider yourself forgiven for your Egyptian blood. I'll have a blade like this if it kills me."

His brothers clustered close about him, exclaiming over Belsunu's work. Sneferu looked at Abram and shared an appreciative nod with him. His mind formed the silent words: *Everything's all right. We're accepted.*

On the second day after Lot's party settled in the Plain of Siddim, between Sodom and its twin city, the seaport Gomorrah, and Zoar to the south, messengers arrived from Bera, king of Sodom, summoning Lot and his wife, Zillah, together with their personal servants, to the city. Lot, as a rich foreigner newly settled in the area, was enough of a novelty to lend interest to the table of any of the kings of the valley; Bera's messenger was respectful and deferential, and the invitation was couched in properly flowery language.

Lot and Zillah decided to wear some of the jewelry confiscated from Psarou, as well as the sumptuous Egyptian-style dress they'd inherited from the fallen scribe. For an exotic touch they decided to bring Shepset, dressed in the style of an Egyptian house-slave at a party.

Shepset, apprised of the order, sought out Zillah. "My lady," she said. "Please . . . I was told that I'd have to accompany you . . . that you wanted me to . . ." She bit her lip, feeling miserable, and tried to say it.

Zillah's bony face twisted in a lewd smile. "But child," she said. "I understood that going naked was nothing to you Egyptians. Besides, it'll be fun. Don't tell me it won't. Why, if *I* could get by with it . . . if I were as young as you . . ." She tried to pull the girl to her. "There, now. I won't take no for an answer. I'll even do your hair myself. And look: here's a bracelet for your arm. You can wear my very own. You'll be lovely." And all of a sudden there was a hard edge to her voice, and Shepset knew that there would be no arguing with her.

So it was that when Lot's party went through the gates, Shepset, walking miserably at heel, was bare as an egg again. But this time there was no innocence about it. Canaan's customs were not Egypt's. The casual nudity of childhood in Egypt was now a calculated thing, and the calculation was to titillate, to provoke. She bore, silent and wretched, the stares and insinuating remarks of the guards at the gate and noted that a high percentage of the men in the streets as they made their way to Bera's house seemed no more than casually interested in her nakedness—seemed, in fact, to be rather more interested in one another, for all the fact that she was blatantly, shamefully nude before them. It was as if she were in some way even less than a slave: a dog, perhaps, walking at heel behind its master and mistress on a stroll through the city. Her face burned with shame; but she forced herself to walk erect, to look directly ahead, to avoid the eyes of onlookers, to play the part of unfeeling chattel as she walked the streets behind Lot and Zillah, every iota of her brown skin on display before anyone who chose to watch—merchants, housewives, beggars, even fellow slaves. And all, secure in their finery or their rags, could look with disdain at her, the least among them, a slave denied even the smallest rag to cover her.

She stood behind Zillah's chair at the feast, cup-bearer to the two of them. As the wine flowed free, bleary-eyed faces, their mouths lolling open slack-lipped, turned her way and looked her up and down. She forced all expression from her face, determined to keep some small scrap of personal dignity in the face of the shameful way in which she was being used. She ignored the remarks—they grew more openly sugges-tive with every passing moment—that the men of the party made to Zillah about her, as though she were not a human being with feelings but a statue, a picture-girl painted on a wall.

For a long time none of them spoke to her. But there came a time when the party's mild pixilation suddenly seemed to turn into a boorish drunkenness, and she felt rough hands, male and female, pawing her. She winced and moved away; but stationed as she was behind Zillah's chair, there was little room to move. She submitted to the rough caresses, the smutty re-marks, answering no one, her eyes fixed on a crack in the wall opposite her. And the party went on. . . .

It was later, much later. One of the guests after another had insisted that the pretty cupbearer share his or her drink. Shepset's head was reeling. Her body was bruised and sore from all the pats and pinches. Some-one had brought a troupe of dancing girls in from the desert, and now Shepset was no longer the only naked person at the banquet. Through blurred eyes she could see a man and a woman coupling in the corner on a pile of cushions. Someone thrust a cup into her hand. "Wine, girl!" a voice said (whose? Lot's? Bera's?). She took the cup and headed for the alcove where the wineskins lay. As she did, a hand reached out from the floor and grasped her bare ankle. She tripped and fell. The hand shifted position to her thigh. "Please," she said. "Please. . . ."

Someone shoved her roughly onto her back. A burly body, robes hiked up to its waist, mounted her and took her, painfully. "No!" she screamed in a surprisingly weak voice, a voice heard as if far away. "No, please. . . ."

She twisted her head to one side, looking for help, just as a rough hand slapped her face first this way, then that. The last thing she remembered seeing across the room, before she passed out, was the face—the red, distorted, drunken face—of Lot, turned her way, giggling hysterically at her predicament.

CHAPTER EIGHT

I

"Here you are, sir." Ahuni, hands and face blackened by the forge, grinned at the customer, holding up the mended blade to let the light glint on its metal shaft. "Good as new."

It was noon. Behind the boy's small forge the tall walls and taller main gate of Mari loomed, thick and forbidding. The customer, a rich merchant from down-river whose ceremonial sword had come loose from its handle, took the implement from him, looking at it closely. "Not bad at that," he said. "I'm surprised. Frankly, from the look of your forge, I'd thought . . . well, set up outside the gates this way, and you a slave . . ." He let the words trail off. His gaze was friendly.

"Life is full of surprises, sir," the boy said smiling. "Look, I ran a metal shaft up inside the handle. It won't give you the same trouble again, sir."

"Hmm. I've seen that trick before—but it was far away, and in a city that no longer stands. I wonder how you got hold of it."

"My master, sir, was once a master armorer. He was trained by a man from Ur."

"Ur! Now there's a word to conjure with, boy." The merchant smiled broadly. "I remember it well, for all that I was hardly more than your age when I was there last. What a tragedy! The Queen City of the Old Empire . . . my father owned a shop in a bazaar near the West Harbor, just below the southern wall of the Temenos, with a fine view of the ziggurat of Nannar from its front window. A city of artists and artisans, boy. What other city was ever governed by a professional musician? Why, my father used to tell me that Shulgi, who reigned in his youth, played eight different instruments and was a wizard on the thirty-stringed lyre." He sighed. "Well, perhaps it might have been better governed by a warrior in the long run, but . . ."

"Url" the boy said. "I'd love to have seen it, sir."

"Ah, it was lovely." The old man's eyes were far away now, and a small smile played over his wrinkled face as he reminisced. "In my grandfather's day it was still partly made of mud-brick, but by my time it had all been replaced by burnt brick. The ziggurat itself was faced with it, and its color was a rich red. The staircase of the tower was threefold, with each stairway having a hundred steps or more. There was a lovely shrine at the top, where the king, on ceremonial occasions, cohabited with the goddess." He looked down at the boy, smiling. "Well, perhaps it was only with the *en* priestess, although the folklore there was that the goddess was said to possess her. Every city has its own beliefs, and when you've traveled as much as I have . . ."

"I'm certain it was a wonderful ceremony," the boy said. He was wondering: *Should I ask him about Babylon? Surely he does business there*. But prudence asserted itself. He gave the merchant a sharp look out of the corner of his eye. *Remember: you're wanted in Babylon for a serious crime. Why take chances?*

"Ah, yes, it was a marvelous place," the old man said, letting his mind wander again. "On all sides the canals stretched out, fed by water from the mighty river . . . downriver, past Eridu, the lagoons connected the river cities with the Lower Sea. There was trade with strange exotic places . . . my father bought a shipload of goods once from a place called Dilmun, many days' sail down the coast of the Lower Sea. . . ." He shook his head, shaking away the old memories, and came back to the present. "But all that's long gone, boy. Look, I like your work. I'll be here another day or two. Perhaps there'll be more work for you. Where is your master?"

"He's inside the city, sir. On business. If you could . . . ah, but here he comes. Zakir! Zakir!" His smile was radiant, his every gesture suddenly suffused with youthful enthusiasm.

The old man's eyes narrowed. "Zakir?" he said. "Now where have I heard that name?" His eyes followed the boy's pointing finger. Through the crowd at the Great Gate a burly figure, topped by a round black-bearded face, moved toward them. His left hand held a purse of leather; his right . . . The old man's eye took note of the missing hand; his face hardened slightly. A thief?

"Zakir!" the boy said. "Come meet someone. This honorable merchant is from . . ."

The bearded man's face broadened into a smile, although a wary note of reserve tempered his speech. "I know where he's from, Ahuni. We have met before. This is the honorable Nabousakin, one of the most respected merchants along the Great River." He bowed slightly to the old man. "Your servant, sir. Zakir, sometime armorer and worker of gold and silver to the king of Babylon and the priesthood of Bel. In better days I enjoyed your custom at the Bazaar of the Three Palms, on the bank of the Euphrates."

"Ah," said the old man, his cracked voice trailing off into a sigh. "*That* Zakir." His eyes searched the ex-smith's face, then went to his ruined arm, then returned to the bearded face once more. "Why, you were . . . you were the finest metalsmith in Babylon. You wouldn't believe the prices I used to get for your work in Eresh and Nippur. But how . . . ?" His hand gestured impotently at the grubby, plebeian marketplace outside the city walls. "This is no place for a man like you."

"Why, sir, it suits us fine just now," Zakir said. "Perhaps it won't suit us in a month or two. We're living cheap and saving money. With that money we'll buy a place in one of the bazaars inside the city." He smiled a sad and knowing smile. "The gods raise a man high and they cast him down. Perhaps the gods that forsook me a while back will look with favor on me again. Or if not me, perhaps on my son here." He grinned at the boy.

"The honorable . . . uh, Nabousakin . . . he liked my work, Zakir," the boy said enthusiastically. "He said . . ." Then his face went blank. His mouth flew open. "Your *son?*" he said, uncomprehending.

Zakir grinned and handed the leather purse to the boy. "Now don't drop it," he said. "In it are the tablets that officially manumit you and identify you as the adopted son of Zakir, an itinerant tinker."

The boy's hand went to his throat. His eyes, glazed over with tears, went rapidly back and forth between Zakir's beaming face and the old man's small surprised smile. "Zakir . . ." he said. But he could find no more words. The precious purse clutched in one sooty hand, he started to step into the ex-smith's arms, but drew back. "Zakir . . . I'm so dirty."

"It's all right," Zakir said. "You have the rest of your life to hug me in, Ahuni. It'll keep. And thanks for thinking of my . . . uh . . . finery." He indicated with some irony his clean but ragged workman's clothing. "You see, sir? The gods frowned on this boy of mine for many years. He can remember no father or mother. Now fortune gives me the chance to make him free and whole, and perhaps teach him a trade. Fate changes. At the moment I'm down myself. Perhaps that'll be my lot. But who knows? All that could change tomorrow." There was still some reserve in his voice, though; he didn't trust the merchant not to turn away from him. So many others had done so.

"Well, now," the merchant said slowly. "This is a special occasion, isn't it? A young man doesn't get his freedom every day, eh? Or find a father either, I dare say." His eyes took in the two of them gravely. "I congratulate the both of you. Zakir, you've a fine son, and one you'll come to be proud of." He gestured with the ceremonial weapon still in his hand. "Who knows? He may even develop a skill as great as yours." He nodded at the boy. "You couldn't possibly be apprenticed to a better man, my young friend. In all the area north of Ur I have seldom seen the like of this man's work." He sighed. "What a waste! But that's fickle destiny for you. Look, both of you. This is a festive occasion. Unfortunately I've business in the city which will occupy me for another day. But . . . my caravan is encamped downriver. You will find it easily by the green banners atop my tents. These are well-known up and down the river for many days' sail. If you will come to my tents the day after tomorrow, at this hour, you'll be well paid for your work today. And who knows? Perhaps I can do something for you. You can tell me then what has happened with you, and how you came to this place." His hand waved away—dismissed —their grubby surroundings as irrelevant. The other hand holstered the repaired sword and reached inside his garment, emerging with a small clay disk, which he handed to Zakir. "Here. Give this to my personal bodyguard when you approach my camp. It has my seal on it. Without this you won't get past the outer ring."

"We thank you, sir," Zakir said, bowing again. "It has always been a pleasure to serve you. Ahuni?"

"Yes, sir. Thank you, sir. And . . . good fortune to you!"

Ahuni, bright-eyed and radiant, came back from the banks of the canal, the soot scrubbed from face, hands, and body. "Zakir," he said, "I'm so happy. I don't think I've ever been so happy in my whole life."

The ex-smith grinned at him. Ahuni rushed into his arms; the two rocked back and forth, patting each other on the back. "I've been meaning to do this for some time, Ahuni. I bribed the scribe to put me ahead of another couple of people in the line. It cost me a bit. But there's still enough left over for us to go to the tavern, inside the city, and celebrate. Here, let's close up the forge. I'll find us one of the off-duty city guards to mind our tools for us. We'll promise him a good price on a breastplate; it's time you learned how to make one anyhow."

Ahuni stepped back to hold Zakir at arm's length. "Zakir," he said. "Going to the taverns . . . are you sure that's a good idea, now?"

"Oh. I see what you mean. No, no. I'll have a few drinks. So will you. Imagine! Your first drink as a free man! No, it'll be all right. I . . . I'm past that time. Before, I drank for oblivion. Now I don't *need* oblivion. It's all right. I'm perfectly in control."

"But Zakir . . ."

"Ahuni," said the ex-smith. "When are you going to start calling me Father?"

They ate at an outdoor stall at dusk: at the edge of the bazaar someone had an ox turning on a spit over a fire of white-hot coals. The smell was ravishing, and the taste of the well-done meat, hacked fresh off the slowly roasting carcass, was even better. Zakir had an appetite after his hot and irritating day of waiting in line at the scribes' stalls and went back for seconds. Ahuni, who had grown used to a Zakir who pecked away listlessly at his food, watched with delight as the one-time smith gnawed the meat from the bone. There was a warm, happy feeling inside him, and his heart was full of love for Zakir. "Father," he said between bites. "It's as if you were yourself again. The way you were before."

Zakir paused, thought about the matter. "I don't know, son. I feel a lot older and wiser. And I feel as if something had gone out of my life. But . . . a man needs to be able to give people something. It isn't good for a man to go around empty-handed. You have to be able to give somebody something. And the more you give away, the more you have. And . . . I haven't had anything to give anyone in such a long time. Such a . . . can it only be a summer? One that is drawing to an end?"

"But Father, you've always given everyone—"

"No, no. At best my accounts drew even now and then. But . . . ever since we arrived in Mari—no, longer —I've been wanting to give you those tablets I gave you today. You've still got them, haven't you? Good. . . . Well, now that I'm able to do it, I feel . . . I feel like a man again. Ahuni . . . you know what I'd like to do? I'd like to go to the taverns and find a woman. Someone my age, maybe; someone who wouldn't be too picky. Someone who wouldn't make me feel bad about . . . about my hand being gone. I've hardly looked at a woman since . . ." He held up his cup to the wine merchant, who signaled his slave to refill Zakir's drinking vessel.

"Of course, Father, if that's what you want. I'll mind the forge, the tools. And when you return in the morning . . ."

"Ahuni. Perhaps it's time to come along with me. Yes, you. Gods, how the women are going to love you! You're already turning into a handsome devil. Bah! One can tell you're no natural son of mine. *I* never looked like that." He took a big draught of wine and wiped his lips with the stump of his right arm. "I had to get by on charm," he rasped, grinning.

"Father, don't you think you'd have more fun without me?" he said timidly. "I'll be glad to . . ."

"Ahuni, today's the day you're free for the first time. You've been a man for some time. How old are you?"

"I don't know. My last master listed me with the tax-gatherer as twelve."

"And your sexual parts are those of a man. And . . . gods, boy. Do you know when you became a man in *my* eyes. When you decided to come back for me and help me, that's when. A man is someone who takes responsibility for his actions, and makes up his own mind about his life." Zakir's left hand, broad and strong, lit on the boy's shoulder. "Now it's time for you to learn the joys of being grown-up. The love between man and woman is sweeter than anything you've ever known, son. Even if it's for no more than an hour, the time one spends with women can be lovelier than any other time you could possibly spend doing anything." A cloud passed briefly over his face. "And it's the most terrible and frightening thing that . . ." He shook his head. "But there's time enough to learn that. You'll never for a moment be as vulnerable to any man as you are with the woman you care for, and nobody can hurt you so much as . . ." He sighed and smiled. "Ah, but that's another story I'll tell you sometime. Time enough, later, for you to learn the darker side of love. For now it's enough to begin learning the sweeter side. Soft breasts. Tender thighs. Lips sweeter than honey from the hive. The sweet soft laughter that comes after love, in the golden moments after both man and woman have exhausted themselves, and she lays her head on your chest and sighs that dearest of sighs. . . ." Zakir drained his wine and smiled at Ahuni, his round face radiant with love and largesse.

"I don't understand, Father," Ahuni said.

"You will, son. Come. I feel after this long and loveless summer that I myself have much to learn, at my age. Come, let's go learn together."

II

"What kind of girl is this Etillitou?" Zakir asked. He lay back against the cushions, the picture of contentment, and watched the woman Tavas-Hasina walk across the room, the ample globes of her brown bottom undulating enticingly. For a moment he considered letting himself be enticed again; on second thought, the relaxed and peaceful mood of the moment lulled him once again into stretching, yawning, taking his ease.

Tavas-Hasina poured wine from a jug into a copper goblet. "Stop worrying," she said. "Everything's going to be just fine. Etillitou is going to be just right for him. She'll make him feel like the greatest lover in the world." She walked back toward him, her body golden in the lamps' glow. "Now it's time to get dressed. Time for me to get back onto the floor and circulate. The dancers will be going on in a moment or two." She lifted one artificially darkened eyebrow theatrically, an amused smile playing on her full lips. "Unless, of course, you've other ideas. But no. Look at you. It'll be another hour before you're ready to go at it again, you big bear. And by that time you'll be snoring contentedly in a corner somewhere."

Back on the tavern floor, Zakir again ordered wine and settled down to wait for Ahuni. He took a seat at a communal table—and immediately saw his neighbor at the table stand and move down the long board to settle two seats away.

If it had stopped there he would have taken no notice. Zakir's skin had grown thick in the months that had passed since the loss of his hand. But the man who had shied away from him had been drinking heavily; he turned toward Zakir now and, very pointedly, spat on the floor at the ex-smith's feet. "In the name of all that's holy," he said in a husky voice thick with irony, "how have I offended the owner of this place that after many years' custom I must now share a table with thieves? Convicted felons? The scum of the earth?"

The proprietor moved into view. His eyes went from Zakir to the speaker, then to a stout stick that stood in a nearby corner. "Here," he said. "Let's have no trouble now. This man has paid his tab in advance, which is more than . . ."

"Paid it, has he?" the other man said, standing up. He was large, heavyset, a head taller than Zakir and nearly as broad. "And with what? Coins stolen from his betters? Blood money? Counterfeit? Hah! My friend, I *was* going . . . I'd *planned* to go upstairs with the women. But the idea of following into a whore's bed a one-armed felon, or the scruffy ex-slave he's dragged with him . . ." He spat on the floor again. Zakir looked at him. He was building up a rage, bit by bit. Once it reached a certain level . . .

Zakir stood up. "I've paid my bill," he said quietly to the proprietor. "I think I'll wait outside, if it's all right with you. When the boy comes out, would you tell him where I am, please?"

"Here, now," the proprietor said. "You don't have to leave. *You,* sir!" he gestured at the complainer. "Look here, if you can't behave yourself I'm going to have to ask you to—"

"No, that's all right," Zakir said. "It's not your fault. I'm sure it'd be best if I just left." He smiled at the owner and turned to leave.

Outside, in the street, he stretched languorously and looked up at the gibbous moon. What was it about the few days before and the few days after the full moon? Men who ordinarily followed their paces in dull lives suddenly burst forth and turned into man-eating lions who . . .

Something large and heavy hit him from behind with terrific momentum. It was as if a full-sized bullock had plowed into him; the attack knocked the wind out of him and sent him rolling head over heels in the hard-packed dirt street. The unprepared fall led him to reach out with both arms, the whole one and the mutilated one, to shield his face from the hard street; the sensitive stump hit the hard ground, sending a stabbing pain through his whole arm. He cried out.

"Yes, whine away, you thieving bastard," the phlegmy voice said. Zakir, shaking his head, tried to get his feet under him, but the big man rushed him again, bellowing an incoherent curse. His heavy fist caught Zakir on the temple just as he was rising and bowled him over; the hard leather sole of the man's sandal came down on Zakir's injured arm, and his heel twisted back and forth on it. Zakir howled in pain and tried to roll to one side. Another wild kick caught him on one shoulder and slammed him against the brick wall of a nearby house. Something dark in Zakir's eyes shut out the moon; licking his upper lip, he tasted blood. If he could just get his hands on the man's throat . . . his hands, his strong, competent smith's hands. . . .

There were other people in the dimly lit street now, looking at him, watching the beating he was taking. He cursed his handless arm and ducked under a wild swing of the other man's fist. And stood, just in time to take another sweeping swing full in the face. The blow was the sort of thing Zakir's own good right hand had dealt many an opponent in his youth; but now he had no right hand to deal such a blow with. His head reeled; stars danced before his eyes, bright and many-colored. Groggily, he tried to stand once again—and winced in advance, waiting for the death blow. . . .

But as he stood, and got both feet under him for the first time, no such blow fell. Instead, through already bleary eyes, he could see something in the shadows lash out and batter the big man before him to his knees. And into the pool of moonlight in the middle of the street danced a figure as slim, as evanescent as a moonbeam. The figure was that of a man, but as slight and long-thewed as any girl's. Its movements were quick and decisive, and as unpredictable as the dancing flames in a fireplace. The wraithlike figure wielded a short stick, no longer than the width of a large man's shoulders; with this it lashed out, poked, fenced, leaped forward to deal short deadly blows that drove the big man, twice his height and heft, backward down the moonlit street.

Zakir stumbled, thick-headed, blood in his eyes, after the pair of them. "A-Ahuni!" he said in a thick voice. "Don't take any chances . . . I'm coming. . . ."

But the ghostly figure continued to drive the monstrous bulk before it, punishing the big man right and left with painful jabs of the short stick, poking viciously at face and belly and groin indiscriminately, dealing out pain like an avenging spirit. The stick flashed to and fro. . . .

And suddenly the giant let out a bellow of rage and counterattacked. The big hand reached out, grasped the swinging stick. The other hand held it, raised it high to smash it over one heavy knee. And the big man's arm lashed out, catching the boy a glancing blow on the side of the head that dropped him onto his back. The attacked became attacker. The big man stooped over to reach for the neck of the supine figure. . . .

Zakir let out a low bellow of rage and charged. His stocky body moved with the speed of a sparrow snatching food from the mouth of a feeding lion. He took to the air; both of his broad feet, their soles protected by thick soles of hand-worked leather, caught the big man in the kidneys. The giant dropped as if his brains had been dashed out with a bronze-studded war club. His big body landed atop the boy, who cried out involuntarily with the sudden pain.

Zakir stepped forward and kicked the fallen giant in the head. He did not move. Only then did he reach one powerful hand down and, grasping his unconscious enemy by the hair, pull his heavy torso off the boy's bruised body. "Ahuni," Zakir said. "Are you all right, son? Because if this bastard has hurt you, I'll . . ."

"Zakir! I'm . . . I'm all right. I'm just . . . a little winded." The boy allowed himself to be helped to his feet. Father and son embraced.

"All right," Zakir said. "That's all, people." He turned as he spoke, addressing the circle of watchers in the shadows. "You've had your show. It's all over. Time to go home." He stood over the fallen giant. "Of course, if he has any thoughts about getting up again . . ." He bent over and watched the immobile face on the ground, with its expression of inexpressible pain. He stood and spoke with the same loud and commanding voice. "But no," he said. "You'd better go home. Unless there's anyone among you who wants to face the two of us."

Ahuni grinned at him, his young teeth white and gleaming in the moonlight. *"The two of us,"* he whispered.

III

The bodyguard was very nearly the biggest man either Ahuni or Zakir had ever seen. He was a full handspan taller than the man they had fought two nights before, and his massive torso, seen mainly from below, loomed above them like the trunk of some gnarled old tree. His weathered face was ageless: he could be anywhere from twenty-five to fifty.

Zakir juggled the clay disk in his left hand for a moment before handing it over. "Here," he said. "My name is Zakir. The honorable Nabousakin is expecting us."

The behemoth scowled down at the two of them: at their spotlessly clean but nonetheless ragged clothing, at the slave-mark still on Ahuni's arm, at Zakir's conspicuously missing hand. Most of all, his gaze took in, and registered disapproval of, the bruises and cuts on their faces, bodies, arms. The strong noonday sun picked it all out and put it on display, mercilessly.

"Wait here," the big man said in a deep and terrible voice, and turned with surprising agility on one heel to march away into the inner ring of tents.

Zakir turned to Ahuni and shrugged. "Well, we *don't* look like your usual sort of visitor, after all," he said. "It'll be days before the swelling goes down in that eye of yours."

"It's all right," Ahuni said. "You look worse than I do."

"I bet I feel worse," Zakir said ruefully. "Gods, Ahuni. I can't get over seeing you tackle that monster. Where did you learn to fight like that?"

"In the slaves' quarters of ... well, it was about three masters back. I was little and skinny, the smallest kid there. I lost a lot of fights. Everyone used to pick on me. Then one of my master's drovers took me aside and taught me some tricks. He'd been a soldier when he was younger, but a sword wound had crippled one of his legs."

"Well, he certainly knew what he was about. Me, I seldom had to fight in Babylon. I was strong and looked it, and people thought twice before bothering me. They knew that if I ever got these hands of mine around their necks ..." He sighed and held up hand and stump together. "But now? Well, no matter. I'm a lover, not a fighter." He grinned at Ahuni. "I ran into Etillitou in the street. She asked after you, asked when you'd be back. I think she looks on you as something special."

Ahuni bit his lip. "I ... she's a nice girl. I enjoyed myself. But Father ... ?"

"Yes?"

"I was a little disappointed. I mean, it was enjoyable, but . . ."

"Ah. You wanted more. Well, son, sometimes it gets to *be* more. Much more. That time will come. In the meantime, give thanks for the blessing the company of women can be even when you know it could be a lot more. And Ahuni, women appreciate it when you're the kind of fellow who wants more. Women like a man with a bit of soul about him. They like him a bit better even when the relationship doesn't totally come off. After all, Ahuni, the world is full of cold sons of bitches. Women have to put up with a lot of *their* kind. They don't value that kind of man any more than you or I do. And if they find you're the other kind, the kind that cares, well, they'll let you know it. They'll hang out the 'welcome' sign for you and turn another man away for you."

"Look, here he comes," Ahuni said. The big bodyguard was headed their way; behind him was Nabousakin, square-shouldered and vigorous-looking, for all his white hair and beard.

Zakir bowed; the boy followed suit. "Greetings," he said. "Zakir, sometime smith to his majesty, King—"

"There, there," Nabousakin said. "Save the formalities, my friends. Come! I've been waiting for you." He smiled benignly, waving the bodyguard away, and strode toward the large central tent. Zakir nodded to Ahuni to follow.

They seated themselves cross-legged on cushions; their host called for wine. But when the servant had come and gone, Nabousakin got down to business immediately. "Zakir," he said. "The boy has talent. How much does he know? I mean, about weaponry?"

"He knows all the techniques," Zakir said. "During his training he has not had the material with which to do fine original work. With the proper material, I think I could coach him through work not much inferior to what I did at my best. It's just a matter of practice. He has an armorer's fist, all right."

"He does," Nabousakin said, looking Ahuni directly in the eye for a moment before turning back to Zakir. "Perhaps more than he knows. I shall have more to say about that. But for now ... well, I've decided to take a hand in your affairs, if you'll allow me." He inclined his head in a minute gesture of deference to their will.

"Oh, sir. We'd be honored if—"

"All right. Perhaps I owe it to you. The gods are witness to the fact that I certainly made enough money selling your wares up and down the river in my time. Some of it I even sold here in Mari." He paused to let this sink in. "In a word, I have spoken to some highly placed friends of mine here. And if you will apply to any one of several names I will give you when we're done here today, you will find that you can secure several contracts for the provision of weaponry for the city guard. There have been several raids on outlying possessions of the city's, and the guard is being augmented."

"Sir, your generosity is—"

"Never mind about my generosity. Some of the people involved already own examples of your work. The captain of the guard himself owns a ceremonial sword of your devising. He is saddened to hear of your falling on hard times." He held up one hand. "Oh, I know how you lost your hand. I employ one man on the Babylon waterfront to do nothing but collect gossip. And ... well, Habasle and that androgynous son of his are a scandal in the city. I shouldn't be surprised to hear, one of these days, that Habasle's extremely poor stewardship had come to the notice of the king himself." He held up that restraining hand again. "All right, all right. To be honest, several of the other merchants and I have prepared a report upon his activities. He will learn that there is much peril in trifling with the financial leaders of the city. But no matter. I see you are thinking, 'I can go back to Babylon!' This would be the worst sort of folly. You have, in fact, broken the laws, and the laws remain and will still be there when Habasle has been put to death with that abominable offspring of his. Forget the idea of returning."

"But, sir . . . if we can't return . . . ?"

"No. Your destiny lies elsewhere. Perhaps in places you could not have imagined. As I say, I have arranged contract work for you here. My assistants in the city will be glad to advance you the credit for working materials and provide you with guarded work space within the city walls. They are in fact under orders to do so as of yesterday."

"We are in your debt, sir."

"Don't interrupt, Zakir. Old men like to hear themselves talk. The wise man humors them in this. I continue. There is a price for everything. There is, in fact, a price for my, ah, 'generosity' to you in setting up the basis for your future security. You are, of course, at liberty to refuse."

"We are in your hands, sir."

"Thank you. You indulge me. That's good. Now, I do this only partly for personal reasons. I am also a businessman, and an uncommonly shrewd one. You will be surprised to know that I have kept records on you back in the city. I know your business reputation, your record of reliability. I know that until the unfortunate incident with Soulai you had a good name in the bazaars as well as in the higher circles in which your work circulated. If you had a weak spot it was the fact that you had not married, settled, accepted responsibilities. Businessmen like a man with responsibilities. Children, wife, property. That sort of thing."

"Well, sir, I'm a different man now. I—"

"I know. You've a son now. This was part of the reason I decided to intervene. And a fine son he is. Ahuni, do you know who you are?"

"Why, sir, I'm a freed slave who has been adopted by—"

"No, no. Never mind. Zakir as much as told me you were born in slavery. I take it that's the story you were told. Well, I have reason to believe it isn't so at all. I think I knew your father once. And Ahuni, he was no slave."

"My—my *father?*" Ahuni said, leaning forward. "But who . . . how—"

"That birthmark of yours. I knew a man who bore it. Zakir, have you ever heard of an armorer named Belsunu? A man trained in Ur? I gather he was well thought of in your trade once."

"The name . . . no, sir. My old master, Mousezebil, who trained me, was from Ur. He might have known this Belsunu."

"B-belsunu?" Ahuni said. He wiped the corner of the one eye that still opened and shut on his bruised young face. "The name—"

"It may come back to you yet, my boy. Belsunu was, it appears, a master armorer. Unlike you, Zakir, he specialized in armaments; he did little ceremonial-sword work, or that sort of thing. He had no patience with the making of jewelry, and gold had little interest for him. He was a weapons man, pure and simple. Well, one day he left wife and family behind and came north to Mari, here, to do some contract work. I met him once, in passing. It was right in the middle of a period in which the tribes between the Two Rivers, men from west of Nuzi and Asshur, were growing bold and making raids on the outlying settlements." The old man paused to moisten his throat with a draught of wine.

"Family?" Ahuni said. "He had a family?"

"Why, yes. A wife, and a daughter just coming to womanhood . . . and a boy of perhaps three or four. Anyhow, he returned from his trip to Mari to find his village in flames, his wife and daughter dead . . . and no sign of his young son. Ahuni, that son would have been around your age now. And . . . mark you. He bore the paw print of the lion on his body, as his father and his father's father had done before him."

Nabousakin paused, watching Zakir comfort the boy. When Ahuni had regained his composure, the merchant continued. "Around this time Belsunu disappeared. Some said he went into Media, others into Elam. But let me show you something." He reached into a chest beside him and drew out two swords in plain scabbards. He pulled the blades free and handed one to each of them. "Ahuni," he said. "The sword you hold was made by your father, Belsunu."

"My father!" the boy breathed. He held the blade high.

"Gods!" Zakir said. "What a weapon *this* is! I've never seen the like of it! And whose is this, sir?"

"This one came to me by a circuitous route that began in Damascus. And I agree: it's a marvelous piece of work. But compare it with the one Ahuni holds."

"You're right, sir. Gods! They're identical. Except ... Ahuni's is much older. And this one from Damascus ..."

"Exactly. My point exactly. Made within ... what? A year? Two years? Of course, someone could have copied an earlier pattern, but ..."

"No, they couldn't, sir. In all due respect. You can steal a pattern, but you can't steal the *feel* of a sword. I could copy this ... and it'd feel different. It might fool someone in the bazaars. It might even fool a merchant like yourself, whose knowledge is more general than particular. But it couldn't fool another metalsmith. No, sir. These are from the same forge, made by the same hand. Ahuni! Your father ... he may still be alive."

"Now, now," Nabousakin said. "Don't go getting his hopes up. Belsunu was a sick man when he lost his family; he may be even sicker now. His lungs were bad. You could tell that, just meeting him casually as I did that one time. But—"

"But there's a chance! Zakir! If—"

"Now, now, boy," the old man said. "It's a very small chance as it is ... and at any rate news—letters and whatever—take a long time to get here from Damascus, when they get through at all. But from Padan-Aram, now ..." He paused, looking at both of them, a small smile playing on his lips.

"Padan-Aram, sir? You mean ... Haran? Up in the mountains?"

"Yes. Zakir ... I have need of a representative to

handle my interests in Haran. The last man who represented me there was dishonest—and cheated me out of a fortune. I'm thinking that Ahuni, say next year after you've put him through the rest of his accelerated apprenticeship here in Mari, could find plenty of custom up in Haran, arming the men of the city against Hittite and Hurrian raids. And in the meantime you can be doing well for yourself as a merchant allied to my own enterprises. A merchant doesn't need two hands, you know. Not even to keep records. He hires a scribe to do it for him."

"By the Gods! I . . . I don't know what to say."

"Then I'll tell you what to say. Or perhaps Ahuni will. Son, how would you like it if you could stand a chance of tracing your father down? And get at least moderately rich in the process?"

"Oh, sir! Zakir . . . please. . . ."

"See?" Nabousakin beamed at the ex-smith. "Give up, Zakir. You're outvoted, two to one. Say no more. I'll consider the bargain all but sealed. Now, let me tell you. You can make other commitments right here in Mari, over the winter. It will be to the advantage of the ruling caste here to have a . . . well, spy isn't the word; a covert representative in Haran, you know. I think you can count on a fat purse from them as well. And as my own trade representative . . ." He waved a hand at the servant beside him. "Call the scribe, please," he said quietly. The servant vanished through the flap.

"But . . . when . . . ?" Zakir said, looking at Ahuni's radiant face.

"You'll winter here. No use trying to leave for Haran in the fall. You'll freeze to death trying to find your way into the mountains. You can leave in the spring. By then Ahuni's 'fist,' as you call it, will be adequate to whatever work he finds in Haran. A metal-smith—an armorer, anyhow; make sure you train him well in that end of the trade—always finds work in that part of the world, where they haven't stopped battling since the Great Flood destroyed the world and Utna-pishtim landed his great boat on the top of Mount Misir. And look you, Haran is a thriving marketplace.

A man with his wits about him—a man in my employ
—will do well there." He smiled, looking hard at
father and son. "Do we have a contract, my friends?"

Zakir gulped, smiling broadly. He reached for Ahuni's arm and squeezed it. "Done!" he said enthusiastically.

CHAPTER NINE

I

Coming in from the fields to Sodom, Rekhmira found his path barred by a new line of pickets posted by the rulers of the city. They were an odd lot, he decided almost immediately. They bore little resemblance to the battle-hardened, flinty-eyed troops of the Sile garrison, many of whom he had got to know in his years with Psarou. They had a soft, overweight look about them, for the most part; *Conscripts,* he thought. *Not a real soldier in the lot.*

After a brief question-and-answer session they let him through; but even here Rekhmira could find fault with them. In their position he'd have made it a lot harder for a stranger, a slave otherwise unidentified, unrecognized, to find his way past the city's first line of defense. He shook his head and went through their lines toward the city.

It was odd, he thought, how little these people of the Cities of the Plain regarded the threat to their existence. If a slave like himself, a man without resources, could keep up with the progress of the advancing armies by listening and asking questions of travelers who passed through, surely the kings of the cities couldn't be unaware by now of the strength and ferocity of the forces that were bearing down upon them. Toward El-Paran the slaughter had reportedly been terrible indeed; the soldiers of the Four Kings had given no quarter and had killed man and woman, child and graybeard alike. He'd met one traveler who had seen the rape of Ashtaroth-karnaim, and his account of the carnage was a thing to stand the hair up on the back of your head. Rumor had it, too, that Enmishpat had fallen, and that Chedorlaomer's troops and their allies were striking northward. Any way you looked at the matter, it was obvious there was going to be big trouble. But try to get anyone to take it all seriously around here.

Coming down the low hill where Rekhmira had encountered the pickets, he looked out over the Salt Sea. To the north a dark cloud stained the sky, high above the shimmering haze that hugged the waterline night and day in the present season. It was a deep muddy brown, with black smudges here and there. Yet . . . it was strange. It didn't have the shape of a thundercloud, broad at the base and hugging the land on the western coast of the sea as it should have done.

He stopped. And thought about the matter—and about the rumors that had come down from passing caravans of the current actions of the armies of the Four Kings. Striking northward, were they? Northward? When the Cities of the Plain lay not to the north, but to the far northeast of Enmishpat? Why northward? Now was the time to hit the rebellious cities from below, from the plains of Arabah—or to strike across the folded hills of the Wilderness of Zin and take the defenders by surprise. It made no sense at all to go as they appeared to be going, as if to turn the armies' path east at Beersheba and cut across the mountains on the easily defended trade route that lay between Arad and Zoar. Besides, other rumors—rumors from a runner from Abram's own camp at Mamre's Grove, as a matter of fact—had placed the armies of the Four Kings north of Beersheba, and . . .

North of Beersheba? *North?*

His first thought was for Abram, whose party lay almost directly in the path of the advancing columns. But then he dismissed the thought; Abram could take care of himself, with that tough Egyptian mercenary Sneferu running the show. No, Abram wasn't the problem he had to think about now. No, it was something else. . . .

II

The same pillar of smoke stained the sky to the east of the little wadi where Sneferu, looking down from a height, was supervising sword drill. He tried not to look at it, but found his eyes wandering upward time after time. His annoyance at this lent an additional force to his increasingly sour comments on the progress this shift was making at the gentle arts of hacking and stabbing.

The squeak of a dry wheel grating in the axletree drew his attention. He turned his head to see Mamre, grizzled and broad-beamed, steering a supply cart down the wadi toward him, cursing at the two short-legged asses at the end of his reins.

Sneferu turned back to his work. "No! No, damn it! You with the long hair—get your back into it. What in the name of ten thousand devils do you think this is, a mating dance? Follow through with the stroke! Follow through! If you do you'll hack a hole in him, sure as I'm standing here—and you'll be in position for a backstroke you can take his head off with! Come now . . . all of you. If you're going to swing wooden swords like a bunch of women, how much worse are you going to look with these metal ones our friend Mamre is bringing us over here now?"

He grinned down at the fifty-man class, letting it sink in. Then, as the cheer went up and they started to break, he bellowed them back to attention again. "All right, look sharp there! Dress right, damn it! I haven't said you could have the things yet, have I? Have I?

Frankly, I don't think you've earned them, not a one of you. But . . . You! Quiet down there, I'm talking!"

He stood legs apart, hands on hips, looking down at them with mock contempt. "What I was going to say was that the threat of war forces a certain amount of haste on me. Look behind you there and you'll see what I'm talking about. That smoke is what's left of Hazazon-tamar, and the Four Kings have just burned the damned town right down to the ground, if I'm any judge. They'll do the same to the southern cities, too, most likely, and then, with the taste of blood in their mouths, my friends, they may get to thinking about those ragamuffins they let slip through their paws up at Mamre's Grove. And this time we won't be able to bluff the bastards like we did a day or two ago."

He grinned sourly down at their indignant faces. "Oh, come now. If they'd decided to fight us, they'd have wiped up the ground with us, in the state we were in. Most likely that's what they'll do with us a week or so from now, if you continue to act as if those things you hold in your hands are for paddling children. By the gods! I ought to wash my hands of the lot of you. To think I passed up a good job as captain of troops for Arioch of Ellasar!" He turned to watch Mamre pull the asses up sharply and dismount. His nod to the Canaanite chieftain masked a solemn horse-wink. "Well, there's nothing for it. I've got to arm you. I've no choice. All I can hope is that you won't stab yourselves in the leg returning the bloody things to their scabbards. *Sergeant!* Get up here on the double and organize a detail for passing out these things." He turned on one heel and let the subordinate take over. "Mamre," he said in an everyday voice. "How are you?"

"If I hadn't had a look at this batch of weapons your smith just turned out, I'd say I was in the worst of dispositions. I had friends in that town across the hills there." He nodded curtly at the column of smoke. "Well, when the confrontation finally comes about, perhaps I'll get even. I'm itching to break some heads." He pulled the sword Belsunu had made especially for him. It was plain, as Belsunu's swords went, but you could tell it had that exquisite balance from the joy in Mamre's face as he made two practice cuts in the air before holstering it again. "Abram and I both contributed leatherworkers for the belts. Nothing special about the work—it's almost an insult to the smith to hang his swords in journeyman work like this—but it'll do the job."

"Of course it will. I take it you're not displeased with our Mesopotamian friend."

"The smith? If you were to tell me he was Sir Adroit-and-Cunning himself, the Divine Smith of the legends, I wouldn't lift a brow. But swords alone won't win a battle. How is the training progressing? Are these idiots responding to that tender treatment you've been giving them?" His head inclined slightly toward the training class in the wadi.

"Well, I wouldn't invade Nubia with them, if that's what you mean. But if it comes down to a fight, and if I get to pick the ground we fight on, I suppose they'll break a few heads. Of course, you never can tell who's going to run and hide until the fight has begun."

"Ah, yes. They're not, uh, blooded, as you say in the trade."

"That is right. But . . . well, about the same percentage of men turn tail in any new unit. I've found some decent leaders among them: tough bastards who won't *let* anybody run on them. One of them is that big, skinny brother of yours. Eshcol."

"Oh, yes. Quite right. He's been that way since he was a boy. Used to fight me, that was half a head bigger and three years older. You'd have to knock him cold to get him to stop hitting you, even when I was ten and he was seven. He'll whip his men into line, all right." Mamre's eyes went to the plume of smoke in the eastern sky again. His brow furrowed with worry.

III

Paghat, wife to the commander of the Sodom garrison, was two-thirds of the way home from her shopping trip in the two bazaars when she stopped in the street and turned to the slave beside her. "Look," she said. "You take the parcels home and tell your master I'll be along soon. I'm going back. Perhaps there's something I can do."

"But my lady," the slave said. "My lord would not approve of your going back to the bazaar alone."

"Not to the bazaar, you goose. To the well. The girl there—the slave. I've been thinking about her ever since . . . well, I'm going back."

"Please, my lady. My lord will be angry with me for letting you—"

"No, he won't. Not if I tell him afterwards that it was my idea. Besides, now that I come to think of it, he won't be back yet. I ran into a friend at the bazaar. She told me all the officers are back on the lines. There's been some sort of trouble."

"Please, my lady. If—"

"Oh, don't worry. I'll be all right. Who would bother the wife of Yassib? Anyone who did would find himself in deep trouble. And everyone knows it. Everyone knows Yassib. No, run along. I'm going back. Somebody ought to do something."

"But—"

"Go along with you. Or *I'll* be angry with you." The last word said, she turned and moved back down the narrow street.

At the cobblers' bazaar she turned right and made her way to the well. The girl was still there, sitting dejectedly on the step, naked and dusty. Two urchins were taunting her; they scattered as Paghat approached. Paghat's sharp tongue was well-known in the bazaars, and her husband's arm was, as she had said, a long one. "You, girl," she said. "What's the matter? I noticed you on the way through."

The girl looked up. Her face was blank; but there was something in her eyes—a dead emptiness, a hopelessness—that begged for further questions. "My lady is kind to concern herself with me," she said in a flat voice. She sighed dejectedly. "But . . . I'm wanted at my master's. I should go. Thank you, my lady, for—" She rose to go.

"By the gods! Just look at you! Under the dirt you're all over bruises and bites and I don't know whatever. Look, you might just as well sit down and let me have a look. I have a reputation as a busybody and meddler to live up to, and I haven't done any meddling today. Heavens, girl. Who did this to you? Your master? Or someone in the city here? Because slave or no slave, there are laws. I should know; it's part of my husband's duties to enforce them."

"No, please." The girl tried to draw away, but Paghat held onto her thin wrist with a grip like a wrestler's. "If my master . . . you'll only make it worse. If he—"

"Who is this master of yours? Hah. He did do it, didn't he? Now don't try to deny it. Look, stand up, I want a better look at you. Huh. A fist did that, I'll wager. Well, let me tell you, young one. Nobody's going to get by with that kind of treatment around here, slave or no. Not while I'm alive. What did you say your master's name was? You're not Canaanite, are you? No, you're too dark for that. Don't they give you anything to wear? Are they too poor to afford a few rags to cover up the harm they've done you? Speak up."

Shepset looked at the old woman's determined face and then, a tremor of shame running through her, avoided her eyes. "I . . . his name is Lot. He's not from here. He and his wife just moved into the city. He—"

"Lot, huh? Are those his flocks on the slopes above? And he's decided to live in the city, has he? Curious how quickly some people acclimate themselves to the worst the city has to offer. I thought those flocks were owned by Bedouins."

"No, my lady."

"Look, child. I'm going to take you to my own house, and you'll wait there while I send a message to my husband. When he hears..." She stopped, stood straighter. Listening. "Here, what's all the commotion? I wonder what that is. The... the voices. Bellowing like that. Far away. If... you, boy!" she barked in her deep voice at one of the reappeared urchins. "Go find what all that noise is. There's a coin in it for you if you do." The boy disappeared around a corner on dirty bare feet. "Curious," she said. "It sounds like some sort of riot. Perhaps in the bazaar. But no, it's too far away for that... but now. Hear? That was closer. The first noise—that was outside the city. But this? This is..."

A man and his small son went past them in a loose jog. The father's face bore a frightened expression. "Here, you!" she said in an imperious tone. "What's happening?" But the pair kept on running.

Shepset, paying attention to her surroundings for the first time, stepped to the corner to look down an alley. "My lady... you'd better get home. Everyone's running... there seems to be some sort of panic."

She was almost bowled over by an old man in a red-trimmed robe who hurried past her, a determined expression on his face. Paghat stepped into his path, though, and barred his way. "Pabil!" she said. "You know me. Paghat, wife to Yassib. And I demand you tell me what's all this fuss? Why are you running?" She stepped aside as a clot of people pushed their way to the center of the little square and dispersed down the side streets. The noise was louder. It seemed to be getting closer.

"Excuse me," the old man said. "I... I've got to get home to my family. If the guard at the gate can't hold them..."

"Guard? Gate? What on earth are you talking about?" The old woman, angry now, grabbed him by the arms and fairly spat the words out. "Pabil! You tell me what's happening right now or ..."

The old man's eyes came back in focus. He looked at her. "You haven't heard? But surely you of all people would have been informed. Your husband—"

"What about my husband? I've been shopping all morning. Quickly, now. What's happened?"

The old man's voice shook as he spoke. "It was a ... a surprise attack. The way I heard it. They ... they struck just before the changing of the guard. The entire force to the north ... wiped out."

"Wiped out? From the north? What are you talking about?"

"Your husband, ma'am ... he was inspecting them when the enemy struck. He was killed. They ... his head on a pole ... oh, it was too awful! I watched from the city walls. They're here! The Four Kings! And they ... they're at the city gates! The whole garrison below the city ... you can see from the walls. They're being driven into the marshes, into the tar pits. It was a complete surprise."

Paghat, one hand to her mouth, let him go. For a moment she stood staring at a blank wall before her, seeing nothing. Then she stepped aside as running people poured past her, headed in a variety of directions. "Yassib," she said. "Yassib? Dead? But ..."

Shepset had turned to go, but now she saw the stricken look on the old lady's face. She stepped forward and took Paghat's white-robed arm. "My lady," she said. "You're in their path. If you'd just move over here, so they won't—"

"He—he meant it," Paghat said. "My husband? Dead? His head cut off, mounted on a pole? But just this morning—"

"My lady. Come. I'll get you to safety."

The commotion grew louder. It was a riot, a full-scale riot. Shepset, hurrying the old woman before her, stepped on something long and thin, and looked down. It was a spent arrow—from outside the walls.

The gate held for a while. Then, under cover of a deadly rain of arrows aimed at the defenders on the walls, a dozen of the attackers moved a battering-ram forward and began a steady battering of the stout doors of the city. *One* . . . a pause . . . *Two* . . .

The door came splintering open. It flattened one defender against the wall behind him, dashing his brains out against the mud-bricks. Soldiers, two abreast, leaped through the breach, the sunlight gleaming on their already bloody swords. Their faces, smeared with soot and gore, were terrible to behold. One young guardsman stood his ground and killed two of the attackers before a blow from a metal ax hewed him down in his tracks. The advance proceeded over his fallen body. Just as he felt the life going out of him, he looked up to see a soldier waving a long stick with something atop it. Something like a brown ball splashed with red, a ball that bore a black beard like a man's, and black beetling brows above eyes that were splashes of red. . . .

Horsemen followed the foot soldiers through the door. The resistance was almost nonexistent now. The cavalry, armed with swords and spears, herded the fleeing civilians before it with a jab here, a roundhouse swing there. One rider, drunk with the sight of blood, speared a runaway child with a wild, nervous laugh. The child died under the hooves of the horse that followed him through the streets.

"Please, my lady," Shepset said. "This way. You told me your house was this way. If we can get you inside, maybe they won't—"

"You go away," the old woman said. "Look, they'll let me alone. What am I but another old woman? They'll burn my house down, but they'll take no notice of me. But you? Run, child. You've no idea what they do to a young woman they find in the streets. Why, my husband told me . . ." Her face went blank again. "My . . . my husband. . . ."

Shepset suddenly felt the old lady slipping from her grasp. Paghat slid to the ground in a dead faint—or perhaps worse. Shepset hesitated for a moment; then she looked down the alley. There were—there were soldiers! Men with swords! She turned and ran—but not before they caught sight of her. *"Hey! Stop! You, girl! Say, did you see that one?"*

Naked, feather-light on tough bare soles, she ran like the wind, hardly knowing where she was running. Anywhere would do, so long as it was away from the men with the swords, the men with the grimed and bloody faces, their teeth gleaming in the filthy faces like wolves' fangs. *Hurry . . . hurry . . . this way . . . now up the alley where they can't follow . . . over the wall, now . . . hurry, hurry. . . .*

And then there were hoofbeats pounding the hard-packed street behind her, and, in a dead panic, she increased speed. Horses! Men on horses . . . behind her . . . gaining on her. . . .

"You! Stop there!"

She came to a corner, turned into the street—and found herself in a blind alley. She came up against a closed door and tugged at the handle. It was stuck shut, barred from the inside. "Please!" she screamed. "Help me! Open the door! Open!"

The hoofbeats drew closer . . . and suddenly the horseman appeared in the neck of the cul-de-sac, looming large and male and brutal-looking. The horse snorted and pawed the ground. Its rider grinned down at her, a death's-head's smile with no humor in it at all, only a fierce look of victory, of exaltation.

"Please!" Shepset screamed hysterically. "Someone help me!" She looked up at the shuttered windows. There were frightened faces behind those shutters, faces whose owners knew that if they once opened that door below, the fall of the city would at last come home to them too. "Please!" she shrilled. But her voice had a dying fall to it. The hope had gone out of it. She turned, small, naked, defenseless, to face the man on the horse as he dismounted. And suddenly the little dead-end street, with the saddled and bloodstained horse barring entry or exit at the other end of it, be-came a small pocket of horrified quiet in the middle of the commotion that attended the city's violent death.

IV

Late in the afternoon Sneferu came in from the hunt, grimy and covered with animal blood. He dismissed the men with him and made his way to the forge even before stopping to clean himself up. He strode, hot and tired, past the row of small forges the Mesopotamian's assistants had abandoned at noontime, when Abram's announcement of the feast had come down. His well-muscled body, with its scars and calluses, showed his fatigue in every way: the heavy shoulders drooped, the knotty arms hung straight down, and the usually powerful and purposeful walk was a lurching stumble.

He found the smith sitting on the ground, his back to a large rock. Sneferu grunted a coarse masculine greeting. Then he took another look—and came closer to kneel before his friend. "Belsunu?" he said. The great head lolled on the stringy shoulders; the cavernous eyes opened and fluttered. "Belsunu. Are you all right?"

The smith sat forward a little—and Sneferu noticed the effort it cost him. "Oh," he said. "I was just resting a bit ... I must have slipped off." He tried to get up, but fell back. "Here," he said in a hoarse voice. "Could you give me a hand there?"

"You sit right here," the Egyptian said. "I'll send someone after Hagar. You don't know where she is, do you? But no, of course you wouldn't."

"No, no. She's at the well. And ... oh, yes. She got a call from Abram's camp. She was going to stop there on the way over and bring some water for the forge. I sent one of the 'prentices with her, a big oaf who'll shoulder the jugs for her."

Sneferu looked his friend up and down. "Well ... I'll find someone else. Or perhaps I'll go look for her at the well. I'm a mess anyhow. Would you believe me if I said there was a lion on the upper slopes? He killed a sheep and was dragging it away when we found him. Big bastard, too. We lost two quivers of arrows in him, and in the end I still had to take a spear to him." He wiped his dirty brow with an even dirtier hand. "Gods, man. You don't look good at all. Have you had another attack?"

Belsunu's dark eyes looked up into his comrade's. "Look," he said in a weak voice. "This time I won't lie to you. I think this is the time, my friend. I sent Hagar away intentionally. She was going to wait and go to Abram's tent later . . . but I didn't want to have her see me vomiting my insides out with every damned cough." The words came out one at a time, without emotion. It was as if he had been discussing the impending death of a stranger.

"Huh," Sneferu said. "I won't insult you by disagreeing. I think you know how you are right now better than anyone. And . . . look, we've been good friends. I don't think I've ever had a better. One of the things I've liked about you from the first was the way I could talk straight with you."

"Egyptian," the smith said with a faint smile. "I love you too. And . . ." The weak hand that had once been so strong reached out and touched Sneferu's bloody arm. "Look," he said. "I could last an hour, or I could last a day. It's just as if all the strength had gone out of me, suddenly. It's happened two dozen times during the summer, but it's always come back. Now I have the feeling that it won't. Not any more." He swallowed. "I . . . my throat's dry. Is there any water?"

"Here," Sneferu said. He pulled a half-full waterbag from his grimy shoulder. "Hold your head back, now. Easy . . . easy. . . ." When the smith was done drinking, Sneferu stoppered the bag and gently wiped his friend's lips with one hand. "There," he said. "If you want more . . ."

"No, no." The voice was an old man's now, faint and without body. "Look," he said. He put his hand on Sneferu's forearm again; the Egyptian was shocked at its palsied weakness. "It's a time for favors," he said. "Among my people this season is the New Year. The same with Abram. You ask him for the girl tonight."

"I will," Sneferu said. "It's the right time."

"Yes. And . . . I'd like to ask . . . something for my-self."

"Done," the soldier said fervently, covering the weak hand with his own strong one. "Ask."

"Please . . . at the New Year, in the Land of the Two Rivers, it's bad luck to refuse a favor. Please. If you'd . . ."

"I'll make the offerings for you," Sneferu said. "I'll ask Abram about the customs up your way. I'll bury you in a cave on Mount Hebron."

"No, no. I don't care. In a week I'll be carrion . . . it doesn't matter. But, my friend . . . my true and very dear friend . . . if you should ever find trace of . . . of my son . . ."

Sneferu suddenly felt his eyes abrim with tears. "Of course," he rasped. "I'll raise him as my own. Of course. Set your mind at ease. And . . . as the occasion permits, I'll look for him, as you did. If he's alive, that birthmark will identify him. No, if there's any chance, I'll find him. And—"

"Tell him . . . about me, will you? Please? And tell him . . . I'm sorry. Tell him . . . I tried. . . ."

The smith pulled himself forward; pulled himself to his own knees, his weak fingers digging into Sneferu's flesh. The friends embraced, the strong and the sud-denly weak; and it was the strong one who wept, openly and without shame.

Some of Mamre's scouts, ranging well beyond He-bron, found him by the side of the path on the track across the Wilderness of Ziph to Arad and the Arabah. His ass had fallen and he himself had broken a leg. The animal could not be found. "Who are you, friend?" they asked good-naturedly; he posed no threat to them.

"Rekhmira," the man said through parched lips. "Slave to the lord Lot, nephew of the lord Abram. I..."

"Abram?" one of the scouts said. "Go on."

"I... have a message," the slave said in obvious pain. "Sodom... the Cities of the Plain... they've been destroyed. The armies of the Four Kings struck at dawn. The lord Lot and the lady Zillah, and their flocks and herds... they're spoils of the raid. They've been carried off. Look." He parted his matted hair to show an ugly wound just beginning to scab over. "Somebody knocked me out when the horsemen came through.... I awoke in time to watch the last of the slaughter. Someone had cut this ass loose... it was wandering on the slopes."

"Here," one of the scouts said. "You, Aqhat. Ride like the wind, to Mamre. We'll bring our friend here along with us later. And... oh, yes, they'll want to know. Which way were the armies going when you saw them last? I gather they didn't head across the hills the way you did."

"No, no... they doubled back. They'll have hit Gomorrah by now, or Zoar, or Admah. It won't matter. Nobody will have much of a chance against them. I tried to warn them... I saw the smoke at Hazazontamar."

"It's all right. You did well. You've warned us, for one thing. We'll take care of you, don't worry. You! Aqhat! What are you waiting for, man? Ride!"

V

On the mountain it was dark now. The last glow in the western sky had faded, and a chill had come over the air, particularly above the little stream where the water gushed forth cold and fresh from the living rock.

In the valley below, Abram's people celebrated over a huge feast. But Hagar and Sneferu were not among them. It was to have been the night that Sneferu asked to have the slave for his wife. He was on his way to Abram's tent to do this when Hagar intercepted him. She had begged for one night—this night—alone with the soldier. Alone on this blooming mountainside. How could he possibly refuse?

Sneferu had built a fire, a small soldier's fire whose bright flames danced merrily on their brown bodies, and they did not feel the chill. He looked with pleasure for the thousandth time at her dark hair framing the almond-eyed face with its broad cheekbones and full lips, and a long contented sigh ran through him.

"You're happy," she said. "I've never seen you happy before, I think." Her own smile was small and troubled; the somber look had never left those great eyes, not even in the heights of passion. She put one soft hand on his broad chest. "Oh," she said. "Another scar. You've been hurt so many times. Poor darling."

"That?" he said. "Oh, yes. That one almost cashed me in. Do you know how old I was when I got that? Fourteen. I can remember it as if it were yesterday. I was on patrol, and I came around a big rock outcropping to find this simply monstrous Nubian coming at me. I—"

"Oh. *Fourteen*. You were a baby. Only a baby. And you were in the army then?"

"I was in the army when I was eleven, my darling. Do you know how long I've been a soldier? Twenty-five years. No, it must be closer to twenty-eight. Twenty-nine. Something like that. I stopped counting at twenty-five. Ah. And now it's all gone. After this it's just a matter of going through the motions . . . and hoping your change of heart doesn't make you soft and kill you."

"But . . . you spoke of the war in Siddim."

"Yes. And unless I miss my guess, *that* one begins at dawn tomorrow morning. The messengers ought to be reaching Abram right about now—if they got through."

"Messengers? I don't understand."

"The clouds on the horizon lifted for a while when I was hunting, up above here but on the eastern slopes. You could see another pillar of smoke, just like the other day. They've taken Sodom and Zoar, I'd guess."

"Sodom," she said softly. "Shepset—"

"I forgot," he said gently. "You've got friends over there, haven't you? Well, we'll do what we can for them. I hope we're not too late. But I'd wager a month's pay that the message is already in Abram's camp. Hagar," he said. "That's the hell of it. I don't want to leave you. Now or ever." His big hand ran up and down her arm, as if he were a blind man trying to memorize every curve.

"I don't want you to leave," she said simply. "I'm afraid. Without you, I don't know what will happen." She shook her head and suddenly covered her face with her hands. Then, as suddenly, she removed them. And now her face was more composed, and resolve was in her eyes. "No," she said. "I won't do that to you. No, no. Don't think of me tomorrow. Not until the end of the day, when you've won your battle. Please. Don't worry about me. Please." The face she turned to him was full of concern.

"Ah, Hagar," he said, his voice deep and reassuring. "Would you try to change me back to what I was before I met you? You couldn't do it, you know. My life has changed. Forever. You've made me over. I'm what you've made me. And I'm not a soldier any more. Not a regular, anyhow. Don't worry. I can do my job, and damned well. And nobody is going to kill me or hurt me, and I'm coming back to you in one piece. But . . ." There was a curious hesitation in his voice as he continued. "My heart isn't in it any more. It was a profession once. It's a job now. No more. A job. And it's a job that will build a home for us. That's all it'll be good for."

Suddenly her eyes were large and soft and warm and there were big tears in the corners of them, visible in the dancing light of the flames. "Sneferu," she said in a voice with a tiny tremor in it. "Hold me. Hold me tight. Yes. Now. *Now.*"

She awoke at dawn to find his place beside her empty. In a sudden panic she sat up and called out for him. But as she did she could see over the lip of the pool below, where the water gushed out of the hillside into a shallow pond.

Sneferu, brown and brawny and naked, stood ankle-deep in the shallows, splashing himself with water from the spring. He stretched; his mighty chest expanded; the muscles in his arms and shoulders rippled. He looked like a god come down to earth, powerful and elemental and male; but a god covered with old cuts and scar tissue and the marks of whip and saber and spearhead. It was the body of an old lion in the last days of his prime, proud and competent and confident. A small thrill ran through her, watching, remembering the night before—and remembering the tremendous fund of gentleness and sweetness that lay hidden in that proud, dominant, hard warrior's body.

Now he looked up and saw her, and his smile was broad and loving and accepting. "Hagar!" he said. "I didn't have the heart to wake you. Good morning! I love you." He reached for the clean loincloth he'd brought along the night before and wound it around his loins. Then he reached for the sword belt at his feet.

"Wait," she said. "I'm coming down." She didn't bother to dress; she scrambled down the bank and walked to him in the shallows. She wanted to show herself to him naked again, before he left; most of all she wanted to feel his hard body against hers, feel it with every part of her. She rushed into his arms. "Sneferu . . . do you have to go?"

"I'm afraid so," he said. "There's a lot of commotion down the hill in the camp. I called to one of the scouts. He said a survivor of the attack had got through with the news. I have to get down and take over, on the double. Ah, but . . ." He hugged her happily again. "It *is* hard leaving you, it is. Hagar, I haven't felt like this since . . . no, I can't remember ever feeling like this. Not ever. I'll be thinking of you every spare moment I have until I return. And I'll come back to you, Never fear." He released her and looked her up and down, holding her at arm's length. "Ah, look at you. Was anything, anyone, ever so beautiful? I'll carry that image in my mind's eye with every step I take. And . . . don't worry about me. The thought of you makes me stronger, not weaker."

"I know. I know."

"Look," he said, letting her go and finishing the buckling of the sword belt around him. "I have to go ahead with a contingent of troops. Eshcol and me. I'll go south and hit them from there and try to drive them up the valley. Abram and Mamre and Aner will go across the hills to Hazazon-tamar and trap them coming north. If we can bottle them up in that slushy ground around there, we've got them." He grinned at her, a suddenly boyish grin. "Don't worry. I feel good. I feel happy. Happier than I've ever been in my whole life. You're good for me."

She sought his arms again: the solace of their hard and protective strength, the warmth of his body. "Oh, please," she said. "Come back for me. Please."

Sneferu's troops marched away singing to the beat of the drums. It took a long time for the sound to fade. The last thing that Hagar heard was the dying fall of a fierce Canaanite song, wailing in the dusty distance above the slow throb of the drummers' sticks. And then there was nothing but the normal sounds of the camp stirring to life. She walked past the picket on the hill, hardly nodding to him, and made her way toward the smith's forge.

She felt numb, lifeless. All of a sudden a deep depression had fallen upon her again, the same depression that had come over her the previous afternoon, when she'd first heard the news. It should have been the happiest day of her life, as it had been the happiest day of his. But . . .

In the bright sunshine, in the clean mountain air, she could hear the many sounds of the camp. Below her, on the flat, Mamre's grandchildren were playing a noisy children's game, dancing in a circle and shouting a singsong refrain in their shrill little voices.

Children, she thought.

Suddenly, her destiny had changed in a day—and changed forever.

It had changed the moment Abram called her to him and explained his decision. His own destiny demanded a child, he'd said, and his wife was barren. Therefore he'd decided to take a concubine, a younger woman who would bear his child and allow him to raise it as his heir. She, Hagar, had been chosen for this honor. It would mean a changed position in Abram's household: prestige, perquisites, status—almost the status of a free woman. And her child, if it was a son, would be raised in a position of honor and would inherit Abram's goods and place in Canaan—a place that would come in time to be a nation of kings. She would be the mother of a line of kings, and he, Abram, would be the father.

VI

Mamre's woman came to Belsunu at midday with food and a shallow dish of tepid water. He sat up and sipped delicately at the water, but waved the food away. He had decided to take no more food until he died. Water he would drink, as much of it as they cared to give him; he had no wish to know the cramps and pangs of dehydration. But starvation was a benign narcotic, as able to ease pain as any sacred mushroom, as any product of the art of vintner or brewer. You simply grew weaker, and so did your perceptions of all things physical, be they pleasure or pain. If you lasted long enough, your mind began to hallucinate, and often there was much pleasure in this. The only way pain could enter this last state was if you started to care again.

He had seen this before. Dying himself, he had seen a fallen friend through the last hours of starvation during a long siege up in Hittite country. His friend had cried out—however weakly—toward the end, trying to tell him, Belsunu, of a sudden bright and vivid vision which had come upon him in his last moments. He had seen and spoken with his own long-lost twin, dead these twenty summers. The expression in his friend's eyes, in that moment, had been one of exaltation. Belsunu wondered if . . . but no. He had been close to death before, and he had had no visions. It was at best a hope forlorn, one which a wise man did not waste his time and spirit entertaining.

Yet . . .

Bah, he thought. *Superstition.* He picked up the bowl and drank again, cautiously. And one of Gilgamesh's songs came back to haunt him, running again and again through his mind. A song with a pleasant lilt, one he hadn't heard in a dozen years or more:

> After all this roving over the empty steppes,
> Must I now lay my head in the heart of the earth
> And sleep there, silent, through all the years?
> No, let my eyes look now upon the sun
> And let me have my fill at last of light!

He put down the bowl and sat up straight. And, gathering the last of his fading strength, he managed at length to stand, weaving to and fro, and, a small triumphant smile on his parched lips, felt his way to the doorway.

The light should have been blinding; he shielded his eyes against it. But as he stepped forth into the autumn afternoon, the air was cool and clear and the light in the sky was muted. A cloud had drifted over the sun; others lay behind it, moving slowly across the heavens. *Fall,* he thought. *Another fall.*

He steadied himself with one hand on a guy rope and blinked out at the pale pastel colors of the grove. Who would have imagined he would end his days here, he who had grown up on the banks of the Great River, where water alternately fed the land richly and, in floodtide fury, washed it away? Well, that was destiny. Now he would sit in the shade of this spreading terebinth and watch the day fade as his life faded, and quite possibly, as night drew on . . .

He eased himself down, his back against the tree. Mamre's tents were on a rise, and he could look down into the little vale below. His eyes closed, opened anew. . . .

. . . and then he woke again, and Abram was sitting beside him, cross-legged on the ground, his sharp eyes searching his face for signs of life. "Abram," he said. "How good of you to come." And indeed a great warmth grew inside him to see the old man next to him now. He smiled wanly and saw his countryman return the silent greeting. Abram took his hand in his own two horny old palms.

"Ah, Belsunu," the old man said. "My heart is full. I . . . the god visited me last night and spoke to me once again in my dream." Belsunu suddenly noticed that both of them had gone back to the language of their youth. "He promised me a son. A son of my own! If I . . ." But he stopped, his face suddenly somber. "I'm sorry," he said. "I was going to say something stupid. Something about 'Do you know what it feels like to be promised a son after . . . ?' But of course you know. Better than I. And here I am burdening you with . . ."

"No, no," Belsunu said, his heart suddenly going out to the old man. "Look, it's all right. I . . . I lost my son so many years ago. . . . It was just a dream, finding him again. I suppose I should have found another woman, made new children. But . . ."

He looked in Abram's eyes and felt the bond of sympathy flow both ways, in abundance. He had been about to tell Abram about Hagar and Sneferu, to intercede with the old man for the two of them. But now he looked into Abram's honest, trusting old face, with its message of hope long deferred and quickened now in his old age; and he could not do anything, try as he might, to spoil the old man's simple, childlike joy.

But Abram was talking now, wasn't he? ". . . always the chance that the boy is alive. Rest assured, if I ever find anyone the right age who bears a birthmark like that, my heart will go out to him, mine and my heirs'. If you drop the torch, I and mine will pick it from your hand and carry it as far as we can carry anything. We will not forget."

"That's kind of you," Belsunu said. He blinked; his vision seemed to be growing . . . well, strange. For a moment there black was white and white was black. "I . . . I was thinking about my family a while back, Abram. Not my boy so much. I can hardly remember what he looked like. I can remember the girl only slightly better. But my wife . . ." He paused, gasping for breath.

Abram squeezed his inert hand softly. "Tell me about her," he said.

"Oh. Well, you know how women are. She often thought me a fool, and she never hid her feelings from me on the subject. She used to call me . . ." He stopped and a faraway smile played briefly over his face. "But never mind. Her harshest word would fall upon me like a caress now, or at any time during the last ten years. Or—how long *has* it been? Five? Eight? It doesn't matter now, I suppose. Anyhow, I think of her in certain attitudes. I remember a certain curve to her body, as she stood trying to hang wet clothing on a line against the wind: a long graceful curve of calf and haunch and behind . . . she had short legs. I never wished them longer. Women never understand. We fall in love with their defects, not their perfection. Her nose was a little crooked. It gave a certain quality to her smile, as she sat giving the baby the breast sometimes, crooning a tuneless little tune. She never could carry a tune. I wish I could share with you the beauty, the . . ." He sighed. His eyes were far away. "I do not think a day has passed that I have not thought of . . ." He sighed again and looked at Abram, his eyes in focus again. "I talk too much."

"Tell me," Abram said. "Tell me more."

"There's not much more to tell." He coughed once, twice; Abram winced at the violence of the convulsion that shook the fevered body. "Abram. I've never been able to swallow all that talk they used to throw at us about the gods. It's all fairy tales. The kind of stuff they used to scare children into obeying. All my years on the road, the years after I came home and found ..." A cloud passed over his wan face and he frowned it away fiercely. "Abram. This god of yours. . . ."

"Ah. Would you believe, my friend, I know little of Him myself? All I know is that He spoke to me, and ... and somehow I knew that in that moment my whole life was weighed in the balance. If I did not respond, my whole being would sicken and die. There was a choice I had to make, and I had to make it right then, once and for all."

"There ... there used to be a fairy tale about Adapa, the son of Ea. When they brought him the bread of life and the water of life, he did not eat or drink. And the chance at eternal life passed him by forever."

"Yes. Yes, it was like that. And ... and from that moment I have followed the word of the God blindly, and every time I have turned my face toward Him in complete trust all my affairs have prospered. All but one. And when I have waited and waited, and my faith has flagged, well, as I wavered, He would appear to me and speak to me again, and I would draw strength once again from this."

"I envy you. No one speaks to me in the dark hours. I lie awake night after night, thinking, and my thoughts go always to . . ."

Abram looked at him, and his two hands closed comfortingly over Belsunu's long fingers. "I wish I could know what to tell you," he said. "This is no time for dissembling between you and me, my friend. I think we do not have long together. All I can say is that if this God—He seems to have several names, and the only one I've learned so far is El-Shaddai; I get the impression I will learn more in time—if this God that speaks to me somehow speaks to you as well in the time that remains to you, well, you know what to do. I—"

"Abram. How do you perceive Him, this God of yours?"

"Sometimes He is a man—but I never can seem to remember anything about Him afterward. Most often

He is a light too bright to look at." He sighed and smiled at the smith. "Everyone thinks me a fool. But I pass them by. If I falter for so much as a moment, bearing the burden I bear, how many generations of my seed will curse me—curse me until the world is old and the sky goes dark and all the wells run dry? Because that's the way I see it. I've been given a responsibility. And while I bear it I am blessed. And if I lay it down . . ."

When he looked back at the smith, though, he saw that the light in his friend's eye was failing. He squeezed the big hand softly and felt an answering squeeze, as feeble as a newborn child's. "Belsunu," he said. "I think there's not much time. All I can say is that I will make the sacrifices for you. I will make the sacrifices to El-Shaddai. Many of us here have come to love you. There is much good in you, and you have suffered enough. I pray night and day to Him, and I understand little. I hope to understand more. I will go to Melchizedek of Salem when I can. I am told he is a priest, and adept, of El-Shaddai. Perhaps he can help me understand. In the meantime, all that I know to do is turn my face toward Him when He appears to me and do whatever He says to do."

Having said this, he sat back and watched the smith's wan face. Belsunu's breathing halted for a moment; Abram leaned forward. He waited patiently for any words the smith cared to say.

Belsunu looked once at him, and his weak hand stirred in the patriarch's. Then his eyes went out over the broad land, to the rain clouds on the horizon. A bright butterfly flitted past his face, darting merrily, and landed on the lowest limb of the terebinth. "I'm . . . not afraid," he said. And then with a sudden sinking rush the earth fell far, far away beneath him and his head spun wildly and when he closed his eyes there was only Light.

CHAPTER TEN

I

Zakir, for the tenth time, reached into the pouch at his side and withdrew the hardened clay tablet he had received from Nabousakin that morning. Blinking against the semidarkness in the tavern, he read it as much with his memory as with his eyes. By now he knew every word of it by heart. And now, as he traced the cuneiform indentations with his left-hand fingers, he took his eyes off the tablet and looked up at the noontime crowd around him.

As he did, the door burst open and the din of the street, screened away by the thick earth walls, came in once again. He blinked even more rapidly at the sudden light, and, framed in this, saw a soldier of Mari in battle dress, fists on hips, legs spread, looking about. The face, he could see now, bore an uncharacteristic fierce beard and the strong hooked nose of a Hittite.

Zakir half rose, a smile on his round face. "Aziras!" he said. "Over here!" He waved his good arm enthusiastically, and, grinning hospitably, sat back down. As he did he carefully returned the clay tablet to its stiff-sided pouch.

Aziras of Kanish, his expression half scowl and half harsh, masculine grin, waved to Zakir; but he stopped and intercepted a servant on the way to another table, taking the slave's tray with its jug of wine and two bowls and handing the surprised menial a coin without even looking to see what denomination it was. Enroute to Zakir's table he turned the jug high with one powerful hand and drank from it. As he approached, he put the jug back down on the tray and wiped his mouth with the back of one forearm.

"Zakir," he said, sitting. "Greetings." He put down the tray and poured himself a bowl of wine, drinking it right off in a single thirsty draught. "Here," he said as he put the bowl down. "Have some. Don't mind me. I'm fresh from the field and I'm all dust and dirt inside. It will take getting drunk as a pig to slake this thirst of mine."

Zakir smiled and poured wine into his own bowl; but he sipped from it slowly, his eyes on his Hittite friend. The mercenary was, as he'd said, dusty and sweaty from the road. He'd obviously come to the tavern even before washing up. "I'll bet you've just dismissed the troops," he said.

"Right." The Hittite poured himself another bowl and took a healthy drink from it before putting it down. "As I say, don't mind me. I've a thirst. I'm going to drink a bit of this good stuff here, and then I'm going down to the troops' camp and we're all going to get so drunk we can't stand. Only then we'll be drinking the kind of bellywash the army provides for people below the officer level. Ugh. But I couldn't disappoint them by not drinking with them. They've earned any tribute I can give them."

"Ah," Zakir said. "The relief of the garrison went well, then?"

"Damned right," Aziras said. "My boys fought like old soldiers. You'd never know they were wet behind the ears at all." He nodded thoughtfully. "Well, now they're not. No, sir. If they're not blooded now, they're never going to be. Let me tell you, my friend, we killed some Assyrians yesterday. That'll teach the greasy bastards to raid a post of Mari's." His eyes shone for a moment with a fearful light. "Drink up," he said. "It's on me."

"I was going to ask," Zakir said, his smile thoughtful. "Is this Aziras of Kanish at the table with me? The cheapest, most miserly, coin-hoarding—"

"All right, all right," Aziras said. "Drink up, damn

it. You've earned anything I can afford to buy for you, you one-armed ape—you and that son of yours."

"My son? What has Ahuni to do with . . . ?" Zakir stopped. "Ah," he said. "Ah. The weapons."

"Damned right. That boy's got the magic touch, my friend. You've taught him well." Aziras, pausing with the bowl at his lips, said in a less boisterous voice: "No. It's more than that, isn't it? I have an instinct for these things. You were no armorer, were you? I asked around. You were a goldsmith, a maker of rich folks' play-pretties. You . . ."

Zakir's blood burned hot for a moment; then he responded with a sigh to the rough sincerity in Aziras's eyes. "You're right," he said. "I taught him what I could. But he's already passed me—in this end of the business, anyhow." He thought of the superb sword Nabousakin had shown him—the one purportedly made by Belsunu. "There's something downright mystical about it. The damned ore loves him. Metal loves him. He's like a farmer with a green thumb, or the kind of fisherman—" Here the skinny, naked figure of Binshoumedir danced laughingly before his eyes. "—who always instinctively knows where the fish are. I couldn't teach him that."

"Ah," Aziras said, sitting back against the wall. "You two don't look much alike. Are you really—"

"Father and son? No. I adopted him recently. He's not sure who his father was . . . but we think he was a man named Belsunu, who—"

"Ahhhh." The soldier's sigh was one of deep satisfaction. "Then my sergeant, Pushuken, was right. I showed him this sword Ahuni made for me." He drew it and held it up for inspection. There were still spots of blood on it; Zakir winced. "He said he'd seen another like it, once when he was young." Putting the sword down and reaching for his wine bowl, he said, "This Belsunu was a famous man among the armies of the area. And . . . yes, I'm willing to believe the boy is of his blood." He drank deeply and touched the sword again. "Look, Zakir. You wouldn't mind if I took Ahuni down to the encampment and introduced him to the troops, would you? I mean, they'd all enjoy meeting him after today. I tell you, we slaughtered those Assyrian sons of—"

"Ahuni? You're not going to get him drunk, are you?"

"Not very. Unless he decides to on his own hook. What I want to do is let him hear about his old man. Some of the troops remember Belsunu—the older ones. Anyhow, all of them have heard about him. They'll be tickled to learn their present arms are being made by the son of Belsunu. And Ahuni—"

"Ah. Yes, yes. It'd be good for him to know whose blood runs in his veins." Zakir's voice, by now very fuzzy around the edges, did not carry much conviction. And a spasm of jealousy tightened his features. A few minutes later, making his excuses to Aziras, Zakir rose heavily to his feet and left the tavern.

II

The shadows were lengthening in the little glen; the impromptu feast had died down for a while, then begun to gather intensity again as the drinkers and celebrants got their second wind. The air was full of dancing motes of dust that sparkled in the dappled sunlight, and the whole roasted ox turning on its spit at the mouth of the little depression had begun to cast its delicious, savory smell across the cool fall air.

Ahuni, nursing his half-empty bowl of bad wine, sat atop a fallen tree trunk and watched happily as Zakir and a burly sergeant of pikemen, bellies flat against the rocky ground and facing each other, arm-wrestled, grunting and sweating. The bulging cap of muscles atop Zakir's powerful left shoulder knotted; his thick neck grew even thicker as he hunkered down and applied the pressure. Around the two a circle of bettors had gathered, each side profanely egging its man on to victory.

A heavy hand fell on Ahuni's shoulder, and he looked up to see Aziras grinning down at him. "Here," the soldier said. "I'll join you." He sat down heavily a handspan from Ahuni, spilling some of the wine in his own bowl as he did. "Ohhh," he said wearily. "I'm not the boy I once was. Time was, I could fight a battle, drink a hogshead of wine, dance all night, and futter ten women before morning. Now? Now I disgrace myself by growing tired before the party's half over."

Ahuni looked him up and down. "But sir," he said. "You're hurt. There's that cut on your leg, and . . ."

"Nonsense." The soldier tipped up the bowl and drank. "I'm full of aches and pains, but that sort of thing wouldn't have slowed me down a couple of years ago. No, boy, I'm over the hill." His eyes, glassy no more, lit thoughtfully on Ahuni's stringy young body. "Ah, to be your age again, son. With all of it ahead of me." He stopped and made a bad face. "But no. At your age I was miserable. Just miserable. And if I had those next twenty years of my *own* life to live over . . . Ugh!" He drank again, as if cleaning his mouth out, and spat the last of his wine onto the ground. "Well, let's hope your next few years will be better than mine. Most likely they will. If you continue as you've been going, you have a fine career ahead of you. With a father like that . . ." He stopped, belched.

"Yes, sir," Ahuni said. "Zakir has taught me well. Here, sir. Take the rest of my wine."

"Thank you, boy. Good of you. No, I don't mean Zakir. I mean Belsunu. Now there was an armorer. He—"

"Belsunu?" Ahuni sat up suddenly, his eyes aglow. "You know about Belsunu?"

"Why, of course, boy. He was a famous man up this way. Yes," he said, looking Ahuni over again. "You could be his son. You've his shoulders. When you come into your weight and size, you'll be built like him. He had a huge chest and large hands. You'd never think anything was wrong with him. But poor devil, he had the lung disease, and after a day's exertion you'd hear him coughing . . ." The soldier stopped again. "Say," he said. "If you're a son of Belsunu's—if you're really a Child of the Lion—you'll bear a red birthmark. He got his from his father."

Ahuni stood and lifted his tunic, baring the scarlet mark above his hard young haunch. "Like this?"

"Ah! To the life!" Aziras grinned. "I wasn't sure whether to believe the story. But now? You're the right stuff all right, boy." The drunken air fell away from him. He drained the refilled bowl and stood up.

"Attention!" he bellowed. "Attention, you hogs, you rutting hinds! Shut up and listen!" The commotion thinned out a little; faces turned his way. "Quiet! Quiet, all of you!"

He stepped atop the log and addressed them, his voice booming out over the little hollow. "That's better," he said. "You've won a fine victory today. I want to congratulate you." He waved away the cheers, halted them with an impatient gesture of one dusty and still blood-smeared arm. "No, no! Before you get to congratulating yourselves and thinking you're ready to take on the Egyptian army—I want you to meet somebody." He waved Ahuni to his feet. "Up, boy! Come on, now."

"No, please," Ahuni said. "I don't want—"

"Who gives a damn what you want?" Aziras said. "Look at him, now, you dogs! You've been thinking the Assyrians were so easy to kill because your arms had grown suddenly strong? Nonsense! The Assyrians are just as tough as they ever were! The reason you won stands before you. Yes, this boy here! He's the man who armed you, for all the fact that most of you are twice his age. And those arms—the swords, the pikeheads—you used to slaughter the Assyrians with were made by him!" He held Ahuni's hand high. "Meet your new armorer—Ahuni of Babylon!"

The cheers were loud and lusty. Ahuni, embarrassed, looked nervously from face to face, expecting resentment, contempt—but seeing nothing but admiration and acceptance everywhere.

"That isn't all!" Aziras bellowed. "Good armorers don't fall out of the sky like hailstones. You can't pick them off a tree like berries. They're not only made but born. Do you remember my telling you of a man named Belsunu, whom I served with years ago!" He paused, seeing the comprehension, the awakening memory, dawn on face after face. "Well, Ahuni is the official son of our friend Zakir here—but he's the blood son of Belsunu! He bears the print of the lion's paw, just as his father did. And after today, anyone who says Ahuni doesn't have his father's fist at the forge will have to settle with me!" He held Ahuni's hand again. "Come on, now—let's hear a cheer, a big one, for Ahuni of Babylon . . . son of Belsunu!"

Ahuni let his arm fall, listening to the roar of the crowd in the glen. There was a marvelous thrill about the moment. He felt like a man newborn into the world. He took the brimming bowl someone thrust into his hands and drank from it. Then he held the bowl high, toasting the men, toasting the strong arms who had wielded his blades and, for the first time, made a full-fledged armorer of him. Up to now he'd been a metalworker. But when a man had made weapons that struck and smote and killed and maimed, he was once and for all an armorer—a soldier's, a conqueror's, right arm. There was a heady power in the feeling. And he rejoiced inside at the thought that they were cheering him, and his father through him. *Ahuni of Babylon . . . son of Belsunu!* It was the most exciting thing that had ever happened to him, and his first thought was to share his elation with Zakir. He looked brightly to left and right, an eager look of anticipation on his young face; but the ex-smith was nowhere to be found.

Once inside the city wall—it took a bribe to a friendly, but money-minded, guard to get him in after hours—the sounds of the revelry in the soldiers' camp faded to insignificance and soon were lost in the many sounds of evening in Mari. Zakir, head high, his walk a trifle stiff, made his way to the pleasure quarter of the city, trying not to think of anything. This was not easy; he searched his already tipsy mind for drinking songs, bawdy songs—anything that would by its monotonous melody and repetitious rhythms so monopolize his thoughts that none of his present feelings could invade

them and make him once again a victim of the despair
that lurked always at the edge of his thoughts.

He made his way on unsteady legs to the house of
Yalampa the courtesan and, his voice hoarse and
slurred, shouted her down from her second-floor apart-
ment to help him up the stairs. She was by turns
annoyed; waspish; mollified (he took pains to drop a
purse heavy with coin on the floor before him as she
brought him wine; it made a satisfactorily substantial
sound); forgiving; friendly; amorous . . .

. . . and in the end matter-of-fact; a little distant;
perfunctorily reassuring; and, through it all, more than
a little annoyed all over again. No woman liked to do
her best to arouse a man, only to have him go limp as
an oyster on her. Least of all did a professional courtesan appreciate this—a woman who prided herself on
her amatory skills and charms. Zakir picked up his
wine bowl, looked at it, and put it back down again
without drinking. "I . . . I'm sorry," he said. "The spirit is willing but the flesh is weak."

Yalampa, still lusciously nude, voluptuous as a girl,
for all her thirty summers, made a wry face. "Come
now," she said. "The spirit was fifty days' march away
and the flesh wasn't there at all. Zakir, what's bothering you anyhow? You've been off your feed for a
month. Or is this your usual manner, and was it the
way you were earlier that was the unusual circumstance
in your life? I'd like to know. Just my normal feminine
curiosity."

"Damn it," Zakir said. He drained the bowl,
reached for the jug, and poured his bowl full again.
His voice was still slurred, but his mind was clear. All
too clear. "It's not you. May all the gods bear witness
to that. You're . . . you're a vision of loveliness. You're
Ishtar incarnate. A man couldn't ask for a more desirable bedmate. But—"

"Then what is it that makes a capon of you? Have
you . . . ah . . . changed your game? Look, I can do
anything a boy can do, and better. If you . . ."

"No, no. I know you can. . . . I know you're the
best, my dear. The best ever. And I'm no boy-lover.
Look, Yalampa. Don't you ever find yourself . . . well,

distracted? Something preying on your mind? Something that may have nothing at all to do with—"

"Hmmm," she said. She sat back on her trim little heels, her long, lovely body all on view for him—and all the pleasure he could take from the sight remained purely aesthetic, intellectual. It was as though she were a model sitting for a maker of images. "Yes, yes. I can understand that. There are times when . . . well, when men come to me, and with the best will in the world I'm not in the mood. Something's bothering me, whatever. Usually my astrologer tells me the stars aren't right for me. And of course business has to go on, whatever I happen to feel like."

"That's it exactly. Here," he said, pressing the purse into her hand. "I don't know what's in there. Whatever it is, the purse is heavy enough to buy a night of your time, my dear. So what if I may need to talk a little more than I need to . . . well, you know. By the Gods! There are times when a man needs a friend, a nice, reassuring friend, more than anything."

"All right," she said, weighing the purse in one slim hand. "Here, I'll put something on."

"No, no. If you don't mind . . . even when I'm not aroused I'm still . . . well, some of me is still the artist I used to be, back before I lost my . . . uh, back before I fell on bad days. I like to look at you. Even so. Just like that, in the light. Your skin is the color of burnished copper, with the flames dancing on it like that."

"Well, your tongue seems to be working all right," she said, smiling. "Tell me more. You seem to be quite aware of what it is that's eating you. Out with it, Zakir."

"Ah," he said, sitting back, smiling, his mutilated arm resting on his naked belly. "That's my girl. Now . . . Yalampa, it's this son of mine. The one I adopted a while back. He's . . . he's found out who his father is."

"Ah. And who is he?"

"That doesn't matter. Or maybe it does. The father . . . he may be dead. But the father . . . he seems to have been an armorer. A metalsmith like me, but a specialist in weapons. And a famous one. And now the boy is down at the soldiers' encampment partying it up with troops who have just got finished slaughtering an Assyrian raiding party with weapons he made—the boy—and . . ." He shook his head and reached for the jug again. "I suppose I'm not making sense."

"Maybe you are. You're jealous. Not that *that* makes sense. I take it the boy's enjoying this hugely?"

"I left before I could see."

"No matter. You know exactly what to expect. You —you've been wanting to be everything to the boy, eh? Father, mother, master, teacher, everything? Anyhow, that's the impression I got from talking to you earlier."

"Yes, yes. Yalampa, what have I got left? I mean, if I don't have Ahuni, what have I got?"

"Come on, now. You're not living through the boy, are you? Not that way. This purse in my hand—that's not all Ahuni's earnings, is it? Look, I have a pretty good idea what everybody in town makes for a living, my friend. Just based on the notion that they all spend a certain percentage of what they make on the likes of me. After all, when someone's wife finally tells him, look, my friend, I've had enough damned children—"

"I understand. And you're right. Some of this is my retainer from Nabousakin. I'll be going to Haran to represent him next spring."

"So you told me. Look, you damned fool, you're not just living through Ahuni. You have a new profession —a whole new profession. You don't seem to realize how lucky you are. You don't have to be dependent upon the boy—not for money, or for standing in the metalworking trade, or—damn it—for affection or reaffirmation of your worth as a man, as a father, whatever. I've met the boy. He's a fine lad. He has enormous respect for you. So what are you doing getting jealous just because he finds out who his blood kin are? You don't have to compete with his blood father. His blood father's not here. He can't run to *him* for comfort when he feels down, can he? No, he's got you for that. For most men that'd be enough. Time enough to worry about that blood father when you meet him—and all the odds favor his being dead anyhow, don't they?

Honestly, Zakir, you men are so stupid and helpless. If you didn't have a woman around to tell you when to . . ."

But she saw the gleam in his eye now and she stopped. And smiled. And came as close to blushing as she'd come in five years. In an uncharacteristically coquettish gesture her slim hands went to her breasts, hiding them. Zakir's eyes roved up and down her lush body, and she found herself suddenly goose-pimply and girlishly aroused. She pressed her thighs together convulsively. She shivered. "Come here," he said. But this time his voice was low and steady and full of musk and desire.

CHAPTER ELEVEN

I

Up ahead Lot and Zillah rode horses, looking beaten and shabby in their dusty finery. Complaining constantly, they rode; behind them, her wrists tethered to a long rope fixed to the soldier's mount, Shepset, her naked body burnt almost black by the sun, jogged along. She was downright gaunt by now; slaves, in the great retreat, were fed only once a day—and this slave, bound hands or no, had developed a reputation as a young lioness. The last warrior who tried to get close to her while bringing her food had had his hand bitten through to the bone.

Lot and Zillah, of course, were ransomable. It made sense to keep them in relatively good shape. If the time came when they had to be traded to the enemy for considerations, they had to be ... well, hardly the worse for wear. But who cared about a slave—particularly a girl slave, weak and slightly built?

Shepset understood everything—and forgave nothing. Her thin face, honed by starvation and thirst to knife-blade sharpness now, held a perpetual look of intense concentration into which a number of expressions could be read: hatred, determination, contempt —anything on the negative side of the coin. Her mind held little of any of this. Her thoughts remained doggedly practical: they tended to focus on the moment, on the necessity of doing whatever was required to survive.

At first the pace they were making on the retreat had been almost too much for her. Keeping up with the pace even of a walking horse was not the sort of thing she had ever had to do, even on the great march across Sinai desert and the Negeb. In the first day or two of the retreat she had fallen once—and had learned the penalty for falling was to be dragged behind the horse, for the soldier on its back would not stop it. Sobbing, muttering incoherent Egyptian curses, she had gotten to her feet and, bleeding from a dozen small cuts, had forced herself to keep up. Now, after five days on the march, she had begun even to get something like a second wind after the first hour of each day's trek. She could even, if she had to, manage to bandy insults with the soldiers who passed and made lewd remarks to test her temper.

This soldier was named Tahash. As soldiers went, he wasn't too bad; he would even slow the horse to a near-crawl four or five times a day to give her relief. Of course, hating him was a matter of reflex; she simply hated him, perhaps, less than the rest.

Now, as she padded tirelessly after Tahash's mount, she saw another soldier, mounted on a tall steed, join him. His horse's hoofs kicked dust in her eyes; she sent a look of hatred after him until he quieted the animal. Dust, dung: she jogged along through whatever they threw at her. She could take anything, she told herself. They couldn't break her. They couldn't even bend her.

"Tahash!" the second soldier said. "I've been back with the command wagon. I think we're going to make a stand sometime tomorrow."

"Good!" Tahash said. "It's about time. I wonder why we've waited so long."

"Well, I asked . . . and I listened. I overheard quite a bit. You know, we almost got ourselves slaughtered back in Siddim. I didn't know it at the time, but they had us in the middle of a pincer movement on the west bank of the Salt Sea. Thank all the gods that Arioch of Ellasar saw what was happening and cut us a path through them. Another few moments of letting their northern arm move into place, and we'd never have been able to break out of there."

"Who would have imagined they'd turn out to be so tough? And ... well, there aren't that many of them, really. And here they are hot on our heels, and all we can do is run for it."

"Huh. That's over, as of tomorrow morning. Amraphel knows the area around Heshbon very well. At dawn, instead of packing up and heading north again, we're going to turn and counterattack. We'll see how they like that."

Shepset could stand it no longer. "That's just what they've been waiting for, you cowards!" she said. "You'll see what it's like fighting troops trained and led by an Egyptian!"

The soldier turned, looked her up and down, laughed. "Tahash," he said. "Where did you get that one?"

"I'm minding her for Tidal. He's taken a fancy to her. Don't get too close: she bites. Of course Tidal likes that kind. 'If they don't struggle,' he says ..."

"Well, let him have her. A little skinny for my taste anyhow." He changed the subject as if she had never spoken to him. "At any rate, if we're going to make a stand, I'm glad it's not going to be in a place like the Sink. Whatever one says, they did a devil of a job on us down there before we broke out."

"Just as they're going to do again!" Shepset yelled at him.

"Shut up!" the soldier snarled. "Unless you'd like a taste of the whip."

"Easy," Tahash said. "Tidal won't like that. Not if it shows."

"Oh, all right. But she'd better keep her mouth shut or we'll simply have to explain to Tidal that she tripped and fell, and that's how she got that black eye I'm going to give her."

"Come on, calm down. But ... you're right. They damn near pulled the same stunt on us that we did on Bera earlier, boxing him up down near the asphalt pits."

"Gods, yes! I thought we were goners for sure. Well,

there's none of that up ahead. Nice solid ground—and we'll encamp on a height. We'll hit them before they're even wholly awake."

"Good! I didn't really get into the thick of things last time. And one of the bastards managed to get an arrow into a good horse of mine and I got stuck with this nag later. There's nothing so humiliating as having a horse killed right under you and not being able to do anything about it."

"I know just what you mean."

"But . . . let me tell you something. I heard a rumor that there's another army somewhere. The one that was going to close us in between Sodom and Hazazontamar. The word is, it was coming north along the west bank of the Salt Sea. If that's the case we may have some trouble waiting for us up in the Jordan Valley. Maybe earlier."

"Huh. I'll ride back and ask around. Maybe someone there knows something I don't. If I pass along the information, there might be a little purse attached."

"Share it with me if there is, eh?"

Shepset, bouncing along in the easy lope she'd fallen into, watched the second soldier ride away. She found herself smiling a small, triumphant smile. So they were going to turn and fight tomorrow morning bright and early, eh? And hit Sneferu's forces with a surprise counterattack? Well, perhaps she'd have something to say about that. Perhaps she'd decide to give Tidal a little satisfaction tonight—however much it turned her stomach to do so. And perhaps he'd free her hands then. If he did, that would be all she needed. By now she knew the pattern of an encampment among the Four Kings as well as any of the soldiers did. More: she knew which of the night guards was vigilant and which was not. It would be a simple matter, with Tidal drunk and asleep, to slip out into the night. There was an almost-full moon, and all she'd have to do would be to retrace her steps along the present track until she reached the first pickets of the advancing army. Surprise counterattack? They'd see some surprises after all. A lot more than they'd bargained for.

Bastards! Wretched bastards!

Hagar had a tent of her own now in the camp at Mamre's Grove. It was set a bit apart from those of Abram's closest household, most likely at Sarai's urging. Hagar accepted this as she accepted everything these days. Ever since her planned marriage with Sneferu had fallen victim to Abram's own plans, the highs and lows of life had passed her by. Everything, everyone around her she perceived without feeling. Her new existence was much easier in many ways—the heavy work went to others now, and she was even being assigned a servant of her own—but she took little joy in it.

Now, trying on the clothing Sarai had sent over—hand-me-downs, to be sure, but expensive hand-me-downs, made, as often as not, of the best Egyptian cloth; bribes given Abram's wife by the pharaoh who had wronged her—she was able to note her own increased attractiveness and mentally register the fact; but the effect on her was, at best, less pleasure than comparative absence of pain.

Turning, she saw a figure at the tent flap, a woman of middle age in slave's dress, her arms burdened down with another richly colored load of robes. "Oh," Hagar said. "Are those from the lady Sarai too? Bring them in, please."

The woman, looking once in her eye and then casting her eyes down, complied. She laid the pile of clothing carefully upon a rug and started to back out the doorway. But something Hagar noticed in the woman's face in that brief glance caused her to say, "Here, I know you. But . . ."

The slave made a perfunctory bow. "I'm Katsenut, my lady," she said deferentially. "I was in service in the household of the lord Psarou in . . ."

Hagar rushed forward, eyes wide and on the verge of quick tears, her hands extended to take the woman's wrists. "Katsenut! Oh, my dear . . . how could I not have recognized you? But . . . but just look at you. You're . . ."

"I've lost a lot of weight," the cook said. "No wonder my lady doesn't know me."

"Oh, please," Hagar said, pressing her hands.

"Please, no 'my lady.' I couldn't stand that. Not any more. Not between you and me, as long as we've known each other. How good it is to see you! I—" She stopped. There was a look of puzzlement on her face. "You're not ... not the 'servant' they were sending me?"

"Yes, my la—"

"Oh! Oh, my dear! Oh, my friend!" Hagar clasped the cook to her gorgeously robed bosom, rocking happily back and forth. "Oh, Katsenut ... this is the first nice thing that's happened to me since ... since ..."

Katsenut couldn't think of what to do. The protocol didn't allow familiarity. But Hagar seemed to invite it. She hugged back, timidly; then she found herself comforting Hagar, who had slipped off into full-fledged tears. "I'll be happy to be with you, ma'am. You were always good to me. I always thought we were ... well, friends, sort of, for all that our ranks were so far apart."

"Ranks!" Hagar said between sobs. "There are no ranks here. I'm a slave just like you. Only where I used to be the slave who fetched water for the lord Abram, now I'm the slave who has to make a child for him. N-no, my friend, my very dear friend. We're on a level, you and I." Her tears subsided and she looked Katsenut in the eye. "But how good that you're going to be with me. I need a friend. Oh, you don't have any idea how badly I need a friend just now. Sarai ... she hates me. And the only friends I had here ... well, they're all gone. Shepset ... poor darling, I wonder where she is now? Belsunu."

"Oh, the poor man. Well, he has to be happier now. If there is anything to this business of another world." Katsenut sighed, smiling sympathetically. "Pardon me, ma'am, but we heard you'd made friends with the soldier too, the Egyptian. If ..." But she saw almost immediately she'd said the wrong thing. She stood with her hand over her mouth. "Oh, I'm sorry. Really I'm sorry."

"It's all right," Hagar said. "If we're going to be friends, you'll hear about it sooner or later. Sneferu and I ... we were in love. He was going to ask Abram for me. But the day he left, Sarai gave me to Abram. For a concubine. And ... here I am, and ..." She closed her mouth and said no more for a moment. She sighed. Her mouth was a straight line, bitter and despairing. "Oh, I just know I'll never see him again. Ever. I've had such horrible dreams, ever since Abram and I ... ever since ..."

"There, now, ma'am. There, now. Don't think about it."

"What good is it to not think about it? Look, I've learned to trust my dreams. Just before the guardsmen came for Psarou I dreamed ... bad things. And it all came true, all of it. All of it. And now? Now I dreamed Sneferu was dead, lying lonely and dead on a battlefield somewhere. I dreamed he called for me. Only—his voice ... he knew somehow that he'd never see me again. I dreamed of him dying, alone, in despair."

"Please, ma'am."

"The only thing that holds me together right now is ... Katsenut. How does a woman know she's pregnant?"

"Pregnant? Why, ma'am, you can't know. Not this early ..." She stopped and looked at Hagar. Her face went blank. "Ma'am. You can't mean ... but you couldn't know about that either yet." She looked in Hagar's eyes and knew she didn't have to confirm it out loud. "Ah. But how long has it been, ma'am? I mean, since—"

"The night he ... the night before he went away. Look, if I—"

"But ma'am. That's still too soon. You couldn't know."

"But I know," Hagar said. "I know." Her dark eyes, still wet with tears, flashed with a fierce defiance. "They'll take it from me. They'll raise it as Abram's. I'll be shoved off in the corner like some old maiden aunt, and they'll all treat me as if I didn't matter. But I'll know, always. And that'll be one thing they'll never be able to take away from me. Never! Never!"

II

The moon was high. Standing on a height with the scout Hazo, Sneferu could see many details of the plain below, as well as the lights of the enemy camp on the opposing hill. "Well," he said, "it looks peaceful enough. Just wait until tomorrow, though. Some poet will come along afterward and name it the Field of the Abattoir, or something like that."

"Then the attack is on, sir?" Hazo said.

"It'll have to be. The messenger from Abram's camp, over near Jericho, came in a while back. I sent a man along the same route to tell Abram to cut them off. We've got them cut off—this wing of the army, at any rate."

"This wing, sir? Then you think . . . you mean that's not the whole army over there?"

"By the gods, no. You've never seen the whole army because we've never faced it whole. It's been mostly skirmishes so far, except for that one battle near Zoar. The damned fools. There have been at least five places where they could have turned on us and most likely slaughtered us. But for some reason they've let the chance slip by again and again. No, that's the army of Tidal—although there may be some of Arioch's troops left behind with them to bolster their strength. They're just the rear guard. Chedorlaomer has left them behind to slow our advance. Most likely he's halfway to Damascus by now."

"But . . . sir . . . I thought they outnumbered us."

"So they do. But we—you, too, my friend, you and yours—gave a good account of ourselves in Siddim. I think we scared the hell out of them."

"Then they're running from us?" The younger soldier looked unbelievingly out over the moonlit plain at the lights of the encampment on the ridge.

"Not really. To be sure, they've had it easy so far; until we intervened they'd mainly been in the business of killing women and children. Nevertheless, they're no cowards. What they're doing is drawing us away from our sources of supply, up into unfamiliar country. Country they know better than we do. The idea is to trap us and fall on us up there somewhere—" His hand made a vague gesture northward. "—and attack from all sides."

"Oh. And in the meantime?"

"Outfits like the one over there are to weaken us. If we deal with these, they'll station another rear guard up the road a day's march or so and those fellows will attack, too. They'll lose troops, but so will we." He looked reassuringly at the scout. "At least that's the way they'll be looking at it. It's a war of attrition the way they're doing it, and it's our job not to let them make that kind of war out of it."

"Oh. It . . . it sounds like such a game. And yet—"

"And yet what it really is is butchery. You know that and so do I. But don't worry. I've fought people like these many times before. I really doubt there's anything that they can throw at me that I haven't seen several times. For instance, camping this far away, I think I've fouled up someone's plans—plans for getting up early and attacking us at dawn."

"Really, sir?"

"Yes. They could have marched another hour. Yet they stopped on the height."

"I see, sir. But why don't we attack them, sir? I mean . . ." But the young scout realized he'd gone too far. "I'm sorry, sir, I—"

"Don't be sorry," Sneferu said. "No way you can learn without asking questions. For one thing, we don't know where the hostages are."

"Hostages?"

"Yes. Abram's nephew and niece, for instance. And there are others." He turned suddenly and looked back toward his own camp. "What's the commotion back there? Look, son—go back and find out what's happening, will you?"

"Yes, sir!" The young man turned without another

word and disappeared into the deep shadow of an oak.

Sneferu looked down into the plain again. *Ah,* he thought. *You sure sounded confident just now. If you only felt that way.* But of course you never really got confident. The moment you did some damn fool would sneak up from behind and skewer your guts for you. He'd never seen it fail.

This contingent across the plain, now. Probably the poor damn fools over there didn't have any idea that Chedorlaomer was sacrificing them to save his own worthless hide. They thought they'd been picked out for something heroic, and they would be all worked up over the idea of doing something glorious in battle. Well, they'd get a surprise or two, they would.

This little army of his own, now—they had no right to be as good as they were. He must, he decided, have been doing something right, training them. And there must have been something there in the first place. They were made of the right stuff. Back there in Siddim, they ought to have broken at the first counterattack. But they'd held their ground like old professionals, not like the amateurs they were. They . . .

There was a noise behind him. He wheeled, hand on his sword hilt. "Who's there?" he said.

"You said you wanted to see the messenger from the lord Abram, sir, when he'd been fed and rested. And . . . sir, there's something I think you ought to see." The young scout stepped aside.

The messenger was a pleasant surprise. Throwing protocol aside, Sneferu embraced him with rough affection. "Enosh!" he said. "It's good to see you. I'm sorry I wasn't available earlier. If I'd known it was you—"

"Yes, sir. I feel the same way about you, sir."

"Well. What's the news? How is Abram? I sent word back with my own runner, you know. He's to hit them from the flank."

"He'll do it, sir. He's very impressed with you, sir. He was with our unit when we headed off the flight north along the west bank of the Salt Sea. He saw what you did to them on the asphalt flats."

"Only thing to do. How's my friend Belsunu?"

"I . . . I hate to be the one to tell you, sir. . . ."

"Ah." Sneferu frowned and didn't say anything for a moment. "Come over here by the fire and have a drink of wine with me," he said in a hoarse voice. "He . . . he didn't make it, then?"

"No, sir. He was a gallant man. We all respected him greatly."

"No surprise in that. He was one of the great ones. Here, drink to his spirit, over on the other side. If there is one." He drank himself and handed over the goat-skin bag. "Sometimes I envy Abram his faith. *Often* I envy Abram his faith. One wants to think that . . ." He took the skin back and drank again, with a great thirst. "Belsunu," he said. "Well, I hope his last hours were good."

"The lord Abram was with him at the end. He says Belsunu died at peace with himself. 'I am praying to El-Shaddai for him,' he says."

"Good old Abram." He sighed. "And how is he— the old man?"

"Oh, fit as they come, sir. Imagine, at his age he's taken, and bedded, a concubine. He says 'El-Shaddai has promised me an heir. The girl will bear,' he says. 'It is the word of the God.' "

"I'm happy for him. He's a wonderful man and a good friend. I hope the girl is good to him, whoever she is. Sarai . . ."

"Oh, I think you know her, sir," Enosh said, taking the wineskin from him again. "She's of your people. One of the slaves the Egyptian king gave the lord Abram in the delta country. A lovely dark girl named Hagar."

Sneferu's head jerked his way. There was such a look of sudden shock on his face that Enosh almost dropped the wineskin. "Excuse me," Sneferu said. "You said her name was . . . ?"

"Hagar, sir. She was the girl who waited on the lady Sarai. He's freed her now. She has her own tent and a servant of her own, and she is treated with respect."

Sneferu leaned back against a tree trunk. "Hagar," he

said. His voice was tight and constricted. "Tell me," he said. "When did this take place?"

"Oh, let's see . . . he announced it at the festival on the night before you left for Siddim. I thought you'd have heard. But someone told me you weren't at the party."

"The night before we left," Sneferu said dully.

"Yes, sir. And he took her officially for a concubine the next day. You'd have been on the march then."

"Yes I would." He sighed and looked at the goatskin bag. Then he handed it over to Enosh. "Suddenly the wine seems sour. I must have eaten something that didn't agree with me."

"I'll get another, sir. Something better."

"Yes, please do. Please do." He leaned back hard against the rough bark of the tree. He shut his eyes. *Hagar!* And . . . she'd known. And she hadn't told him. She'd known how the news would have unmanned him on the night before a battle. Always thinking of him, of his welfare. *Oh, Hagar.* And suddenly, with his eyes shut tight, he could call the picture of her up no more. He tried to visualize her as he'd left her that dawn . . . but the image steadfastly refused to come.

He'd failed her. Belsunu had known. He had seen this coming. He'd warned him, Sneferu, to ask Abram for her immediately. And if he'd done what Belsunu had told him to do, Abram would never have refused him; the bond between them was too strong for that. If he'd only spoken for her. If only he'd let Abram know that he was in love with Hagar.

And instead he'd ruined her life. And his own. What was left of it. Because now that he'd lost her he no longer knew what there was to live for. He'd lived for his trade for so long, and he'd lost that. After that the only thing he'd had to live for was the thought of Hagar, of living with her and making a home with her. Virtually every waking thought not occupied with the minutiae of war and pursuit had gone to her—and now he could not even summon up her image. He'd failed her. And himself.

And now he remembered, as clearly as if he were

hearing his own voice speaking the words, what he'd told her the night he'd first declared himself. "If I fail you," he'd pledged, "may I die when I least expect it, when the hope shines brightest in my own heart. May I die on the doorstep to happiness, with everything I ever wanted in plain view."

The omen was clear and simple. He'd died the moment he'd failed her, just as he'd said. The rest was just a matter of going through the motions.

Enosh, and a young soldier behind him, a man Sneferu did not know, interrupted his thoughts. "Sir! This is Elon, a picket from the outermost line. He has someone to show you."

Elon stepped forward, bringing with him a small figure in a long wraparound cloak. The figure was that of a boy—or a girl, perhaps—and the face was unmistakably Egyptian. "Sir, this girl claims to be a slave of the lord Lot. She says she escaped from the camp on the heights across the plain."

"Oh?" Sneferu said. Business; back to business. "Here, my friend, what's the . . ." He stopped. "I know you," he said to the slave. "You're Hagar's friend. Shepset."

"Yes," she said in a hoarse voice. "I was given to Tidal tonight. I let him have his way—my hands were tied, what could I do?" She held out her thin wrists, poking them out of the robe's folds. They were bloody, the flesh around them hanging in shreds. Sneferu started, in anger. "Afterward I asked him to cut me free for a while. When he did I hit him on the head with an earthenware jug and ran out into the dark."

"Gods!" Enosh said. "The bastards!"

"Let her continue," Sneferu said in a low voice, his anger barely in check. "Lot and Zillah . . . are they with this group?"

"They were. But Tidal sent them ahead to Chedorlaomer this afternoon."

"He's just signed the warrant for his own death," Sneferu said. "Are there other hostages?"

"No," Shepset said. "There were . . . but they could

not stand the pace. I have been tethered behind a horse. When I fell the horse would drag me. I have been starved and repeatedly raped. But see for yourself."

She stepped closer to the fire and loosed the cord at her neck. The robe fell to the ground.

There was a universal gasp of astonishment from the soldiers closest to her.

Her naked little body was emaciated, weathered, burnt dark by the sun. There were cuts and bruises all over it—and bite marks here and there, and the marks of a recent beating on her narrow back. She turned slowly, her face a mask of hatred, and showed where the lines of blood ran down the backs of her legs. "I did not wash myself," she said. "I wanted the soldiers of the lord Abram to see how Tidal uses a woman. I . . ."

But suddenly her pose of self-confidence deserted her. The look of hatred was replaced by a mask of pain and humiliation and self-loathing. She reached for the robe and sank down on the ground before them, trying to pull the cloth around her thin shoulders. "Please . . ." she said. "Help me. Someone help me, please. . . ."

Enosh gently took her away, murmuring soft words of reassurance in her ear. Sneferu turned to his captains. "All right," he said. "Do we wait for these bastards to smite us at dawn? Or . . . Well, look up there. There's enough moon for me. What about the lot of you?"

Mamre's stringy brother Eshcol stepped forward. "Perhaps I could wait myself," he said, "but this fine sword Belsunu made for me keeps crying out in hunger. If it doesn't get to bite into somebody's neck before morning, it'll never let me have another moment's peace."

"So be it," Sneferu said, his voice all barely controlled rage. "Get them together. But keep it quiet. The less noise we make, the fewer men we lose. If I have anything to say about it, we're not going to lose anybody."

"Very well," Eshcol said coldly. "One question: do we take prisoners?"

"We do not. Feed that hungry sword of yours." Sneferu's voice was savage. It was good to feel something again.

III

The runner reached Abram's camp shortly after nightfall. Exhausted and sweaty, he was shown through the lines with no ceremony. The guards, however, halted him at Abram's tent. "It'll have to wait," the principal guard said. "The lord Abram is at prayer."

The runner was Korah, one of Eshcol's men. He scowled and spat into the fire. "Look, friend," he said. "I've just finished running a good horse virtually to death to bring a message from the lord Sneferu. It's a matter of life and death—and of the lives and deaths of friends of mine and of yours. Surely His Worship can break up this mystic communion of his with the birds of the air or whoever."

"He left orders. Besides, it's not a thing we do around here."

"Look, if you won't go in and call him out, I will." Korah stepped forward, hand at his sword.

The guard lowered his pike. "You try it and I'll spit you like an ox at a feast."

Korah unsheathed the blade, his hand closing tightly around the plain, unornamented handle, feeling the fine balance. "Damnation," he said. "You outlanders are a contentious lot. In the best of worlds you'd be saving some of that feistiness for the enemy. But as you wish." He circled slowly to his left, his eyes wary.

"Here!" Abram's voice came from the open tent flap. "What's this, now? What are you up to? In my own camp, now?"

Both men lowered their weapons. "Sir," Korah said. "I have an urgent message from the lord Sneferu."

"Ah!" Abram said. "Look, my friend," he said, turning to the young guard, "any messenger from Sneferu must get to me immediately. It's all right. Let him speak." He turned back to Korah. "And Sneferu says . . . ?"

"He says he wants you to come across the track from Jericho to Heshbon—and immediately. As fast as you can travel. He expects to do battle with Tidal's forces around dawn. He wants, then, to join up with you to chase Chedorlaomer's troops up the Jordan Valley. But time is of the essence."

"Ah, so it is," Abram said, his eyes young and bright in the old face. "Is there word yet of the lord Lot and his wife?"

"No, sir."

"Very well. I'll give the order to mount immediately. There's clear moonlight. We should be able to make fairly good time. Meanwhile, you've done nice work tonight, reaching me before we bedded down. You must be hungry. Go draw your ration from the cooks —but don't eat too heartily; you've more exertion ahead of you."

"Yes, sir!" the runner said, saluting.

Spread out in five columns, Sneferu's striking force made its way slowly and cautiously across the valley. There was a minimum of the usual cursing and complaining; Sneferu had made it brutally clear that the first person who made a noise audible to him, up at the point of the middle column, would face his, Sneferu's, sword after the battle. No one wanted to meet Sneferu in single combat, particularly when one was plainly in the wrong. All of them had by now seen the Egyptian in action, and there wasn't a man in his army who didn't fear him—with the single exception of Mamre's saturnine brother Eshcol, who, people said, was still trying to figure out the meaning of the word *fear;* by now he had come to think of himself as a slow learner, considering the number of people who had been at pains to teach him the word.

Now the five columns neared the base of the hill on which Tidal's army had encamped. The two flanking arms of the attack force moved to the side, while the middle three made their way directly up the side of the low hill.

There was a dim light in the eastern sky when Sneferu poised himself behind a projecting rock, waiting for the outermost guard to pass. Hearing the even footsteps, he drew Belsunu's sword; and when the guard passed his perch, he swung the sword with all his strength, hitting the man on the temple with the flat of the blade. The guard dropped in his tracks. Sneferu grinned and turned in time to see the first direct rays of the sun peep forth over the eastern hills. He looked to left and right; swords flashed in the morning light. The other guards had met the same fate. He felt the blood pounding in his temples; his hands were hot with blood. His arms quivered with anticipation, as they always had before a battle. He raised his own sword high and saw the others raise theirs, waiting for his signal. They would come in quickly, taking advantage of the fact that Chedorlaomer had taken most of the bowmen with his own group. They'd hit the camp in a rush, making a fearful din—and they'd kill every man they found.

Suddenly, as he stood there, arm raised high, he caught a glimpse of Eshcol, standing within plain sight of him. The cold self-possession of the man, the bloodthirsty gleam in his eye, sent a sudden chill up Sneferu's spine. *It's true,* he thought. *This man doesn't know what fear is. What kind of monster is he anyhow? Every man feels fear.*

Gritting his teeth, he controlled the shaking of his arm—and suddenly swept the sword downward with a shrill scream of rage. The scream was echoed by all the men in his command as they swept through the scrub and fell on the just-awakening camp, swinging swords that changed color from copper to bright red in a matter of moments.

Sneferu killed until his arm was weary; then, like the old soldier he was, he switched hands. The magic sword fit the wrong hand as well as it had the right one. He felt invincible, invulnerable; time and again he seemed surrounded, outmanned—and time and again the splendid weapon hewed his way through his attackers. It was no longer rage that enlivened him; now it was the sheer animal joy of the battle itself. He would have been shocked at this if he'd had time to reflect; he hadn't felt this way in years. And as he hacked and cut away at the angry, frightened faces before him, another curious transformation occurred; he found the power, the strength of youth beginning to flow back into him—the kind of second wind that came only in youth, and that was instead flowing into his aging body at the end of his soldiering life. Now a Canaanite guardsman came at him, sword flailing; he parried the blow effortlessly and swung at the man's face, seeing the seemingly enchanted blade hack into flesh and bone as if it were unresisting belly flesh. A low animal cry of power and menace rose from his throat. *Bastards!*

He looked around him. Everywhere his men were winning. But Tidal—where was Tidal? He'd seen the Canaanite king once, hewing his way out of a hole—but had not been able to get across the clearing to him. Now he was nowhere to be seen.

A Canaanite guard came at him with a pike. He shoved the weapon to one side with his bare hand and rammed the sword into the man's innards up to the hilt. He yanked back on the sword to let the man fall ... and as he did he caught one glimpse of Tidal, slipping through the bushes, heading north. He looked to right and left; no one had seen the escaping king. A fierce grin on his face, Sneferu gave chase. As he did, a Canaanite bowman saw him and, picking up his weapon from the ground where it had fallen, followed him, pausing only to ascertain that there were only two arrows left in his almost-exhausted quiver.

Tidal loped easily out over the rocks. Ahead, the hill narrowed to a long spur, deeply eroded on both sides. There was a narrow causeway of rock that connected the hill with the next. As years passed, the causeway itself would be eroded away; now it stood, wide enough for one man to pass—one man, not two. Tidal made for this, sword swinging at his side.

Sneferu loped easily after him. The strength was in his legs, his arms, again as it had not been in a decade. He bellowed in the voice of a young man: "Tidal! Tidal, king of Goïim! Stand and fight, coward! Stand and fight in single combat with Sneferu the Egyptian!"

Tidal, up ahead, tripped and fell—and as he rose he turned to see Sneferu in hot pursuit. He stood and drew his sword. "All right!" he said. "Come and fight."

Sneferu's trot slowed to a walk. "Ah," he said in the same young bull's voice—but with the authority of an older man, the controlled force of a man at the peak of his power. "Good. I wanted you for myself. Tidal, did you know the girl made it to our camp? The slave you raped?"

"What's another slave?" Tidal said. He stood at the entrance to the narrow bridge of rock, with it and the sheer drop at his back. "Come and fight, Egyptian."

"I'm going to kill you, Tidal. The girl was a compatriot of mine, and a friend of a friend. No matter. She'll be the last woman you rape, ever. I'm going to kill you and make a capon out of you. It doesn't matter a damn to me which I do first."

The Canaanite king was large, fleshy, strong-looking. He stood half a head taller than Sneferu himself. He looked formidable. "Kill me first," he said. "Then do what you will. Only you'll find the killing part more than you bargained for."

Sneferu, approaching, slowed for a moment—and then attacked, driving Tidal back onto the narrow bridge with a ferocious combination of cuts and thrusts. "What's the matter?" he said between thrusts. "Can't handle an armed man ... quite as well ... as a little girl-child with her hands tied?"

With a scream of rage Tidal counterattacked. His blows rained down on Belsunu's strong blade; Sneferu switched hands and, parrying with his right, flexed the left, still aching from the shock. He gave ground ... and then halted the Canaanite's advance with a parry that almost disarmed Tidal. Backward he drove the Canaanite, backward, across the narrow causeway.

The bowman, limping from a leg wound, made his way to the edge of the scrub. He stopped and sat on a rock, holding his aching thigh, moaning with pain. And he looked ahead and saw the two fighting on the narrow bridge, with a yawning drop to either side. In pain, he reached behind his back to his quiver and withdrew the next to the last arrow. It had lost a feather; he'd never be able to count on its accuracy. Nevertheless, he notched it and drew the bow. He sighted along the shaft at Sneferu's brown back, quite visible in the clear postdawn light. He let the arrow go; it flew wide, as he'd expected, and fell into the depths. He wearily reached for the last shaft and notched it.

Tidal was quite a swordsman. Even Sneferu had to admit that. He hadn't given a body's length of ground since that second furious, lunging attack of Sneferu's. His forearms were huge, thick, sinewy. They seemed to have added reserves of strength beyond a normal man's. Sneferu, a sinking feeling in the pit of his stomach suddenly sapping his reserves, abruptly became aware that he was dealing not only with a fighter of advanced skills—but with a man stronger than himself.

Unfortunately Tidal came to the same realization at almost the same moment. And, a gleam of triumph in his eye, he cried aloud and attacked with redoubled ferocity. His wild roundhouse swing caught Sneferu's blade broadside, forte to forte; the shock jarred Sneferu's hand, and he almost dropped the weapon. He gave ground, looking for an opening in Tidal's attack. As he did, Tidal slashed at his face, opening a deep cut over Sneferu's right eye. Blood flowed down his forehead, half blinding him. He faltered, gave ground . . . and drew the rush he had been looking for. Tidal came in after him, fast—too fast. His guard opened up. Sneferu's point jabbed him in the gut—a shallow wound but a painful one. Tidal dropped his sword arm, covering. And, thrusting with every vestige of strength left in his quickly tiring body, Sneferu lunged —and buried the entire tip of his sword in the side of Tidal's neck.

Rich arterial blood spouted wildly. Tidal clutched his neck; the sword fell from his hands, bounced once on rock, and clattered over the side into the depth below. In a red rage Sneferu swung his sword—again and again, cutting Tidal's forearms to bloody ribbons. He feinted at the stricken giant's neck, drawing his arms high, and then slashed wildly at Tidal's exposed belly, gutting him as one might gut a fish. The giant swayed on the stone bridge; swayed, and slowly turned and fell.

Sneferu let out a bellow of delayed rage and triumph. "Die!" he yelled . . . and found his voice cut off in the middle of the next word. Something hit him hard in the middle of the back, knocking him off balance. He swayed precariously atop the narrow causeway, the abyss on both sides of him looming fearfully. The motion, however, shifted the position of the arrowhead the bowman's lucky shot had driven deep inside his chest. There was a sudden, sickening pang of pain; half-fainting, he felt his legs falter under him . . . and fell heavily on his back, driving the arrow all the way through his body.

Supine on the stone slab, he looked down through half-blind eyes to see the arrowhead protruding from his chest. He reached over to touch it—but the motion shifted the path of the shaft inside him again and the pain became excruciating. His hand pawed ineffectually at the wooden stick with its bloody and jagged metal head. Then his hand fell limp on his chest.

So this is what it's like, he thought. *It was only a matter of time anyway.* It was pretty much as he'd known it would be, from the night before. He'd begun to die from the moment he'd failed Hagar and left her to be taken away from him. "May I die when I least expect it . . ." he'd said. Well, the gods tended to forget all your other prayers, but they always remembered that kind. Make that one wrong turn, and you could never get back on the right road.

And he'd lost everything: the hope of Hagar, the hope of a home and a peaceful old age and sons and daughters to gladden his heart. The warm light of the home campfire at the end of a long and painful and dusty road. . . .

He coughed, and the pain was so intense he knew there wasn't much time left. He closed his one good eye and tried to remember her. And, miraculously, he managed for a moment to bring back a vision of her—Hagar, looking just as she'd looked that day, that magic day at the pond when he had first committed himself to her: small, dark, standing slim and erect, the round bare breasts proud on the slim body, those great brown eyes searching deep inside him, the expression on her face trembling on the brink of trust. . . . "Hagar," he said with his last breath. And felt himself slipping easily away into the last long sleep.

The bowman walked to the causeway's edge and looked down at the man he'd killed. The face had a curiously peaceful look about it, under the mask of blood. *Well, rest to him now,* he thought—and found himself curiously wondering for a moment which of the two had deserved his arrow the more. Tidal had not been an easy man to follow.

Well, no time for that. Here he was unarmed, and for the sounds of the diminishing battle behind him the skirmish had become a rout. Most likely these outlanders didn't take prisoners. It was time, then, to find a quick pathway down the hill and take off for the north. Perhaps he could catch up with Arioch and Chedorlaomer.

Better to go armed, though. He looked down at the body of the man he'd slain. A bronze sword lay by his fallen hand; the bowman stopped to pick it up—and immediately felt the fine balance, the welcome rightness of the weapon. He swung it once, grinned, and stuck it in his belt. And, with one quick look backward, began scrambling down the goat path toward the valley floor. Above, in the clear pastel sky of morning, a second vulture joined the first, soaring, circling. And presently the sounds of battle came to an end.

IV

Abram's party found the site of the morning's raid as much by the now augmented ring of predatory birds in the sky as anything else. Climbing the hill, they found Eshcol rallying his men for pursuit of the remaining armies to the north. He had brought up the supply wagons from the previous night's camp and was now pressing for quick action, striking up the ridge with one arm of their force and up the Jordan Valley with the other, following the trade routes as—nobody doubted—Chedorlaomer had done. His eye was cold and his tone bloodthirsty. "The time to strike is now," he said in a voice with an edge on it.

"How many of our friends have we lost?" Abram said.

"Oh . . . three, four. No more. It was the finest piece of soldiering I've seen."

"And Sneferu? Has he been found yet? Because if he's gone . . ."

"True," Eshcol said. "Losing him is like losing fifty men—a hundred. He . . . but look. I think Mamre has found him."

The two men turned. Eshcol's stocky brother was advancing from beyond the copse, carrying without apparent effort a familiar-looking body easily as large and bulky as himself. His face bore an expression equal parts mournful and angry.

"If you're looking for Sneferu," he said, "I've found him." He knelt and laid the body out gently. Standing, he blew out and said in a tired and bitter tone, "Three of my men found him on the ridge. Below him we found Tidal, broken on the rocks—but cut to ribbons in single combat with our friend here." He sighed. "Sneferu—he was a mighty man. Tidal had a reputation with the sword."

"I think no man with a sword would have been able to kill him," Eshcol said. "How did Sneferu die then?"

"I pulled an arrow out of him before I picked him up. Some cowardly bastard got him from behind."

"Ah," Eshcol said. "Then we did let someone get away. Well, let him go—all the way north to wherever his masters are hiding. Let him spread fear of us, and turn their backbones to jelly."

"Yes," Mamre said. He turned to Abram. "Well? Do we pack up and strike north? There's plenty of day left for traveling—"

"And leave our friend unburied?" Abram said. His voice was low and calm and thoughtful.

"But . . . the hostages," Eshcol said. He looked to his brother for support; but Mamre's beetling brows were knit.

"He's right," Mamre said. "Chedorlaomer will keep. And he doesn't dare kill the hostages."

"But—you should see the way they've mistreated the slaves. There was a girl who escaped from them—"

"Nevertheless," Mamre said, "Abram is right. I'd think poorly of myself if I couldn't stop long enough to lay a comrade like Sneferu to rest. Plenty of time to dirty our swords on those bastards." He laughed bitterly. "Now listen to me, will you? Hear how we are talking—and me the worst of all—as if we'd already killed our game and had nothing left to do but eat it. And Chedorlaomer's men still outnumber us three to one. Maybe worse."

"Sneferu put heart in us all," Abram said. "It is because of him that we think we can win. That we *know* we can win. All the more reason to honor him, if it costs us a day."

Eshcol frowned; then he shook his head and said in a tight voice. "I . . . I suppose you're right." His hand closed tightly around the hilt of his still-bloody sword. "It's just—"

"I know," Mamre said. "You've still got the killing lust in your system and your blood's still hot. It's all right. You'll fight the better for it tomorrow." He sighed again. "What a week! To lose Sneferu and the smith together." He nodded his head angrily. "Well, we'll make an occasion of it. We'll mourn both of them. And then we'll go break some heads. I think I know where they've gone. At least I know where I'd go if I were Chedorlaomer."

"Where?" Eshcol said. "Not up the coast—"

"No. Inland. He'll provision in Gerasa; he'll pass Rabbah by, knowing he's got us right behind him."

"Toward Damascus, then."

"Most likely. Along the trade route."

"I'm sure you know best," Abram said. "But let us talk of this later. It is time to say farewell to our friend. And while we are doing so we can give praise to the living as well. Eshcol, you have struck a good blow today. Your brother has told me of your valor . . . but I see he has hardly done you justice."

Disarmed, Eshcol fidgeted and blushed. Mamre, watching, smiled to himself. Perhaps there was something to Abram's dream of dominion over the land, he thought. One didn't run into a real leader often, and one could surely tell the difference when the real thing came along. Here he'd managed to pull Eshcol's teeth without unmanning him or demeaning him—and had managed to compliment him at the same time. Any man who could handle men that way might well become the father of a king.

The funeral feast went on into the night, well after they'd laid Sneferu and the handful of amateur soldiers who'd died with him to rest in a cave in the hillside. During the afternoon a small guard detachment was sent back to Mamre's Grove with Shepset and a few of the wounded who could not make the big push northward. And in the dawn hours of the next morning they set out, marching tirelessly and singing the songs of Abram's people, the songs they'd sung on the long trek across Sinai to the land Abram's God had promised him. By the end of the first day Eshcol and Mamre were joining in the singing, having picked up the words by rote without knowing or understanding them.

During the second day they passed Mahanaim and, hailing a scout from a passing caravan, asked for signs of the armies marching north. They learned that Mamre's feelings had so far proven true: the war party had kept inland, and avoided even the easy marching afforded by the Jordan Valley. Smiling his fierce smile, Mamre ordered the drummer to pick up the pace.

Then, on the day following, they made contact with the enemy once more. A contingent of Arioch's troops, lying in wait for them in a mountain pass near Ashtaroth, ambushed them from above, inflicting serious injuries and killing five of Abram's servants and one of his distant kinsmen. The party fell back and regrouped; Mamre and Eshcol confronted Abram. "Well?" they said almost in a single voice. "What do we do now?"

"What else should we do?" Abram said mildly. "We fight again—but we send bowmen up the flanks to hit them broadside as we attack."

"Ah," Eshcol said. "That's more to my liking."

The second battle of the heights was short and vicious. Mamre's bowmen enfiladed the entrenched enemy and inflicted great damage; and Eshcol's powerful push up the hillside drove through the enemy position like an armor-tipped arrow. Mamre even looked up from the serious business of cleaving heads to see Abram, standing tall and powerful despite his age, hurl a javelin with a stripling's eye and arm and pin an Ellasarite soldier to a tree trunk. "Well struck!" he bellowed, and turned to his own opponent with redoubled rage. By nightfall, when they passed down the other side of the mountain, they had left a handsome feast for the vultures and scavengers of the Amorite wilderness.

The emissary from Chedorlaomer arrived shortly after dawn. The Great King's troops were encamped at a place called Hobah, Damascus having refused them sanctuary. The final battle was imminent. "The Great King says peace to his brother Abram," he said, mouthing the memorized words carefully. "He offers the lives of the hostages as a token of peace between us."

Abram spoke slowly and carefully. "Tell the Three

Kings, who were Four before they opposed us, that if the hostages are returned alive and unharmed by the time the sun is at its height, we will not dishonor the bodies of king or vassal alike once we have killed them. Tell Chedorlaomer this: the hand of the Most High God has come down in the night and touched the foreheads of the Three Kings and all who follow them, and marked them all for death. Tell them the sun will not rise twice upon them, and that they will do well to put their affairs in order. And if the hostages are spared and returned to us, we will bury you with honor and dignity. But if the hostages' lives or limbs suffer from them, so shall you suffer. And the second sun will shine upon your white bones, picked clean by vulture and jackal alike and scattered to the four winds. Tell them this."

The emissary, brows knit with concentration, nodded gravely. "I think I've got most of that, sir," he said. "Good day, sir. I think you'll not see me again."

"As you will," Abram said. His face had not lost its calm for so much as a moment, and his words were measured and unhurried. A slight inclination of his head signaled that the interview was at an end. The emissary left; and Abram turned to the brothers beside him, his face unchanged except for an almost imperceptible glint in his clear eye. "Sharpen your swords, my friends," he said. "We have work ahead of us."

V

Katsenut had searched for her mistress the better part of the morning before, encountering one of Mamre's women at the well, she learned Hagar's whereabouts. Retracing her steps past the campfire site, she turned right instead of left this time and made her way to the little height where Belsunu's forge had stood.

The rough masonry was still there, and the smaller forges, but there was a desolate feeling about the place. Everyone avoided it now, with the smith gone and all the menfolk off to war.

It was a strange place to find Hagar; but as Katsenut topped the small rise and looked down, she could see her mistress sitting quietly on the ground, her back against the spreading terebinth that had sheltered the smith in his last hours. Hagar did not look up as she approached, taking notice of her only in the last moments. "My lady?" Katsenut said in Egyptian. The two had taken to speaking together in the old language of late.

"Ah," Hagar said. "Come sit with me. Or ... is there something urgent?"

Katsenut did not speak for a moment. "My lady," she said. "I ... I don't know how to ..."

Hagar looked up. Her mouth was drawn and her eyes were red, but her face was composed. She drew up her knees, tucking her long skirt modestly around her sandaled feet. "I heard the party had come in bringing the wounded from Jericho," she said. "I suspect someone has bad news for me." Her voice was dull and flat. "It's Sneferu, isn't it? They've killed him, haven't they? I dreamed about it last night, and the night before ..."

"Yes, ma'am. I'm so sorry."

"Come, sit. Please." Hagar made room for her. "I ... I was expecting it. I have done all my weeping for now. It has been some time since I slept well. The terrible dreams kept waking me. Perhaps now that I have heard it confirmed I can sleep again. How ... how did he die?"

"I did not hear the details. There are people with the party who know, I'm sure. And—Shepset is with them. She escaped and made her way to our camp and they brought her in. But ... my lady, there seems to be something wrong with her. She won't talk. And she's all over bruises and cuts, and the men say she was terribly abused by the people who took her."

"Oh, the poor dear. I'll have to go to her." Her

voice remained as flat, as unemotional as ever. "I'll go in a few moments. But now . . . now I want to sit and think."

"I'm in the way, ma'am. I'll go."

"No, no. I could use a friend near me now. Sneferu, he died well? I hope so. It would mean something to him, I think." She thought of something suddenly and her face grew somber. "I wonder . . . I wonder if he knew about me and . . . and Abram."

"Maybe there's someone to ask."

"I'll see. But perhaps later. I've been . . . well, trying to sort out my thoughts and feelings here. For some reason it seemed to make sense to come sit here, where Belsunu died." She looked at the slave now and her eyes for the first time held traces of emotion. "So Sneferu's dead, my Sneferu. I think one of these days the real shock of it will hit me and I'll come apart altogether. But now . . . all I feel is weary. I feel . . . oh, somehow suddenly so old." She looked at Katsenut, sudden surprise in her eye. "That's it. My youth . . . it's gone. Overnight. My youth has passed me by. And now I must get down to thinking of other things, just as Sneferu had begun thinking of other things. He said he'd stopped living for himself and was going to start living for home and family . . . and for me."

"He must have been a fine man," Katsenut said lamely. She couldn't think of anything better to say.

Hagar ignored her. "Yes. Yes. That's it. And what I have to do now is find something new to live for. The child. The child inside me."

They visited Shepset some time later. The girl wore a plain unbleached robe, with a hood that covered her head; she had been put to work grinding grain for bread. She did not look up from her work for some time. Then she said over her shoulder, "Hello, Hagar."

"Shepset," Hagar said. "They told me you'd been captured and taken away . . ."

"Yes," Shepset said. She looked up just once, her eyes flashing with hurt and resentment. "I'm sure they told you everything. Everyone in camp knows now, don't they? Everyone knows what I went through up there. Only they don't. Nobody knows. Nobody knows but Lot and Zillah. They watched what happened, before I escaped. The rest of you—"

"Shepset, no. No one's talking about you. We're . . . we've all been worried about you."

"Well, thank you." The girl's voice was constricted, low-pitched. "Thank all of you. Only . . . I'd appreciate it if you'd leave me alone."

"But Shepset—"

"Please!" She looked Hagar in the eye now, and there was painful pleading in her gaze now under the anger. "Please! Hagar . . . the only way I can bear it is to . . . to not think about it. Please! If you all keep bringing it up—"

"Well, of course, my dear, if you like—"

"It's what I'd like. Yes. And thank you, but . . ." She bit her lip and, still on her knees, put the pestle down atop the half-ground meal. "Hagar. I . . . I met your Sneferu before he died. He was a wonderful man. He . . . killed the man who raped . . ." But she started the sentence and then could go no further. Her thin chest rose and fell rapidly in dry sobs as she bit down hard on her scarred knuckles. Her shoulders shook uncontrollably.

Hagar knelt beside her; Katsenut took her other arm. "Shepset. You don't need to finish that. We'll do the work. You come with me. Katsenut will spell you here—won't you? Now, dear. Come with me."

"No!" Shepset said, suddenly angry. "No, leave me alone! I need doing this. I need having my hands busy. I need some nice hard work right now. It keeps my mind occupied." Hagar rubbed her back; she shook off Hagar's hand, near hysteria. "Please . . . I can control myself. But not if you . . . if you keep on trying to . . ."

Hagar held her for a moment; then she released her and sat back on her heels. "I think I understand," she said. "Or at any rate I can understand something of what you feel, if I can't understand what you've been through."

"Been through! Been through! Oh, leave me alone, won't you? Just leave me alone!"

Hagar thought for a moment; then she rose and

stepped back. Shepset did not look up at her. Hagar
nodded to Katsenut; the slave stepped away from her
and went to Hagar's side. "All right," Hagar said. "But
remember what I said a long time ago. I'm your friend.
If you need me—if you need anything I may possibly
have to offer—all you have to do is call upon me. I
have some status here now. Some privileges. Not
much, but some. Abram would listen to me, I think, if
there was anything I really asked him for. He might
even do a favor for me. If there's something you need,
something you want—"

"Thank you," Shepset said, her voice still low and
tight. Her words came out measured and controlled, as
if she were holding in a great anger—or perhaps some
emotion she found even harder to control. "Thank you
very much, Hagar. I appreciate it. If I need you I'll
call for you. But now I have work to do." She did
not look up. She put her hands back on mortar and
stone again and waited patiently for the two women to
leave. "Thank you for coming," she said. "Good-
bye."

VI

Mamre rode over to Abram's position at the center
of their ragtag little army. He'd captured a fine Canaanite horse in the last encounter and lost no opportunity
to ride the animal and solidify the still uneasy relationship of man and beast. As he dismounted, he saw
Abram talking with a sturdy-looking slave, whom he
recognized as he drew nearer. "Ah, Abram!" he said.
"You ought to free this man Enosh here. He's a lion.
He fights like two men. If you do not free him, I will
buy him from you and free him myself."

Enosh beamed—and then recovered his sober expression. He inclined his head respectfully. He did not
speak.

Abram looked at him once and then nodded to Mamre. "I had indeed thought of this," he said. "I am not pleased with Eliezer and have felt so for some time. I had hoped to make Sneferu my second in command, but . . ." He shrugged; but the last thing one might read in the shrug was indifference. "Well, if we survive this," he said, "I will consider the matter. I have been giving some thought to the whole business of slavery. It now seems to be most strange, when you come to think of it. I have lived around the custom for all my life, and I have never totally gotten used to it. When Terah, my father, raised me, I played with slave children until a certain age and then we became no longer equals, but master and vassal. Yet often as not the slave had as good blood as I. Sometimes better, for all I knew; a man may be a king's son one day and a slave the next. And there was no change in myself, or in my childhood friends. Only our status changed, and forever. I was puzzled at the time, but I accepted it. And that is the strangest thing about it all—that people accept it, both master and slave. No one questions that a man should own another man as one owns a sheep or an ox."

"Sir," Enosh said. "I think I see some activity over there." He pointed out over the bowlike valley that lay between Abram's positions and those of the Three Kings.

Mamre grunted, squinting into the noonday sun. "Yes," he said. "You've sharp eyes. You're right. They're beginning to move." And sure enough, as the small plumes of dust began to rise all along the wide line deployed upon the opposite height, there came across the still valley a low wailing sound, from perhaps a thousand throats. The armies of the kings had struck fear into their enemies during the whole of their summer-long campaign of destruction with just such a sound. It was meant to demoralize, to unman an enemy long before the two lines met in combat.

Enosh shivered. "It sounds terrible," he said. "It's very effective—unless you've fought them before, and know they are only men who bleed when you cut them."

"Good man," Mamre said. "You have the guts to admit your fear and face it down. That's what makes a man, my friend." He kept his eyes on the field, on the attacking army; but his words were for Abram. "This is a man here, Abram. Not a chattel. I shall hold you to this when we're back in camp."

"I shall listen to you respectfully," Abram said. "Enosh, ride over to Eshcol's wing and ask him to hold the counterattack until I raise my hand—so—and drop it. He is prone to haste, and everything depends upon delaying the action."

"Yes, sir!" Enosh said, breaking into a trot along the ridge. The two watched him go; then they turned their eyes back to the scene below.

The advancing enemy maintained no precise line as they marched forward. The terrain was dictating their alignment, and some soldiers were far ahead of the rest. "Huh," said Mamre contemptuously. "Look at them come. No more discipline than a bunch of sheep. Why don't we have the archers hit them right now— the advance men, anyhow? That won't be good for their morale. It might even open more holes in that line of theirs."

"A good idea," Abram said. "But wait until they cross the dry wash. The archers can hit them just as they show their heads above the bank."

"Good!" Mamre muttered to a servant at his side; the servant set out to his own flank. "You know, Abram," he said, "I've been skeptical about this 'God' of yours . . . but it's curious. I have this strange feeling of strength, of invulnerability. It's as if—"

"There's nothing strange about it," the old man said serenely. "They have been delivered into our hands by the Most High God. Look at them—like ants on a hill. By evening they will all be dead." He turned to Mamre for the first time, his voice calm, his words measured. "And after this I do not think anyone will contest my place in this land, or yours."

"It would be nice to have people think twice before raiding one of my outlying herds, or moving onto my lands without my permission." He turned his eyes back to the field. "Gods! There certainly are a lot of them."

"It does not matter. It would not matter if there were ten times as many. Look, they are crossing the wash. Signal to your bowmen."

"Yes." Mamre raised his arm, pumped once. There was an answering signal from the right flank. The bowmen notched their arrows. "I must say, Abram, if we're fated to win or whatever, your 'God' has chosen a tactic to my taste. I like this business of making them come to us. Easier on the legs. They'll be tired out before they get here." He shrugged. "But of course that was Sneferu's idea, wasn't it? Not this 'God' of yours."

"The God sent Sneferu to me—yes, and Belsunu too. They were his instruments. Their rest will be serene; their names will be honored." There was a great cheer on their right; the bowmen had launched their first shafts, and they could see the first infantrymen stagger and fall back into the wash as the rain of arrows hit them. "Now," Abram said. "Hold them up. Hold the bowmen. Wait until they've cleared the bank now. Wait until the last of them has passed the discoloration in the soil—right there, see?—and then hit them again. One volley only. Then I'll have Eshcol hit them from the flank. While they're occupied with that we'll attack them head on."

"Splendid," Mamre said. "Sneferu speaks with your voice."

"All honor to his memory. He has taught me much —and he has given my children's children a kingdom."

Mamre looked at the old man, incredulous. *There he goes again with those 'children' of his,* he thought. *Well, let him. All men of any substance are a bit mad anyhow.* He loosened his sword in its scabbard, and, raising the other arm high, signaled again to the bowmen on the left flank.

High on the opposite heights, above Chedorlaomer's camp, Mesha, leader of the guard the Three Kings had left to mind the hostages and the stolen herds, watched the first assault on the enemy positions falter and then fail. He watched the counterstrike on the Ellasarian flank, and blanched as Arioch's crack, battle-hardened troops fell back under the fierce, barbarian attack. "Why don't they *hold?*" he wondered aloud. "Cowards! Damned spineless bastards! Stand and fight, damn you!"

The hostage Lot spoke at his side, in a sarcastic voice. "It's the beginning of the end, isn't it?" he said. "I told you. I told you my uncle would come after you and kill you all. You wouldn't believe me."

Mesha turned to him and started to answer; but at the sight of the supercilious expression on that weak face, and epicene posture of that soft body, he turned away in disgust. "Hold your tongue," he said. Lot started to say something else and Mesha turned on him. "Shut up, I said! Shut up or I'll smash your face in."

"No you won't," Lot said. "You know good and well what will happen if there are any marks on us when they come after us."

"There won't be anyone coming after you. Get that through your thick head."

"Oh, won't there?" Zillah said. "Look. Abram's men are attacking from the heights now. Look, your people are falling back."

"Shut up!" Mesha said. He turned to Lot, his face red with rage. "Look, you. Keep that bitch's tongue quiet or I'll drop her off the cliff."

"Oh, you will, will you? And what will happen when your master hears of this? If indeed he's alive by dusk at all?" There were still traces of paint—of makeup, like a woman's—on the hostage's dusty skin; they lent a strange, unreal quality to Lot's dissipated face. It looked like a death mask—but what it resembled was the death mask of an old woman. Mesha's nose wrinkled in disgust, looking at him. And how old *was* the androgyne anyway? Forty? Surely no more.

Mesha turned away and watched the rout on the field. That was what it was—a rout. The soldiers of the Three Kings were falling back. Some of them were throwing down their weapons and running. The ones who ran fell under a hail of arrows from the barbarian bowmen on the left. *Stand, you cowards! Stand and fight!*

Lot drew Zillah aside, his eyes still on the field below. "Look, my dear," he said. "I think we'd better let him alone for a while. He's upset—and there's no telling what he'll do."

"Strutting Canaanite peacock! I hope Abram's men impale him."

"Abram wouldn't allow that. You know what a fuss-budget he is. But the thing to remember, my dear, is that we're no real good as hostages anymore. Not since the message came over that Abram wasn't going to be making any deals with anyone, or taking prisoners or whatever."

"I don't understand," Zillah said, brushing at a smudge on her robe.

"Why, what I'm trying to tell you is that he no longer has to keep us alive. If we can't be ransomed, then we can't be used to buy anyone's escape." There was a touch of irritation in his high-pitched voice. "I wish Abram hadn't done that. How dare he take such chances with my life?"

"You mean . . . this man could . . ."

"He could kill us and have done with it. And bolt and run. *I* certainly would, in his place, let me tell you. At any rate, my dear, I wouldn't twit him much more if I were you."

"You started it," she sniffed.

"Yes, I know. But I wasn't thinking. Now I've thought about it . . . and frankly, my dear, I'm not too happy with our present situation. We've no protection at all. Not any more. Oh, Abram, how could you do this to me?"

"The old fool! Let me tell you, if we get out of this I want to settle as far from him as possible. Always meddling, moralizing."

"I've been thinking about that. Abram's winning, you know. He'll be a power in Canaan when all this is over. I have no wish to live close to him either. And—Zillah. I like it in Sodom. There's such freedom

there. Around Abram I've always felt someone was
looking over our shoulders whenever we had a party.
Even back in Egypt, where . . . where the customs are
a bit looser. But . . . well, we'll be very big in Sodom if
we settle there. Bera will rebuild, you know, and we'll
have a bit of status there, as the niece and nephew of
the new power in the land. The city will be regarded as
being under Abram's protection, although he's sure to
pay it no mind at all. He hates cities. But it won't
matter. No one will dare attack it now. And we'll be
people of property: big people in town. So many of the
old rich, the old powers in the city, died in the raid.
We'll be virtual leaders of society."

"Ah. Now you're talking a language I understand."

"I thought you'd come around. But look, I think the
best course right *here* is to convince this fellow we'll
put in a good word for him—or perhaps that we'll
misdirect Abram's men when they come after us and
he takes off for the hills."

"Ah. You *are* a clever man, darling."

"Stay by me, my dear. By spring we'll be running
the most decadent salon the Valley of Siddim has ever
seen. For once you'll get your fill, perhaps. You'll
spend half your waking hours with your heels in the
air. Who knows?" he simpered prettily. "Perhaps I
might have a bit of fun too, myself. You will leave a
few of them for me, won't you, my dear?"

"Hmm," she said appreciatively. "Boys or girls?"

"Oh . . . let's leave that open. One mustn't be too
rigid about these things."

The Canaanite turned and faced him suddenly;
Enosh, in his headlong haste, almost ran him down.
The Canaanite aimed a vicious swing at him; Enosh
parried, as Sneferu had taught him to; feinted high;
and slashed low, opening the man's naked thigh almost
to the bone. The Canaanite let out a howl of pain and
rage and dropped his sword; Enosh ran him through,
kicked the body free of his sword, and, not waiting for
the man to fall, turned and looked around him.

Abram, tall and erect, a pike in his hand, stood atop

a knoll watching the rout. Rout? It was a slaughter. Below him Eshcol virtually beheaded a Canaanite warrior with a mighty blow, ignoring the red network of cuts that laced his own bare torso. His face was a mask of fury; it was something beyond anger, this spell that was upon him. As Enosh watched, he hit another soldier with the flat of his sword.

There was a noise behind him. Enosh turned and saw a Canaanite bowman stand and draw his bow. Abram! He was aiming at Abram! Enosh rushed forward. The bowman tried to turn, the arrow still notched, the bow drawn; but Enosh's sword knocked the weapon aside and the bolt flew wide. The bow fell to the ground; the bowman reached for the sword in his belt. Enosh looked down at the weapon and a sudden flash of hot rage ran through him. "Why, you bastard!" he said, incredulous. "That sword—that's one of ours. You took it off one of our dead!"

The bowman attacked; but the hot blood was in Enosh, and his hands suddenly seemed as strong as a blacksmith's, his arms as solid as oak. He battered the attack aside, drove the man back. "You son of a bitch," he said. "You scavenger—killing one of ours and taking his leavings! I'll teach you to . . ." He didn't finish the phrase. He didn't need to. The bowman's guard faltered; Enosh battered his point down with two quick, powerful blows and thrust at the man's face. The bowman screamed and put his hands to the red place where his right eye had been. Enosh slashed once; then he raised the sword high and struck mightily downward.

When the bowman fell, something made Enosh look down. The sword Belsunu had made lay at his feet. He looked to right and left, saw no immediate attackers, and stooped for it. He felt the magical power of the blade almost immediately. The handle clove to his hand like an extension of his arm. He opened his mouth in a fierce grin, swinging the weapon to and fro with exhilaration. He knew this sword! He'd helped its owner buckle it on . . . Sneferu's sword! His own!

Near him a Canaanite rushed Eshcol's unprotected

flank. Enosh bellowed a wordless battle cry and went after the man, his heart beating fast, the great sword singing in his hand.

VII

Brooding dark clouds had hovered over the imposing bulk of Mount Hermon through the whole of the battle, and a chill in the air which had gone all but unnoticed in the heat of the struggle now became oppressively noticeable. Now it was no longer a matter of fighting, of a contest between equals; it was a matter of pursuit and slaughter, of the tracking and killing, one man at a time, of what remained of Chedorlaomer's striking force. And, distasteful as the job was, it had to be done in cold blood, one weary stroke at a time. To compound the depressing aspects of the work, a chilly drizzle, rare to the east of the great mountain even in this, the season of rain, began to fall.

There had been numerous escapees from the punishing wrath of the amateur soldiers of the south—men who had turned tail and run at the first charge, and who had been seen seeking exit from the valley, either across the dry country toward Damascus or into the great eroded bulk of the Mount Hermon massif itself. "Let them go," Abram had said. "They will spread the news of our victory as a dozen bards could not." But now, with battle become rout and rout become debacle, the men of Mamre and Eshcol ranged through the field chasing down stragglers and hacking them to death one by one.

Enosh, bone-weary and chilled to the heart by the gray skies and sodden rain, plodded doggedly after one of the escapees. He had long since reached the point when the killing urge had left him; at the moment all he wanted was a quiet, and preferably dry and warm, place to rest for a while. Now, however, he followed the great, dejected-looking bulk of the man before him, his legs leaden, the breath coming in great gasps. For the life of him he could not narrow the distance between the two of them. He had tried—and his tired muscles had refused to cooperate. And, more times than once, he had thought fleetingly of turning back; but he was, he remembered, pursuing this man on Abram's particular command, and it still seemed important to him to impress Abram with his loyalty, fidelity, and valor.

Just as his legs felt as though they might give way under him, the man up ahead stopped, turned to face him. Enosh faltered in his steps; his hand tightened its grip on the great sword he had won on the field of battle. "You!" the man ahead said. "Go back now. Go back or I will kill you."

Enosh stopped, perhaps twenty paces short of his quarry. As he did there was a low rumble of thunder in the distance, and almost imperceptibly the gray drizzle became rain: the drops became larger and closer together. He shivered. "It is no use," he said. "Kill me you may. It is the only way you will get rid of me. Do we fight it out now, or . . . ?"

The big man looked at him, his expression one of bitter resentment. "You are a slave," he said. "In this country a slave does not raise his hand against a free man. Much less a king."

"King?" Enosh said. He took a step or two forward, blinking against the rain. "I see no king. I see only a drab, overweight man, wet as a drowned rat. As for who I am and what I am, I was born with as good blood as the next man's."

"You speak to Chedorlaomer, King of Elam . . ." Thunder, louder than before, cut off his other words. He straightened; Enosh could see he was a tall man, carrying perhaps too much weight for even his own great height despite the long days' march and all the fighting. Enosh suddenly wondered if, before this, the Elamite had done any of his own fighting or marching at all.

"I see only another poor devil like myself, and one my master has ordered me to slay." Enosh wiped his eyes with his free hand. "Come, let's get on with it. I'm cold and tired. Come, King of Elam. Kill me if you can."

Chedorlaomer sighed visibly, and advanced on Enosh, a broad sword, a little longer than the average, in his big hand. His eyes flashed with sullen rage; but all of the lines in his aging face drew inexorably downward. Enosh saw in his enemy a man even more weary than himself. As he advanced, Chedorlaomer slipped on the slick ground underfoot and went down to one knee; righting himself, he showed the measure of his fatigue. Yet the eyes held menace; Enosh, circling slowly toward better ground, remained wary.

Suddenly, from some hidden wellspring, the Elamite drew upon a reserve of vigor—and attacked. His first blow Enosh parried just below the hilt of his own weapon; the sheer power of the stroke shocked his whole arm, and he almost dropped the sword.

He gave ground before the attack. Chedorlaomer slashed, hacked, beat him backwards; most of his frantic parries, learned only months before at Sneferu's hands, fended off the sharp blade, but one sweeping blow caught him a glancing blow on the left shoulder, leaving the whole left side of his body covered with fresh blood. He gave ground once more, and would have been quickly killed if the Elamite's foot had not slipped again on the wet, uneven terrain.

There was no time to think. Enosh counterattacked, trying desperately to take advantage of his enemy's slip. He beat Chedorlaomer backward with wild, roundabout swings, none of them connecting solidly, most of them parried with a skill much greater than his own. Chedorlaomer fell to his knees in the mud; but Enosh's foot slipped and he landed heavily on his own rear end, unable to finish off his opponent.

The dank, dismal rain battered away mercilessly at them both as they slowly rose, struggling to find solid footing on ground that the rains had turned to slush. Suddenly a cold feeling of nausea dug at Enosh's guts, and depression gripped his heart. What a way to die— wretchedly tired, covered with small cuts and bruises, his shoulder hacked to pulp, ankle-deep in greasy, foul-smelling mud . . . and at the equally dirty hands of a man as wretchedly weary as himself. And all this under a sky of blue-black clouds in a dismal gray setting, with a ghastly, near-freezing rain drubbing the two of them, numbing body and soul alike.

So this was it. This was his last day. Or the other man's. There was a way in which it hardly mattered. For the winner there would be no victory. There would only be a marginal survival, and no glory, and afterward the feeling of having been dirtied, sullied, devalued by the whole experience. He spat into the mud, baring his teeth in the dirty face. "Come," he said hoarsely. "Come and kill me. I'm tired waiting for you."

Chedorlaomer rushed him—and went down again. Enosh raised his blade high and swung it backhanded. The blade cut through the Elamite's neck just below the corner of his chin, severing the big artery there. The Elamite had just been rising. The blow drove his head back; the blood spurted. Enosh swung the sword again and again. There was no science, no skill, in his wild swings; only desperation. Chedorlaomer's hands clawed at the mud, trying to find his dropped sword. His great shoulders cringed at the rain of blows. He tried to speak once, but the words would not come. He fell face-down in the muck, twitched once, and did not rise.

Enosh, weaving drunkenly above him, vomited up his guts, weeping uncontrollably. Then, mastering himself, he set to work cutting off his slain enemy's head. He had to have something to take back to Abram.

It took a day to gather the herds stolen from Siddim and to arrange for mounts for the seriously wounded. But by the next morning Abram's little army was ready to climb the hills and trek through the pass where there was ample graze for the animals. Keeping the huge bulk of the mountain on their left, they gained the path of the traders and made their way through a mountainside forest of oak and wild fruit trees into the valley beyond in bitter cold—cold that became visible on the slopes of the mountain above as the year's first snows struck the peaks of Mount Hermon. The trade route forded several rushing streams whose water was cold enough to numb their bare legs; but they comforted themselves by remembering that this was Jordan water —water that would wind eventually down to the Jordan and its lakes, to the Ghor, to Siddim itself. It was running water that pointed the way home.

The rains were heavy in the valley below, and they continued all the way to the sacred groves of Tal. When the gray cloud cover lifted for a day, they drove the herds down the river, through dense woodlands of trees, blackberry bushes, and flowering oleander. Willows clung to the river's banks, interspersed with the chaste trees.

They detoured past the swamps of the Hula fens— and the Egyptians in the party, displaced slaves all, wept at the sight of tall clumps of papyrus growing above the water. Yet in the waning days of fall, with little wildlife visible beyond the coots and wild ducks that dotted the ponds and sloughs on the fringes of the great swamp, there was an air of illness on this part of the land. The swamp-dwellers of the region were a sickly lot; their children—naked, sun-blackened—had gaunt looks, spindly legs, and swollen bellies. Humanity, Abram's people saw, did not do well here. Nowhere near so well, say, as the great flocks of pelicans that swooped majestically down on the water, raiding the great bounty of fish life in Lake Hula. They came by the hundreds, a great line of pelicans sailing low over the water, driving the fish before them. When they had concentrated the fish in the shallows, they would then come in even lower than before, trailing their pouched underbeaks just below the surface, coming up with great mouthfuls of the lake fish, their pouches streaming water as they took again to the skies.

Below the Hula fens the Jordan cut its way through a V-shaped defile and began dropping in a series of rapids toward Lake Chinnereth, bouncing merrily over black rocks amid dense clumps of oleander. And when they camped on the slopes above Chinnereth, with the blue water below them and feasts of fresh fish to be bought from the fishermen on the banks below, even the gray skies could not dampen their enjoyment.

Enosh was a minor hero by now: Abram had publicly commended him and had led the assembled members of his party in a mighty cheer for the man who had bested Chedorlaomer and driven the oppressor from the land. Enosh, blinking and trying to smile, had stood and received their cheers at Abram's insistence —but in his heart he thought, *Am I a hero then? A mighty warrior? Me, who barely managed to keep myself from being killed at the hands of a better fighter?* Common sense prevailed, however, and he held his tongue, deprecating the event privately whenever anyone brought up the subject. This, if anything, only made the situation more distasteful to him, since people tended then to comment upon his modesty. This drove him in upon himself; he grew even more quiet and withdrawn, while remaining polite and helpful when approached.

Abram, however, had begun showing him more attention of late. Now, as the Jordan, below the great lake, meandered slowly through cultivated land, Abram marched beside Enosh for as much as a morning at a time. For lengthy periods neither would speak; Enosh sensed that his silence was one of the things Abram liked about him just now. But at other times Abram would share his thoughts with the slave, as though they were equals. This Enosh was careful to cultivate; it gave him hope that his promised freedom would come soon, once the party had reached Mamre's Grove again.

It was understood that Abram, for the time being, would remain quartered in Mamre's country. Their purposes lay together for a time, and until the word had got around to the whole of Canaan that the combined might of Abram and of Mamre and his brothers had defeated—slaughtered—the invading, marauding armies, it was thought best to keep together. Once their reputations had been established there would be time for Abram to find new territory.

As the river wandered through bottomland and even

dense jungles, the land changed. Abram's eye lit up with pleasure, seeing the richness of the land, which, no more than a day's march from land as barren as Siddim itself, now sprouted impenetrable thickets, with forests of mixed tamarisk, poplar, and willow trees crowding the banks, laced with creepers. Hunters from Abram's party ranged ahead of the slow-moving herds, striking deep into the forest to slay game—and returning, on two occasions, with the skins of half-grown bears, already somnolent in the fading days of fall and easy prey for bowmen. One hunter claimed to have heard a lion's roar in the thicket, but no signs of the big predators had been seen by the time they left the forested strip. Encouraged, they encamped within sight of the forest, with Tell Azur looming high above them on the right.

After a double guard had been posted over the flocks, Abram took Enosh aside. "Come," he said. They made their way to Mamre's campfire, downstream from their own. "Mamre," Abram said without ceremony, "I'd like to ask a favor. Could you lead the party back to the grove without me? Enosh, here, and I have an errand."

"Errand?" Mamre said, looking up from the mending of a broken spear. "What errand?"

"I'm going to Jerusalem. I must speak to the High King there, Melchizedek. I think he has something to tell me, something I need to know."

"Ah. I'd almost forgotten. Well, you're right, it is a good time to do something like that, if that's what you've a mind to do. Go in peace. We'll get everyone home in good condition. But if I'm going to do you a favor, you'll owe me one in return. The one you promised me."

"Which?" Abram began. Then he stopped, smiled slowly, and nodded his head. "Yes," he said. "You're right. It's time. It's past time. Very well." He turned to Enosh. "So be it," he said. "We'll make things formal later. For now, consider it done. You know my word is good, and here's my hand on it." He extended his thin old hand to Enosh.

"I don't understand," Enosh said. "Pardon me, sir, but . . ."

Mamre's voice was gruff but good-humored. "He means you're not a slave any more. Do you hear me? You're free. As of this moment, before witnesses. Congratulations, my friend. You've earned it." He chuckled. "Go ahead, take his hand. He's not your master any more. He's your employer."

"And your friend," Abram said. "Your very respectful friend."

VIII

Enosh, still a little dazed after a sleepless night spent in thought, left with Abram early the following morning. The brothers, Mamre, Aner, and Eshcol, supervised the breaking of camp and, taking Abram's people in charge, integrated them with their own servants and slaves. The sun was high, however, when Mamre, awaiting news of the disposition of the stolen herds and holding the departure of the great caravan, finally saw Aner riding up from the rear of the column, an annoyed look on his face. "Well?" said Mamre. "What's the problem? Did you augment the herdsman and the rear guard?"

"I did that while you were still snoring," Aner said disgustedly. "No. Its that . . . that nephew of Abram's. He says he isn't ready. It's something about his wife."

Eshcol joined them just in time to hear Mamre's snort of derision. "What's the matter?" he said. "We've been ready to move out for some time now."

"I'll give you one guess," Aner said.

"Lot?" said Eshcol, his voice harsh and cutting. "By all the gods, Mamre, this time . . ." He shook his head. He spat into the dust. He pounded his fist into his palm. "No, damn it, I'm *not* going to hold my temper this time. Abram's not here. I know what you think about humoring the old man, but . . . I'm right, am I not? It is Lot. Him and that damned painted bawd of his."

Mamre looked at his two brothers, one by one. Then he spoke to Aner. "Were they ready when you left them?"

"No. The woman wasn't even dressed. I told her to cover up that lascivious rear end of hers, I didn't give a damn if she wore a bearskin. I told both of them they'd better be ready by the time I got back."

"Look," Eshcol said. "I'm going back and tell them a thing or two. I've had enough of this."

"All right," Mamre said after a moment's pause. "But—Aner. Go with him. Anything you say to Lot, Eshcol—I want a witness to it. For when Abram rejoins us. For some reason he favors this kinsman of his. And . . . mind you, I think a lot of Abram."

"So do I," Eshcol said. "But if this popinjay is blood kin of Abram's I'm a mongoose. I smell a cuckoo's egg there."

"Be that as it may, Abram is a valued friend of ours. Go ahead and say what you wish to Lot and Zillah, if it makes you feel better. But keep in mind that we still want to leave as quickly as possible. And for the love of all the gods, don't do anything that will cause a breach between us and Abram."

"Of course I won't," Eshcol said. But as he turned and spurred his horse down the path, Mamre could virtually feel the raw anger and nervous energy in him. He nodded to Aner, who set out after him, ten paces behind.

When the two dismounted, they saw Lot sitting on a fallen log, holding his chin high while a slave shaved him with a long, thin blade. Eshcol, fury in his eye, looked around. Lot's tent had not yet been taken down, and inside it a woman's voice hummed a familiar Canaanite tune whose words, both brothers knew, were the rawest sort of gutter utterance.

Eshcol stood for a moment, the rage boiling inside him. Then, drawing his sword, he strode over to the tent and slashed through the guy ropes. The tent collapsed, to anguished feminine screams. But when Eshcol turned back toward Lot, he saw that Abram's nephew had not even interrupted his morning toilet. There was a tolerant, amused smile on his weak features. He shrugged prettily. "Well, Zillah," he said, "you can't say I didn't warn you." He lowered his voice, speaking to his barber. "Easy there," he said. "Cut me and I'll have you flayed."

Eshcol let out a strangled cry of inarticulate anger. He raised his sword and hurled it point-first at the ground, where it stuck halfway up to the hilt. In one bound he reached Abram's nephew, elbowed the slave aside, and picked Lot up by the folds of his robe, slamming him against a lightning-splintered oak stump and holding him there, his frantically kicking heels a handspan off the ground.

"Look here," Eshcol said in a voice full of undiluted acid. "The rest of us have been ready to leave for a hell of a long time now. The only thing holding us up is you. If you think we're going to put up with this sort of thing, you're—"

"You let him alone!" Zillah, emerging from the collapsed tent in her shift, attacked him from behind, clawing with long talons. Eshcol, releasing his grip on Lot, backhanded her with one hand, knocking her sprawling. "Aner!" he bellowed. "Restrain this bitch for a moment, will you?"

He turned back to Lot, still holding him with one hand. "Look, you. I'm going to say this once and that's it. We're moving out, men, animals, and chattels, as fast as I can get back to the head of the column. You have that long to pack it all up and get mounted, you and that roundheeled alewife of yours, or we're leaving both of you here for the wolves."

"Look," Lot said, "you can't talk to me that way."

Eshcol cuffed him across the mouth, his face a mask of rage. "Be quiet and listen!" he said through clenched teeth. "I don't know what it is, this hold you have over Abram, but where I'm concerned, it won't work any more. Do you understand? Abram took off for Jerusalem this morning at daybreak. He left the whole column in my hands, mine and my brothers'.

That means that until this caravan is back in the grove our word is law."

Lot tried to speak again but Eshcol's hand went to his throat. "One more thing," Eshcol said. "The girl slave, the one who escaped from the enemy and made it back to us. Some of the wounds and bruises and flogging stripes on that poor skinny little body of hers were new, and could have been made by Tidal and his scum. But there were old stripes beneath these, and nobody could have made them but you."

"The girl," Lot said in a shaky but defiant voice, "belongs to me. I will do what I please with—"

Eshcol grunted and, coiling and uncoiling like a pit viper, buried his fist in Lot's soft belly, doubling him over in pain. Then Eshcol straightened him out again by sheer brute force and stared into his eyes, his voice shaking. "Hear me," he said. "I've been getting reports about you." He turned his head rapidly, addressing the slave. "You! Barber! Have either of these two touched you? Propositioned you? Answer me, or I'll—"

"Sir, please, I only do as I'm—"

"*You!*" Eshcol turned back to Lot, slapping him across the face, humiliating him. "You cowardly, buggerly bastard! You'd do it with an animal, wouldn't you, if the animal didn't have any choice in the matter? Both of you pigs!" He grasped Lot by the throat again. "Look," he said. "Hear me, once and forever. I'm keeping an eye on you from now on. And let me tell you this. You touch another slave of yours—or of anyone else's either, for that matter, damn your eyes—and whether you touch him or her to pat them on the fanny or flog them, news of it will reach me. Either of you, do you hear? That little girl who showed us her wounds . . . if you ever lay a hand on her again, in any way—if you give her away for a night to one of your damned pervert friends, or cause her any discomfort in any way again—"

"Eshcol!" Aner said in a cautionary tone.

"Quiet, Aner. I haven't finished. If *either* of you lays a hand on that girl again, or causes a hand to be laid on her, either in lust or in anger, so help me, I'll kill you. I'll kill you slowly. I'll weight your ankles down

with rocks and I'll sit you down on a sharpened waist-
high sapling and let that fat gut of yours drag you
down until the stake comes out of your eyes." He
slapped Lot again, hard. "And if the woman's guilty
too, so help me, I'll sell her into a whorehouse in
Damascus, minus her tits and nose. Do you hear that,
bitch?" he bellowed over his shoulder at Zillah. "Just
try me. Try me once."

Then he threw Lot away from him as if he'd
touched something contaminated with a vile disease.
"All right," he said. "Get it all packed. I don't care
how you do it. By the time Aner and I have reached
the head of the column, this caravan will be moving
out. Whether or not you care to join it is up to you.
But I've been away too long. I want to be home, and
anybody who delays me from here on in has made an
enemy he won't forget in a hurry. I don't give a damn
what Abram thinks of the matter. Do you understand?"

He waited for a moment for an answer and got
none, from either of them. Then he turned and mounted his horse in three steps and a single high vaulting
leap.

Enosh yawned for perhaps the fiftieth time, sitting
cross-legged atop a low earthen wall that lined the tiny
marketplace off one of Jerusalem's many squares. He
scanned the faces that passed. Would Abram never
come? Enosh must have dozed off; he felt a tug at his
arm, his eyes flew open and gazed right into Abram's
radiant face.

"Wake up, my friend," Abram said. "Wake up and
hear my news. I'm glad I came. So glad."

"Then your meeting with Melchizedek was produc-
tive?"

"I could hardly have asked for better. I hope you've
had lunch. Yes? Good. The High King fed me like
royalty. He blessed me, as one whose enemies the Most
High God had delivered into my hands. He told me the
God has laid his hand on me—that special things are
going to happen to me. Oh, Enosh, my friend, all these
years I have been working on nothing but faith—faith

in the dreams and visions which the Most High God has caused me to see, to experience. All this time I have been sustained by nothing more than my own faith in the veracity of my vision, of my mission. And now . . ."

"Yes, sir?" Enosh looked at the old man, at the near-ecstasy in his face. He wondered suddenly if he'd ever, in all his days, seen anyone so happy.

"Now, Enosh—I've met, and spoken with, one who has, like myself, heard the words of the Most High God, of El-Shaddai. One who heard the words before I heard them. One older in faith than I. I have spoken with a priest of El-Shaddai, an adept of the God. And . . ."

"Yes, sir?"

"Enosh, he confirmed everything—everything—that I've known in my heart for all these years, but have had no one to discuss it with. His experiences with the God were the mirror of my own."

"That's wonderful, sir!"

"No, more. They were a mirror of my own with one very important exception. The God has spoken with me about a covenant which is to come, a covenant between Him and me, and my heirs, forever. El-Shaddai, all praise to His name, has spoken to me of this . . . and he has not spoken so to his priest, Melchizedek. It is curious. Melchizedek spoke of me as one possessed by the God, as one chosen for great things . . . things which he knows will not happen to him or to his own seed. He blessed me. He spoke of a prophecy—a vision he had had that a man blessed by the God would come, and make peace in Canaan at sword's point, and found a great kingdom." He sighed, shaking his old head happily. "Enosh, I'm so happy. You can't imagine how happy I am just now."

Enosh bowed respectfully and said nothing for a moment. Then he spoke in a quiet but forceful voice. "Yes I can, sir. Begging your pardon, I think I can imagine it."

IX

And then Abram and Enosh rode home, and in a day the caravan followed them in, and things went back to normal in the settlement at Mamre's Grove. Only there was a subtle difference. Bera of Sodom visited them and greeted Abram with respect as one might greet an equal. Lot and Zillah, who had kept to themselves since their return, found their status with Bera much enhanced; they began making plans for a return to the Valley of Siddim—a permanent return—as soon as repairs could be made to the house they had purchased there.

There were visitors from Hebron, too—Abram said afterward to Mamre that their purpose seemed to be to reassure themselves that Abram's warlike ambitions were put aside—and as the weeks passed it became more and more evident that the word had been passed around: there was a new power in Canaan, one which had to be considered at all times by everyone in the region.

Lot's party was preparing to leave in the morning. To Shepset's dismay, Rekhmira was being left behind. His broken leg had not healed properly, and he would be left with a permanent limp. Abram had agreed to trade him for an able-bodied herdsman and to set him to less arduous duties. Shepset found him packing his few possessions a little before sundown. "Rekhmira," she said. "I've come to say good-bye. I'll miss you so. Tomorrow we go to Siddim . . . and with you gone I haven't a friend left there in the world."

"Ah," he said with a sad smile. He put down his blanket and gave her a brotherly embrace. "I'll miss you too, my dear. I wish you could stay, too. I thought for a while that Hagar was going to ask Abram for you."

"She did ask. Abram thought about it . . . and forgot. He has his mind on other things. Hagar's pregnant."

"Oh. That's too bad. I mean it's too bad for you. But . . . well, you've more friends than you think. Do you know a man named Ezbon? A slave of Lot's?"

"Yes. He worked for you on the hills above the city."

"Well, I had a talk with Enosh the other day, and he told me to tell you something. Look, Lot and Zillah have eased up on you since your return, isn't that right?"

"Yes. I suppose they're on their best behavior around Abram."

"No, no. It's not Abram they're afraid of. It's Eshcol. Mamre's brother, the one who lives down by the brook that bears his name, where the figs and pomegranates grow."

"I know who Eshcol is. But what has he to do with me?"

"He seems to have appointed himself your guardian. He admired the way you escaped and ran to warn Sneferu of the coming attack. And on the way home he had a row with Lot, and beat him up, and told him and Zillah that if he ever heard of their beating you again, or . . . trying to do anything with you . . . well, he told them he'd kill them if he ever heard of their mistreating you in any way. And . . . he's asked Ezbon to report to him if there's any trouble. So if they ever try to . . . well, do anything, anything at all . . . you just get a message to Ezbon. He'll get the message to Eshcol. And let me tell you, my dear, I wouldn't like to be the person Eshcol got mad at. He has a violent temper. Enosh says he fought like a hungry lion in the field, and he's strong as a bullock."

"Thank you. You reassure me. But it'll be lonely without you."

"Farewell," he said, shouldering his little pack and moving away in his painful cripple's gait. Shepset watched him go, her heart empty. Losing her only friend in Sodom would once have been the sort of thing to make her cry; but now her eyes were dry as dust. She was sure she'd never cry again.

X

Now came the season of rains, and Canaan turned as green as the Nile Delta. The hills were alive with narcissus and cyclamen and winter crocus, and in the meadows mandrake grew among them. The dripping boughs of the trees bowed low, and their leaves, already turned, began slowly to fall. Beneath them mushrooms and other fungi sprang up. The bead tree was bearing now, and the evening and the night were full of fruit bats, swooping down to eat the berries. In every puddle there was the croaking of frogs.

Winter came on little by little. It was a time of rare birds in the skies, a brief and fleeting time: flamingoes, black storks, cranes settled on the ponds to the north, and in the Jordan Valley the starlings came in great black clouds, darkening the sky. The trees were bare now, bending against the cold winds. Wild mammals of the region had their winter coats, and as Abram's hunters ranged far and wide in search of food, they returned, often as not, wearing capes made from the furs of the animals they had killed.

Then, imperceptibly, the weather began to turn. The air grew warmer and the grass more lush. The anemones came into flower all over the green land; in the south they were joined by irises, and to the north on the shores of Lake Chinnereth by fragrant hyacinths, as pale as the blue skies above. Pink cercis blossoms poked out of the ground, forerunners of the flowering trees and shrubs. Now even the Negeb and the desert came into full bloom, and in the riverless land white broom covered the rolling hills. Birds nested; the air was sweet with their songs.

Then came the season of the full flowering of the Negeb, and iris and tulip and stock and mallow shone in the yellow fields of dandelions. Oak and terebinth came into flower, their green leaves dotted with red. The styrax and arbutus bloomed. At the feet of the great trees rich undergrowth came abundantly to life: orchids, iris, tulips. In this profusion of color moved the newborn young of the mammalian life, while above in the higher branches the larger birds sat on their eggs. The smaller birds had already begun the spring migrations.

Then, in a day, the brief flowering of the Negeb was done, and the blossoms began to die all over the waterless land. To the north the woods remained in flower, and the mountain streams were thick with fish. In lands watered by the streams that flowed down to the Jordan, iris and buttercup lined the banks, edging aside the flowering annuals. The spring migrations of birds were in full swing now, and the sky was dark with great flocks of storks, with oriole and nightingale and turtle dove and rufous warbler. Along the scarp of the Rift the great birds of prey drifted north, their wings hardly moving as they sought the upward air currents and rode them, watching always for signs on the hillsides below, of the unwary young of the ibex and gazelle herds who grazed below. It was a time of great beauty, and the air was fresh and clear. The world had grown old and had been made new again.

And, one spring morning, the life inside Hagar stirred for the first time. She opened her eyes in the pale predawn light, instantly awake. Had she dreamed it? Or . . .

No! There it was again! A single tiny movement . . . then a stronger kick! She put her hand to her already-hard belly to feel it. *There!*

She pulled herself up onto one elbow. "Katsenut!" she said in a loud whisper. The slave lay on the blanket next to hers, the pastel light of the morning sun going halfway up her covered leg. She sat up, blinking. "Yes? My lady? Did you call?"

"Katsenut! It *kicked!*" Hagar sat up, her bent legs splayed before her under the robe. "It's alive in there!"

The slave blinked again . . . and smiled a sleepy smile. "Oh, how wonderful, my lady!" she said. Her words had a slightly perfunctory sound—the words of someone who had seen the whole cycle come and go many times over in the past—but she thought to add, "Here—may I feel it?"

"Yes . . . try it right here." Hagar guided the woman's hand to her belly. "Now . . . just wait . . . there! There! Did you feel it?"

"I certainly did. And a nice strong kick it was." The slave pulled her hand away. "Oh, look, my lady. We simply have to tell the lord Abram. He'll be so happy."

"Oh, let him wait," Hagar said, lacing her fingers snugly over the bulge in her front. "He'll be taking over everything soon enough. Let the baby be mine a little longer—just mine alone, something little and helpless and alive that's growing inside me."

"Yes, ma'am."

"There! There he goes again! Oh, Katsenut . . . I just know it's a boy! I just know it!"

"I hope you're right, ma'am. It'll mean so much to—"

"Did you hear me?" Hagar said irritably. "Can't we forget him for only a moment." She shrugged then, and let her narrow shoulders droop. "Oh . . . you're right, of course. You're always right, my dear. I'm sorry I was short with you. But . . . but isn't it wonderful?" She didn't wait for an answer, looking downward at her own distended belly. "How many months is it now?"

"Six, I think. We figured you'd have him by midsummer."

"Oh, how I wish Abram had astrologers here— someone to tell me what his destiny will be."

"The lord Abram broke with those people before he left Ur, ma'am. I heard from—"

"I know. I know. His religion. His precious religion." She sighed. "Well, I suppose I shouldn't complain. There are so many others who aren't doing as well as I am right now. Shepset. You."

"Oh, it's all right, ma'am. Really."

"No it isn't," Hagar said firmly. "But I can't do anything about it." She shook her head, as if to shake away the thought and all that went with it. "But you're right. I should go tell Abram immediately. Come, let us get dressed before he's up and about. He's supposed to be going somewhere today, on a trip."

"Yes, ma'am. Up to Jerusalem. In the mountains."

"Well, let us go." It was a duty, not a pleasure.

The few moments' delay in the tent, however, had cost them valuable time. Abram had arisen early and left for the grove shortly after dawn. In his place stood Sarai, hands on hips, a look of implacable hostility on her still-handsome face. "Yes?" she said. "What do you want?"

"Please, ma'am," Katsenut said. "We wanted to tell the lord Abram—"

"You!" she said. "You speak when you're spoken to. Do you want to be whipped like a tavern slut?" Her eyes flashed at the slave; then she looked at Hagar, and her expression did not soften in the slightest. "You, now. What business do you have with my husband?" She emphasized the last two words with considerable subtlety.

"Please, ma'am," Hagar said, softening her voice. "The baby . . . it moved inside me. I thought the lord Abram would be pleased."

"Ah. And no doubt he would. He talks of nothing else, more's the pity. But you . . . you're just here to curry favor with him, aren't you? Here to remind him once again that you—his concubine—can do what his legitimate wife cannot? You—"

"No, please. . . ." Katsenut stepped forward. When she did, Sarai lashed out at her with the fly whisk in her hand. The implement caught Katsenut across the face. The slave went to her knees, her hand across her face. Hagar caught a quick glance of fresh blood under the woman's hand.

"Get out of here!" Sarai shrilled at Katsenut. "Never show your face before my tent again!" Katsenut slunk away. "And you! *You!* Parading your big belly before me so shamelessly . . . I'll show you who's the wife around her and who's the servant!" She advanced on Hagar, the fly whisk poised, her face a mask of hatred.

Hagar backed away carefully, testing the ground behind her with a timid foot. "But . . . my lady . . . the whole idea of giving me to the lord Abram as a concubine was yours in the first place."

"I don't care! I want you out of here! Do you understand? You and that bastard in your belly! I want you away from me—you Egyptian slut!"

"Please, no."

"And as for Abram—well, let me tell you something. I complained about you and your uppity ways to him last night. And he told me, 'Do as you will with her.' "

"No! Abram wouldn't say that! He—"

"He wouldn't, would he?" That was all the coherent speech Hagar could dig out of Sarai's furious tirade. The rest was all screeching, bilious curses—that, and the blows she continued to rain on her pregnant and unsteady-legged rival. Hagar took the blows on face and head and shoulders, shielding her big belly with her arms. When she finally fell to the ground, she continued to shield her belly with her hands; but Sarai had turned on one heel and walked angrily away.

Hagar sat up and looked around. She held her belly. *Oh, please,* she thought. *Let the child be all right.* She saw several of Mamre's slaves watching her silently; as her eyes met theirs, she saw them turn their heads away and draw apart from her. "Oh, gods," she whispered. "She's humiliated me before slaves."

She got up carefully, holding her middle. Her eyes were full of sudden bitter tears. And, one hand still on her belly, she began to walk, hardly knowing which direction she was taking. Any direction would do, so long as it led away from Sarai, who had tried to kill her and the child inside her.

The sun was high. Hagar's sandals had begun to fray; she cast them aside and walked barefoot over the hard ground. Atop a rise, she looked before her, to where the spring sun had already begun to blast the waterless Negeb. Across that way, many days' walk, lay Enmishpat, and after that the lifeless stretch of Sinai, and after that the green delta lands she had left as a slave so many months before. She knew she would not reach there alive, and that the life inside her would not survive either Already the hot sun burned her unprotected brow; already the thirst had begun to plague her as if she had been marching for days rather than . . . but how long had it been? No, it didn't matter in the slightest, did it? Not now—now that there was no place for her in the world.

Someone missed her around noon. Mamre called his servants and slaves together and pieced things out. "Aner!" he cried. "Eshcol! Bring three mounts! Quickly! She can't have gone far."

But his heart sank as he said it. For one thing, he didn't know how long ago she had left, or in which direction she'd gone. And the slaves differed with one another on the severity of the beating she'd taken, but they all agreed Sarai had knocked her to the ground. And this late in her term, there was no telling how little it would take to force a disastrously early labor and a miscarriage.

Her face parched, her tongue swollen with thirst, Hagar sank down on a large flat stone. "I'll rest here," she told herself aloud. "Or perhaps . . . perhaps I won't go on. Perhaps this is where it all ends."

She blinked at the mirage in the distance. The horizon seemed to curve up and away from her; there was a lake of some sort in the sky. And in the lake there was . . . what? A man, walking on the surface of the water as if it were solid ground. A man dressed in white.

"Y-you," she said. "Whoever you are, go away. You'll die here. You'll die like me."

The man walked forward and stopped. He smiled and picked up a small stone and casually dropped it into a depression. She started to speak, but he held one finger to his lips. He gestured to her to wait; then she heard, from the depression—actually it was a hole in the ground, wasn't it?—a tiny splash. He smiled again and gestured at the hole. "Nobody's going to die," he said. "See? It's a well. Fresh spring water. Your instinct led you here, to safety."

"Who are you?" she asked.

"It is not important who I am," he said. She tried to fix his face in her mind but it kept changing. "You are Hagar, maid to the lady Sarai. But where are you going, Hakar?" His voice was calm and soothing.

"I . . . I was running away from my mistress," she said. "She wants—"

"Never mind what she thinks she wants," the man said. The only part of his face that did not change was the eyes. They were large and compassionate and friendly. "Sarai is confused and does not know her own mind. Come, get up. Go back to your people and do as you should do. You have a destiny to fulfill—a child to bear."

"My child?" she said. "But—"

"There, now," he said reassuringly. "It'll be all right. I can tell you now he'll be a boy, just as you've hoped. You'll call him Ishmael."

"Ishmael? But—"

"It's a good name," he said in that same calm voice. "It means 'God hears.' And the God has heard your cry, Hagar. He will make you the mother of a great nation. Your son will be a man of power, a free spirit, as untamed as the wild ass. He'll be strong and independent and nobody will be able to get along with him." His smile was warm and accepting now. "He'll be wonderful. And you'll be blessed for bearing him. Come! What better destiny could a woman want?"

His hands stretched out to her, comforting hands. She reached out to him, weeping openly and unashamedly. "Oh, yes!" she said. "Yes, yes."

Clouds drifted over the sun. The desert cooled. They found her there, not a double armspan from the well, sleeping quietly, her breath even. When she awoke she tried to tell them about the man who had spoken to her; but Mamre, avoiding her eyes, shook his head. Other than their own, no footprints but hers led to the well from any direction, any direction at all.

CHAPTER TWELVE

I

Zakir's first plan had been to start for Haran with the first spring thaws; but in the winter an order had arrived from downriver from Nabousakin for arms for the king's guard, and completing the commission took Ahuni another month of hard work. Then, as Zakir once again began to round up supplies and mounts for the long trek up the Euphrates, a second order arrived by messenger—this time from the Port of Mari itself. Standing in the marketplace while Ahuni packed his forge and tools, Zakir read the tablet, his face breaking out slowly into a big smile.

"Ahuni," he said. "Would you believe it? The noble Nabousakin has come to see us off!"

Ahuni's smile matched his own. "Wonderful, Father! Where is he?"

"Down at the Port Inspector's. How much more have you to do there?"

"I won't be long. Why don't you go meet him and I'll join you as soon as everything's secured?" The boy tugged at a strap, and Zakir noted once again the new muscles on his adopted son's chest and shoulders. *By all that's holy*, he thought. *He's getting to look like a real blacksmith.*

"All right," he said. He went away smiling, looking dapper and prosperous. Ahuni watched him until he disappeared behind a wall; then he set back to work drawing his parcels tight. On his knees in the dust, he hardly noticed the normal workaday crowd around him; but after a time he became aware of a presence quite nearby. He looked down at the street and saw a purple robe, a pair of slim, sandaled feet. His eyes followed the robe upward, and his face broke out into another grin. "Tavas-Hasina!" he said. "Hello!" He stood and brushed off his hands.

The courtesan looked him up and down, approving what she saw. "My, my," she said. "Can this be the same Ahuni who first came to my rooms to meet Etillitou last summer? Or was it last fall? Goodness, you're turning into a real man."

"I'm a smith," he said, pleased with her praise. "How nice to see you!"

"Well, if you haven't seen us lately, whose fault is that? And here I see you preparing to leave us for good. Shame on you."

"Well . . ."

"Oh, I understand. You've got to go where your destiny calls. But let me tell you, you'll leave a trail of broken hearts behind."

"Really?"

"Don't tell me you haven't noticed. The butcher's girl. Several marriageable daughters right here in the market. Etillitou herself—and you know, she isn't easily impressed." She watched him blush and fidget, then let him off the hook. "And now I think of it, I'll miss that big bear Zakir more than I can say." Her voice changed, softened. "I *will* miss him. A woman likes a man she can talk to . . . afterward, I mean."

"Awww—"

"I know. You don't know what to say. Well, maybe that's one reason the women like you. You never hand them a line of nonsense. You talk straight. Never forget that, Ahuni. Women like moonshine, a little at a time, in the right places . . . but only where it isn't important. In the important places they like having you be honest with them. They're very practical. They have to be. It's your impractical men who make up all the songs and poetry. Poetry isn't what we're all about."

"But . . . why do the men make it up, if it's not for you?"

"It's the way their minds work. The gods put them in that impressionable frame of mind so we can snare them and make husbands of them." She sighed. "Husbands. Ah, well. Anyhow, the men make up the songs because they think it'll please us. When, after all, the thing that pleases us is the attention. Why, look. Look at you, now. You're paying attention to every word I say."

"Of course, Tavas-Hasina."

"Of course. Well, let me tell you, if it were the baker or the rope-merchant I were talking to, there wouldn't be any 'of course' about it. They'd be pounding dough or picking at stray fibers. And that's where the difference lies. Ahuni, don't let anything that happens to you in life change that about you. You keep right on giving a woman your whole attention when you're talking with her. You hear?"

"Yes, Tavas-Hasina."

"Good. Now don't forget. That's as valuable a piece of advice as you'll ever get in your life, my young friend, and you're getting it for nothing—and from Tavas-Hasina of Mari, who never gives anything for nothing." She frowned slightly, smiled, and thought about something far away. "Well, almost never. For Zakir, perhaps . . . but look. Tell him to drop by and say good-bye, won't you?"

"Yes, I will . . . and ma'am?"

"Yes?"

"Thank you for the advice."

Ahuni stood watching her go, thinking. He smiled a small, appreciative smile. Then he turned and looked around the marketplace. A skinny urchin of perhaps ten lurked at the edge of the retaining wall, his eyes warily on Ahuni, his nervous, bony body ready to run at a moment's notice. "Hey," Ahuni said. "What's your name?"

The boy stared. His mouth worked but he said nothing.

"That's all right," Ahuni said. "You don't have to tell me. Believe me, I understand your caution." He switched to the all-but-unintelligible thieves' argot of the city, his voice low. "What's the matter?" he said. "On the run?"

The boy answered with his eyes.

Ahuni continued in the gutter *patois*. "Don't worry. I won't tell on you. Look, damn it, a year ago I stood where you stand right now. Only it was in Babylon, and if you think being on the run is tough here—"

"You? I don't believe it. Let me see your slave-mark."

Ahuni grinned and lowered for a moment the bracelet on his thick bicep. "See? The crossmark through it hasn't been there long. But you're right not to trust me." A sudden impulse ran through him; a disturbing, thrilling thought. What if . . . ? "Look. We're leaving town soon. How'd you like a new chance? A chance at freedom? Huh?"

"Are you kidding?"

"No, I'm not. And I can't guarantee anything. But I'll try. In the meantime . . . watch these things here, would you? Until I get back? See that nobody runs away with anything? Not that anybody's likely to try. The parcel with the tools weighs as much as a young water buffalo."

"Watch it? What do I do if anyone tries to steal it? Call the guards?" The scorn was heavy; but there was a friendlier tone to the voice than before.

"Are you crazy? Raise some kind of a ruckus. Knock over a vegetable stand. That'll bring the guards running, all right—and the people who're trying to steal my belongings will take off quickly enough. Then you can double back and meet me outside the walls at sunset, below the third lantern, where the caravan's forming. All right?"

The wary eyes flashed; but the head nodded yes.

The giant bodyguard showed Ahuni through the line of guards to Nabousakin's tent at the river's edge. Zakir and the trader stood outside, looking out over the water; both smiled as he approached. "Ahuni!" Zakir said. "Look at this, will you?"

Ahuni saluted the trader politely and only then looked at the implement in Zakir's left hand. "Why, that's . . . that's one of ours, isn't it?"

"No it isn't," Zakir said. "The pattern's ours, but the work is someone else's." He held up a distinctive-looking fisherman's gaff. "And guess where our noble patron found it?"

Nabousakin intervened. "I have, as you may have guessed, a new supplier—not only of fisherman's gaffs, but of rope. As insolent a rogue as I've met in years—and as endearing, too, in his way. A blackened, emaciated scoundrel from some benighted village a day's sail up the Euphrates from Babylon. But he does good work, and—"

"Binshoumedir!" Ahuni said, delighted. "Have you seen him, sir?"

"Yes, I have, my boy—and he sends you his best, both of you. Well, you may prefer having him put it some other way. 'Tell those two half-drowned river rats I picked out of the waves last year,' he said, 'to have a drink on me.' He went on a bit in that vein. I suppose you know what to expect from the likes of him."

"We do," Zakir said. "A great friend of ours, to whom we owe our lives and more. A cuff from Binshoumedir is like a caress from someone else."

"Well, be that as it may, I suspect that you've paid your debt to him—if that gaff is a pattern of yours, and if you've given him the right to market it. Nobody on the waterfront from Babylon to the Gulf will use anything else now if he can help it. I have orders backed up for a month or two. And although he's only been in business since the solstice, his shed at the Bazaar of the Three Palms now sells more, because he has better rope and gaffs, than any in the city."

"Oh, I'm so glad," Ahuni said. "How I'd love to see him."

"Well, I can't do anything about that," Nabousakin said. "He's too busy to take time off. He's going to be a rich man, and that village of his will be a city before he's much older. Cities have been built on weaker foundations than that, let me tell you. But you two, now: are you ready to go?"

"Ahuni?" Zakir said. "Is the forge packed?"

"Yes, Father. And . . . Father? Could I have a word with you?" Zakir pulled closer to him; Ahuni whispered in his ear.

Zakir stepped back. "Well, it's risky, but . . ." He turned to Nabousakin. "Some nameless urchin he's befriended. He wants to smuggle him out of the city. But the guards . . ."

Nabousakin looked at Ahuni. His contemplative frown turned to a thoughtful smile. "Ah," he said. "You remember your own beginnings, don't you, my boy? All the better. You'd be a much worse person if you didn't. How well do you know the child?"

"Not at all," Ahuni said. "But . . . I looked at him and saw myself. And suddenly I knew that I had to try to give him a chance. If somebody had given me one when I was his age . . ."

"Think no more of it," Nabousakin said. "I'll see that the caravan gets a day's march up the river before anyone thinks of inspections. I enjoy a certain relationship with the customs and border officials hereabouts. And since the treaty with Haran last winter, one doesn't have to present quite so many credentials as before. Just tell them he's a slave of yours. My name carries some weight in Haran."

"We're in your debt, sir," Ahuni said.

"Ah," Nabousakin said. He looked out over the great river, his eyes misty. "You're about to set out on the Great Adventure, my boy. The world is wide beyond your remotest imaginings, and it is full of an infinite number of people—people speaking a hundred tongues and owing allegiance to a hundred lords. You haven't the smallest notion, right now, how complicated your life will have become by the time you're my age, or half my age. But the one unifying factor in it all will be debt. Your life will be a neatly interlocking network of debts, large and small, and only some of them monetary. Look, I am indebted to a dozen people already today—from the soldier who saluted me respectfully even before knowing who I was to the woman who smiled at me in the street without *caring* who I was. All of them, all, enrich my life. And how can I repay them? Well, I'll tell you. I can't. It is one of the oddities of this world that we can never quite repay the precise people to whom we owe the intangible debts. All we can do is to pass the favors along. Look, I'm pleased with you. You're doing the right thing. It justifies my faith in you. It tells me that I've chosen the right people to represent me in Haran."

"Thank you, sir," Zakir said. "We'll do what we can to keep right on justifying your confidence in us."

"Yes, sir," Ahuni said. "We'll make you proud of us, sir. Just you watch!"

The boy was gone when Ahuni returned to the forge. He hired porters to carry their gear to the caravan outside and spent the afternoon supervising the loading. Then, at dusk, the guards lit the lanterns before the main gate to Mari. Zakir left to go inside and say farewell to Tavas-Hasina; Ahuni looked around for his little friend. His eyes had swept the scene three times before he realized that he was, in fact, standing almost within arm's length of the boy, who stood frozen against the wall, half hidden by a tall basket. "Hey," Ahuni said. "It's all right. You can come out."

"The guards came," the boy said. "I did as you said."

"Look, we're going to take you with us. You—"

"Take me with you?" the boy said. "Where?"

"All the way to Haran, if you like. Look, it's all right. Really. We have protection—from a pretty powerful source."

"But—"

"I know. You don't believe it. Well, I wouldn't have, either. But I'd have been wrong." He looked at the urchin's knobby ribs. "How long has it been since you've eaten?"

"Y-yesterday."

"Gods. Well, come with me. I'll get you some gruel. You probably won't be able to handle anything more.

And I'll show you where to bunk down. You'll need to get a good night's sleep. We're going to march your tail off tomorrow."

"Tomorrow?"

"Of course. We leave at dawn." He looked around. The darkness was coming on fast; a cool river wind stirred the flames in the lanterns. "I was going to ask your name, but it'll keep. Come on." He turned on one heel and set off, leaving the boy to follow. Then he stopped and looked around. "Come *on*."

"Belanum," the boy said. "My name is Belanum."

In the caravan encampment some of the ostlers and porters struck up a song. It was a slow march, but there was nothing of sadness in it for all its slowness. Ahuni caught a word here and there, a word in a dialect of Padan-aram. The song was one of thanksgiving. A song of homecoming. It was a song of Haran.

CHAPTER THIRTEEN

I

In the night a vision came to Abram. At first there was darkness, and then there was a soft light. And the light grew more intense, and soon it came to blot out all else. Abram—he seemed to be standing somewhere, but he could not place it—held his hand before his eyes, but the light struck him down to his knees. He trembled with fear, as he had done so many times before. He was in the presence of the God.

He was sick with fear; but in a moment there came a voice to him, a voice inside his head. It was as if he did not have to hear it with his ears. And the effect on him was calming, but it did not calm him altogether. He remained on his knees, his hands shaking, his eyes struck blind by the great light.

"Don't be afraid," the voice seemed to say. *"I am the shield that guards you from harm. I am your reward and your blessing."*

"Blessing?" Abram said in a weak voice. "How have I deserved blessing? I am nothing and nobody. I deserve nothing."

The voice went on as if he had not spoken at all. *"I am He who brought you from Ur to take this land for your own, yours and your descendants'. Listen, Abram. You tremble. You disbelieve. You are afraid to believe. Rise now, and come with me. Go to the herds, to the butchering pens, to the dove coops. Select me sacrificial animals: a heifer, a ram, a pigeon, a turtledove. Quickly, now! Quickly, while all the rest are asleep. Quickly, to the hills! I will give you a sign."*

And then he was awake, sitting erect and blinking about him in the thin predawn light. He shook his head; then, quietly, he stole from his bed and went out into the chill of the morning. I must be mad, he thought, knowing the arduous ritual of sacrifice, knowing what was expected of him. I must be a fool. But he went to the pens and selected the animals asked of him, and the birds; and he led them to the hilltop above his camp, to a small depression atop the hill where he had built a small stone altar. There he butchered the animals and killed the birds according to the prescribed ways. Then he sat on a flat stone before the altar and waited. The sun rose high. He had brought nothing to eat or drink. He sat, patiently, prepared to wait. When the birds of prey began circling over the freshly killed animals, he pelted them with stones, driving them away; but this required great vigilance and persistence.

Shortly after noon one of his servants started up the hill after him; but Enosh, spotting him, called the servant down again. The standing order was that nothing was to intrude upon Abram at these times. "But sir," the servant said. "It's a hot day. Out there, with his head uncovered, he—"

"Never mind," Enosh said. "I appreciate your solicitude. But he wants it this way. And nothing is to disturb him, or break in on his thoughts. It's the way of things. I'm not going to change it. Not if he dies up there. But he won't, you know. He has a stamina you or I might envy."

And the hours passed, and the birds circled, and Abram stood his vigil. And the sun grew low.

At sundown Hagar's pains began. "Ah!" she cried. "Katsenut! Please! Help me! Ahhhh . . ."

The slave held her. "Now," she said. "Breathe deep, my lady. Deeply. Slowly, if you can. There, now. When it hurts, squeeze my hand. Yes! Hard! Harder!" She looked with some misgivings at Hagar's distended belly. The child was a good two weeks overdue, if she was any judge. The girl's belly was huge: the child would be a large one, and a lusty one, from the powerful kicks she'd felt earlier under her hand. She called to a passing slave. "You! Get help! The lady Hagar is in labor!"

The dusk winds struck up, and there was a sudden chill in the air. Abram sat where he had. And soon, as all but the swallows abandoned the skies, a great drowsiness came over him. And his head slumped onto his chest.

Suddenly he felt, in his dream, a pang of intense horror and fear. A feeling of deep foreboding came over him, and he trembled with terror. For somehow, he knew for the first time, truly, that he would indeed be the father of a nation. But now it was those descendants of his—the ones he had hardly dared believe in before this—that he feared for. Somehow, the terrible fear that had come over him now had to do with them.

"Please," he said. "What's happening to me? Help me, please. I can't understand. I'm afraid . . ."

And little by little the vision came into his mind. He saw a son, another son; he saw daughters and grandchildren. He saw his seed multiply and pair off and generate, and he saw them spread out over Canaan, looking down on it all as if he were a bird flying above it. He saw the land black with the descendants of Abram. He saw a time of growth, and of expansion and building; he saw . . .

"No!" he said. He covered his eyes. But his hands had no substance in this vision, and he saw through them as if they had not been there at all. The terrible vision darkened. He saw his people, the people of his blood, enslaved, taken prisoner in a foreign land. There they labored in bondage for many generations. Children were born, grew, matured, married, had children, grew old, died—all in slavery, all in subjection to foreigners. Centuries passed.

Then the darkness began slowly to lift. He saw them

come together, pool their forces, throw off the foreign yoke. He saw them march into the wilderness singing. He saw them return to Canaan, tough, hardened fighters; conquerors. He saw the nations fall before them: the Kenites, the Kenizzites, the Kadmonites, the Hittites, the Perizzites, the Rephaim, the Amorites, the Girgashites, the Jebusites, all of Canaan. A great nation, sundered once and now made whole, and all honoring his own name, father of nations, forever. And his heart leaped up to see them: his sons and daughters all, spreading out over the land, making children, their hearts full of the praise of the God for all time.

The contractions continued. It was a difficult labor. "Hold on, Hagar!" Katsenut whispered into her ear in a warm and soothing voice. "Now . . . push! Push!"

Hagar's screams carried far out into the evening air. Men, passing, winced and made signs against evil. Married women bit their lips; the unmarried and those who had not borne children yet sat with wide eyes and felt Hagar's pain for her, the cold sweat on their brows.

Abram opened his eyes. It was dark; the moon was high and the stars were thick over the hillside. He shivered against the chill and felt for the first time the pangs of a hunger he had not recognized through all his long vigil over the sacrifices.

It had all been a dream. He frowned. A dream. And now he could not feel the presence of the God at all. He could feel only the chill of the night fog in his old bones. All of a sudden he felt old. *Well,* he thought, *it's about time you started feeling your age. And perhaps acting it. You've had a hallucination, and . . .*

And then, before the light appeared at all, he felt it once again, and a totally different kind of shiver ran through him. He fell to his knees. He clutched his skinny biceps through the thin robe he had worn onto the mountain.

The God was in the grove with him.

And now the light was something different. It was

not the cold light of the morning's vision. Now it was that of a blazing, all-devouring flame. Fire that required no fuel to burn: hot, hot. . . .

And from the great cauldron of fire came a single flame, and it rose and flew to the altar where he had laid the animals' carcasses, and as he looked, the flame licked at the butchered remnants of heifer and ram and consumed them, and the birds as well. A jaunty, lusty flame, burning brightly and merrily until all trace of the meat was gone.

And then it all began to fade. And the flames grew small, not as if they were going out but as if they were going rapidly farther and farther away from him. And he watched them disappear without dying, leaving behind only the blasted altar and the moonlight and the hillside, and a thoroughly chastened Abram, who stood, shivered, and looked back once at the altar before slowly turning to find the path down the hill.

Hagar's face was a mask of pain. "It's tearing me apart!" she said in a hoarse voice between piercing screams. "It's . . ."

And then the real pain began. It was more than she had ever been asked to bear. It was more than anything she had ever imagined. Others held her arms and legs. She kicked, screamed. She . . .

. . . and all of a sudden the pain lifted and she almost fainted for a moment. And the hands still held her arms and legs; but down there someone held a pink-and-red thing high, covered with blood and trailing a long wet string of something. And there was, in the sudden silence left by the absence of her own screams, a tiny wail, insistent, nasal, high-pitched. A cry of pain at coming into a new world.

She reached her hands up the moment they released her. But somehow her coordination was all off, and for some reason she hardly had the strength to raise her arms. She tried to speak and her voice was a soft, weak croak. "Please . . ." she said. "Give him . . ."

"My lady!" Katsenut said, bending over her. "It's a boy! A man-child! Large and lusty and strong!"

"Give him to me," Hagar said. Her voice failed her halfway through. "Please. I want him."

"Please, my lady. Wait a moment. They're tying the cord. Just rest, rest now. You've had a . . ."

Hagar pawed at her arms with hands grown suddenly a mite stronger. "No," she said. "Give him to me. Give him to me now. He's mine. I have to . . ."

Mamre's wife held up the child. It continued to squall loudly. Hagar, blinking in the half-darkness, made out closed eyes, a wide-open mouth, features contorted by crying. Tiny ears. Little arms and hands, waving impotently in rage and pain.

My son! she thought. *Mine!*

Somehow, after another glance at the tiny, naked body wriggling in the woman's hands in the light of the dancing flames, Hagar managed to get the strength to raise herself on one elbow. "Give him to me," she said in a hoarse voice that was quickly losing its weakness. She sat up, took the baby from Mamre's wife, lay back down with it, held it to her, her hands on its tiny head and back, pressing it to her naked breasts. "There, there," she said. "There's my own. There's mother's darling. There he is. There. . . ."

Katsenut leaned over her again. "Oh, my lady, I'm so happy. He's a beautiful child. He's a giant! A big strong bear of a boy."

Hagar suddenly found herself weeping; sobbing. *He will be a man of power,* she was thinking, remembering. *A free spirit, as untamed as the wild ass. He'll be strong and independent.*

But now? Now he was tiny and helpless; he could do nothing in the world for himself—and he was hers. He was hers as long as she could keep him. In time Abram would want to take him away: *"His* son." The man always treated the matter that way. When puberty came, the rituals would intervene between mother and child and he would be turned over to the men who would certify him as a man like themselves, and he would never again live with women in the same way.

She felt the warm, wrinkled, soft skin under her hands and, her eyes still streaming, crooned softly into the tiny ear so close to her mouth, hearing the crying abate little by little. *You're mine,* she thought. *The men's notions will come and go, but you'll have me forever, little one. And they'll never take you away from me, never.*

"My lady, I sent someone to tell the lord Abram."

Hagar looked up at Katsenut. She sighed and felt weak again. "Yes," she said. "He should know. He'll be so proud. He'll . . ."

But there was another presence around the little fire. All of them could feel it. Katsenut turned . . . and there was Sarai standing above them. She looked down once, hard, at mother and child, and Hagar shivered at the malice in her glance. She hugged the child closer to her, still crooning hoarsely into its ear. She looked Sarai in the eye and suddenly felt a fierce surge of pride. Her own eye flashed, and she saw Sarai wince. And the look of hatred that came back at her a moment afterward was enough to strike terror into Hagar's soul. Then Sarai turned on one heel and stalked out of the circle of women that surrounded the new mother. She had come and gone and said nothing, nothing at all.

Hagar turned back to her baby. "Look at him," she said. "All that dark hair, and so big and strong. . . ."

She held the child to her cheek, feeling the delicacy, the softness of his skin. "Give me something to cover him with," she said. "He's cold. There, now, my darling . . . there, my own."

Katsenut smiled at her, timidly. "My lady? Has . . . I mean, have you thought of a name for him?"

"Yes," Hagar said, passionately. "His name is Ishmael. 'God hears.' Yes, yes. Ishmael!"

Down in the grove the trumpets sounded and were answered from a post on the hill above. They announced the birth of a boy-child, the coming of a dynasty long deferred. The coming of a king in Canaan.

BOOK
TWO

CHAPTER FOURTEEN

I

The great gathering took well over a month to come together. First to arrive were the tribesmen of Canaan itself, from Dor south to the Negeb. Then these were joined by parties from Bashan and Moab, and emissaries from the dwindling Phoenician settlements along the banks of the Great Sea: Sidon, Tyre, Berytus, Gebal. By the time two weeks had passed, Mamre's Grove had played host to visitors from Ugarit, up in Hittite country, and to fierce Bedouin tribesmen from the Midianite wilderness far to the south. Gifts, too, had been received from seafaring peoples whose ships called at Canaanite ports and who had reason to wish for peace between their peoples and those of Abraham, once called Abram but now called by a new name, which meant "Father of Nations." (His wife's new name was Sarah, meaning "Princess.")

The deference paid him followed the protocol of the region; Abraham, an uncrowned king in Canaan in terms of wealth, power, and prestige, commanded after fourteen years' stay in the lands between the Jordan and the Great Sea the attention and reverence of all peoples within the area, although he had never demanded tribute in tangible form. Now, when he called a great spring festival to celebrate the thirteenth birthday—and the coming to official manhood—of his firstborn son, Ishmael, it was expected that every tribe and every city would send its complement of visitors and emissaries. And as the festival wore on, the hills and valleys below Mount Hebron were covered with the encampments of Abraham's neighbors.

Now, however, astonished scouts on the fringes of Abraham's domain sent runners to the grove to announce a truly unexpected sort of visitor: an Egyptian official, apparently of high rank, accompanied by a crack troop of fierce Shairetana warriors. The sight of an Egyptian war party was so far beyond the commonplace that some members of Abraham's party feared for their safety; but Abraham, calm as ever, kept his head and sent his own hastily assembled troop of guards ahead under Enosh's command, with instructions to welcome the representatives of the Lord of Two Lands with all possible courtesy.

The armed guard once disposed of, Enosh escorted the ranking visitor to his sovereign lord's tents. He was plagued by the thought that somewhere he had seen the officer before. But where? He shot one nervous glance after another at his companion, trying to put a name to the face. He had been introduced to the officer by rank alone, first in flowery hieratic Egyptian, then in passable Canaanite; but no name had as yet been attached to the haughty, hawklike Egyptian who limped along silently beside him.

As they approached Abraham, Enosh began his involved and overstated introduction, as he'd been told to do; but halfway through it the Egyptian held up his hand. "Peace," he said. "The lord Abraham and I know each other, I believe." He grinned and bowed, at once courtly and offhand. "Nakhtminou, commander of the garrison at—"

"Ah!" Abraham said, stepping forward. His smile was warm and accepting. "Nakhtminou! Yes! It's good to see you!" He held his arms out; the two men embraced formally. "Enosh," Abraham said. "This officer was the emissary of the Egyptian king at Sile when we left Goshen. Don't you recognize him?"

"Ah . . . yes, sir. I was trying to remember where I'd . . ."

But Abraham turned away from him, motioning Nakhtminou toward his tents. "Well, sir," he said. "It's pleasant to see a familiar face after all this time." He looked the visitor up and down. "You've remained fit, I must say."

"Relatively," the Egyptian said. "As you can see, my fortunes have changed somewhat, as have yours. It's aged me some. I've a bad leg now, from an old war wound that didn't bother me much when I was younger. I'm a lot grayer. But you? You don't seem to have aged a day."

"It's a family characteristic," Abraham said. "We're long-lived in my family. Come, you'll take refreshment with me, won't you? Here, I insist upon it."

Nakhtminou looked at his host again, his sharp eyes missing nothing. *If anything he's grown younger,* he thought. *And grown half a handspan taller.* He shook his grizzled head and grinned incredulously. "As you wish," he said.

Three courses of viands came and went, and two flagons of home-grown wine from the slopes of Mount Hebron. Nakhtminou's appetite had not diminished; he drank heartily. This had brought on a reflective mood. "I can't get over the change in you," he said. "You've certainly grown into the role of leader here." He belched unconcernedly. "Incidentally, the Lord of Two Lands was most pleased to hear of your turning back that Elamite incursion some years ago. You saved us from having to mount a large and very costly expedition ourselves."

"It cost us little to do the job," Abraham said. "All thanks to Sneferu, who trained our men and led them through the first battles. I think you knew him?"

"Ah, yes. An old friend indeed. We served together far up the Nile as youngsters. We were hardly more than children at the time. Funny, I was thinking of him as we were coming in. . . ." But a cough interrupted his thoughts; a racking cough from deep inside his chest.

"Here, some wine," Abraham said. "You've been ill."

"Well, yes," Nakhtminou said, once he had mastered the spasm. "In a way that's why I'm here. I mean . . . I had worked myself to a place of some

eminence in Lisht . . . but I'd picked up a touch of the
lung disease in my travels, and it laid me up for a
while. When I was better I found that my job had been
given to someone else . . . and the Lord of Two Lands
had made his feelings known. He didn't want a lunger
around him. Too depressing. So it was back to the
hinterlands. Actually it's been good for me. I spend as
little time at that damned, damp Sile as possible, and
as much as I can out inspecting his majesty's far-flung
domains. And—like this Canaan of yours—those tend
to be dry places with thin air. If I keep on the road
enough I may last another ten years."

"Well, I wish you the best of health," Abraham
said. "We lost a good friend to this disease . . . but
here, I see you wear a weapon he made. That can have
come from no other hand."

"This?" Nakhtminou held up his sword. "I got this
masterpiece from Ka-Nakht before he retired. You
knew the man who made this? I envy you. But you say
he died?"

"Yes. Some years ago. He was a great man, a man
much loved among us. Named Belsunu." Abraham's old
eyes grew misty for a moment. "I think," he said, "that
he was the loneliest man I have ever known. It hung
over him like a cloud." He told the tale of Belsunu's
loss of his family and of his fruitless pilgrimage in
search of his lost son. "It is curious. Now that I have a
son of my own I think often of Belsunu. I think I
understand more clearly the extent of his loss."

"Yes," Nakhtminou said. "One of the ways you can
tell I've aged is the fact that I seem to have lost all the
armor on my soul. I used to be cynical about these
things. But now when I look about me and see some of
the misery that descends upon so many of the people
in this life . . ." He shook his head. Abraham, looking
at him, began to see in his somber face signs of the
illness that lay upon him. "Well, anyway, this Belsunu
was a hell of an armorer. I'm proud to have a weapon
of his. If I had a son to leave it to—"

"Ah. Well, it's not too late."

"Perhaps. Look at you." Nakhtminou, thinking
suddenly of a dark-skinned boy he'd seen on the way

into camp, felt a sudden thought run through his mind. "Anyhow, you've made yourself a son, and at an age greater than mine."

"By far. And he's a fine, strong lad too. His name is Ishmael. His mother was a slave in the household of Psarou the scribe, in Sile. Now she is my concubine."

"Ah. Your wife, then, is—"

"Barren so far. Of course, if she were to conceive, it would be her son, if son it were, who would become my heir under our laws. But for now, I have Ishmael. A fine, strapping boy, healthy as a wild ass, high-spirited. I'm afraid I spoil him a great deal."

"And this festival? It celebrates his majority?"

"In part. His, and the majorities of a whole group of young men sired by their fathers during our first year here and born the following spring. It will also be a festival of the sealing to our God of the people of my blood and those who follow them."

"I see. I understand you practice circumcision here."

"Yes. It is common through the whole area, among those who follow the false god Baal as well as among us who follow the word of El-Shaddai." Abraham saw the light of interest die out in his visitor's eye, but went on. "After this our custom will be to circumcise all male children on the eighth day after their birth. All of us have already been sealed to our faith thus. But I bore you with our tribal customs."

"No, no. I was thinking . . . I have some work to dispose of. I take it there's a feast here tonight?"

"Yes. At dusk. We will be honored to have you as our guest." Abraham looked up; Enosh stood at the doorway. "Yes, my son?" he said.

"The lord Lot has arrived."

"Ah, yes," Abraham said, rising to his feet in the tent. "My brother's wayward son," he explained. "I promised my brother on his deathbed that I would look out for his son. I often think I have failed him. I should have disciplined the boy more when he was younger. Now, grown, a man in middle life, he . . . well, I'm afraid he doesn't amount to much. I hope I have the sense to raise my own son better."

"Ah, yes. But now I'll take my leave of you, sir. It's

good to see you again. You've done well for yourself here. I'll make no secret of the fact that part of my mission here is to assure you of the friendship and support of the Lord of Two Lands."

"Which is reciprocated as far as my poor powers can reach."

"I'll tell him that. And now, until this evening."

On the way back to his own quarters, Nakhtminou spied on a hillside a group of boys playing. He stopped to watch. Two of them, husky lads, crept up on a third and attacked him from the rear. He was a dark-skinned, well-built boy, and as he turned to face his attackers, Nakhtminou could see that it was the boy he'd noticed earlier.

Yes! And what a boy he was. He actually welcomed the attack! As Nakhtminou watched, the boy grasped one of his attackers by the neck and threw him over his shoulder, to land flat on his back gasping for breath. The other was as quickly tossed to the ground and pinned.

Then the boy saw him looking at him and, turning his back on his vanquished opponents, came forward to look him over. "You're Egyptian," he said.

"That's right, boy."

"And you're a soldier."

"Right again. Why? Do you want to be a soldier?"

The boy's eyes shone. "I want to be a leader of soldiers. Not a follower. I want to lead men into battle, and fight, and conquer new lands."

"Well, good luck to you. I wanted much the same thing myself at your age."

"Did you get your wish?" the boy said.

"More often than you can count, I'll wager. I have fought in more battles than you have had meals, I'd guess."

"Yes? And did you win them?"

"I'm here, boy. That answers your question, doesn't it?"

"Well . . . you could have run."

"But I didn't. And I'll wager you won't either."

"No." There was no deference at all in the boy's tone.

"Look, boy, my name is Nakhtminou."

"Pleased to meet you, sir." Ah, a trifling amount of superficial politeness at last. But it seemed perfunctory, insincere.

"Well?" Nakhtminou said.

"Oh? Oh, yes. You don't know my name. You're a stranger. I forgot. Everyone around here knows me."

"And?"

"My name is Ishmael. Son to the lord Abraham."

Nakhtminou's face slowly broke into a smile of complete understanding. "Well, greetings to you, Ishmael," he said. And, with a curt nod, he turned and strode away, favoring his bad leg.

II

Keret, eldest son of Eshcol, nudged his pony in the ribs as he followed his father's tall, rigid form down the broad, flat course of the wadi. The sword banged against his thighs as the pony made its way along the stony path, and for the ten-thousandth time Keret wished he had been conveniently absent when his father had called for a companion to go with him after the missing herds.

Not that it would have much difference in the long run. His father would have found him if he'd been anywhere within the domains of Abraham and Mamre. And, having found him, he wouldn't have settled for any companion other than his son.

Keret looked once again at his father's straight back, at the still-powerful arms and shoulders that rode above the animal's back as easily and naturally as if he'd been born part of the horse. His seat on the beast was martial, manly, bellicose; a harsh and dominant maleness exuded from his very stance, his quick and sure motions.

Keret sighed. *Father, I love you,* he thought, *although you are easier to fear and respect than to love.* He shrugged and shook his head. How much easier it would be if he hated his father, if relations between father and son had broken down totally. If he could simply dismiss Eshcol's rigidity and single-mindedness and fight him head on, it might be a totally different life. Even if the prospect involved meeting his father head on in battle, say—his father, the fiercest, most widely feared warrior Mamre's Grove had known since the death of the great Egyptian warrior Sneferu—even that might be preferable to living with him a divided man, bound to the older man by love and loyalty. Keret was unable to accept his father's high-handedness, his insistence that his sons be measured always against the rigid standard he had set for himself.

He shook his head again, just as Eshcol swiveled in the saddle and yelled back at him in a gruff voice, "Come on there! Are you going to lag behind forever?" And Keret, stifling a sharp-tongued answer, nudged the pony again. The animal, finding a more stable footing, jumped forward and drew up alongside Eshcol's mount.

"That's better," Eshcol said matter-of-factly. "I wanted you to see the sign for yourself. There!" He pointed with a long, bony arm down the path. The winds of the previous day's twilight hour, the hour when the wind in a valley always changed direction diametrically, had all but erased the tracks they were following, but Keret could see what his father was pointing at—the signs of desert scrub close-cropped near the ground level, cropped closer than horses or asses or cattle would crop it. "Sheep," the older man said. "They take the scrub right down to the dirt, leaving nothing behind for other grazing animals that might follow. We're on their trail."

"I'm certain you're right," Keret said. "Do you know whom it is that we follow, Father?"

"Bedouin of the Arabah, of course," Eshcol said. "Just such as your uncles and I sprang from. I told you

I spotted tracks of horsemen. Who else has tamed the horse here? Who else prefers so noble a beast to the lowly ass? But as for which Bedouin of which tribe, I could not say. Not yet, at least. But why do you ask? If you had listened to all I have tried to teach you for all these years, you would not have to ask me such questions. Bah!" His father spat into the trail beside his path.

Keret, his face reddening, stifled another sharp retort. "I defer to my father's wisdom," he said in a tight voice.

"Damn it, don't defer," Eshcol said. "Notice things. Pay attention. I'm not going to be around forever. You're going to have to do these things for yourself. What'll happen when I'm gone and some tribe that hasn't learned the meaning of proper fear and respect comes to steal your herds? What then? Will you send them some sort of coward's message to bring them back or you'll ... oh, hold your breath, or throw a tantrum, or—"

"Damn it!" Keret said. He reached over and grabbed the reins of his father's horse, pulling both animals to a stop. He looked into his father's face, his eyes blazing. "Look," he said. "I've listened to about enough of this. I'm no coward, Father, and my arm is as strong as yours. I can fight any man you can, and acquit myself as well. It's just that ... damn it, my blood isn't as hot as yours. My temper isn't as quick. If you think—"

"By all the gods!" Eshcol said, his face breaking into an astonished grin. "The mouse stands up on its hind legs and roars like a lion! What wonders will we see next?" His eyes grew cold. "Well said, mouse! But if your hand isn't off those reins in two blinks of an eye ..." He left the matter of what would happen if he were not obeyed an open one. His tone was flinty; the grin faded.

Something inside Keret, goaded at last beyond endurance, broke loose. "Ah," he said, his own voice edged with ice, "what will you do then, Father? Kill me? Butcher me like a hog, as you've so often threatened to do to Lot?" His hand tightened on the leather reins. "I'll tell you what. Why don't you try to make me. You'll find you're not dealing with a frightened stripling any more." His voice grew more powerful as the long-deferred rage built in him. "Come on, damn you! I've taken enough of your abuse! From this moment I follow no damned order of yours that you're not prepared to enforce with the sword. From this moment you will ask me to do something, as you would ask a friend—or you'll do it yourself and the hell with you."

Eshcol, his long, lean biceps bunching suddenly, yanked the reins free. "All right, puppy," he said in a voice thick with phlegm. "Dismount, will you? And face me with this newfound manhood of yours? Yes, yes. It's time. It's long past time. I've been wondering when you would find your manhood. Come now. Down on the ground. Face me with that sword of yours, that nice virginal sword. If you've the guts required to use it, and the strength required to swing it." He stepped down onto the flat saltpan, his own reckless youth flowing easily back into his veins with the touch of the desert sand beneath his feet.

Keret dismounted, and hobbled his horse before turning to face his father.

"Come on, boy," Eshcol said. He planted his feet on the hardpan, two handspans apart. His sword was drawn; he held the hilt in one hand, the blade in the other. He tapped his left palm with the blade impatiently. "Come on," he said. "I'm tired of waiting."

"You never could wait," Keret said. Calmly he unsheathed his own sword and faced the older man. "And that's your only idea of how to be a man, isn't it? I'm differently made, and slow to anger . . . but you won't hold with that sort of thing being manly, will you? You won't put up with my being anything but your own shadow, will you? If I'm not exactly like you—"

His words were cut short as Eshcol, his face a mask of rage, attacked. He feinted a thrust, beat Keret's point aside with a quick-wristed stroke, and lunged. Keret's recovery was lightning-fast; he parried, wrestled Eshcol's point to the ground by brute strength, and disengaged, stepping back with a curt salute.

Eshcol returned the salute. "Ah," he said. "By all that's holy, boy, you've got a forearm of steel! I'm proud of you! Where have you been training, to play a maneuver like that on me?" He put his guard up and circled his son slowly, wary-eyed.

"I've been taking lessons with Enosh," he said. "Enosh, who killed Chedorlaomer of Elam in single combat and won his freedom." He spat the words out. "Do I have to do the same with you, Father, if I am to win my freedom?"

"Well, find out!" Eshcol said, and attacked. He feinted low, engaged his son's sword forte against forte, and spun his blade. Keret parried, beat his father's blade down, and lunged—but pulled the lunge up short at the last possible moment. The sharp blade touched his father over the heart, with a touch as light as a maiden's kiss. A tiny drop of blood appeared over the spot—a drop that would have been a gout of red if the younger man had not called back the thrust.

"Touch!" the young man said.

"By the gods, yes!" Eshcol said. "Well struck, boy! By the gods! I've been *waiting* for you to talk up to me! Come! Come, try that again!" He sprang forward like a man half his age, a fierce joy in his every movement.

His first lunge was cut short as Keret parried; then Eshcol unleashed a mighty swing that jarred the blade from his son's hand. Eshcol sprang forward while Keret's blade still lay in the dust before him. He raised his sword high . . .

. . . and then something shook his whole stringy, long-muscled body. Keret was to remember this moment the rest of his life. His father's eyes changed. His hand shook on the upraised weapon. His mouth opened. He said, "Son, I . . ."

And fell slowly forward on his face. Keret dropped down to one knee, his hand on the blade in the dirt.

A long-shafted arrow protruded from Eshcol's back.

Keret's eyes swept the two sides of the wadi. His hand closed tight about his sword. He remained in a half-kneel, his muscles tight and ready, his eyes quickly scanning the saltpan.

Then a wild whoop erupted from the area just to his left. Keret wheeled—and saw two mounted Bedouin bearing down on him, bearing swords. One of them wore a strung bow, hung hastily over his back. Keret poised on the balls of his feet, the adrenaline running high in his body, the blood rushing to his extremities.

At his feet Eshcol tried to rise. "Son," he said. "Stop them. Don't . . ." Then, with a gasp, he fell again on his face, one hand pawing the dirt impotently.

Keret picked up his father's sword and faced the two, a sword in each hand. His own sword, an instrument of recent manufacture, hung in his right fist; the other instrument warmed to his left hand. Gods! What a weapon! No wonder his father swore by it!

The horsemen came to the gallop, boxing him in between them. He feinted to one side, then dived toward the other. As he did, rolling under the hooves of the horse on his right, he stabbed blindly upward with his own sword. The weapon sank into the horse's unprotected belly and the animal carried it away, buried in its innards almost to the hilt. The horse went two steps past him, shuddered, whinnied, and staggered to its knees. Its rider fell forward over the horse's head and landed on the back of his neck with a sickening crunch. He groaned and lay still.

The other rider slowed, wheeled, turned, and looked at him. Then he charged, with a bellow of rage.

Keret changed his father's sword to his right hand and crouched in wait, shifting uncertainly from side to side, ready to dive either way, depending on the horseman's movements.

"K-keret," Eshcol said at his feet. The young man looked down. His father had rolled to one side, a grimace of mixed pain and rage on his whey-white face. "Watch . . . watch for—"

"It's all right, Father," Keret said. He stood up, planting his feet. "I'm standing my ground. He'll touch you again when I'm dead, not a moment sooner." He raised his head and his young voice boomed out. "Come and get me, you Bedouin pig-eater! Come and kill me, you scum, you lover of boys! Here!" He opened his robe to show his naked chest. "Here's my heart. See if that blade of yours can find it. Or is it good for anything but pig-butchering?" The insult, he knew, was a mortal one. All the tribes of the area, including his own, considered the pig beneath the notice even of a starving man.

The Bedouin kneed his mount's flanks and charged. Keret made a strong body-feint to one side and then, standing still as the horse churned past, swung the magic blade with both hands. It cut through the rider's ribs and knocked him off the animal onto his back. The horse charged past, riderless.

Keret leaped to the fallen man's side. "You!" he said, raising his blade high. "I'm going to . . ."

But then he saw the great wound in the man's side, and his inner parts oozing forth from the wound. The rider waved feebly at his wound. Keret could see he was sinking fast. "You!" he said in a fierce whisper. "Of what tribe are you, who steal our herds? Quick, now! You're dying. Will you have a quick and merciful death at my hands, or shall I ride away on that beast of yours and leave you here to die slowly, in great pain?"

"I . . ." the rider said. A brief flash of hatred animated his face.

"Quickly, now! I'm losing interest. In a moment or two the pain in your guts will hit. The cramps'll start. You'll beg for death, quick death, but I won't be here to give it to you."

"I . . . I am of the tribe of Yatpan," the Bedouin said. "We raided you . . . a fortnight ago."

"Quick! Where does Yatpan live?"

"Two day's ride south of here, at the well which bears his name. Please . . . the pain . . . it . . . aggghhhh!"

Keret looked down; breathed deep; and, gritting his teeth, stabbed—once, twice. Life fled from the Bedouin with an audible sigh.

Keret shook his head . . . and turned back to his father. But when he knelt over Eschol's body, the thin

man's face had lost its saturnine cast and now bore a
look of peace, the first Keret had ever seen there in all
his seventeen years.

He sighed. He looked at the blade in his hand. And,
with another sigh, set out after the Bedouin's riderless
horse, which pawed and snorted restlessly nearby. Eshcol's mount had long since fled. He walked easily, not
wishing to scare the one free animal remaining. He'd
need both horses to bring his father's body home for
burial.

III

Katsenut, coming back from the southern encampment in midafternoon, found Hagar gathering dried
dates. "Here, my lady," she said. "Let me do that.
Please." But her voice was bone-weary, and when
Hagar looked at her old servant she could see that her
heart was not really in her words. Katsenut had aged
in the years since Hagar's emancipation, and her legs
gave her trouble now. Her face was gray, and her
stamina was ebbing with every year of service.

Hagar smiled gravely at her. "No, no," she said.
"You've had a long walk. I've been thoughtless; I
should have sent someone younger over there."

Katsenut had momentarily rested against a downed
tree trunk, but now her pride made her stand up again.
"No, no," she said. "I'm all right. Please. You'll be
putting me out to pasture . . ."

"No, I won't," Hagar said. "You'll have a place at
my side as long as you live, my old friend. But these
long, tiring errands . . . surely I can hand them over to
someone who won't feel the fatigue as much. Here, I
won't have you worrying. What did you learn?"

"Oh, I left a message for Shepset," she said. "She
was out somewhere with Lot's daughters. I imagine
they run her a merry chase; they're very wild, the

women say. As who wouldn't be, growing up in a wicked place like that?"

"Oh, hush now. You know nothing firsthand of Sodom."

"No, ma'am. But . . . well, everyone says—"

"Let them say. You stay out of it. Now, how's Shepset? It's been so long since we've seen one another. Five years, is it? No, Ishmael was seven, that would be six years. What did you hear of her?"

"Well, ma'am . . . it depends on whom you're talking to. A lot of them there . . . well, they think she's snooty. Although how you can say that about a slave—"

"Shepset told me once she had a sort of protector. It seems the lord Eshcol, Mamre's brother, took Lot aside once and told him if he touched her again he'd break his neck. He had a spy in Siddim who looked out for her. It gave her a strange sort of status. She was technically a slave, but there were limits past which they did not go in disciplining her, or . . . or whatever else they did."

"Oh, they're bad people, ma'am. They've taken up with the gods of the city. They . . . well, someone told of orgies, and—"

"I wouldn't talk of that if I were you. I mean, telling me is all right, but you don't know when that sort of thing is going to come back at you."

"Yes, ma'am."

"But of course you're right. They're terrible people. And from all I've heard, the little good influence Lot's daughters get is all from Shepset. She does what she can. Or did. But I think that from what you say that's still her main job, raising the girls."

"They call her—the other slaves call her—'the Princess.' Very sarcastically, you know. But only behind her back. She's said to have a sharp tongue in her head."

"Oh, poor Shepset. We've all been unfortunate in one way or another, but I think she's had the worst luck of all. Well, I hope she does come visit me, as I suggested. You left the message with someone reliable?"

"Oh, yes, ma'am. This man Ezbon. I think he's the one who reports to the lord Eshcol."

"Lot," Abraham said, "I have to say this. I've heard . . . well, reports about you. In Sodom." His face was solemn, almost worried-looking. He and his nephew sat cross-legged in Abraham's tent, a single cup of wine on the rug between them.

"Reports, Uncle?" Lot said. "What kind of reports?" His fingers drummed on his knee nervously; the quick motions were at variance with the artificial calm of his words.

"In a word," Abraham said, "I hear you have adopted the ways of the city. Of Sodom."

Lot tried to brush it off. "Well, Uncle, we *do* dress after the fashion in Siddim. One doesn't want to look out of place—"

"Dress? What is dress? That doesn't matter. I understand that you have different standards. You do not live the kind of life your father lived. You hark back to your great-grandfather, my father's father, who lived as a city man in Ur. From all family reports he was not a man to get his hands dirty, either. Well, that's all right. There is honor in trade if you choose to live that way. And you're certainly wealthy enough not to have to soil your hands with business, if that's the way you look at things. I'm traditional-minded and cleave to the ways of my father for the most part; but I can understand someone differing from me in this. It is a large world, and there is room for many ways of life in it. But—"

"But, Uncle?"

"You tell me, Nephew." The old man sat back and looked hard at Lot—not unkindly, but with a steady and unavoidable gaze. "You tell me. I know you do not sacrifice to El-Shaddai. I know you are not raising your children in the ways of the God. This is a great hurt inside me. But . . ."

He waited for a moment, but Lot said nothing. Abraham, his voice slow and thoughtful, chose his words carefully. "Have you taken up the religions of the city?"

"Oh, Uncle," Lot said. "Of course not." He tried to wave the whole subject away with one hand; but Abraham's eyes bore unblinkingly into his. "Well, of course I don't believe in . . . well, all that superstitious nonsense of theirs. Please, Uncle. Give me credit for some intelligence."

"But . . . you pay lip service to the customs of the people there."

"Uncle! One has to . . . well, accommodate those one lives among. I don't go out of my way to insult the people there. I know that . . . well, living separate from people, the way you do, you can afford to be uncompromising about your attitudes, about your ways. But I—"

"The question is, where does lip service end and the business of sliding into an acceptance of those foreign ways begin?" Abraham reached out and touched his nephew on the knee. "Lot, it is an unshakable custom among us, from the very first days, that the family shall remain intact, that the family unit shall be sacrosanct. I will be blunt. The people of Sodom have a reputation for . . . certain sexual improprieties. Several *kinds* of sexual improprieties. Now, I have not visited the city myself, and I can speak only of hearsay. And I do not give too much credence to that. But . . ." His eyes searched his nephew's puffy face, hoping against hope. "You and Zillah . . . is all well between you?"

Lot fancied he caught a weak spot in Abraham's line of attack. "Uncle!" he said in mock indignation, his voice rising almost to a feminine pitch. "*You* speak to *me* of . . . of the sacrosanct family unit? You who have fathered a son on a concubine? On a freed slave? You who have put your own wife aside to—"

"You go too far!" Abraham said, bristling. But Lot could see the vulnerability in his face. He pressed on.

"But no, Uncle. Look, I'm a person of mature years by now. I'm no stripling that you can question me about the intimate details of my married life and not expect me to throw the same sort of thing back at you! If you get to question me, then I get to question you! If you think—"

Abraham held up his long-fingered old hand. "Peace," he said. "You've made your point. But you must know, I haven't put Sarah away. Far from it. And the concubine—Hagar, her name is—I've never lived with her, that way, since she first became pregnant. And . . . Lot. It was the command of the God that I father a son, an heir. I was told in a vision—"

"Uncle. *Please*. I don't *want* to know. Do you understand that?" Lot felt a thrill of smug awareness. He'd turned the tables. He'd found his uncle's weak spot and forced him to give ground. If only Zillah could see this! She'd never believe it as it was. "The point is, Uncle . . . if *I* don't pry into *your* affairs—if I don't go snooping around after you, well—"

Abraham shook his head sadly. "I have no answer ready for that, Lot. It's just that . . . I promised your father, my brother—"

"I understand, Uncle. And I appreciate your solicitude. But you must give me the benefit of the doubt now and then. And not take the word of the first lying sycophant who seeks to curry favor with you by—"

Abraham sighed. "The reputation of Sodom is bad. You know that. License. Promiscuity. Homosexuality. Incest. And when I hear that you have been giving parties, festivals—and festivals timed to coincide with the festivals of the gods of Sodom—"

"Strictly diplomatic, Uncle. It would probably surprise you to learn that I'm quite a good businessman. I've actually increased my wealth since I came to live in the Valley of Siddim. I suppose you think—I'd wager, as a matter of fact, that you've been thinking—that I've been dissipating my portion, tossing it to the four winds."

Abraham sighed. He looked at his nephew, at the carefully tended mustache and beard, at the pursed lips between them. He sighed unhappily. Lot had always been able to get around him. He had a devious tongue. Well, perhaps it was given to him as compensation for the masculine strength he had always lacked. "Ah, well," he said. "You realize I was only asking—"

"For my own benefit? Of course, Uncle. And I appreciate it, really I do. But—Uncle, I'm a grown man. You can't go on treating me as if I were sixteen."

"You're right. You're right, of course." Abraham looked up, his face drawn and miserable, to see Enosh standing in the door. "Excuse me," he said to his nephew. He raised his voice. "Enosh," he said. "You wouldn't presume to interrupt us if it weren't important—"

"No, sir," Enosh said. "Keret, son to the lord Eshcol, just came in with his father's body draped over the back of a Bedouin horse. There was an arrow in his back."

"Ahhhhh." The word tore itself out of Abraham's chest. "Lot, if you'd excuse us, please? It's important."

"Yes, Uncle," Lot said. He looked at Enosh. A slow smile spread itself over his fat face. "Pardon me," he said. "Did you say . . . the lord Eshcol?"

"Yes, sir," Enosh said. "He was out tracing a lost herd. Keret says the herd was stolen. Keret killed his father's assailants, and—"

"Oh," Lot said. "What a great pity. My sympathies to his kin." A very strange expression had replaced the smile on his puffy features. It didn't seem to match his sympathetic words at all.

Shepset sat by the edge of the pond, her feet tucked up underneath her. She watched Lot's two daughters splashing in the shallow water, their bronzed young bodies glistening in the late afternoon sun. Adah, the elder of the two by a year, was getting too old, by Canaanite standards, to go naked like this. Her breasts were already small but ripe, and the bottom of her body was already adorned by a rich growth of hair—dark, curly hair that gleamed with drops of water now. When her sister, Elisheba, splashed her, she instinctively covered her lap with one hand; but the little patch of hair was by now almost too big to be covered by her slim brown hand.

Elisheba, on the other hand, was physically not as well developed as her sister. But Shepset knew this to have little effect on her sexual development. The girl bore no more breasts than a boy, and her little pubis was as bare as her hand; but she had already shown signs of sexual precocity that would, in Sodom, land her in trouble soon if steps were not taken. Indeed, as Shepset watched, the girl unashamedly put one hand to her flat little belly and caressed herself, smiling wickedly at her sister—and then, knowing in advance the effect of this, smiling the same mocking smile at Shepset.

"Stop that," Shepset said in an even voice. "You know what I've told you about that."

"Pooh!" the girl said. "Mother does it all the time. So do her friends, all of them. Just because you've no interest in such things—"

"Silence!" Shepset said. "Do you want to go to bed without your supper tonight?"

The girl, standing ankle-deep in the cool water, spread her legs another handspan and stood facing her, flaunting her narrow and as yet hipless little body. "Just try it! I'll go to father, and—"

Shepset stood up, ready to kick her sandals off and go in after the two of them. But a voice from behind her broke into her thoughts. "Shepset?"

She wheeled. "Oh. Ezbon. You startled me." She watched the slave's eyes run up and down the two naked bodies in the pool, then return to her—a little reluctantly, it seemed. "What is it?"

"Uh . . . the lady Hagar. She left a message for you. She wanted to see you if you had time."

"Fine. I'll go when—"

"Uh, there's another thing. The lord Lot returned a few moments ago. He says we're all to make ready to leave for Sodom, 'as soon as I can decently get away,' he says. 'As soon as I can get free.' "

"Get free? But of course he's free to come and go—"

"It's a matter of, uh, manners, ma'am. He doesn't want to offend anyone, he says, if he can avoid it. He's hoping the funeral takes place quickly. Most likely it will. The lord Abraham wants to send a detachment after the murderers as quickly as possible."

"Funeral? Murderers?" Shepset stood looking at

him, her eyes wide. "I don't understand. Who's dead? Who's been murdered?"

"Why, the lord Eshcol, ma'am. A band of Bedouin got him. They were stealing a herd of his, folks say. The lord Abraham says . . ."

Shepset stared at him open-mouthed. She didn't hear the rest of what he had to say. Eshcol . . . dead! But with him gone . . .

"Please, ma'am," Ezbon said. His eyes stole to the two cavorting youngsters in the pond, but lingered on them as they would not have had the girls really been youngsters, pure and simple. Then they came back to her again. "In the meantime the lord Lot wants to see you. Right now. I'd make haste if I were you. You know what he's like when he's mad."

Shepset, her heart sinking, tried to say something; but her mouth was dry. "I . . . I'll be right along," she said.

CHAPTER FIFTEEN

I

An unparalled three years' famine had settled on the lands of Padan-aram. It was a time when one crop after another had failed, either through the extended drought or through one kind of pestilence after another. Then, when the drought broke, and the early spring thaw brought torrents of water pouring down from the heights into the dry land only to be followed by heavy rains, drought became surfeit and washed away all the newly planted grain. The only vegetation that survived the torrential rains and floods was the green brush on the hillsides, and when the rains ended for the season the brush soon faded from green to brown.

In the hills a shepherd, minding another man's flocks, drank himself into a stupor on homemade wine. Sparks from his ill-tended campfire ignited the brown brush near his sleeping body. By the time the smoke awoke him he was surrounded by flames. He died drunkenly trying to stand up, to get his singed legs underneath him. And the fire quickly became a prairie holocaust, surging its way through parched brush and dry grass alike. It closed the trail from Haran to Carchemish for better than a week, as the fires raged unchecked.

Then, when the first travelers set out from the Hittite city toward Haran, they were turned back by guards posted by the people of the city. A darker cloud than any fire could produce now hung over Haran: plague. No visitors were allowed to go through. Caravans on the great semicircular route between the Great Sea and the Land of the Two Rivers were rerouted and in some cases canceled outright; the drain on alternate wells not meant to handle fully equipped caravans was too great, and some travelers reported encountering dry wells where oases had been expected.

Inside Haran, the disease raged. A victim would first experience chills and a high fever, a rapid irregular heartbeat, then stupor, loss of motor control, prostration. Then the infected person would note the growth of buboes in the groin and armpits: fat, pus-filled pouches the size of a child's fist. Shock and a terminal coma followed soon after. There was no known cure. Half the town died within the first month. The city lay under a severe quarantine; food and supplies were deposited before the city gates by residents of the outlying areas, who withdrew quickly. Only when their benefactors had retreated an hour's march did the few able-bodied people of the city go out to pull the abandoned wagons inside the city walls.

The quarantine proved effective in controlling the spread of the disease; there were a few isolated cases of plague among shepherds living and working almost in the city's shadow—bats coming down to feed off the sheep spread the diseased fleas they bore to the flocks, and the masters of the infected animals came down with the dread symptoms. But there were few shepherds, and they tended to keep to themselves.

Zakir and Ahuni, stranded through the whole period in Carchemish, fretted their way through the times of flood and fire; when the news of the quarantine found its way into the Hittite settlement where they had gone to sell weaponry, Zakir, gray-bearded but still powerfully built and vigorous, called a council of war at the tavern where he, Ahuni, and Belanum ate their meals in the foothill town.

"I've been thinking," he said over a third cup of wine. "I wonder if our days at Haran are not over. What if we were to . . . well, not return at all?"

Ahuni looked at him, his knife poised over a lamb joint. "Not return?" he said. He looked at Belanum, beside him; then he nodded to Zakir. "You have the floor, Father. And our respectful attention."

Zakir took another draught of wine and wiped his lips fastidiously. "Well, since the death of the noble Nabousakin, I, for one, have been pretty much a free agent. And with my natural markets at Mari and in the Valley of the Two Rivers mostly dried up, I'm very largely out of business. Besides, if I know the superstitious bent of the locals, there's going to be little a trader from Haran is going to be able to do for some years now, until the taboo is off the city."

Ahuni looked at Belanum for corroboration. The younger man, trained as a scribe at his and Zakir's expense in Haran, had been in charge of their joint and separate accounts for some years now. "Well, Belanum?"

Belanum smiled admiringly. He'd never quite got over his hero-worship of Ahuni. "I think Zakir is right, Ahuni. I think we can forget Haran for some years to come. It will be all the city can do to find some sort of equilibrium now, much less reestablish trade connections with other cities. Besides, I don't feel any too well myself about the matter of going back to a town only recently cleansed of the disease."

Zakir waved his left hand over the cup. "See?" he said. "Look, what are we leaving behind? A house, some possessions . . . we've got the wherewithal, among us, to make our way virtually anywhere. We have established personal credit in Kizzuwatna and the coastal cities. We could settle in Ebla, Ugarit, Arvad, anywhere. We could press north of here and try our luck in Kanish, Ankuwa, Hattusas, Malataya. We . . ."

Ahuni's sharp glance caused him to cut short his speech. Zakir sat back and looked at his adopted son. Then Ahuni's stiff demeanor softened. "Excuse me, Father," he said good-naturedly. "It's just that . . . well, I'm a creature of habit, and new ideas——"

"I know," Zakir said. "But . . . well, just think about it, will you? Both of you. And consider where you'd like to go to start our business again."

"I gather, sir, that Carchemish isn't your idea of a place to settle." Belanum's tone was deferential.

Zakir shrugged. "We already know Carchemish. We've spent the whole season of the rains here, concluding our business. I happen to know that both of you are as bored here as I am."

"Ah." Ahuni grinned affectionately. He turned to Belanum, a knowing smile on his handsome young features. "The fleshpots and taverns of Carchemish have been weighed in the balance and found wanting— and by an expert of experts at that." He chuckled. "Father, you'll never change. Never."

"Well," Zakir said, taking up the cup again and playing with it, his eyes on its contents. "Of course, one *does* tend to think of such matters from time to time. Life isn't all business, you know."

"All right," Ahuni said. "I'll think about it, Father, as you suggest. And I'll give my consideration to which direction we ought to take. But do you yourself have any suggestions as to where? Any preferences?" He turned again. "You, Belanum?"

Belanum made a self-effacing gesture. "I defer to the noble Zakir," he said. "What do you think, sir?"

Zakir sat back on his stool, his shoulder blades against the earthen wall of the tavern. His hand rested on his left knee and rubbed it. "Well . . . maybe someplace not too wet and not too cold, if I had my choice in the matter. The season we spent in Mersin, with that cold winter wind coming down from the hills, and the humidity from the Great Sea, all my joints ached constantly. Ah," he sighed. "I'm getting old."

"All right," Ahuni said. "That lets out Ugarit and Malataya. Now that I know what you don't want, I'll give the matter some thought." He stood up. "Now, if you two don't mind, I'll take a stroll out by the city gate."

"Please, sir," Belanum said. "May I go with you?" Ahuni nodded; Belanum bowed to Zakir and went out one pace behind the young armorer.

Zakir sighed, drained his cup, and held it up for the alewife to see. She padded to his side on silent bare feet and refilled it for him from a tall amphora. Then she put it down and looked at him. "I couldn't help overhearing, Zakir," she said. "You want to leave, but you're not sure where you want to go."

Zakir looked at her. The face was plain but the figure was ripe. His glance lingered for a moment on the mature bare breasts, then went to her brown eyes. "You heard right," he said. "Do you have any suggestions?"

"Only that there are times when a soothsayer comes in very handy. Are you superstitious?"

"Oh, I used to be. There was a time, many years ago, when I would hardly make a move without consulting my astrologer. Why? Do you know someone here?"

"In fact I do. A mystic from Damascus named Barhaddad."

"An astrologer? A numerologist, perhaps?"

"No. A mystic. He speaks from a trance. He is well-known here, throughout all the southern lands of the Hittite empire. He foretold the plague of boils that fell upon Ghazir of Ugarit, to the very day. He foretold the plague in Haran—"

"By the gods! Does he specialize in plagues?"

"Of course not. He also predicted the great fortune that came upon Azitawadda of—"

"Enough," said Zakir. He drained his cup and put it down, his hand already unsteady. "I've had enough to drink that I can appreciate him, and not so much that I won't remember what he's told me. Lead me to him."

But when the seer's assistant showed him into the presence of the visionary, Zakir almost backed out, superstitions or no. Barhaddad, it appeared, was a madman: a drooling spastic whose head lolled this way and that, whose eyes rolled in his head, almost totally beyond his control. His words were unintelligible; the assistant put a hand on Zakir's forearm, whispering low beside him. "He speaks only Aramaic," he said. "I will translate. You have the money?" Zakir handed over a purse. "Very well. But you must be patient. Hold out your hand. No, your other hand."

"I have no other hand."

"So be it. Your left hand, then." Immediately the afflicted man's long bony fingers sought Zakir's and clamped down on them with a madman's powerful grip. "Relax," the assistant said. "Now think on your problem. Think on what it is that has brought you to Barhaddad of Damascus. Think of . . ."

But his words were drowned out by a flurry of broken, high-pitched Aramaic. Zakir felt the fleshless talons grip his hand, relax, grip it again. The madman droned on. "What's he saying?" Zakir said. Behind the lunatic the candle flame danced merrily—although there was not the smallest trace of a draught in the room.

"He says," the assistant said, "that you go south into a land of peril. A land which will be visited by the gods of the fire. You go to lands which will know the breath of death. Fire will rain from the skies. Death will lie upon the lands below the mountains' rim."

"Go on."

But the madman interrupted them again with another burst of rapid-fire speech in the southern tongue. His head wobbled crazily from side to side; his eyes opened and shut rapidly, crossed themselves, went in opposite directions. His nose ran, dripping a loathsome pendant of phlegm from the end of that broken beak. Zakir, who knew a little trader's Aramaic and could make his basic needs known in the language, still hadn't made out a word.

"He says," the assistant said at the first pause, "that you must walk through the fire to find the healing waters. You must walk into the jaws of death if you would find safe harbor at the end of your life. He says you are a lonely man, a solitary man, and you have sought an end to loneliness all your days. He says that you will find your heart's desire . . . but you must first face the things you fear most. You must lose the one thing in life that you love before you can find your heart's desire. You must . . ."

Zakir, suddenly stone cold sober, swallowed. "No," he said in a hoarse voice. "No, please. . . ."

"He says there is no alternative. These things you must do. And you will pass through unhappiness to find the things you have sought all your days. It is your destiny to do this. There is no escaping your destiny."

Zakir stood, his hand masking his eyes. His voice croaked, "No! Stop! I'll hear no more!"

The assistant stepped back, smiling. The idiot's head fell forward on his chest, like that of a puppet whose strings had been released by the puppeteer.

Zakir kicked his chair to one side and stumbled to the door. "Ahuni," he said. "Ahuni. . . ."

II

The moon was high, and one could see well into the foothills by its light. The silvery beams glinted on the sluggish waters of the river as it wound its way past the city in a wide curve. The fires of half a dozen encampments outside the walls dotted the gentle slopes. The air was clear and cool; Ahuni threw his head back and sniffed it through his nostrils, savoring the richly mixed smells of the night. "Ah," he said to Belanum at his side. "It's a fine place."

"Yes, Ahuni." Belanum wasn't commenting. He had grown exquisitely attuned to those moments when Ahuni wanted to think out loud, when what he really wanted of a companion was the occasional evidence of his presence and attention.

"But it's not for me. And you know, Zakir is right. Our time for being in Haran, for using it as a base for our activities, is at an end. While the noble Nabousakin lived, it was all right . . . but his sons have divided his leavings less like the sons of a rich father than like jackals dismembering a corpse. They have no use for us. And we have no markets in our home country. It's time to move on."

Belanum fell in step with Ahuni as he walked slowly

around the high walls of the city. "I agree, Ahuni. But where to? Have you any thoughts on this?"

"Not yet. I'll be honest with you. I have a feeling something will tell me where to go."

"Ah. An augury of some kind?"

"I don't know. I just have a feeling, which grows stronger as I think upon it, that there is a particular place for us just now, a place we are destined to go to. Belanum, do you believe in destiny?"

"I don't know. I used not to believe in anything. Since I met you and Zakir, I have never ceased to believe in luck."

"I know what you mean. But it's more than luck. I mean, the concept is a larger one. I have had the feeling for many years—since before we met you and left Mari—that my life has not been a matter of drifting with the impersonal tides." He stretched languorously, and Belanum noted the rippling muscles in Ahuni's broad back, the great bunched muscles at the point of his broad shoulders. "I feel that something *wants* me to do this or that: that I am somehow being pushed by some destiny toward some undisclosed direction. I have had this feeling before. I felt it when Zakir bought me as a slave, when Binshoumedir picked us out of the Euphrates, when Nabousakin befriended us—"

"Yes?"

"And I feel it now. I feel it very strongly now. Something will turn up. Some portent that will guide our steps. The two young men fell silent and continued on their way, little suspecting how soon Ahuni's presentiments were to be fulfilled.

III

Zakir did not come home that night. Instead he wandered the streets, thinking. The visit to the mad seer had sobered him up completely, and to his chagrin there was no trace left of the alcoholic haze that had hung upon him before and that might else have cushioned him against the head-on assault of fear.

In the end he barged into a saloon just as it appeared to be closing, threw his purse down on the table, and persuaded the innkeeper to keep the place open as long as he cared to continue to buy drinks.

In the course of a long night he grew thoroughly inebriated, sobered up again, and drank himself once more into a semistupor. As morning came on, having exhausted the coins he had brought out with him, he left, walked out into the chill of morning, vomited up about half of what he had drunk, and made his way slowly and unsteadily back to the rented dwelling he shared with Ahuni and Belanum.

Ahuni awoke when Zakir slammed the door and, giddy, leaned against it for a moment to get his balance. "Father!" he said sleepily. "We were wondering where you'd gone." He sat up, rubbing his eyes. "Ah," he said. "You've been out on a carouse. Well, now. You haven't been on one of these in quite some time. I'd thought you were done with that sort of thing. Well, let's get you to bed now. We've had some extraordinary adventures of our own tonight. We'll tell you all about it when you wake up."

Zakir stared at him, breath coming in little gasps. "I . . . had a bad experience," he rasped. "All the wine in Carchemish could not drive it away, or efface it from my mind."

"Poor Father," Ahuni said. "Is there anything I can do?"

"No, no . . . I'm probably just being stupid. I'm in a bad mood. Things prey on my mind. I . . . perhaps all the events in Haran . . . the knowledge that we've no home just now . . . it all brings back the time when you and I first met, I suppose. Whenever I get to thinking about that period, I go into one of these moods. Sometimes I wake up with the cold sweats. But that hasn't happened in some time."

"Well, just lie down and take it easy for now. Do you want something to eat?"

"Eat? Gods."

"Well, whenever you're ready. In the meantime, I can't keep back my news any longer. It may turn out to be the answer to our prayers."

Zakir eased himself down into bed—but he remained in a sitting position, looking miserably at Ahuni. "News?" he said.

"Yes. I met a man who had a sword made by Belsunu. My natural father—if that's what he was after all."

"Belsunu?"

"Yes. And it turns out that Belsunu was employed by a rich sheikh named Abraham down in Canaan as recently as . . . oh, twelve or thirteen years ago. The sword was used in a war there. This man we met bought the sword from the widow of a man who fought in that war. There are nicks and scratches in it from that battle."

"In Canaan?"

"Yes, Father." Zakir's heart sank at the joy, the anticipation, in the young man's voice. "And there's a good chance that there might be work for us down there. And . . . well, we *were* looking for a place to go."

Zakir shook his head, trying to clear it—and immediately wished he hadn't. There was a stabbing pain just behind his eyes that made him feel faint for a moment. This was followed by a wave of nausea. "Gods," he said. "I won't be able to drink anything but goats' milk for a month." He lay down on the pallet, carefully. "Go on," he said.

"Well, Father . . . there was a chance . . . at least I thought there might be a chance . . . that . . . well, that Belsunu might still be alive. And if he's still alive, maybe this rich sheikh—his name is Abraham—might be able to tell me where he is now." He looked cautiously at Zakir. "That is, if he's alive."

Zakir closed his eyes. *Well,* he thought. *They told you you were going to lose him. And there are more ways than one of losing the son you love above all else. Some are worse than others, too. And what worse way than to lose him to his real father?*

He opened his eyes and looked at Ahuni. The young man's eyes were focused on something far away, much farther away than the blank wall he appeared to be staring at. "Just imagine, Father," he said ruminatively. "What are the odds against my running into someone who knew of Belsunu in an out-of-the-way place like Carchemish, way off the trade routes? It's almost as if there were some sort of destiny involved. Something pushing me toward finding him."

Suddenly the pain in Zakir's heart was worse by far than the pains in his head and belly. Destiny. Destiny indeed.

They sent Belanum to purchase livestock for the trip. This was the sort of thing he did well, driving bargains and extracting the greatest possible return from any expenditure. He purchased three fine horses, brought up from Arabah where the Bedouin horse-breeders and trainers were reputed to be the best in the known world. Two of the horses were big, strong draft animals with thick legs, built for heavy work. They'd need to be to carry the rotund Zakir and the tall, athletic, big-boned Ahuni. For himself he settled on a gentle but serviceable mare of another breed; Belanum's tastes were for the reliable, the unexcitable, the steady.

He drove a far better bargain for asses than he had expected to be able to. The dealer was a man with a gaunt, sharp-tongued shrew for a wife, a woman who ridiculed virtually every word, every phrase, that managed to find its way out of her beleaguered husband's mouth. She kept her husband so badly off balance that he hardly noticed it when Belanum talked him out of a concession that he would regret for days afterward.

At the end of the day he headed for the tavern where he had promised to meet Zakir and Ahuni, bearing with him a thoroughly pleasant feeling of accomplishment. Belanum knew his own merits and was understandably proud of them. However much he might admire Ahuni's unparalleled craft and his dashingly masculine ways, Belanum knew better than to undervalue himself. He had grown up small, skinny, physically insubstantial. The intensely conservative streak in his nature tended to agree with his build, and he habitually withdrew from physical encounters, as he had from his street childhood.

No, there were people who were good at physical things, and there were people who were good at things of the mind. And it was no good wishing you were something you were not, and thus selling short your own merits and strengths. He, Belanum, was a good businessman. This had been evident from the first. Not only had he an ability to make a good bargain; it had seemed from his first apprenticeship at the scribe's trade that he would possess the unteachable secret of keeping long lines of figures in his head, and of always knowing where he and his partners stood financially. He had also a sixth sense for divining the proper time to buy or sell for maximum profit. It had been Belanum who had prevailed upon his friends to liquidate much of their holdings in commodities other than real estate before they had left Haran and to convert the money to workable gold that could be traded—or, as the occasion demanded, turned into even more valuable jewelry by Ahuni, under Zakir's expert tutelage. And now the two of them had Belanum to thank for their present relative prosperity, while all the other exiles from Haran had been ruined by the plague and the quarantine.

Something had sat on his shoulder advising him then. Why, he wondered, did no interior voice speak to him now, when the three of them were making ready to travel into new lands? Why—when so much depended on their making the right choice—did his inner sense desert him? It was a thing to puzzle over. It was not as though something were wrong with him; the deal he had driven for the asses had been ample proof of that. The conscious skills for which his friends valued him were still much in evidence.

The road lay along a rise in the land. He climbed it to the top of a low hill, from which the road wound down to the city with its high walls.

There was a strange light in the sky.

He turned to look at the sunset. He'd never seen anything even remotely like it. Is was an explosion of color, with virtually every hue in the rainbow represented. Orange bands defined dark blue clouds; high in the sky stripes of violet vied with stripes of pink.

He looked around him. Shepherds on the hillsides knelt and made signs against the evil eye. Herdboys, hurrying their cattle homeward, scampered nervously beside the jittery animals, purposely averting their eyes from the gaudy atmospheric display in the west.

An omen? Belanum frowned disapprovingly. He'd always taken a dim view of the common superstitions of his contemporaries. Things were what a man could make them, most of the time, aided by his own intelligence and a little luck. The notion that portents would appear in the sky to guide one seemed ridiculous. Of course, around the intensely superstitious Zakir he'd kept his own counsel; but his opinion had remained his own. But this? This mad display? The strange coppery tint of the air around him? What could this mean?

Shivering against a cold he had not felt before, he hurried down the hill toward the city.

CHAPTER SIXTEEN

I

Walking in the hills, thinking, pondering, Abraham came upon his son playing with two friends. The boys were down below him, in a box canyon where Mamre's horsebreakers had penned the wild horses the raiding party had retrieved from the tribe that had killed Eshcol and stolen his herds. Abraham looked over the edge, his face somber, his thoughts dark and melancholy.

It was easy to pick Ishmael out of any group of boys his age. He had grown enormously in the last year and would challenge his father in height within the year. Then, too, he was powerful, burly, and—dark. Dark even among swarthy half-Bedouin boys like these grandsons of Mamre, Mesha and Hanniab. His hair and brows were as black as any Hittite's ... or any Egyptian's. And his naturally olive-hued skin remained much the same hue through the winter, when the tan skin of the other children had faded.

He was a fine son for any man, Abraham thought. But the thought gave him no pleasure now. He shook his head in pain, remembering the vision of the night before. *Dreams,* he thought. *I must keep reminding myself they are a blessing ... if only to drive away the nagging suspicion that they are a curse.* Shivering, he made the sign against evil. Yet the moment he did so, the doubts came back as strong as ever. What if ... ?

What if the voice that had spoken to him all these years, the spirit that appeared to him, spoke to him, in his dreams . . . what if the spirit were no god at all, but the spirit of a demon? Of a false god? Of a . . . ?

He shut his eyes and, his heart suddenly pounding fast, begged the forgiveness of the God for his doubt. *Please,* he thought. *I didn't mean it. But . . .*

Wringing his hands, he looked down at the boys playing. Mesha and Hanniab stood, hands grasping hands, barring the way of one of the horses back into the fold. Ishmael, a coarse rope in his hard young hands was approaching the animal, muttering soothing sounds. "Here, horse. Nice horse. There, now, I'm your friend, really I am. I have fruit for you. There, now. A little closer. Come, horse."

Look at him now. Why, those are Mamre's horses. If the boys are caught trying to ride one, they'll be beaten. And I'll have to go along with it; they'll deserve it richly. Yet, Abraham reflected, it wouldn't make a bit of difference to Ishmael, and the boys with him would rather take the beating than lose Ishmael's respect, brave his withering scorn. Ishmael was that kind of a boy. A leader, an initiator. Fearless, confident: see him stalking the horse now. And surprisingly patient when it came to the point where nothing but patience would do. "Here, horse. Nice horse. . . ."

He was the stuff kings were made of. And he had been for the thirteen years of his young life an uncrowned prince in Canaan. And now . . .

Suddenly Ishmael deftly slipped the noose over the horse's head and stepped back, pulling it tight. The horse shook its noble head, its big eyes rolling. It reared, pawed the air with its sharp hooves. Ishmael, laughing in triumph, danced merrily out of reach. The animal bolted—but with no place to run, it quickly settled for a tight circle. Ishmael stepped nimbly aside, giving the horse room—but keeping the noose pulled tight around the animal's thick, muscular neck. The boy laughed a victor's laugh: hearty, unrestrained. And took up the slack in the rope, drawing closer to the animal by a finger's length with each frenzied circuit of the narrowing ring.

A prince, Abraham thought. *Someday to be a king. . . .*

The thought, strangely, was a sword in his heart. He should be happy, he knew. He should be jubilant, after the night's dream. But . . .

Little by little the trot slowed to a walk. Little by little the animal's fear gave way to calm, to something remotely akin to trust. *Amazing!* Abraham thought. He has the hands of a horse-tamer! Where has he learned this? Or was it a trick of his mother's Egyptian blood?

My first born he thought. *The first child of my camp to be circumcised and dedicated to the God in this new land the God has given us. And now . . .*

And now what? "I will ask of you many sacrifices," the God had told him those many years ago. And he had undertaken them all willingly until now. Until now, when . . .

With a single quick, vaulting leap—how could a boy his size jump so high? He must have the legs of a lion—Ishmael sprang onto the horse's broad back. His strong thighs gripped the unsaddled back of the beast; his face bore a fierce expression of triumph. "Now!" he cried. "Now, horse! Unseat me if you can. . . ."

The horse reared; the boy held his precarious seat. Then the animal came down and, with a twist, vaulted high into the air. It came down with a stiff jolt and went back up again. Ishmael, yanking on the noose, held on for dear life. The boys below him danced out of the way, frightened. Their eyes went again and again to Ishmael's jubilant face. "Ride him, Ishmael! Ride him! Tame him!"

My firstborn son, Abraham thought with a sinking heart. *And is he to be one of those sacrifices I must make to the God? This strong, healthy, brawling boy who enforces respect in child and adult alike by sheer force of personality, as a king does?* The bitter thought was a spear through his heart, and for the hundredth time that day he begged the God to ask something else of him to prove his faith; anything, anything at all.

II

Coming down the coast they had simply kept the sea on their right—dazzlingly blue, almost always visible from the coastal track that united the port cities of the Crescent. Now, on their left, Ahuni, Zakir, and Belanum found themselves following the gigantic massif of Mount Lebanon as they passed through the sparsely settled Phoenician country east of Sidon.

Now, as they bypassed Tyre, they found themselves entering a rolling upland, covered with low maquis growth. The trees were not tall and they grew closely together. Many had more than one trunk, and creepers connected them with other trunks to make for a thicket-like growth that was well-nigh impassable to a man on foot who dared to stray more than a few steps from the center of the road. Much of this brush growth between the oaks and terebinths was hard-leaved deciduous growth, armed formidably with sharp spines and thorns.

Nevertheless, to a man who stayed on the path as he headed southward the land seemed suddenly lush and generous after the stunted garigue of the Phoenician-settled country. Gone now was the pale green growth of the ruined hillsides of the North. In its place was a riot of color: lizards of bright green scuttled through the underbrush below the blazing-red trunks of the flowering arbutus trees, with their hanging clusters of cream-colored, bell-shaped flowers. They saw bay trees growing trunk by trunk with plane trees and maples, and even in the dense thickets that grew in the ravines they could see the lovely white blossoms of the wild pear trees. Here, too, insects buzzed in the flowering styrax, and the blooming of the wild cersis trees painted the hills with pink.

Ahuni's heart sang as he nudged his horse along the track. *Truly,* he thought, *it is a land of milk and honey. Will this be the place where we can settle for a time? Where Zakir can put down roots? He grows old and tired of the trail, and there will come a time when I will have to move on and leave him behind.* The thought was a white-hot spear in his heart; but he knew the time would come. And when it did come, he hoped the country in which his adoptive father settled would be a green, well-watered, and pleasant land much like this one, a place where a man could grow old in peace and comfort, a place with a mild climate and . . . He sighed. "Father," he called over his shoulder. "From what I've seen I like it. I like it very much."

"It does indeed look very pleasant," Zakir said. "Of course we know nothing of its people. They could be hostile and warlike."

"All the better," Ahuni grinned. "The more custom for my forge. That was the problem with all those other cities to the north of here. They were too peaceful. What use could they possibly have for the likes of me?"

"Agreed, agreed," Zakir said. "Nonetheless, there are times when I almost wish you'd followed a little more closely in my own footsteps and become a maker of golden baubles and ceremonial ornaments. The people who buy that sort of thing generally live in places with stable economies."

"Stable?" Ahuni said. "Like Ur, for instance?" He laughed. "I'm sorry, Father. You were an artist at the forge. I'm an artisan. My hand simply didn't turn naturally to the making of things whose beauty was independent of any question of utility. I have a good fist—but only for the making of practical things."

"Practical?" Zakir said. "Is the hewing of arms and legs, the crushing of skulls, practical?"

Ahuni shrugged. The argument was one that resurfaced from time to time, never very seriously. After all, he was more than half sure by now that he was the son of an armorer, and one of the greatest armorers of the known world. What could be more natural than for him to follow in the footsteps of his natural father?

What a pity, though, that Zakir had to be so sensitive on this subject. What a shame that he had to take it personally, the fact that Ahuni's talents lay in a different aspect of the smith's trade than Zakir's! Of course, it was all perfectly understandable: Zakir had lost his own trade and—particularly now that the long business association with Nabousakin was over—he was reduced, to some extent, to living through Ahuni.

Ahuni sighed. Somehow Zakir had to be brought around to living for and through himself. If he didn't learn this soon, he would wind up growing more and more dependent upon his adopted son, with disastrous results for the very real and deep affection the two had for each other. Because, after all, Ahuni *did* have a trade, a life's trade, and it was one that would require him to keep pretty much on the move for the rest of his life. They had managed, father and son, to put off this aspect of Ahuni's life for some years due to the lucrative contract Zakir had made with the great trader who had befriended him. During those years, Haran, being located at the nexus of a veritable hotbed of bellicose tribes and nations—the Hittites, the Hurrians, and the men of Padan-aram, plus the men of Mari and upper Assyria—had proved a perfect base for his own short trips into other lands to sell his wares and his expertise. Then, too, the work for Nabousakin had kept Zakir so busy that he had had little time for worrying about Ahuni's frequent absences.

Now? Now it was a whole new situation. And wherever they settled, he'd have to find some enjoyment for Zakir, something that would keep him too busy with his own affairs to allow him time to worry about Ahuni. But what? He'd racked his brain for days. All the solutions he'd come up with so far seemed so . . . so temporary, so shallow.

Up ahead Belanum stopped; turned his upper body to halt with a gesture the two who followed him. "Ahuni," he said. "There's someone coming."

Ahuni followed his pointing finger. Below them on

the slopes leading down to a lateral valley, which cut inland below a jutting mountain—Mount Carmel—a group of horsemen, armed, stood athwart their path. The horsemen were dressed almost like Bedouin; they looked strong and competent. There were six in all: burly fellows, in plain robes. Three bore bows across their broad backs. One, a trifle taller than the rest, armed only with a sword but sitting his horse with the proud stance of a man who had tamed the animal himself, appeared to be the leader. His face was sunburned, but youthful.

Ahuni pulled up next to Belanum in the narrow path. "Let me go ahead," he said. "I'll talk to him."

Belanum made way for his friend, and Ahuni nudged his horse down the curving path.

At a dozen paces he halted the horse. "Peace," he said in serviceable Aramaic, holding up one hand in the universal sign of nonbelligerence. "I am Ahuni of Haran, an itinerant smith in search of a patron. This is my father and my friend. We come in peace."

The young man before him looked the three of them up and down. His face had a fine, manly, straightforward look about it, and Ahuni liked the way he sat tall and proud. "Keret, of the Grove of Mamre," he said. "Son of the lamented Eshcol. You will pardon my inquisitiveness . . . but your accent is not that of Haran."

Ahuni grinned; the young man had risen in his respect. "You have a good ear," he said. "I was born in Mesopotamian lands. We have lived in Haran for some years, as representatives in Padan-aram of a famous trader of Babylon and Mari."

The stranger still made no move to clear their path. Ahuni could hear Belanum's horse snort impatiently behind him. "Welcome to the land of Canaan," the stranger said suddenly.

Ahuni reacted in surprise. Then he bowed. "You do us great honor," he said. "We were thinking of making camp in the valley below. We have ample food for all; would you do us the additional honor of being our guests at supper tonight?"

"Our camp is already made," Keret said. "And the

honor will be ours. It is a custom among us. We have been up this way selling horses, and we are on our way back to our own country. You are a smith, you say?"

"A smith and the son of a smith," Ahuni said with pride.

"Then perhaps once we have talked you might like to ride south with us. A smith will always find custom among us. My people are the people of Eshcol, and they have especial affection for a good horse and a good sword. In no particular order." He looked Ahuni in the eye, and Ahuni suddenly felt a great strength in the young man's steady gaze. "The better a smith you are, the better we will like you. Are you a good one?"

Belanum broke in now. "The best!" he said. "The best in all the north country."

The young man inclined his head. "All the better," he said. "The men of the north are famous for their hands with forge and fire. I'm looking forward to seeing your work."

Thus the six became nine; and as the western skies, at dusk, once again for the eleventh straight evening began their wildly undisciplined display of reflected color, two of Keret's men built a blazing fire that did much to cut the gathering chill in the little glen as the evening fogs lay low on the banks of the river.

One of the men of Keret's party had found a stray sheep wandering on the hillside; killed and butchered, it provided the nine men with a hearty meal of roasted mutton. They washed this down with wine from the jugs Belanum had packed on the backs of their pack asses. At a suitable time in the evening Ahuni, smiling, nodded to Belanum, who went to their packs for a bundle which he proceeded to carry back to the camp-fire with as much ceremony as if it had been a pallet bearing a golden crown.

Keret looked up with interest. "What is this, then?" he said.

"You asked whether Ahuni was any good as a smith," Belanum said, his eyes bright with pride for his friend and benefactor. "Open the parcel and decide for yourself." He put the package down before Keret and stepped back, his face deliberately noncommittal.

Keret looked at Ahuni. "Examples of your work?" he said. "All right, let's have a look." He untied the knotted cord around the parcel and unrolled the soft cloth. Three weapons gleamed upon the fabric in the dancing light of the campfire. A sword, a mace, a battle-axe. The light of the leaping flames was warm on the glinting copper implements. Their shapes were at once graceful and deadly. Keret's eyes shone; he picked up the axe, hefted it, felt the balance. He put it down, his mouth open, the breath coming in long, deep draughts through his nose. He picked up the mace and felt the sheer power flow from its heavy bludgeonlike tip down the shaft into his hand. Only when he had tested this, and then placed the weapon on its cloth again, did he approach the gleaming sword.

"Ah," he said, his voice a half-sigh. "How my father would have loved these. How he would have loved them." He held the sword, sighted along the sharp blade. "My father," he explained, "was a man who loved battle more than virtually anyone I have ever known. He loved a good fight as even a professional never does. I remember when I was a child, how excited he was when the call to war came. A light shone from his eyes. . . ." He sighed and softly laid the long blade against his bare palm, holding it as if it were a thing of no more potency than a child's toy. "It's a curious thing," he said. "I have my mother's word—and no more honorable woman ever drew breath in this life—that I am my father's son. Yet I am myself so unlike him in this that I wonder at the blood that runs in my veins."

One of Keret's men demurred. "Keret would have you think he is no fighter. His father, Eshcol, was killed no more than a matter of two moons ago, ambushed by a cowardly bowman who struck from cover. Keret killed those two Bedouin who attacked his father." There was a fierce pride in the man's words—pride for both Eshcol and Keret alike.

"Here," Keret said, smiling. He put the sword down gently, respect in every motion. "Don't listen to my friend here. I am my father's heir . . . but while I have trained myself to fight, as a man must, I take no joy in it. My pleasure lies elsewhere. I am no man to the battle bred. Take it from me. I have met real warriors —people who lived for the fight—and I can tell the difference." He passed the wine to Zakir solicitously, and Ahuni, sharp-eyed, noted the gentle grace in his motion. "I have known Sneferu the Egyptian, for instance. These lands have never known a greater warrior." He paused. "I suppose I talk too much."

"No, no," Ahuni said. "We enter a new land. The more we know of it, especially from the lips of a friend, the better. Please . . ."

"All right," the young man said. "There never lived or breathed a more complete soldier. I used to watch while he trained his troops—farmers, herdsmen, ordinary people—as if they were elite mercenaries." He smiled, and once again Ahuni was impressed by the young man's precocity. He had the maturity—the feeling he gave of controlled strength—of a much older man. "He would sometimes talk to me, child though I was, as though I were someone worth talking to. Ah, I loved that man."

"What happened to him?" Ahuni said.

"Oh, this war he was training everyone for. The one against Chedorlaomer of Elam—"

Ahuni started. "Excuse me. Did you say the Elamite War?"

"Yes. I was a child then. My father fought in it. Poor Sneferu died in it—victim, like my father, of a coward's arrow. But it was his training of our people, his planning, his professionalism, that won the war for us, that allowed an amateur army drawn from the followers of my father and uncles and from the lord Abraham's camp—"

"Abraham!" Ahuni said. He leaned forward. The sword belt bound his middle; looking down, he unbuckled it and pulled it off, laying it down before him, the battered sword still in it. "Did you say Abraham?"

"Well, yes, but his name was Abram then." Keret glanced down and saw the weathered leather, the blackened sword handle. "Well, now," he said. "That can't be one of yours. It's older than you are. What sort of smith is it who carries a personal weapon made by another man?"

Zakir leaned forward, his face a mask of dismay; but Ahuni, oblivious to his pain, smiled eagerly. "A smith who has had the good fortune to find a sword made by Belsunu," he said. "Here, draw the weapon. Hold it. See what I mean . . ."

"*Belsunu?*" Keret said. "I knew Belsunu. He made my father's sword. Here. See for yourself." He drew his own weapon and laid it beside Ahuni's, looking oddly at the young smith's flushed face. "How my father loved him! All of us did, old and young. Why, at his funeral . . ."

Ahuni stopped and looked at him. His face fell. All the expression went from it. "F-funeral?" he said.

"Why, yes," Keret said slowly. "I remember it well. It took place three days after my birthday—thirteen years ago."

III

Puzzled, a little apprehensive, Abraham watched the three travelers disappear over the crest of the hill. They were an odd sight in these hills: barefoot, plain-robed, unarmed, carrying no provisions against a long and dusty march in a sparsely watered land.

The meeting itself had been even more odd. There was something about them . . . something . . . He shook his head and turned to find Sarah looking at him. There was an annoyed look on her face; Sarah did not like puzzles. He shrugged off the question she had not asked. "I don't know," he said. "I haven't the faintest idea who they could be. But I have the strangest feeling . . ."

"What kind of feeling?" she asked, a slight edge in her voice. Absently she toyed with the tent's taut guy rope.

"I . . . I can hardly explain it. It's as if they were . . . oh, some sort of omen."

"Birds of doom?" she snorted. "Come, now."

"No, no. If anything, the thing they most resembled was . . . well, religious pilgrims. On some sort of quest."

"But they said they were going to Sodom. What sort of pilgrimage ends in Sodom? A sinkhole of every sort of vice."

"That's what I don't understand. Yet, sitting with them over the luncheon you were so gracious as to prepare, my dear, I had the strangest feeling. As if they were . . . well, I haven't felt anything like that in the presence of anyone before, ever, anywhere . . . except once."

"Oh?"

"The time I visited Melchizedek of Jerusalem. No, no, don't go making fun of me, my dear. It was much the same thing. Only . . . there was a strange sort of aura about the tall one." He waved aside her scornful shake of the head. "No, no . . . look, did you know he looked at you and afterwards told me, 'Congratulations, sir, on your wife's pregnancy.' "

"Abraham! How could he know? How could anyone know? I'll not be showing, now, for at least another . . ."

"That's what I mean." He looked her straight in the eye, and his voice was firm. "One thing more. He said the child in your belly would be a son. A son. He spoke with absolute confidence."

"Heavens! Well, of course I hope he's right. A son of your own house for an heir, not some bastard fathered on a servant."

"There, now. Please." He put one hand on her arm, his touch gentle and soothing. "It's no time to get angry. It's a time . . . well, for rejoicing. A son? A son of our own? The son promised me in the covenant."

"Yes," she said. There was passion in her voice.

"Yes, Abraham. An heir. A true heir. A true father of your line. A true king in Canaan."

"Ah," he said. "You know how happy that'll make me. But . . ." He sighed and looked at the hilltop where he had last seen the three pilgrims. "How strange. How very strange. And traveling on toward Sodom? Sodom, of all places in the world?" He wrung his long-fingered hands, his mind far away. "What does this mean?"

Sarah did not answer. Her hand caressed her belly beneath its bright robe. A small smile of triumph played on her thin lips.

Hager dipped the rag once again in the healing oil and, wringing it out, passed it gently over her son's bare back. He winced, but made no sound. She looked apprehensively at his determined young face. "How does it feel? You're sure I'm not hurting you?"

"No, Mother," he said—but his voice made a liar of him. "Again, please . . . again. Higher." She touched his arm and felt the muscles above the elbow tighten and stiffen. Indeed, his whole body was as tense as a young deer's. "Mother . . . you haven't lectured me about this. Why?"

"I don't know," she said simply. She dipped the rag again and rubbed it delicately over the welts on his upper back. "Perhaps I feel that the beating you got for doing this was enough." She patted a place where the whip had broken the skin. "Perhaps I thought that . . . well, that you really hadn't done much that was wrong." There was the smallest hint of stubborn pride in her voice as she said this. "After all . . ." she began in that soft voice of hers.

He turned to her, his motions quick and decisive. "Yes!" he said. "What harm did I do, anyhow? Breaking Mamre's horses for him? I'm a better horsebreaker than anyone he's got already. I did him a favor! And—"

"Turn around," his mother said calmly. "I can hear you just as well sitting as you were."

Ishmael complied; but his muscles did not relax. She could feel the defiant stiffness in him. "And besides

... who is Mamre to discipline me? I'm Abraham's son, not his. And why didn't father support me? It's not fair! If it was anyone else's son—"

"Easy, there," she said. "Calm down." She put one hand on his hard young shoulder. "Your father has a lot of things to think of now. And Mamre is not only his friend, he's his partner. They don't always get along as well as they could. They're having an argument these days over the groves to the east of here. Eshcol's son claims them as part of his inheritance, yet Mamre says—"

"I don't care about that!" Ishamel said. "It'll all be mine someday, anyhow, won't it?" He turned around to face her again, his anger showing in the flashing dark eyes that sought hers. "Well, won't it? Because that's what—"

"Please," she said. "We're not to talk about that. Particularly so loudly. It's a very delicate matter. Your father has plans for you that ... but look. We aren't to talk about them. And we certainly aren't supposed to go trumpeting them to the hillsides. Look," she said, putting a hand on his tense forearm. "You haven't been talking about that with the boys, have you? With Mesha and Hanniab? Come now, be honest with me. Have you?"

He looked away, unwilling to face her clear gaze. "Well, so what if I have? It's the truth, isn't it? I *will* be king in Canaan, won't I? Well, won't I?" But he looked up just then and the words he had been about to say froze in his throat. "Mother ..." he said.

Hagar whirled, looked behind her.

Sarah stood in the path, her thin body drawn up in pride, her arms crossed haughtily over her meager breasts. "King in Canaan?" she said coldly. "Is that the sort of nonsense you've been feeding him, Hagar? No wonder he gets in trouble. What was the beating for this time? Stealing fruit? Insolence to his elders?"

Hagar mastered her own anger and spoke as calmly as she could. "That," she said, her words measured, "is a matter between Ishmael and Mamre." She kept her face expressionless. "And me," she added.

"You forget yourself," Sarah said. "You may be

free. You may have the doubtful status of a concubine to the lord Abraham. But you are a member of my household, and while you are you'll keep a civil tongue in your head."

Hagar looked at her. She felt strangely puzzled. Sarah's words carried none of their usual load of resentment and anger. This cold, controlled behavior was so unlike her that . . . "My apologies," she said with no hint of apology at all in her tone. "Is there something I can do for you, my lady?" The term of deference had a similarly hollow ring to it.

"No," Sarah said. "Other than discontinuing this silly business of encouraging Ishmael, here, to give himself airs. I don't know what's got into you, Hagar. It's not only foolish but cruel to give the child ambitions beyond his station."

Hagar stood up suddenly, her eyes blazing. "Beyond his station?" she said angrily. "He is the true son of the lord Abraham. You know that. The firstborn. The first child in this encampment to be circumcised and sealed into the faith. He—"

She stopped suddenly, embarrassed. She hated herself for having been the first to show anger. She hated the thin, superior smile on Sarah's long face. And something—something she could not define, something she feared the more for it—made her reach out a protective hand toward her son.

And then it hit home to her, and her heart sank. "You're not . . . ?" Then, seeing the triumphant gleam in Sarah's eye, she pulled Ishmael to her with a desperate possessiveness. "But . . . you are, aren't you?" she said in a low voice. "You're pregnant? After all these years? After . . . ?"

But Sarah's silence was assent enough—that, and the suddenly passionate smile on her face, a face to which passion was normally a stranger. Sarah inclined her head slightly in farewell. Then Abraham's wife— his true and only wife—turned and walked with dignity up the path toward her own quarters.

Wild colors once again painted the western sky. Sitting in the door of his tent in the heat of the late afternoon, Abraham dozed off. His head sank on his chest; his hands, folded together in his lap over his crossed legs, relaxed.

The sun, a flat-hued ball, dove sluggishly into the mirage, sinking into a many-hued surface that stood, now, many degrees above the normal horizon. Abraham slept on. Dusk approached. The sky to the east grew darker. A light wind stirred the leaves beneath the deciduous trees. Abraham's sleep, fitful at first, entered a new plateau . . . and then suddenly he awoke. Only it was not like awakening. It was like . . . it was like being disembodied, free of gravity and of physical sensation alike. His point of view was that of a bird on high, looking down on a bare mountaintop whose base disappeared below into impenetrable clouds.

He looked down. Atop the hill knelt an old man, skinny, naked, pitiful-looking. The old man's white hair stirred in a light wind that Abraham, from his vantage point high above, could not feel. The old man down there shivered.

It took a moment for Abraham to realize who the old man was—thin, weak-looking, shivering as much from fear as from the cold. It was himself. Yes, he thought, I look like that, don't I? I'm an old man. I should be weak in the thighs, phthisic, impotent, addled. My life should be nearing its end. Yet . . . He looked at the old man down below and knew the reason for his fear. It had nothing to do with his age. It had to do with . . .

But then the hilltop was bathed in light. Abraham saw the old man's body relax; he could share with him a feeling of ineffable physical calm washing over the old body that knelt so far below.

He was in the presence of the God.

The God was to be feared; was He not the master of life and death? Could He not snuff out a life in the twinkling of an eye? Could He not end the world in a moment?

Yet the God was more than fear. He was reassurance as well. The giver as well as the taker away of life, He acted never on caprice, always with justice. If he asked a man to put away his wife, sacrifice a son . . .

The clouds parted. The old man on the hilltop looked up. And Abraham's viewpoint, high above him, turned to where the old man's eyes sought the horizon.

In the vision that had opened up below him he could see the great Sink of Siddim, with its gleaming blue sea, and with the Cities of the Plain clearly visible below him.

Suddenly his eye, unbidden, focused sharply on a city he knew to be Sodom—on it, and on a smaller city just up the seacoast. Gomorrah, the sister city of Sodom. Gomorrah the wicked. Gomorrah, the procurer to Sodom's whoremaster ways.

The heavens opened above the two cities, and from the skies above a great light shone, two-pronged, upon the cities. A light that gave off a terrible heat. It was the visible finger of the God, touching the spoiled work of Man.

Abraham thought, *Lot. Lot and his household* . . . And he said, "No, Lord. Please. Punish the wicked if you will. But spare the good. Surely there must be good men in the city . . . don't destroy them along with the evil ones. Please . . . there must, there *must* be fifty people there worth saving. Please . . . would you spare the city for fifty people?"

But even as he said it, he knew the answer. The question was a moot one. There were not fifty righteous, upright persons in the doomed city below, the city that stood transfixed by the mighty light from above. "Lord," he said in despair. "Please. Forty? Thirty? Twenty?"

The light still shone with an unshakable resolve. And although no word formed in his head, Abraham suddenly knew that the God would, on his request, spare the city if ten upright men could be found in it.

But no such ten men could be found.

His heart sank even farther. *Lot,* he thought. *Lot; his wife and children; his slaves and servants.* . . .

They were doomed. Doomed to a horrible death in
the coming destruction of the two Cities of the Plain
. . . unless he could remove them somehow, get them
to safe ground.

He did not plead with the God now. He bowed his
head, conscious of the unstated, but unmistakable, fate
of the cities and all who would be living in them when
the God chose to strike. And when . . . when would
that be? In a day? A week? A year?

Suddenly he knew. And, as suddenly, he knew that
the life in Sarah's womb was that of a boy-child—of
the true promised son of his blood.

It would not be Ishmael, the child of a concubine,
with whom the God would make His covenant forever.
It would be the son he had fathered upon Sarah. His
name would be Isaac—the word meant "laughter"—
and his seed it was that would rule the land given by
the God to Abraham. It would be Isaac who would
become the father of nations . . .

. . . and as the new life flowed in the child Isaac's
veins, as the covenant passed to a new generation, the
light of life would die in Siddim.

Sodom and Gomorrah would die on the day of
Isaac's birth. And all the life in the cities would die
with them. With wildly mixed emotions, he bowed his
head—somehow he saw things now from the eyes of
the old man on the hilltop, and the two were one—and
accepted the harsh and impartial judgments of the
God.

Ishmael, he thought. *Poor Ishmael.* But in the general mental turmoil of the moment the thought left
him, and his mind instead struggled between mixed
feelings of joy and foreboding.

He awoke in a cold sweat, shivering against the
evening chill. Night had come on, and cold fogs lay on
the bottoms.

CHAPTER SEVENTEEN

I

They had passed into a wholly different area now—a changed country, with a new and strange weather pattern. The season of winter rains and chill did not, as it did elsewhere, give way to a gradual warming of the land, a slow and imperceptible metamorphosis into spring. Instead, the end of the wet season was heralded by a week of sudden blazing heat, brought on by a hot, dry east wind that stirred a dusty haze in the air along the trail.

Ahuni and his companions had never seen anything remotely like it, and they commented ceaselessly to Keret about it. Eshcol's son tended to shrug the matter off. It was the natural way of things, and one did not question nature. One accommodated himself to it: "It pays to watch your temper when the hot wind blows. In the season of heat a chance word may set off an argument that may lead to a duel, a feud, a blood enmity that will last for years." He smiled. "In the days of a violent-tempered man like my father sometimes the hot wind would sow the seeds of mayhem and death. We used to give him a wide berth in those times. He loved us children very much—but such was the effect of the wind upon him that a misdeed of ours that would ordinarily provoke no more than a harsh word would then provoke a cuff that would make our ears ring for days."

Ahuni, pulling up alongside him, looked around at

the sudden upthrusting of wild grass and thistle. The rainy season had been short here, and the land would have a brief flowering in this dry country. "Is this the end of the rains altogether?" he asked.

"It may be. You never can tell. Sometimes thunderstorms follow the first week of the hot wind. This year? I think not. I think we are in for a dry spell. It does not matter much. We are good at getting the most out of the land here. The growing seasons overlap and as one kind of plant dies another bursts forth. It is even harvest time—imagine, harvest in the spring—in some areas here. A number of Abraham's people have begun cultivating the land north of our domain; they will bring in the hay now, and they'll be harvesting wheat and barley next month. My own people keep bees, and the hives are bursting with delicious honey. The fruit trees and the grape vines are heavy; it will be a good harvest."

"It's a fine country," said Zakir, coming up behind them. "It looks so barren ... but when you get up close it's thick with life."

"Yes," Keret said with pride. He waved to a solitary man sitting, near his tethered horse, at the top of a hill. "Look. One of Abraham's people. We have had some raids from the desert Bedouin lately, as you know. We watch closely these days for banditry, and we police our own part of the trade routes here. For all practical purposes we are in my country now—mine and Abraham's and my Uncle Aner's and Mamre's. Since the Elamite War no one seriously disputes our domain ... but we're determined that things are going to stay that way. That's why there exists a better than usual chance you will find work among us. There is a whole generation coming up since the battle against the Four Kings, and they will have to be well armed against future problems. Our numbers have nearly doubled since that day. I'll have work for you myself, among my own people—but I'll wager Abraham will welcome you as well."

"I'm looking forward to meeting him," Ahuni said. "For one thing, the more he can tell me of Belsunu the

better. I believe you said Abraham was with him when
he died."

"Yes. He can satisfy your curiosity, I'm sure. And
pardon my asking, but your curiosity does seem out of
the ordinary. Was he that famous a smith?"

"Well, yes. But I have reason to believe he was
also . . ."

"Ahuni," Zakir broke in, not entirely disinterestedly.
"Do you know? I've just put two and two together for
the first time. I think I've heard of this Abraham, or
Abram, or whatever his name is . . . back in Haran."
He pulled abreast of Keret. "Did he ever live up that
way? I think I may have done business with people
who knew him—maybe even with relatives of his."

"You may very well have," Keret said. "Abraham—
his name *was* Abram then—came into Canaan from
Egypt, but before that he had spent many years in
Haran. I think you'll find much in common talking to
him. For one thing, he's actually a Mesopotamian like
yourself . . . and like Belsunu."

"A Mesopotamian? From what city?"

"From Ur. From back before the Fall."

Zakir laughed out loud. "Imagine, Ahuni! A countryman who's turned into a rich sheikh here! By all the
gods, I like the area more and more. If we can find
work, I think we'll enjoy it here."

High on the opposite hill another sentry looked
down from horseback. He responded to Keret's wave
with a barely perceptible nod of recognition. He looked
alert, armed, dangerous. Ahuni glanced sharply at
Zakir behind Keret's back; Zakir, eyebrows raised,
nodded back thoughtfully. They were back in civilized
country again. But what kind of civilization would it
turn out to be?

The runner, his horse lathered and dead tired, pulled
up within sight of Abraham's tent. He was in the process of dismounting when Abraham saw him and came
down to meet him. "Here," the old man said. "You're
the messenger I sent to my nephew in Sodom, aren't
you?"

"Yes, sir," the runner said, wiping his brow with a corner of his tunic. "Hanno of Hebron, sir. I joined your service a year ago."

"Oh, yes. My apologies for forgetting. I grow old . . . but look you, my nephew—what does he say to me?"

Hanno reached inside his garment and retrieved a flat clay tablet. "Here, sir. I can't read it. It's in a tongue I don't understand."

Abraham took it and squinted at the tiny cuneiform marks. "Of course. My own tongue. Now let's see . . . 'Speak to my revered uncle, Abraham: I shall not leave the city. Business has never been better. My absence now would be disastrous for some crucial dealings in lands which I have been putting together over two years' time. . . .' " The old man shook his head. "The fool! The shortsighted, stubborn fool!"

Hanno shrugged. "There didn't seem to be much I could do to convince him, sir. Besides, there's some sort of 'Festival Year' thing going on there now. All year. Something having to do with the religion of the city."

"I hear ominous reports of the things going on in connection with just that, my young friend. If even a small portion of them are true . . ." But then he stopped. Of course they were true. What other reasons would the God have for the coming destruction of the city? Depravity . . . blasphemy . . . homosexuality . . . incest . . . "I think I'm going to have to go to Sodom myself and see what is going on . . . and if necessary to bring Lot and his family out of the city myself."

Hanno shook his head incredulously. "I don't think he'll come, sir. I don't think he'll be listening to reason. Not even from you, sir."

A wearily ironic smile flitted across the old man's face. " 'Not even' from me, eh? From me least of all. I've never been able to persuade him. He's always had a mind of his own." He sighed. "Other than all that, were he and his household in good health when you saw them?"

A guarded look suddenly neutralized Hanno's features. "Uh, yes, sir," he said. "In good health."

Abraham was quick to catch the nuance. "Ah. But all is not well there, you mean?"

Hanno's carriage was stiff, his voice restrained. "Their ways are not mine, sir," he said. "I think they are not yours either."

"Ah. You mean, I think, that he has embraced the ways of the city with open arms." Abraham's voice was full of barely controlled despair now; he was thinking about the ten good men. "Please. Be honest with me."

"I'd rather not comment, sir."

"I understand. Well, thank you for the errand. I'll make a point of remembering your service to me. It appears I have to go over there and see everything firsthand." He looked up just then and noted the chagrin on Hanno's young face. "You'd rather I didn't do that, eh? You're being protective of my feelings. Well, my thanks to you. I have seen so much in this long life of mine. But you're thinking I still have some shocks left to see."

"I'd rather not say, sir."

"I see. Well, thank you." His despairing nod dismissed the servant, who turned smartly on one heel and strode away. Abraham's eyes followed him for a moment . . . and then he saw Hagar standing, small and silent, as darkly lovely as ever, looking at him, not ten paces away.

Somehow this saddened him even more than Hanno's news had. "Hello, my dear," he said in a dull voice. "What can I do for you?"

The hurt in her eyes was so great he could not look at her directly. "My lord," she said. "The lady Sarah tells me she's pregnant. Is this true?"

Abraham looked at her, and, chastened, looked away. "Yes," he said. "We're pretty certain by now."

Hagar broke in, her voice plaintive. She was already on the verge of tears. "The lady Sarah says that if she has . . . if she bears a son, my Ishmael will no longer be considered the firstborn son of your house. He will no longer be your heir. This . . . this despite the fact that he is your own true son, the first-conceived child of your blood." She took a deep breath, audibly; it was almost a sob. "He was to have been the heir to all you own. You told me so. He was the first child sealed into your faith, the first circumcised according to the laws of your God. Yet . . ." Now it was a sob, an unmistakable one, which interrupted her passionate utterance.

"Hagar," Abraham said wearily, "it is the laws of my people. The son of a concubine is regarded as the heir only in the absence of issue of the wife of wives. You knew that when—"

"—when I agreed to concubinage? I was never given the option of disagreeing. You know that. I was a slave at the time. I was *told* to do this."

"Yes, but . . ."

"I was told to have a son by you . . . and I did. And he's a beautiful, strong, intelligent son, the best son a man could ask for in the whole world. And now you propose to disinherit him, after thirteen years of promises, just because . . ."

"Hagar, it is the law. The custom. It is—"

"You're a *king* here! In all but name! You can make your own laws! If you do this it is by choice! By choice! You'll be taking away everything you've promised my son—*your* son—just because of your own unwillingness to change a rule which you, as lord and master here, could change with a wave of your hand! My lord, it isn't just! It isn't honest!"

"Hagar, you go too far—"

"Too far?" she said, her passion unspent. "Too far? By all the gods of my people, my lord, how am I going too far when I remind you of promises you made, and remind you that it is the honorable thing—the *only* honorable thing—to honor promises made, even if—" Her voice turned bitterly accusing here. "—even if they've only been made to an ex-slave who has shared your bed at your express command and borne your child at your express command and—"

"Hagar, what can I do? Our laws are handed down by the God Himself—"

"The God?" she said, her voice acid. "What kind of God is it who tells you to ruin my life and my son's, to devalue us on a moment's notice—and after the most solemn pledges—from human beings with status and a future to ... to the place of ... of cattle in your herds? *No*," she sobbed. "Worse than cattle. Worse by far. A cow has a place here. We'll have none at all. You've raised our hopes to the skies ... and then dashed them to a thousand pieces just as my son comes to manhood."

Abraham had a sudden inspiration. "Hagar, Sarah has not yet borne a male child. A male child." He watched the truth of this register on her tearful face. "Think upon that." He put one hand on her thin shoulder and felt real pain when she winced at his touch. "Hagar. It is in the hands of the God."

When she had gone, Abraham, his heart pounding fast, leaned against the bole of a spreading terebinth for support. "Please," he implored the God. "Please don't make me go through this. Her words are a knife in my breast." But the God was not with him now. There was no answer, no sign of any kind that his words had been heard. *I'm being tested again,* he thought suddenly. *I'm caught between hammer and anvil. If I follow the command of the God, I'm guilty of every injustice she has accused me of ... and I'll have to live with the fact the rest of my life.* On the other hand, the only posture possible in the face of the God's explicit command was one of absolute and unquestioning obedience. If he faltered in this for so much as an instant, not only would his own life be forfeit, so would the lives and fortunes of an infinite number of his descendants. ... Worse. Perhaps there would be no descendants at all. Perhaps, if he failed the God, his boy Isaac would die without issue. Perhaps ...

"Is something wrong, sir?"

It was the young man, Hanno, again. Abraham looked speechlessly at him. Then he swallowed hard and said in a hoarse croak, "I ... I'm all right. It's just that ..." He straightened up, mastered himself. "Excuse me. You have a message for me, my friend?"

"Yes, sir. The lord Keret is back from his scouting trip to the northern lands. He's brought some visitors with him ... and he thought you'd want to know as

soon as they arrived. 'They're some of his fellow Meso-
potamians,' he says, 'and most likely it'll make the lord
Abraham feel good to meet fellow countrymen and
talk with them in his own language.' "

Abraham smiled wanly. "How thoughtful of him.
Please thank him and . . . no, I'll come with you. He's
right. It would make me feel better right now. Please,
be so kind as to lead me to them."

Distraction, he thought. *Any kind of distraction.*

II

There was a place on the side of the hill where a
spring burst forth from the bare ground. Below this
was a spot where someone had dammed the little
stream and made a shallow bathing pool. Keret led his
fellow travelers to this place, and, gratefully, Ahuni,
Zakir, and Belanum washed off the dust of days of
travel as Zakir, grinning, taught Keret's men a bawdy
song of the Babylonian stews by rote, a syllable at a
time.

Ahuni washed his tunic and laid it on a flat rock to
dry in the sun; then, going to the packs he had taken
from the asses' backs, he withdrew a leather bottle.
"Keret," he said. "Look. Good wine of Mitanni."

But as he looked up, still wearing only his narrow
loincloth, he saw they had been joined by two men at
the spring. One, a tall, thin, white-haired and white-
bearded man of dignity and gentle bearing, could only
be the patriarch Abraham. With him was a powerfully
built man in his middle thirties, a man with a likable,
open sort of face and a ready smile. Ahuni was rather
drawn to him at first.

"Ah," Keret said. "My lord?" He bowed, then
turned to the guests he had brought back from the
northern country. "Look here," he said. "Here's the
gentleman I've been telling you about." He wiped his

wet face with a clean rag and stepped out of the spring; one of his men handed him his loincloth. "Well, no need to stand on ceremony. Gentlemen: the lord Abraham—and this is our friend Enosh, conqueror in single combat of Chedorlaomer of Elam, King of Nations." He turned again to Abraham. "Countrymen of yours, my lord. Zakir of Babylon, a merchant of Haran. His son Ahuni, a master armorer. Belanum, their friend and scribe."

The three bowed to their host. As they did, Ahuni continued the motion and reached for the bottle he had laid down. "Well met," he said, standing erect and speaking in his native tongue. "And if I haven't forgotten my old local customs by now, my lord, it used to be customary to mark an auspicious meeting with a drink of good mountain wine."

But as he looked at the old man, it was evident Abraham had not been listening. Instead Abraham stood as if rooted to the spot, his mouth open with surprise, his eyes on Ahuni's hard young body. "I ... I beg your pardon," Abraham said. "Did I understand you to say that you are the son of ... of this gentleman here?" He nodded at Zakir, a perplexed look on his face. "Because ... pardon me," he said again, sitting down on a flat stone, his hand over his heart. "Pardon me ... it's as though I'd seen a ghost."

Ahuni stepped forward. "Are you all right, sir?" he said. He glanced over Abraham's shoulder at the thirtyish man—what was the name? Enosh? "Here, sir ... take a drink of this, if you will."

"No, no ... thank you," Abraham said. "It's just that—"

"Oh, I see," Ahuni said, smiling. "You've noticed the slave-mark and the bar through it. Well, sir, if you'll remember, among our people being a freedman is not regarded as a drawback."

"Neither is it among us," smiled Enosh. His speech was accented but serviceable. "I'm a freedman myself, thanks to the lord Abraham."

"Very well," Ahuni said. "In my case Zakir not only emancipated me, he adopted me as his heir. He has since then been father and more than father to me."

He grinned affectionately at Zakir, who was just struggling into a clean garment.

"It . . . it isn't that," Abraham said. "It's the . . . the birthmark on your back. I've only known one man in my life who bore that mark—and let me tell you, my young friend, give you twenty years and you'd be as like him as two peas in a pod."

Ahuni knelt before Abraham, his eyes shining. "Belsunu?" he said. "You—you knew Belsunu? And he *did* bear this birthmark, sir? My lord . . . I can't remember my blood father. I was taken from him when I was little more than a baby. But . . . but I have been looking for him ever since . . ." He swallowed and could say no more. His eyes were abrim with tears.

Abraham stood and raised Ahuni to his feet. His own eyes were damp—and, indeed, a strange quiet had settled on the little gathering around the spring. Every eye was on the two of them—and no one noticed the stricken look on Zakir's broad face.

"Ahuni?" Abraham said gently. "Did I get the name right? Ah, yes . . . look at you. You've his eyes, and his big shoulders. You're a smith, you say? An armorer? Did you hear that, Enosh?" he said over his shoulder, his voice quivering with emotion. "An armorer. It runs in the blood! The legend was right—the legend of the mark of Cain. Ahuni . . . I was with your father when he died. He had searched for you all over the known world, from the Land of the Two Rivers to the borderlands of the Egyptians' domain." He sighed; he was weeping openly now, and so was Ahuni. "I was with him the moment the light died in his eyes. He was as strong as a bear and the gentlest spirit I have ever met in all my years. There was no man or woman or child in all the domain I share with Mamre and his kin who did not know Belsunu and love him."

Ahuni tried once to speak, but failed. He bowed his head, overcome by his emotions.

"Ahuni," Abraham said, a new benevolence entering his voice. "I made a vow to Belsunu as he lay dying. I told him I would continue, for his sake, the search for his son, and I have. And now I have found him. Do you hear, all? I have found the son of Belsunu!" He put his thin, but very strong, hands on Ahuni's broad shoulders. "Ah, feel the sinews there. You're your father's son all right. The disease had wasted him when we knew him—but ill as he was, he had your bulk and heft . . . and you've his power. Yes! *Yes!*" Now he was smiling triumphantly through his tears. "Enosh! Doesn't it fill your own heart with happiness, my friend? We've found him! I've found the lost son of a dear comrade . . . and now I can make good on the promise I made to him."

"Promise, sir?" Enosh said.

"Yes, yes . . . I promised Belsunu I would, if I ever found his son. treat him as I might a son of my own. And so it shall be. Ahuni! Well met, indeed!" And, his own smile gentle and accepting. Abraham took his surrogate son in his arms, crooning wordlessly over the young giant as he might have done over a child.

The day of their arrival, of course, became a festival day—one that brought pleasure to everyone in the encampment who had known the smith Belsunu in the days of the Elamite War. The three travelers were introduced to about a hundred more people than they would be able, later, to remember by name. Ahuni's head swam from the host of new impressions, new faces, and—most of all—the old and long-suppressed emotions the day had unleashed in him.

At the great feast that night Ahuni heard one guest after another tell tales of Belsunu. until he almost felt he was coming to know his lost father personally. From Abraham, too, he heard the melancholy tale of how Belsunu had lost his family in the first place, and of the years he had spent hunting him down. always in vain. He heard of the smith's deep friendship with the great Egyptian warrior, Sneferu, and learned how it had been, as much as anything, the marvelous weapons Belsunu, with his strange new methods and his marvelous touch. had created that had enabled Abraham's heavily outnumbered people to defeat the armies of the Four Kings. Finally—and in some ways this was the most moving and marvelous story of all—Abraham told once again the tragic tale of Cain, the farmer-smith, who fell from grace in the first days of the world and who, with all his male issue, was marked with a special sign that told all nations of the trade they practiced and allowed them to pass all frontiers even in time of war without being harmed: a mark shaped curiously like the paw print of a lion. And he, Ahuni, was one of these—a Child of the Lion! Once again, he marveled at the strange destiny that had led him to being rescued, freed, adopted, and above all, trained by a smith. And here he was among friends, dear friends who had known and loved his father and who extended that love now to him and his companions. He couldn't ever remember having been so happy.

Depressed, Zakir wandered away from the big campfire and the great gathering before it. He felt excluded, unloved, devalued. From Ahuni's only known father he had gone in a matter of hours to a status more like that of a guardian or conservator. The celebration, joyous and expansive though it was in intention, was not for him. Its very reason for being was one that by its nature excluded him from the celebrating.

He'd had quite a bit to drink already, but none of it had done anything to raise his spirits. Indeed, this seemed to be one of those times when drink, strong drink, tended rather to depress than to palliate depression. In spite of this he took with him a leather bag still half full of wine when he slipped away from the feast.

The moon was no more than a day short of full, and hung in the clear desert sky, big and bright. It was no problem to pick his way up the hill to the trail that led back to his own campground. Walking slowly and sure-footedly, he raised the bag again and again, squirting the raw red wine into his open mouth. Finally, the bag empty, he threw it over his shoulder into the scrub beside the trail. Shaking his head, he resumed his way . . .

. . . and then stopped.

What was that noise? Thin and remote, it sounded

like a woman's voice. Calling out. Crying for help . . . a woman's? Or a child's?

He turned his head this way, that; he tried to pin-point the exact location of the repeated cries.

It seemed to be coming from . . . yes, there it was again. Beside the trail. Down the hill. In the arroyo below.

"Help! Please! Someone . . ."

"Here," he bellowed hoarsely. "Where are you? Keep calling, will you! Louder, so that I can hear you!"

"Over here . . . please . . . quickly. . . ."

Zakir pushed his way through the bushes—and almost suffered the same fate as the person who'd called out. By the light of the moon he could see the place where the bank had caved in. He couldn't see very far down, though. "Keep talking," he said. "I can't see you. I don't know how far down you are."

"I'm not far down," the voice said. Now he could make it out: the voice of an adolescent boy, most likely. "But . . . every time I move I slip a little farther. If you could reach your arm down . . . maybe I can get hold of it."

"That probably isn't the best idea," Zakir said, totally sober now, keeping his voice soothing and reassuring. "I've only one arm. If I put an arm down to you I've nothing to hang on up here with, and we'd both get pulled down. Look, there's a tree here. I can hang onto that and maybe hold my legs down for you to climb up on. Do you have both arms free?"

"Yes," the voice said. "Yes. I hurt my leg when I fell, but my arms are all right."

"Fine," Zakir said. "Now just remain still and don't wriggle. I'll sit down here . . . I think I can hang on just so. . . ."

"I think I can reach you," the boy said. And presently Zakir felt a hard young hand on his ankle. The boy's grip was strong, sure. "Now . . . now, if I can only . . ."

Zakir took the whole weight, holding tightly to the small tree. The boy climbed up using only his hands:

an exceptionally strong lad, this. When he pulled himself up alongside Zakir, he found his left ankle would not bear his weight. Zakir helped him up, feeling the chunky solidity of the boy's body. *Why, he's built a lot like me when I was his age,* Zakir thought.

"Here," he said. "Sit down on this stone. Let me have a look ... ah, you really hurt yourself, didn't you? Looks like a bad sprain ... but here, you didn't get those welts on your leg from falling down."

"No, sir," the boy said. "I was caught riding one of Mamre's horses without permission. He gave me a beating."

"Ah, well," Zakir grinned. "I had the same thing happen to me once, many days' ride away from here. Look, I'm Zakir of Babylon. We'd better get to be friends, I suspect; it looks like I'm going to have to try to help get you home, wherever that is."

"I'm Ishmael, son to the lord Abraham," the boy said. "Perhaps if I tried it now ... *Oww!* Oh, oh ... I guess you're right. I thought I could walk, but—"

"It's all right, son. I didn't have anything better to do right now anyway. Be glad to help you. But ... I'm curious. I thought Abraham had no children. He said his wife was pregnant with her first child."

"Oh. I'm his son by the lady Hagar. She's Abraham's concubine."

"I see. I was wondering how it was that Abraham would let a son of his be beaten by another sheikh like Mamre."

"He ... *ow!* He raised me as his heir ... but now he says that if Sarah has a son I won't be his heir any more. It ... *mmmmm,* that hurts! It isn't fair. People shouldn't be able to break their word to you, should they, sir? They should do something just like they said they would."

"I've no disagreement with you there, son. It *doesn't* seem right. Don't repeat what I said. I may need to find work here for me and my son and my friends."

"Here, sir ... down the hill here ... that tent on the right. ... Oh, there's my mother."

At first Zakir could make out no more than a short, slim, rather shapely female body. Then as the full moonlight fell upon her face he could see Ishmael's mother—what was the name, now? Hagar?—was fair of face, with strong Nile Delta features on a wide-cheeked, oval face. Her eyes shone up at him. "Ishmael?" she said. "What's the matter, darling?"

"I hurt my leg, Mother. . . . This man helped me. Sir? This is my mother, Hagar."

"Your servant, ma'am," Zakir said in his best courtly manner. *Really now, she's quite lovely. How old? Thirty-five? And concubined out to a graybeard like Abraham? What a pity. What a waste.*

III

"Ahuni," Abraham said, "I looked around just now and could see no sign of your honorable father, Zakir. And here I had been looking forward to hearing news of my kin in Haran. Belanum, here, tells me Zakir knows relatives of mine there—people who have done business with him in his merchant days."

"That's odd," Ahuni said. "He was right there."

Belanum contradicted him—and managed, diplomat that he was, to make the contradiction sound deferential. "Pardon me," he said. "He's been gone for quite some time. I think he might not have been feeling well. He's been depressed a lot lately."

"Ah," Abraham said. "Zakir, then—he's a sensitive sort of man? I thought I caught that from . . . oh, his speech, his manner."

"Yes," Ahuni said. "It's one of the reasons why we love him, Belanum and I. Zakir has the biggest heart in all the world . . . and that's one of the things that makes it breakable. He's a man of moods . . . and his moods have run on the dark side lately."

Belanum stretched his bony toes out toward the fire. "Yes," he said. "And that isn't all, unfortunately. He went to a seer of sorts in the northern country recently, and he seems to have heard some particularly distressing predictions."

"That's curious," Abraham said, "I've had some disturbing dreams lately myself. Dreams . . . yes, and visions as well. They prey on my mind, too . . . and I'm a lot older and, presumably, less impressionable than Zakir." He offered the wine jug; Belanum refused it, but Ahuni held out his cup. "But is there more," he said, pouring, "to his current depression than this?"

"You're very astute, sir," Ahuni said. "Yes, there is more. We are in the land of Belsunu, my . . . my blood father. And this makes Zakir remember that I am not his blood son. That, in fact, he has no blood son of his own. It is a sore point with him."

"It's worse than that," Belanum said. "He feels he's losing you."

"I know," Ahuni said. "And what a shame he should feel that way, and should be so hard to reassure. How could Zakir lose me? I owe him my life. I owe him everything. And even if I didn't . . . well, how could one not love Zakir and treasure him above all men, even if one viewed him not as father but rather as friend? Tell me, Belanum. Have you ever had so fine a friend?"

"Only yourself." Belanum inclined his head, slightly embarrassed.

"Ah," Abraham said slowly. "If I felt so about another human being, I would not leave him in the dark about my feelings. I think I would take pains to let him know what I thought of him—the more so if I found him a man of moods, and the darker moods in the ascendancy." He held up his two long-fingered old hands and looked at them.

Ahuni frowned unhappily at the ground before his feet. "You're so right," he said. "Belanum, we've been remiss. I wish he were here."

Belanum stood up and fumbled for his sandals. "I'll go looking for him," he said. "By your leave, sir. . . ." He bowed to Abraham and went out of the circle of firelight.

Abraham watched him go. "He's like a younger brother to you, I see," he said. "You're fortunate in your companions, my young friend, be they blood kin or no." He sighed deeply. "I wish I were as fortunate in my own kin. I have a nephew, over in Sodom. I am afraid he . . . well, he hasn't amounted to much." He sighed again. "No, he's worse than that, much as it hurts me to admit it. I'm not sure just how far he *has* strayed from the path, but I have the unhappy feeling that he's pretty far gone now."

"In what way, sir? I mean, pardon my curiosity, but—"

"No, no. Feel free to ask. As Belsunu's son you're as good as family to me—and besides, I feel a curious affinity with you. I would wish the son now stirring in my wife's womb—if son he is—to be much like you."

"Thank you, sir. In so many ways I feel very much at home already—and that's a strange feeling for a rootless fellow like an armorer to have."

"This is your home as long as it feels that way to you, my boy. It will not be your home forever. That's not the way of a true Child of the Lion. But the thought of a home will eventually stir your heart, make no mistake about that. You have found out who you are, and it now remains to make that home for yourself —wherever it happens to be—so that you can train your son to follow in your steps. Otherwise the line will be broken, as Belsunu for so long thought it to be."

"I understand, sir. So far I've known many women, but none has touched my heart."

"Ah. Like Zakir?"

"No . . . I think that Zakir might have settled down with a wife some time back, if . . . well, there's the matter of his arm. He's self-conscious about it. Anyone would be. Over all the known world it's the badge of a thief. It held him back as a merchant . . . and now his second profession seems as much a thing of the past as his first."

"Leaving him, of course, a prey to all sorts of self-destructive thoughts. But like yourself . . . I'd say he simply hasn't met the right woman. Perhaps he will yet. He's still vigorous, I take it?"

"Very much a man, sir. He is a man women instinctively like and warm to. I've never known him not to have a half dozen of them on the string at any given time."

"I see. He *is* a warm man ... and this is a quality much beloved of women." He looked up just then, and smiled. "Enosh," he said to his visitor.

"My lord." Ahuni saw the man he'd first met with Abraham that afternoon. The face was still as guilelessly likable as ever. "You asked me to tell you how quickly we could make ready to go over to Siddim."

"Ah," Abraham said. "I'd forgotten. Thank you for reminding me." He turned to Ahuni and tapped himself self-deprecatingly on the temple. "My memory ... it isn't what it was, I fear. Without an intelligent and reliable friend such as Enosh at my side, I'd be in trouble most of the time. He has just reminded me that I'd asked him to make plans for that trip to see my nephew." A sudden thought raised his snow-white brows. "Ah, but ... Ahuni. Would you like to accompany us to Sodom? Who knows? You might well find some custom there for your wares. And I would enjoy your company—and so would our friend Enosh. Wouldn't you, Enosh?"

"I would indeed, sir." His voice carried in it not only respect, but deep affection for the old man. In a servant, whatever his caste, this was a good sign—and said much about Abraham as a leader. "Belanum showed me some samples of your work, Ahuni. You're a true son of Belsunu. I'd be hard pressed to come up with a better compliment than that." His smile radiated sincerity and trusty masculine friendliness. He turned back, though, to Abraham now. "Sir," he said. "You asked me the other day if I had a boon I might ask of you. I know that you never waste words, or say things you do not mean. I have thought of the matter, and I do have a request which I advance now with the greatest respect and love."

"Name it, my friend."

"The slave Rekhmira. He is able, industrious, gifted at the managing of men and lands."

"He is that."

"He was lamed in your service. He belongs in a

position which will use his mind more than his un-
equal, and unfit, limbs."

"So far I am in complete agreement. Go on. You
have a recommendation."

"My lord is, as usual, ahead of me. I ask one thing:
has my lord gotten better, or worse, service from me
since he freed me after the Elamite War?"

"You know the answer. I do not need to give it to
you. The service went from excellent to ... to superb,
unequaled. You are my right arm."

"I do my poor best, my lord. But the extension of
the question is this: might not the same treatment draw
the same response from a man like Rekhmira?"

Abraham smiled. He looked at Ahuni. "Observe if
you will," he said, "how skillfully this most valued of
retainers works upon me. When a servant is intelligent,
it is a sin in him to withhold his counsel. In this I have
little to reproach Enosh for, let me tell you, my
friend." He turned back to Enosh. "As you say, I am
sometimes ahead of you. Rekhmira is not only a good
and valued comrade of yours, he is a man overdue for
both advancement and emancipation. I have already
given the orders. On the next festival day he will be
given both his freedom and the management of my
southern herds, with, as payment for his services, a
fifth of all relevant revenues ... and a handsome retainer."

"My lord. . . ." Enosh was visibly moved—and
Ahuni liked him the more for it.

"Ahuni," Abraham said, "you yourself have been a
slave. So have some of the finest people I have ever
known. There is no justice in the institution. I have
thought much upon this matter. I shall raise this son of
mine—if son it is—to hate the practice of slavery. And
upon my death I shall leave instructions for the emancipation of every slave I own."

"I . . ." Ahuni swallowed hard, and looked up at
Enosh. The two exchanged glances blurred by tears.
"M-my lord," he said, "you mentioned going to Sod-
om? I . . . I'd be honored to accompany you." He swal-
lowed again. His voice was hoarse when he spoke to
Enosh. "And you, sir . . . you as well."

CHAPTER EIGHTEEN

I

Coming out of the little square into the narrow passageway that led to the broad street where Lot lived, Shepset suddenly felt a rough hand close about her ankle. Her nerves were bad already; she gasped and stumbled forward, trying to pull herself free, trying to stifle an outcry that had been building up in her throat for many minutes and that threatened now to become a hysterical shriek. She kicked; the hand's grip hardened. "P-please . . ." she said.

"Now, now," a gruff voice said. "Let's have a look at you, there, girl . . . don't be so standoffish. All's fair at festival time."

She pulled herself into the light below a lit window, dragging him with her, her fingers tearing at the sill. She could see him now; it might not have been a bad face before drink and drugs had addled it. "Stop!" she cried out. "Let me go! Or I'll—"

"Come on, now . . . you won't do anything. It's festival time . . . you owe it to yourself to—"

"Let go of me!" she yelled, a wild feeling of rage running through her. Her fingers closed around a broken tile that had fallen onto the sill. She picked it up in both hands and, raising it high, brought it down on the offending wrist. The man howled and let go. With a little gasp of surprise she spun away and took to her heels.

She had lost one sandal coming through the crowded

square; now she kicked the other one off and ran, fleet-footed, down the uneven dirt passageway. At the end of the passage, however, caution returned; she stopped and peered around the wall of the end house, looking out into the main thoroughfare.

Down the street a group of revelers, male and female, made their way. Their backs were to her . . . but they stood between her and her master's house. Better to wait. She watched them go, their path lit by the festival torches that hung in bronze holders from the walls of the earthen buildings to either side of the thoroughfare. Their clothing was in disarray, and two of the women were naked; so was one of the men. As she watched, a child scuttled out of the darkness to cross the street; one of the men grabbed it and held it up. "Come here, sweetie . . . there's a girl. . . ."

She put one hand to her heart, feeling its pounding through the thin tunic. Would it never end? The festival had been in session for two days now, and virtually the only sober breath any adult inhabitant of the city had drawn in that time had been spent in vomiting or in snoring away after a drunken orgy.

Somehow she had managed to avoid being raped thus far—but there had been many close calls. The only way she'd managed not to have problems with Lot's guests had been by staying away from them altogether, spending the time trying to ride herd on Lot's increasingly more rebellious, increasingly more wild daughters. By now Adah and Elisheba openly defied her; they had noticed the unsubtle change in the way their parents had treated her since the death of her protector, Eshcol. Worse, they had seen her beaten on Lot's orders. She had never had any authority over them after that.

But now . . . now they were gone, and she could not find them. And she was in great trouble. When she told Lot and Zillah that their daughters had slipped out into the night during festival time, when any man or woman found in the streets was considered fair game . . .

Of course, how could it have been otherwise? Having lost, once and for all, her ascendancy over the two girls, she could not control them. And when, on Lot's orders, she had left them alone while she delivered an invitation to a neighbor, an invitation to the orgy that had been going on for two days at Lot's place, the girls had slipped away. How could she be legitimately blamed for that?

Well, questions of legitimate blame—of fairness or anything like that—were of no use now. The way things stood, she could never count on anything again from Lot and Zillah but abuse. They had stored up so many petty resentments against her in the days when Eshcol had protected her that virtually any action of hers now drew their combined wrath in disproportionate quantities. And, with the girls gone, she would be lucky to get nothing worse than a beating.

Nevertheless, she had to tell them. Something had to be done—and she'd done all she could about finding the girls. Somehow, the implications of their disappearance had to be brought home to Lot and Zillah, no matter how besotted they might be. And someone had to help her find the girls.

Now. *Now!* They were gone . . . the street was clear. She sprinted out into the thoroughfare and ran heedlessly down the road. As she did, she knew her motions were throwing the hem of her tunic up in the air, showing off far too much of her body. She heard a cry of raucous male appreciation behind her; frightened, she redoubled her speed.

She made it to Lot's front door a step or two ahead of her pursuer. Once inside, she leaned, panting, against the door, shoving the bolt home. The man who had chased her pounded on the door once or twice, then quit in disgust. There would be other girls—and most of them would be more than willing.

She looked around her. The anteroom was full of discarded clothing. In the central hall of Lot's house there were sounds of revelry: off-pitch singing, drunken laughter. She took a deep breath and, throwing her shoulders back, walked out into the hall, past the jumbled bodies on the floor, heading for where Zillah sat splay-legged and bleary-eyed before a great table full of half-spoiled food, a cup of wine in her grimy hand. Zillah's hair was stringy, filthy, and hung over one eye. Her headdress had been torn away hours before; one shoulder was missing from her garment. She looked up at Shepset, her face full of sullen resentment. "What do you want?" she said in a slurred voice.

"Please," Shepset said, "Adah and Elisheba . . . they seem to have slipped away. Please, ma'am . . . someone has to help me. I can't find them."

Zillah just looked at her for a moment. Then she raised one hand and tossed the contents of the half-empty cup of wine in Shepset's face. As the girl put her hands to her face, Zillah threw the heavy cup at her. It hit Shepset on the mouth, and the girl shrank away from her. A thin line of blood ran down her chin. "Stupid bitch!" Zillah said. She seemed not to have got the message Shepset had brought. "Think you're so damned smart . . . I'll show you."

She stood up, weaving slightly on her feet, and bellowed out to the crowd around them in a fishwife's voice: "Hear me! Who wants a slave for the night? Who'll pay me for a night with this . . . this baggage here? Eh? You, Magon? Akborat?"

Shepset shrank away; but Zillah pursued her and held her by the neckline of her garment. "Please . . . no. . . ."

"*Shut up!*" Zillah croaked. "You! Akborat!" she yelled at a tall, masculine-looking woman who stood nearby, a supercilious smile on her long face. "Maybe you'd appreciate her more than a man would. Heaven knows she's a cold enough piece . . . but she'd respond eventually, in hands as practiced as yours."

There was no immediate response. Zillah belched and covered her mouth. Her cosmetics had faded and run, and her face was a mask of hatred. "All right," she croaked, "maybe you need a closer look at her."

Shepset shrank away again . . . but it was no use. Zillah, with the strength the alcohol and drugs had given her, tore Shepset's only garment all the way down to the hemline and yanked the shreds from her body. Shepset's hands went to lap and bosom. "Don't" she said in a bitter voice. "Please . . . don't."

She tried to back away . . . but ran into a new and

different pair of female hands: hands that caressed her intimately, insultingly. She stepped forward again, hugging her arms.

"All right. What'm I bid?" Zillah said. Her hand, ungently, patted Shepset's bare behind. "What'll you pay for a night with this slut? Magon? A jar of oil, perhaps? You, Akborat? How about that necklace you're wearing? I've coveted it for some time now."

Akborat stepped forward. Her hand, as big and sharp-angled as a man's, touched Shepset boldly, here, there. Shepset let her face go dead. Her eyes looked flaming arrows at Akborat. "Done," Akborat said. She pulled the golden necklace off her long neck and handed it to Zillah. "Now . . . come, darling . . . I saw a free room down the way. Don't give me any trouble, now . . . I'll make it worth your while, you'll see. I'll give you such pleasure . . ."

Miserably, Shepset let herself be guided down the long hallway. And suddenly she felt the panic in her heart give way miraculously to a cold cunning. She had to find a way out of this, somehow. Perhaps now was the time. . . .

She thought after this fashion all through Akborat's clumsy seduction of her. The cold hatred at the core of her took precedence over her disgust. She faked passion, consummation, exhaustion. She lay her head on one side as if she'd slipped off to sleep. Akborat looked away for a moment. When she did, Shepset's fingers closed around a heavy wine cup someone had left behind. She tensed herself . . . but the woman turned around just then.

"Ah, there," Akborat said. "You're awake. I'd thought you asleep. . . . You're really quite lovely . . . what a pity to see you fall into the hands of a pig like Agbar! I tried to get Zillah to sell you to me instead, but . . ."

"Agbar?" Shepset said. It was the first coherent word she had spoken. She sat up, one hand, buried in the bedclothes, still touching the heavy cup. "I don't understand. What's this about Agbar?" Her tone was wary. Agbar, son of one of the concubines of Bera of Sodom, was a powerful man in the city despite his bastardy. He was also a gross and brutal man who, some said, could get no sexual pleasure any more that did not involve the infliction of pain—pain in increasingly severe doses. Rumors had it that certain of his casual lovers, usually obtained by purchase, had not survived the night spent satisfying Agbar's savage passions.

"Oh ... I thought you knew. The sale's been held up while Agbar was out of the city. But they've been haggling over the matter for days. Rumor says the price now includes certain political considerations. Agbar has great influence in the city just now, and Lot hasn't missed the point. But it's very likely the sale will take place. What a very great pity." Her coarse hand fell on Shepset's naked thigh, stroking, caressing. "Poor dear. Poor darling. If I could have intervened, if I could have made Lot the right offer, I would have. Heaven knows I tried my best."

Shepset had all but made up her mind to keep quiet and, if she could, learn more. But the woman's touch sickened and angered her. Her fingers closed around the solid bulk of the cup—and before she knew what was happening she had swung the vessel and hit Akborat hard over one temple. The woman's eyes rolled back in her head ... and she tipped forward on her face, spread-eagled on the bed.

Shepset, her hands over her mouth, sat up straight, looking down at the gawky form on the bed. Horrified, she said, "What am I going to do now?"

Behind her she heard a sudden high-pitched sound —a female voice, giggling. She whirled, stood erect, her naked body alert, tense, the cup still in one hand.

Adah and Elisheba moved out from behind a curtain. Elisheba was still laughing. "Look, Adah ... Miss Virtue, who keeps telling *us* not to fool around with each other."

Adah's face was stern. "What have you done?" she said. "You're in trouble—big trouble. Why ... why, that's Akborat. She's very rich. Her brother is very big at court. Have . . . have you killed her?"

Shepset made no move to find out. "Where have you been?" she said in a low, controlled voice.

"Oh, we've been around . . . watching it all. Nobody saw us."

Shepset's face was bleak. This was the end. There was no going back now, not from where she stood. If Akborat lived, she would have her revenge . . . and even if she didn't, there was the impending sale to Agbar, She'd heard tales. . . . She turned, looked around the room. Discarded clothing lay in piles here and there. She searched through it.

"What are you doing?" Adah said. "Where are you going?"

"None of your business," Shepset said. "Just stay out of my way." She found a pair of sandals about the right size and laced them up her ankles. Then she reached into the pile and found a tunic, a robe.

The girls watched her dress. "You can't get away," Elisheba said. "Father will have you tracked down."

"Let him," Shepset said. She smiled coldly, triumphantly, holding up her latest acquisition. Someone had left a knife, sharp, elegantly scabbarded, in the pile of clothing. "I've got nothing left to live for here. I'll kill myself before I'll let myself be taken again." She hung the knife and its belt around her neck, then fastened the robe over it. "Don't try to follow me," she said.

The party went on past dawn. The sun was high when Lot heard the pounding at his front door. He staggered to his feet, bumping against the wall as he tried to get his balance. At the door he called out. "Who's there?" he said.

"Chemosh, my lord." Ah, his overseer. "I thought it best to come inside the city and warn you."

"Warn me? Warn me of what?" Lot looked down at his filthy, vomit-stained garment. The stench was overpowering. He made a bad face. "Speak up, man!"

"Very well, sir. The lord Abraham and companions

... they encamped outside the city walls last night at dusk. I think he's here to pay a visit."

Lot's heart almost stopped. Abraham! In Sodom! And in the middle of the Festival of Spring. . . .

II

A drunken reveler reeled into Ahuni, digging him painfully in the ribs. *Why*, Ahuni wondered, *did I agree to accompany Abraham to this sinkhole of a town called Sodom?* He had borne the crowds patiently for some time, but something about the drunken man's boorishness awakened a streak of black Babylonian temper in him. Ignoring Enosh's warnings, he turned and slammed the offender hard against the earthen wall of a dwelling behind him. Trembling with rage, Ahuni whispered between clenched teeth, "You! You mind what you're doing! Do you hear?"

Ordinarily the armorer's great bulk and imposing shoulders spelled enough visible trouble for anyone and instilled caution in any man with a trace of prudence in him. In one disgusted moment, however, Ahuni realized he was dealing with a person too far gone even to take warning. He released the man, who slid giggling down the wall to a sitting position in the street. Enosh pulled Ahuni away just as a thick clot of celebrants elbowed its way into the little square before the ostler's shed.

"Easy," Enosh said. "Don't pay any attention. They're out of their heads, all of them."

Ahuni made a wry face. "I thought I'd seen the worst, back when I was a slave in the gutters of Babylon. But this . . . gods! What kind of people are these?"

"People," Enosh said calmly, "who—Abraham says —lie under a curse of the God of Abraham's people.

He's come here to ask his nephew to leave before the God destroys the city with fire from the skies, he says."

"Agh! I can almost believe it." Ahuni looked Enosh in the eye. "Do you? I mean ... this God of Abraham's? I remember you've been a slave, just like me. It's my experience that few of the slaves I knew when I was one ever believed in anything at all. Anything but people, anyhow."

"I know what you mean," Enosh said in his slow, mellow voice. He turned into a side street. "Shortcut to Lot's place," he explained. "But your question ... I didn't at first; although I went through the ceremonies and was sealed to Abraham's faith, it was mainly for love of the old man. Now? Now I'm not so sure. This El-Shaddai is not a hard master, all in all. And he never embarrasses you with his grossness, as these gods of Canaan do." He pointed at a drunken couple making awkward and ungainly love in the street; on closer inspection, both turned out to be men. "See? And mind you, this is a *religious* festival of theirs. Those pigs in the street ... they're pleasing their gods by acting this way." His face, visible in the light of the overhead torches on the walls, was thoughtful even in its disgust at what he saw. He shook his head. "Another thing. Abraham tells me El-Shaddai is no particular friend of slavery."

"A point in his favor," Ahuni agreed. "Incidentally, someone said you were getting married. My congratulations."

"Yes. A freed servant of Abraham's, a girl of his people named Mibtahiah. Abraham is even providing a dowry. Can you imagine that? What a man he is."

"I'm very taken with him," Ahuni said. The two flattened themselves against the wall in the narrow passage as three revelers passed noisily by. "Ugh!" he said, watching the dirty, mostly bare, bodies go down the street, drunkenly bouncing off both sides of the passage. "Imagine! And they're apparently attractive to one another. I'd rather touch an adder."

"Well, we won't be here long, I suspect," Enosh said calmly. "Abraham is sure to think even less of this than you or I do. I'll bet he's roasting Lot's ears right now."

"Well, I hope so." Ahuni stopped. "Just look at that, will you? Up ahead, under the archway. Right out in the open."

But as the two watched, the man and woman—he wearing only a tattered undergarment, she wearing by now nothing at all—moved out from under the arch and they could see there were two men involved, and one of them was holding the girl's arms from behind. She managed to kick the first man hard in the thigh before he hit her in the face with his fist.

Ahuni flexed his big hands. "Now that's something else. It appears she doesn't want to play. The rest of this isn't my business. That is." He moved quickly down the passage.

Enosh, following him, tripped and fell. When he got up he could see Ahuni put a hand on the first man's arm. There was a flash of metal in the flickering torchlight; the second man lunged forward and barely missed burying a short sword in Ahuni's belly. Enosh broke into a trot.

Up ahead in the passage Ahuni grappled with the armed man; the other man was kept busy fighting the girl, who, encouraged, was doing everything she could to break away. As Enosh lumbered down the street toward them, he could see the man and girl slip back under the arch. He blinked once; Ahuni seemed to be doing all right. Coming to a halt, he ducked inside the arch.

As he did he heard the flat jangle of a sword falling into the street. In a moment there was the sound of a heavy body following it to the uneven cobbles. "It's all right, Enosh," Ahuni said behind him. "Get the girl."

But as Enosh stepped out of the torchlight, something hard hit him on the back of the head and drove him to his knees. A second blow—powerful, pile-driving—landed on his back. He tried to scuttle forward. There was someone up ahead of him; apparently there were more than two of them. The girl let out a muffled cry.

In the outer passage Ahuni reached high on the wall

and pulled down a pitch-soaked torch. Pausing for the blink of an eye at the archway, he tossed the torch, still blazing, into the middle of the enclosed space. Immediately he could see Enosh on his hands and knees, struggling to get up while someone rained blows on his head and shoulders. Drawing Belsunu's sword, he leaped into the little close with a bellow of rage. As he did he parried a wild swing of a sword, feinted once, and buried his blade in his attacker's guts. Then he turned to the man with the bludgeon. "Drop it," he said, "and take to your heels. Or so help me, I'll carve you like a joint of beef." The second man took one look at Ahuni's great bulk and fled.

Enosh struggled to his feet. "Oh, my head," he said. "That'll teach me caution if nothing will." He stooped to pick up the torch and groaned again with pain. "Some conquering hero I am."

But as he held the torch high, they could see the girl now: naked, bleeding, dirty. She crouched against a corner wall, a knife—stolen, most likely, from her attacker in their struggle—in her trembling hand. "Easy," Enosh said. "We won't hurt you." She didn't believe him. He continued in a calm voice. "We're not of the city. We're—"

The girl's mouth opened. "Enosh!" she said. The knife fell. And as the fear left her she suddenly seemed to feel shame at her nakedness for the first time. She cringed miserably, trying to cover herself. "Oh, please. Don't look."

Ahuni stepped forward and pulled off his outer cloak, handing it to her. "Here," he said. And looked away respectfully.

"Shepset?" Enosh said incredulously. "Is that you?"

Cloak and shame were forgotten. The garment fell to the ground. Sobbing, she buried herself in Enosh's arms.

They barred off the door to the little archway in order to talk with her undisturbed. As she spoke, Ahuni, watching her, hearing her words, grew angrier and angrier. Finally he could listen no more. "Gods!"

he said. "And this is Lot? Abraham's nephew? I came here with the idea of doing some work for him—but now there's no coin he could pay me with that would get me to—"

"I'm not going back there!" the girl said. "You don't know what he'll do—the two of them."

"Easy," Enosh said again. "I know what happened. When Eshcol died you no longer had a protector. They resented your having one for a long time, and they're taking it out on you now. Well, I think I'll just serve notice to Lot that you have a new protector, on the same old terms."

"*Two* of them," Ahuni said. "And on even worse terms." The girl turned and saw the rage flashing in his eyes. He shook his head at her. "I . . . I'm a freed slave, like Enosh," he said. "And the idea of anyone treating a slave that way . . ." His long fingers clenched and unclenched around the hilt of his still-drawn sword.

"Excuse me," Enosh said. "Shepset, this is Ahuni. He . . . do you remember the son Belsunu always said he'd lost? Well, he's finally turned up, and you're looking at him. See? He even looks like Belsunu." He smiled and patted her hand reassuringly. "Look, we'll both talk to Lot. And with Zillah too. We can't have that. I'm sure Abraham will back us up, too. Even if you did strike that creature Zillah gave you to—"

"But no!" she said, suddenly terrified again. "I . . . I can't go back! I didn't tell you! They're selling me to Agbar! I'd rather die! I swear to you . . ." Hurriedly, an edge of terror in her voice, she told them what she'd learned about the impending sale . . . and about her prospective buyer.

Enosh looked at Ahuni. "Well, we can't let *that* happen, either, can we?" Grim-lipped for the first time, he pounded his fist against the earth wall beside him. "Damn! If I had the money . . ." He looked at Ahuni, his eyes flashing. "Maybe I can get it from Abraham. Maybe."

"Money?" Ahuni said.

"Yes. Enough to top Agbar's offer."

"It's no good!" the girl said. She was in tears again. "It's hopeless. Agbar . . . he has political power in the city. This is part of the sale."

Enosh's slowly rising rage continued to grow unchecked. "Well . . . with the money I'd also offer Lot something more important than political considerations. I'd offer him protection. Protection against my own anger. Because if he sells you, or mistreats you again, so help me, I'll pull him apart like a cooked fowl." His rage was by now barely within his control. "Don't worry," he said. "I'll get the money somewhere. I'll . . ."

Ahuni put one hand on his friend's arm—a big hand like Belsunu's with the same immense strength in it. "Go talk to Lot," he said. "Tell him just what you've told us. Any money you can't raise by your own means I'll make up myself. Don't worry about it." He saw the doubt in Enosh's eyes, the girl's. "Don't worry about it," he said again. "I have made a comfortable living. Consider it a loan unless—"

"Unless?" Enosh said, still uncomprehending, unbelieving.

"Well, if you're buying her to keep her a slave, you have to pay me back. If you're buying her to free her, consider the money a gift." He smiled a dark smile, haunted by memories, at the girl, reassuring her. "I've been lucky. I owe it to the world to put some luck back in the pot for someone else to draw out—to replace the luck I withdrew myself thirteen years ago."

Then, for just a moment, all the fear and worry and disgust fell away from the comely face she turned toward him, and he could see the great dark eyes that looked up at him. And for the first time he could see what she really looked like.

Hastily dressed, his hair still in disarray, his face bloated from drink, drugs, and lack of sleep, Lot faced Abraham. "Uncle," he said testily, "I won't even ask your pardon for the state of things here. You know better than to drop in unannounced."

Abraham just looked at him. Then he looked around him at Lot's dwelling. Zillah had made a beginning at cleaning up the rubbish in the corners, but the place still stank of spilled wine, human vomit, and other even worse odors.

"Look," Lot said. "My life is my own affair, Uncle. You've no right to judge me, you know. I'm a middle-aged man, Uncle. I've two half-grown daughters. I live my own life, follow my own ways. I . . . here, what are you doing?"

Abraham had risen and was heading toward the rooms in the back of the house. Lot followed, pulling at Abraham's garment ineffectually. "The judgment of the God lies on this place . . . and I can see why," Abraham said, making an obvious effort to keep his voice calm. "But I had hoped to find you better than I had been told. You, my brother's son. I had hoped to learn that the reports which said you had forsaken the ways of your fathers, which said you had taken up the iniquities of the Cities of the Plain—"

"Uncle, don't go in there! Don't!"

"Let go of me. I had hoped to find these reports false—envious lies told to me about you by your enemies. But now I see they were not enemies. They were friends." He opened one door and stopped. Lot, looking past him, could see two bare feet, one male, one female, sticking out from under a long table. Abraham shut the door. "Friends," Abraham said, "who have your best interests at heart. They wanted to see that you were spared the wrath of the God."

"Uncle! I really must insist . . ."

But Abraham would not be stopped. He forced open the next door . . . and this time the sight that met their eyes was that of a pair of naked bodies, embracing after a peculiar fashion upon a rumpled bed. The bodies were young, smooth-skinned, only half-formed. As Abraham let out an involuntary, wordless cry of pain, one of the young faces turned their way, eyes out of focus, features blurred by drink imbibed, obviously, from a jug a former occupant had left there.

"Oh," the girl on the top said. "Father. And Gr-great-uncle Abraham. How . . . how nice. Look, Adah. Look who's come to s-see us."

III

Ahuni came in from the street. Abraham was sitting on a bench, his face a mask of despair. Ahuni was shocked at the change in him, for the first time Abraham looked *old*. "Pardon me, sir," he said gently. "The horses are ready. We can leave at any time."

"Leave?" Abraham said. He looked up uncomprehendingly for a moment; then the light of understanding came back into his eyes. "I'm sorry. I was lost in my thoughts. Yes, I suppose we'd better make ready. I . . . feel dirtied here." He shuddered. "Yes. We must leave." He looked at Ahuni now and really saw him for perhaps the first time. "You know, I always thought it was Zillah. I've never liked her. I always made excuses for Lot. I could never imagine that anyone of my own blood . . ." He shuddered again. The fatigue in his voice was matched by the fatigue that showed in his face, in his stance.

"You can't live another's man's life for him," Ahuni said in a lame attempt at commiseration.

Abraham seemed not to have heard him. "You know what this means? It means the curse lies on Lot as well . . . unless I can get him to leave. And he won't leave. He defies me openly, contemptuously." He wiped his eyes with a trembling hand. "I . . . I told him he would be welcome in my lands if he changed his mind. But . . . I don't think that's going to happen."

Ahuni put one hand on the old man's bony shoulder and noted how frail he seemed. Where did he get the strength from—the strength he showed on every other day but this one, when events had sapped him dry? It must all be strength of spirit . . . and, he thought, this affair of Lot has taken much of that away from him. Yes, the only thing to do was go.

But . . .

"I wonder what's keeping Enosh?" Abraham said.

"He has business to do with Lot. The young Egyptian slave, Shepset—"

"Oh, yes," Abraham said wearily. "Word has got back to me. He's mistreating her again. I should have made him an offer for her a long time ago. After all, the child left Egypt in my care. I should take responsibility for her. But—fool that I was, I've indulged Lot again and again, and let him get by with—"

"It's all right, sir," Ahuni said. "You see, Lot had plans to sell her to someone in town here—someone with a particularly unsavory reputation. Enosh is, uh, persuading Lot that it would be a bad idea if he did." He flexed the knuckles of his big right fist. "Frankly, sir, if Enosh's argument doesn't work, I have a few of my own."

"I see. She's a lovely young woman, isn't she? One of us should buy her—get her out of this place."

"That's our idea, sir. Any money Enosh can't raise I'll put up myself. It's . . . well, a special project of ours. As ex-slaves—"

"I understand. Commendable of you. Tell him to come to me for money."

"Yes, sir." He looked up just then, though, and saw Enosh coming out of the back room. "What did he say?" Ahuni said, stepping forward impatiently.

"Well . . . he tried to hold out on me. But I . . ." He looked down and saw Abraham. Then he motioned Ahuni aside. "I tried twisting that weak neck of his, like a chicken's, for a bit. He gradually came to see the light. He won't be mistreating Shepset again."

"But the sale—the sale!"

Enosh looked his friend in the eye. He didn't say anything for a moment. "Ah," he said with a slow smile. "You're developing more than a purely altruistic interest in her, eh? And on such short acquaintance? Well, good for you. She's a good girl—perhaps the only one in this hell-hole of a city. And she hasn't had an easy time of it in—"

Ahuni broke in impatiently. "The sale," he said again. "Tell me about it."

"Well, it will go through . . . but there'll be some

delay. It appears this Agbar fellow has a hold on Lot, politically. If the sale to Agbar is called off precipitately, Lot will lose a contract to provide food for the reorganized army of the city—which lives on mutton, as you may imagine."

"Go on, go on."

"All right. Our sale will go through, as I say. But Lot has to have some time to delay things with Agbar until he has his contract in hand. He'll give him one excuse after another until the bargain for the herds has been made."

"And in the meantime?"

"You *are* more than usually interested. Well, that's all right. She's very grateful ... and maybe a little taken with you as well. I met her on the way out and told her what had happened. She wants to say goodbye to you—and thank you. And ... well, whatever."

"Damn it, Enosh."

"Don't worry. I told the son of a bitch that if either he or his wife so much as raised their voices to her before delivery was made, both of us would come over and ... well, look. I said, 'Did you see that big ox that came in with us—the one who has to bend over to come in your front door? Well, he juggles anvils for a living. He can climb Mount Hebron with ease, carrying a pack ass under each arm. And if he hears you've given the girl a hard time ...' "

Ahuni laughed. "All right, all right. Look, Abraham is feeling pretty bad. Do me a favor, will you, and try to cheer him up? I don't seem to be able to think of anything that will break his gloom right now. And—" He looked around.

"There's a little garden in back. She'll be waiting for you there. She wanted to fix herself up a little."

"Thank you."

But when Ahuni found her, sitting on a bench in a plain robe, her hair freshly combed, her knees primly together, her slim sandaled feet peeping out from under the garment's hem, he found himself strangely tongue-tied. He looked at her and smiled nervously and said something stupid and obvious about the sale.

She stood and smiled at him. Her face still bore the marks of the beating she'd taken—but those big brown eyes were virtually all he could look at, once she had turned them on him. "I . . . I wanted to thank you," she said in a low, beautifully modulated voice. There was, he could hear now, a trace of huskiness about it that would make the sound of her speech unforgettable.

"Please don't," he said, finding his tongue. His throat was dry. "I . . . I'm usually quite able to express myself," he said. "I don't know why I'm all of a sudden so awkward."

"Enosh tells me you're a good man. A good man through and through. He says you're the son of Belsunu."

"Yes," Ahuni said. He smiled nervously. "I never knew him. I wish I had."

She stepped closer to him. Her eyes were on his. She took his big hand between her own two small ones. Her touch sent a strange thrill through him. "You would have loved him, as we all did. And now, meeting you really for the first time—you couldn't call that fracas in the streets a meeting—I can see him in you. Yes, yes." Her voice, that husky voice, was a caress. "Do you know what he was, Ahuni? He was the strongest man I've ever met, and the kindest, and the most gentle for all his strength. I see all that in you. Yes, and that wonderful honesty of his. He was never the man to volunteer a truth when that truth would hurt . . . but if you *needed* to know the truth about anything, you could go to Belsunu for it. Oh, Ahuni . . . be that way always. Guileless and natural and . . ."

But now somehow she felt she had overstepped herself. She let go of his hand and stepped back, half-turning her slim back to him. "I'm . . . sorry," she said. "I forgot myself. I—"

"No, no," he said, stepping forward and putting one timid hand on her shoulder. She turned to look up at him, and there was a strange, puzzled look on her face. Could she be, somehow, as strangely disconcerted as he was just now? Well, considering the violent experience she'd had out in the streets of this vile city . . .

gods! Imagine ... her having to live here, among these degenerates. No, imagine something even more unimaginable: imagine her being able to live here for so long uncorrupted, a decent human being among swine of the lowest order. Imagine finding anything so fine in this den of jackals.

Suddenly, he was not at all sure how it came about, he found himself reaching out protective and comforting arms to her and holding her close. Protective. And somehow, by some strange magic, that one quality in him—protectiveness—which had never been drawn forth in him by any of the independent-minded, tough, spirited, rough-and-ready women he had known until now ... it opened floodgates of feeling in him that had never been opened in all his twenty-six years. She was so tiny, so defenseless, and yet so brave and strong—she, who barely came up to his chest.

The shuddering sound that came forth from his chest was so strange to him that he could hardly recognize it. She pulled back and looked up at him, her eyes large and questioning. "Why, Ahuni," she said gently. "You're crying."

He could not speak. The mixture of feelings in him was so violent, such a jumble of opposites, that he could not deal with it. With a sob he held her close again, his broad hands nearly spanning her slim back. He buried his face in her still-wet, freshly washed hair.

By the gods! he thought. *We're all so vulnerable. So damned vulnerable. One moment we're alive and the next moment we're dead. So little time. So few consolations.*

"Oh," she said, her voice husky and soft. "Oh, dear. Oh, my dear. Oh, my dear Ahuni."

"L-look," he said, releasing her and holding her shoulders to look into those big, bottomless dark eyes. "I ... I have to see you freed. I'll do that. That's a promise. If I fail you in this ... but no, no pledges. I won't fail you. I'll see you freed, if I have to come over here myself and take you away at sword's point. No, no, please ... listen to me. Hear me out. You and I ... there is a bond between us. I don't know what it is. I've known much of women but nothing at all of love. Maybe this is what that is, the feeling I'm feeling just now. Maybe I'm in love with you. But ... the words don't matter. What you call it doesn't matter. The thing that matters is the bond. Whatever it is."

"Ahuni," she said, visibly moved, "I feel it too. And I can't describe it either."

He broke in impetuously. "Shepset ... I have to free you first, before anything. I don't want gratitude or any other thing between us ... nothing but the bond, whatever it is. I want you free to choose. Then if you choose me—"

She put one tiny hand up to cover his lips. "Ahuni, I think something chose you for me before either of us was born. I ... I think that when I was a child, and used to dream, it was of a man much like you. And the little time I knew Belsunu ... I think he helped me understand the thing it was that I would someday look for in a man. Then I came to Sodom with Lot, and the dream faded ... but every once in a while, in my sleep ..."

Her upturned face, free now of all defenses, all subterfuges, the great liquid eyes boring into his own ... with a sob Ahuni bent and kissed her. Then he found himself covering that soft, bruised little face with kisses, a face so small and delicate that his great hands, on either cheek, almost covered it. "Shepset," he said with a great shuddering sigh. "Shepset...."

A cry came from the vestibule. "Ahuni! We're losing travel time."

"Another moment," Ahuni yelled hoarsely over his broad shoulder. "I'll be right along." But he still held that enchanting face between his hands and looked at her as if he could not tear his gaze away, as if he were memorizing her every feature. "I ... how can I leave you now?" he said. "Leave you here among these—"

"It'll be all right. I listened in on the conversation Enosh had with Lot. Lot won't dare break his word to Enosh. He knows Enosh will kill him if he does. I'll be all right. Don't worry about me, my darling. For the first time in many, many years I have something to look forward to, something to hope for. That'll sustain me. As long as I know that you . . ." She looked at his impassioned face, saw the desire in it . . . yes, and the steadfastness, the honesty, the openness. . . . "You *are* straight and true, aren't you? You *are* just what you seem to be, here in this world of false hearts and false faces." Now it was she who drew his face down to her and kissed it, once, twice, a dozen times. Then she took his hands in hers and kissed them too, lovingly. "But . . . Ahuni, come for me. When the time comes— and you'll know when it is, in your heart of hearts— come for me."

"I will. Nothing in this life or the next can stop me. Not Lot, or the army of Sodom itself."

"Then . . . go, my dear. Your friends await. And keep me in your heart until we see each other next."

"I will." He stepped back, and now his smile was a different one altogether. There was pride and confidence in it, along with the vulnerable soul he had just bared to her. "You know . . . I haven't had time to notice until just now. You're beautiful. You're the most beautiful woman I've ever seen in my life. I . . . I didn't notice. All I could see was the bond. Whatever it is."

"You *know* what it is," she said. And squeezed his hand once more. And let him go.

CHAPTER NINETEEN

I

Ahuni was uncharacteristically quiet all the way home.
Enosh took note of the thoughtful look on his friend's
face and left him alone; Abraham, depressed and sick
at heart, needed his attentions more. And at the end of
the journey from Siddim, Enosh called for Abraham's
personal servants to help the old man to bed, where he
remained for some days.

Ahuni sought out Belanum. He had come to rely on
the common sense of the young scribe, and often, as
now, confided in him on matters which, for some
reason or another, he could not easily bring to Zakir.

Belanum heard him out, in the course of a long,
circular ride around the base of Mount Hebron. He did
not interrupt Ahuni's rambling discourse, waiting until
the end to speak. "Well," he said at last. "It wouldn't
do a bit of good to point out that this is all a bit
sudden. Would it?"

Ahuni's horse snorted; he reached down and patted
the animal's thick neck. "No. I mean, I couldn't be
that wrong. And Enosh knows her, ever since she was
a child. My father knew her briefly, before Lot took
her away to Siddim."

"Hmm. She brings no dowry . . . no family."

"She's a slave. So was I. So were you."

"I can't argue with that. Very well, so she's the right
woman for you. Have you and Enosh the money to—"

"I was going to ask you."

"It's largely a matter of sending a letter back to Carchemish for credit. We have some funds there. We'd have more if the quarantine were lifted from Haran by now, but—"

"Damn. Then we're not as well off as I'd thought."

"It's not that bad. And Abraham offered to help Enosh—"

"I want to do this myself. Look, I talked with Abraham. He hasn't any immediate work for me here ... but he knows an Egyptian named Nakhtminou, who commands a garrison at—"

"Ah, yes. I remember hearing of him. Go on."

"Well, Abraham will give me a recommendation to him."

Belanum thought about this. "Hmmm. It sounds like a good idea. That is, if you insist on putting up the money yourself. Besides, I know you. You're impatient. You'll go insane sitting here waiting for the word from Lot. You'll drive *me* insane, more to the point."

Ahuni grinned nervously at him. "Then it's settled. Do you want to come along?"

"Yes. I've never seen an Egyptian soldier at work. They're supposed to be something impressive."

"What about Zakir?"

"That's another question. While you were gone ... well, Zakir's up to something. I wonder if he truly knows what it is that he's up to. I think he's just following his inclinations, and telling himself that it's something else."

Ahuni slowed his horse as the path wound down the slope. "I don't understand."

"He's befriended Abraham's young son, Ishmael. The one whose mother is a concubine of Abraham's. Do you know the woman? Dark? Egyptian? Very pretty? Mid-thirties?"

"I've seen her. Why?"

"Well, Zakir has, as I said, befriended the boy—but I think it's the mother that he's really interested in."

Ahuni whistled. "Abraham's concubine? That's not very good."

"It isn't. Even though Abraham has reportedly never lived with the girl since she conceived the child."

Belanum raised a brow at Ahuni. "He bedded her only because his wife, it seemed, could not bear—and he had been promised an heir by his God."

"I remember. But now Sarah's pregnant. Imagine, at her age."

"Yes. And Sarah . . . she hates the woman. What's the name? Hagar, I think. Well, Sarah's been putting it out that Hagar has grown too . . . well, she aspires above her station, as Sarah puts it. If that baby of hers is a boy, let me tell you . . . Ishmael's portion won't be any large one."

"It all seems a little unfair."

"Well, of course it is. But it's their laws. And to complicate matters there are the visions Abraham keeps having. His God tells him the new child will be the Promised One of the covenant between Abraham and this God of his."

"Poor Ishmael. Poor Hagar, when you come right down to it." But there was no conviction in his voice. His mind was elsewhere again. Belanum caught the nuance and smiled to himself. Ahuni caught him at it and flushed. "I . . . I was going to ask about Zakir. What has he to do with this? Oh, I see. But . . . that's chancy, isn't it? If he loves a woman who has something very close to second-wife status to Abraham—"

"Exactly. Although I'm not sure how aware he is of what he's doing. He's spending more and more time with the boy. And of course it just happens that this involves spending a lot of time with the mother. It began . . . well, I think it was our first night here. The boy sprained his leg, and Zakir helped out. Now he's giving him riding lessons on his own horse."

"Have you tried to talk to him?"

"Well, no. Not really. You know how hard it is to talk to Zakir about anything when he doesn't want to talk about it."

"Yes, yes. But . . . well, we can't let this get out of hand. Look, I'll talk to him. I'll try to talk him into coming along to Enmishpat, where this Egyptian fellow is encamped."

"Good luck. But I don't think it'll do much good." Belanum thought of something and looked sharply at

Ahuni. "Ahuni. I don't know if you believe in such things, but—"

"But what?"

"I was remembering. Abraham said he had a vision. Sodom would be destroyed by fire—he said 'fire from the heavens,' as if that God of his were going to rain down fire and burning embers from the sky."

"Yes?"

"He said soon. Maybe around fall. I . . . well . . . I wouldn't stay too long at Enmishpat. Not if my girl was in Siddim."

II

Lot sat up, rubbing his eyes. He swallowed hard, tried to get his breath. His heart was pounding fiercely, as if he'd just run a great distance, and his head throbbed with pain. His stomach was sour, and he felt as if he might vomit at any moment.

He patted the bed beside him. It was soaked with his own sweat, as was the garment he wore.

The pounding at the door continued.

"Please," he said to no one in particular. "Let me alone. Just let me . . ."

But the furious pounding on the door continued and gave him no peace. He rose, swaying queasily, and almost fell down again. He steadied himself with one hand against the wall. "Gods," he said in a voice full of fear and phlegm. "A dream. A damnable dream." But . . .

The pounding continued. A familiar voice, raucous, bellowed at him from the street. "Lot! Open this door! I know you're in there!"

"All right, all right," he said. He made his way unsteadily to the door and unbarred it. He turned away from it the moment he had done so, not wanting to face Zillah's wrath. She followed him in, her mouth already working at a fearful pace. He blotted it out to the greatest extent possible, finally holding his hands over his ears as he sat down miserably on the soaked bed.

This didn't work either. Picking up a rag from the floor where he'd dropped it, she slapped him in the face. "You! You listen to me, you bloody fool! If you'd listened to me in the first place, we wouldn't be in this mess! And as it is, it's me that has to go out and try to heal things up, while you snore away in drunken sleep! Not that it does the slightest good, at this stage. You fooled around for so long that now it's too late."

"Zillah, for the love, of—"

"You! You shut up and listen to me! You and your 'pledge' to that damned ex-slave Enosh! It's going to cost us the whole army contract, you know that! Don't you?" She reached down and grabbed a handful of his damp hair and pulled. *"Don't you?"*

"Will you in the name of heaven shut up?" he said, turning bloodshot eyes on her. "It's not bad enough that I'm haunted day and night by these damned dreams. I have to wake to hear that raucous alewife's croak buzzing in my ears, accusing me of every transgression known to man, calling me every name . . ." He reached for something to throw at her, but nothing other than the damp rag came to hand. He heaved it at her head, missing by a handspan.

He was ready to get up and try again, this time with a heavier object, when she finally took note of the dull spark in his small, red-rimmed eyes and, forewarned, backed away—at the same time modulating her attack.

"Look," she said. "I'm sorry you've been having the bad dreams. It's that damned uncle of yours. He's obviously some sort of magus, and I think he's put a spell on you. Mother warned me against marrying into a family from Ur. Home of those terrible magicians, she said. Bad business . . ."

"It was the same dream," he said miserably. "The very same one. The same two men, coming to my door as my guests. I take them in, just as I always do in the dream, and then all of a sudden it seems to be festival time again and all the . . . well, you know, the lovers of boys, and their hangers-on and lovers and catamites . . . they start clamoring outside to make me open the door and let them have the strangers. You can guess for what reason. And . . . I offer the crowd anything, anything I have but they won't listen, it's no use."

She was sitting now, looking at him patiently, her mouth resigned. Waiting for him to finish the familiar recitation.

He tried to swallow. "And . . . and then, just as somebody is about to break down the door, there's this terrible light, and I cover my eyes. And the two men turn out to be . . . oh, I don't know. Divine beings. Messengers of this God of Abraham's. And they tell me that things are so vile in this place that they're going to destroy it. And I'd better get out before it's too late. And——"

"Just as that damned uncle of yours told it to you," she said bitterly. "See? He's put a spell on you. And you won't come with me to the Temple and let me buy a counterspell. Heavens no, we couldn't have that. When I'm on perfectly good terms with the archpriest-ess of Ashtaroth, and she'd be perfectly glad to——"

"No, no," he said, standing up and beginning to pace fitfully back and forth. "I know how many times you've brought it up. And I appreciate your concern. But this is something I'll have to work out for myself . . . some other way. It's just something I . . . I can't do, somehow."

"Well," she said, standing and talking in a sharp-edged voice at his back. "This *is* something we can handle together. We're in deep trouble, let me tell you. Forget the dream and deal with reality for a change, will you? You're not only about to lose that army contract, but perhaps everything we own as well. Do you remember the debt we owed the estate of Bera, here?"

"Yes, yes. But the family hasn't shown any inclina-tion to press for restitution. They've plenty themselves. The son of a king of the city? Besides, they're good friends of ours. Why should they . . . ?"

"That's just it. That's just it. They owe Agbar a considerable sum. And he's accepted as part payment of their debt to him a package of other people's indebtednesses. He's bought *our* debt. Do you understand? Now we owe *him* money—money we haven't a chance of paying him unless we get that army contract. And you know how ruthless he can be. Remember what happened to Sha'il and his family? Sold into slavery, every one of them, to pay their debts. Is that what you want for us? Is that what . . . ?"

"Woman . . . *be quiet!*" His voice, anguished as it was, carried conviction—and a scarcely concealed threat. "I know. I know all this. I knew it before you did. I knew it some time back. Everything but how it would come about. I knew he'd put the pressure on. But . . . I was between the hammer and the anvil, do you understand? On the one hand there was Agbar and those damned debts and all. On the other . . . Enosh—the man who killed Chedorlaomer of Elam—telling me that if I sold the little bitch to anyone but him he'd wring my neck like a chicken's! And when he said this, those hands were around my neck! Squeezing! What could I do?"

She sighed disgustedly. "You *know* what you could do. I've told you again and again. But you won't listen."

"It's too chancy. Enosh has too many friends. And he's very close to Abraham."

"It doesn't matter. He's a loner. We've asked around about him—all these weeks since he was here. The herdsmen know him, know his habits. Have a false message sent to Abraham. Have Enosh called out to deliver the answer. On the way he's intercepted by—"

"Too obvious. He'd never—"

"Well, work it out some other way. But the main thing is, he's standing in the way not only of our prosperity right now, but our freedom."

"No! No! Too risky! Too much chance of Abraham finding out. Besides—"

"*Damn you!*" she exploded suddenly, casting all caution to the winds. She picked up the wet rag he'd sailed at her and threw it in his face. "You'd lead us all into slavery, just to save your own cowardly skin! Well, I won't put up with it! Do you hear? I won't stand by and let you! If you won't take affairs in hand right now and get us out of this trouble you've landed us in, I will. And the hell with all your excuses of why it wouldn't work, and why we shouldn't do this and shouldn't do that! Go ahead—sit on your lazy, cowardly behind and whine about your bad dreams. *I'm* not going to sit here and take it passively."

He looked at her, suddenly exhausted. "What are you going to do?" he said.

"Whatever turns out to be necessary," she said. And went flouncing out, slamming the door behind her.

In one of the narrow streets, the door of a sleazy house opened just a crack. Then the man inside recognized Zillah and pulled the door wide to let her in. "You've been careful?" he said. "No one saw you coming here?"

"Of course not. What kind of fool do you take me for?"

"All right, all right." He lit a pair of lamps and set them on opposite sides of a table in the middle of the grubby room. "Now ... let's get down to business. But first I've got to tell you ... the price has gone up since I talked to you last."

She stared at him, taking in the empty eye socket, the knife scar that had caused it running down his stubbled cheek. She struggled to keep the absolute disgust out of her voice. "Gone up? But I thought—"

"Look, lady. If it were just some other poor devil in the streets, it'd be another matter. But with someone like this Enosh chap ... it'll take three men at least. Maybe four."

"All right. As long as you get him. *And ...*"

"And?"

"There was another big fellow with him. Very large. His name's Ahuni. He's a smith of some sort. How much extra to have him killed as well?"

"Hmm. You want it fast or slow?"

"Pardon?"

"I mean . . . just zip, and his throat's cut—or with any . . . uh, refinements?"

"I don't care how he dies as long as he dies. But it has to be done within the week. No, make that less time. The news of their death has to be back here in Sodom in one week's time."

"Ah. It's going to cost you. Double the price, plus—"

"Look, I haven't much money."

"Lady, do you want them killed? Or do you want to sit here and haggle over it like a couple of rug merchants? Because if that's your game, you can find another man. I haven't got time for that sort of—"

"Double the price and how much?"

"Oh, I'd say . . . half again."

"Half? *Half?* Surely you can do better than that."

"Why should I? I mean, look at it from a business standpoint. I've got my price. I have to oversee this business. If you want a good job done, you pretty much have to come to me. I'm the most reliable man in Siddim. Satisfaction guaranteed, no questions asked. I have to hire the best men for the job, at a reasonable rate, and I'm entitled to a reasonable rate for my own services in setting up the thing. Fair's fair. Take it or leave it. I haven't got time to haggle."

But something in the glint in his one useful eye told her it didn't end there. Not at all. His smile was crafty, knowing, intelligent. "Take it or leave it," he said, a little more gently this time. "Of course, if it's a matter of coming up with the cash in one lump, I can understand how a lady could find herself a bit short now and then. I'm sure that we could work something out."

"Well," she said in a matter-of-fact, relieved voice. "Why didn't you say so in the first place?" And she reached for the brooch that held her robe at the shoulder. When she had unfastened it, she put it on the table. "Here," she said. "Help me with this, will you?"

III

In the heat of the late summer Enosh rode back to Mamre's Grove from the Egyptian camp near Enmishpat across the barren Negeb. The acacias were still in blossom and the rocks were full of scampering lizards, but otherwise there was little visible life in the parched land. Considering the heat, it came as a distinct surprise to see Abraham, roused by the excited cries after the pickets' first sight of Enosh, ride out to meet his former slave. They met on the high road to Hebron.

"Enosh," Abraham said with emotion. The two dismounted and embraced. "Come, sit a moment in the shade. I really shouldn't ride any more. I'm getting too old for that."

"I was going to suggest something rather like that, sir. Although I'm flattered—I can't say how much, really—to have you come out to meet me."

"The truth is, I was lonely. My wife is nearing her time, and she's irritable. There's hardly anyone left to talk to."

Enosh let slip, "There's Hagar—" But then he stopped. "I'm sorry. I shouldn't have . . ."

Abraham sighed. "No, no. It's all right. I know what everyone thinks. And let me tell you, my conscience pains me daily. But in this, as in all things, I follow the express dictates of the God. Oh, Enosh . . . the laws of my people . . . the will of the God. . . ." He sighed again, even more deeply this time. There was one more thing to be done as well as the disinheriting of Ishmael, in the event of a male child, which neither of them wished to talk about. It was just too painful a topic.

"I'll change the subject, sir. Ahuni and Zakir send their best. They've been enjoying themselves hugely.

'This Nakhtminou,' they say, 'he's a great character. He can tell tall tales for a month without repeating himself.' "

"Then . . . Zakir is working too?"

"In a way. Part of the order is for ceremonial gear for Nakhtminou's officers. This was Zakir's specialty. Whenever that sort of order comes in, Zakir supervises the work and Ahuni, as docile as any apprentice, follows his every command. Of course both of them are anxious to get back."

"Ahuni, of course, is anxious about the girl. And well he should be. It's time to get her out of there. Ah, if only Lot . . ." He shook his head in bitterness.

"Lot was being obstructive last time I heard from him. I think it's time for me to put the pressure on again. He's delayed things too long."

"So have you. When shall I announce the wedding between you and that girl of yours, my friend?"

"I was thinking . . . what about the New Year's festival, sir? The fall feast."

"Splendid." The old man allowed himself to be helped up, but insisted on mounting his horse unaided. "And when can we expect our friends home from the Egyptians' camp?"

"Soon—within the month, I'd say. Ahuni's working night and day finishing the order. Zakir works the bellows for him half the time, in relays with Belanum. They're a very good team."

Abraham glanced at him once, a wistful look in his eye. "I miss them," he said. "I keep feeling I won't have them for long." He shuddered against a nonexistent chill in the blazing heat of midday. "I keep expecting somehow to lose everyone, all my friends, all of the people who are close to me now. You too, my friend. I will lose you to marriage and to new duties. I won't be seeing you every day, either. With whom will I talk then?"

"Cheer up, sir. We'll all be within a moment's call whenever you need us." He spoke the words with confidence . . . but for a moment the ghost of the same chill wind blew across his heart.

Hagar, too, came to meet him, on foot and preceded by her bright-eyed, enthusiastic son. Enosh dismounted and reached into his saddle pouch. "Hello, Hagar," he said. "I'll be with you in a moment. First things first. Here," he said to the boy, tossing him a curious item of cast bronze. "This is for you. Zakir and Ahuni made it, after the Egyptian pattern."

"A real Egyptian war harness!" the boy said. Then his face fell. "But I have no horse of my own to—"

"Patience," Enosh said. "Zakir is bringing you a mount of your own. A magnificent Bedouin beast, four generations removed from one tamed and broken by the great Sneferu himself when he was at Timna. And if that won't keep you busy . . ."

Enosh smiled at the boy, "Now, my young friend. Run along, will you? I have to talk to your mother for a moment." He watched the boy go, his smile frozen.

Hagar watched quietly while he tethered his animal. Then she spoke. "Zakir," she said. "Is he well?"

"Yes. Hagar, do you know something?"

"What? Tell me."

"Nothing that makes you or Ishmael happy could possibly hurt Zakir. He's that much in love with you. I think he'd be happy just staying here with you . . . even if nothing came of it, even if you remained Abraham's concubine in name only, even if—"

"Enosh. You're serious."

"I was never more so. You see, Hagar . . . Zakir is a man who . . . how do I say it? He needs to be a father. And he's grown gray-haired and past his prime and he's never fathered a child, be it girl or boy. I think that if one of the thousand girls he's known and dallied with, if so much as one of them had presented him with a little bundle, you know . . . or had had a child of her own for him to raise . . ."

"I often wondered. I thought: *Is he impotent? Or . . .*"

"Far from it. Ahuni says Zakir was—and for all we know still is—a woman's sort of man. Ahuni never knew him to have less than half a dozen girl friends. But none of them ever lasted too long, although it was not for their lack of trying. It's just that . . . well, they lacked the one thing it took to make Zakir fall in love."

"I see. And raising Ahuni . . . took the place of this in his life, then?"

"Yes. And of course now Ahuni's grown. And Zakir is like a boat without a rudder . . . except when he's with you and Ishmael. Now, mind you, my dear. I'm not taking away from your own considerable charms, but it isn't your beauty alone that . . . Well, you know."

"Yes, I guess I do," she said, looking thoughtful. "I must admit I'd wondered. He's as attentive to Ishmael as to me, although in a totally different way." She smiled thoughtfully. "It's curious. I think I'm more flattered this way than I'd have been if he were interested only in me. I feel better about him. He loves the whole me, including the me that has a son." A sudden cloud passed over her face. "A son about to be disinherited. A son about to be declared bastard instead of heir."

"Hagar," Enosh said. "Do you think he cares about that?"

She looked up suddenly. "N-no," she said, taken unaware. But then the bitterness returned. "But what does it matter?" she said. "I'm another man's concubine anyhow. Ishmael is another man's bastard. What can come of it?"

Enosh bit his lip. He couldn't think of a ready answer, no matter how hard he tried.

The scene haunted him through the rest of the afternoon, as he made the rounds of Abraham's overseers, catching up on the current situation in the encampment. Somehow the whole thing had left him feeling guilty, inadequate, a terrible disappointment both to her and to himself. Here he'd done his best to raise her hopes and spirits . . . only to run headlong into rock-hard reality, which dashed all her fragile dreams in a moment.

The question went round and round in his mind, accomplishing little more than his own thorough discomfort. It distracted him from the problems people brought to him and resulted in his providing inadequate answers. He was aware of this, and it only served to make him unhappier. By the time dusk approached he was thoroughly distraught. When the skinny man with the ferret face approached him, his mind was a day's ride away. "Sir . . . beg your pardon, sir, but . . . well, there's a fight going on, and someone's going to get hurt bad if somebody doesn't—"

"Oh?" Enosh said. He struggled to get his wits about him. "A fight? Something serious? Where?"

"This way, sir."

Enosh followed, his mind elsewhere. Perhaps he could ask Abraham to release Hagar and the boy, so that she could . . . but no. He'd never do that, unless . . .

Yes. That was it. That would be the saving of all of them. And in many ways it was the best thing that could possibly happen to them all. Yes. He'd tell Zakir. He'd send him a message immediately, by runner. Yes, yes.

"Here, sir. This way." Enosh nodded and followed the man down the winding path into the little canyon where his herdsmen normally penned their strays. Now, Shepset . . . that was another matter. Something had to be done about her in the greatest possible haste. He'd have to make a special trip over there about her. It was not only the matter of heading off a sale to Agbar; there was also the business of that vision Abraham had had. One tended to discount that sort of thing, particularly now that the strange displays in the sky had ended. Of course that had been no portent, no portent at all. Some mountain across the Great Sea had exploded and . . .

"Here, now, you dog! Stand and fight!"

He looked down into the canyon. Twenty steps down the path two men circled each other, knives drawn. "You!" he said. "This is Enosh. Put those weapons away on the lord Abraham's ground."

The nearer man ignored him. The other looked up at him—no more than a wary glance—and spat on the ground. "I take orders from none but Aner," he said. "You keep out of this."

His opponent lunged; the speaker danced out of the way after a single futile slash at his attacker's arm. "Stand!" the attacker said. "Stand and fight like a man, you coward!"

Enosh unshipped his sword and felt, as always, a little stronger, a little safer, for having done so. The great blade of Belsunu had outlasted two handles since it had been forged. It had been used to kill two kings, first in Sneferu's hands and then in his own. It almost seemed as if the power and authority flowed up his arm from the sword the moment he touched it.

"Look," he said in a commanding voice, calm and unafraid. "If this stops right here and now, I can promise you it'll go no farther. I won't tell Aner, you won't be punished. But if you continue . . ."

The two exchanged glances. They lowered their knives. He stepped forward. "That's better," he said. "Now if you'll just hand over the weapons, please." He held out a welcoming hand, forgiving, conciliatory.

There was a terrific blow to the back of his head. For a moment he swayed, his head reeling, bright shards of light dancing before his eyes. His knees buckled; he felt sick, nauseated, dizzy. He was going to go down. He stiffened himself with a last effort and managed not to fall. The sword hung loose in his limp hand. He struggled with the multiple images that blurred his sight and staggered forward a step or two to get his balance. As he did so he ran headlong into both of the sharp dagger blades that lunged his way.

Both blades did not hit him simultaneously. The first slipped in cleanly, into his lower left side. His own lurching motion tore it from its owner's loose grasp, leaving the knife inside him to rend and tear as he moved. The second knife was in the hand of a more determined man; it caught him in the pit of his stomach and ripped upward. Enosh's sword rattled on the stones below his feet. He staggered forward past them, somehow still standing. He tried to pluck the first knife from his side but somehow it would not move. His hands were suddenly as weak as a baby's. Now he could see the third man, the betrayer, the one who had hit him from behind. He had picked up Belsunu's sword and was looking up at him, Enosh.

"Look at him, will you? He's dead on his feet. But he won't fall." The third man, in a rage, leaped forward, the sword raised high. Enosh parried the blow on his forearm; there was a terrible pain in his arm. The next blow caught him on the side of the neck; bright arterial blood splashed forth.

He fell to his knees. The knife in his side ripped and tore at him. He put one hand on its hilt; then somehow he could not make out which direction was up and which down. He fell forward heavily on his face, driving the knife through him and out his back.

"No," he muttered weakly. "Not finished. Much to do. Must do." The words were so weak he could hardly hear them himself. Or was he actually speaking them? Was he thinking them instead? What did it matter, after all? There was no one to hear, anyway, was there? A pity. So much to do. So much to do. So much left unfinished. Duty. Work. Help. Well, it was other men's concern now. He flexed his hand; it would no longer close. It would no longer open. Lay down your work. Over. At last. Darkness at day's end.

He heard the voices above him, blurred:

". . . cut off his head. Then . . ."

". . . no time for . . ."

". . . bring back sword . . ."

It didn't matter, did it? Everything was dark now. Everything was a soothing gray. Everything was bright as morning.

CHAPTER TWENTY

I

"I was right, then?" Nakhtminou said, stifling a cough. "Abraham is going to disinherit Ishmael?"

Zakir took down the leather bottle of wine and unsealed it. He offered it to the Egyptian commander, who shook his grizzled head. "Yes, so far as I know."

"Then this is your salvation, in a way. Although ... it's damned hard on the boy. You know, being raised to think he was going to be the Number One Son— some sort of tribal chieftain or whatever." This time he did accept the wine; his throat was dry. He had been coughing all day.

"Well, yes," Zakir said. "But I've been thinking of that. Ahuni's grown and independent. He makes more money than I do now—although he'll never make as much, in that end of the trade, as I used to make as a jeweler and artisan to the rich ladies of Babylon. No, he doesn't need my money now—or me either, though it grates to think of it."

"They all have to reach that stage. One must accustom himself to it." Nakhtminou turned that hawk-faced smile on him now, and this time it was tolerant, accepting, friendly. Zakir, remembering Abraham's accounts of their first meeting, marveled at how age and—yes, infirmity too—had mellowed the old soldier.

"I know. Well ... once we're done here I'm going back and face Abraham down. Nicely, you know, but firmly. Hagar's wasting her life with him. What does she get out of this life? And the boy ... the boy needs a father."

"Agreed. But will they let you?"

"You remember Abraham and I are countrymen. If the child *is* a boy, and if he is to be regarded as the new heir, well, it's not just a matter of disinheriting poor Ishmael."

Nakhtminou's brow rose; his sharp old eye fixed itself on Zakir's face. "I see. Ishmael has to be got out of the way. There cannot be two firstborn. The false claimant will remain a danger to the true one."

"Exactly. In the up-country, away from the civilized areas Abraham and I come from, such a child would be put to death. If the mother had kin nearby, this would often lead to a slaughter. Even war."

"Yes. I've seen that before. Go on."

"Well, I'm going to offer to ... uh, remove the problem. Abraham will prepare the documents. I'll take Hagar to wife and adopt the boy. There's no problem about supporting them. I've a large sum on deposit in Haran, and good credit in Carchemish and half a dozen northern cities because of it. I'll take her up that way for a time, get her and the boy away from the scene of so much misery and disappointment."

"Sounds like a fine plan. But ... what does Hagar think about this?"

Zakir looked out over the valley below, where the troops drilled smartly to shouted commands. "I wish I could say for sure. I know she approves of my interest in the boy. Once she gets over the disappointment ... well, you know she still thinks she can *win*."

"And you think she can't?"

"I'm only moderately superstitious ... well, perhaps a little more than moderately. But this Abraham ... he's as lucky as a magus. Don't try playing the game of peas and shells with him, my friend."

"Yes, I know. Who watched him bluff a whole garrison of His Majesty's finest troops? Who watched him—or his God, which is the way he put it himself— put a spell of blindness on the Lord of Two Lands himself?"

"I forgot. Anyhow, if Abraham says the child will be a boy, it will. But back to Hagar . . . I think she loves me. If not, she feels friendly. Perhaps that'll change as time goes by. I have the ghost of your friend Sneferu to chase away."

"Make her happy and there'll be no ghost. But look—this Ahuni of yours. He's a hell of a fellow. I'd like to send him back to Sile if I could. For a while, anyhow. Who knows? He might work his way up the Nile. The divinity Sesostris is rattling the saber these days. An armorer will stay busy there."

"Hmmm. The thing might work. You know, if he's going to be marrying an Egyptian girl—"

"My thought exactly. But . . . look. Here comes a runner. And from Abraham's camp, unless I'm mistaken." He stood up and bellowed down the hill at his guards to show the man up. Raising his voice brought on another fit of coughing, and he sat down hard. In an instant Zakir was at his side.

"No, no . . . it's all right."

"No, it isn't."

"You . . ." He went off into another burst of furious coughing, and it took him a moment to answer. "You're . . . right, my friend . . . but . . . but if you'd do me a favor . . . I'd like to . . . ignore the fact . . . as long as I can. . . ." He coughed again and mastered himself, his face white and drawn. "The final stage comes all too quickly without my going around treating myself like an invalid before I actually have to." He breathed deep, trying to get air. "The rest . . . well, indulge me, my friend. Just this once indulge me. I assure you it won't have to be for long."

The runner was Jakim, a slave of Abraham's; Zakir knew him and returned his salute. The slave was breathless from climbing the rise after a long ride; he took a moment to catch his breath. "Several messages for the lord Zakir, sir. First, from the lord Abraham. . . ." He told, between gasps, the melancholy tale of Enosh's murder. Zakir listened, horrified, wide-eyed. The slave was still speaking when Ahuni came up the hill, carrying a freshly finished sword.

"Ahuni," Zakir said, standing. "It's Enosh . . . he's

been killed. Waylaid by assassins, inside his own camp. Who in heaven's name could—"

"Quick," Ahuni said to the slave. "Jakim, tell it to me just as you told it to Zakir. Please."

"Well, sir . . . this morning we found . . ."

The story was quickly told. Zakir prodded Jakim at the end. "You had other messages. Quickly."

"Yes, sir. The lady Sarah . . . she was already in labor when I left. That was yesterday morning."

"In labor!" Zakir said. "But . . . Ahuni. Remember Abraham's vision. Sodom would be destroyed on the day Sarah gave birth. And here she must be . . . what? Three weeks premature?"

Ahuni looked at him with a sharp eye. "But surely Shepset is in Mamre's Grove by now. I sent Enosh the money weeks ago." He turned to Jakim, his hand on the slave's shoulder. "Look. Do you remember a slave, an Egyptian girl, whom Enosh must have brought back from Sodom . . . oh, perhaps a fortnight ago? A slight, dark girl named Shepset?"

"Oh, I know Shepset, sir." Ahuni's face lightened for a moment, then fell as Jakim said, "But sir . . . she's not in Mamre's Grove. She's still in Sodom. The lord Lot delayed delivery. All her friends in Mamre's Grove—people who traveled to Canaan with her through the Sinai desert when she was a child—they all know about the purchase Enosh had been trying to make. But . . ."

Ahuni's eyes went to Zakir again. "Gods! She's still there! And . . . if there's anything to Abraham's prophecy . . ." But he turned on himself savagely. "But of *course* there's nothing to it! A lot of foolish superstition! Why should I believe . . ."

And then the same thought occurred to him and Zakir at the same time, and father and son stared at each other dumbfounded, speechless, for a moment. Zakir was the first to break the strained silence. "Lot," Zakir said hoarsely. "Who else would kill Enosh? And for what other reason? Enosh didn't have an enemy in the world."

"And if she's still in Sodom . . ." Ahuni's bronzed

face went white. "The bastard. He's sold her. He's sold her to . . ."

Nakhtminou broke the brief silence, bellowing to a guard. "Captain! Have the gentlemen's horses readied immediately. Call the order down the hill. If the animals aren't ready by the time these gentlemen are there to mount them, you and every member of the chain of command will be reduced one rank . . . and you, personally, will have your back reduced by a layer of skin."

"Yes, sir!"

Nakhtminou turned to Zakir and Ahuni. "Move quickly! I'll have Belanum rounded up and sent down after you! Ride like the wind!"

Abraham had put a guard around Sarah's tent to keep people from bothering her. The guard who had come for Hagar brought her through the cordon and made her wait while the latest round of labor pains racked Sarah's aging body. Hagar, already haggard from worry, winced at every scream, remembering. *And I was in my twenties then. . . . How much worse must it be for her now, at her age.*

Then there was silence for a while. The pains ceased. The midwives came out of the tent to fan their own fevered faces and take some sort of break against the three days' tension. It was then that the guard came down the hill to Hagar. "Please," he said. "She'd like to see you." Hagar did not know the man; one of Keret's recent recruits, no doubt. She followed, eyes on the uneven ground before her. When she at last stood before Sarah, she could see the sunken eyes, the drawn face clearly. Sarah lay in bedclothes soaked with her own sweat. She shook as if striken with an ague. "You," she said, recognizing Hagar. "In a few hours, no more, there'll be no need for you here any more. Do you understand? You were never more than a . . . a substitute. For all your high-and-mighty airs."

"Sarah," Hagar said. "Why do you do this to me? I've tried to be your friend, your faithful servant. When that wouldn't work, I tried to stay out of your way, to efface myself wherever possible. And now, as you give birth, my heart goes out to you. Can't we mend whatever it is that has come up between us, once and for all?" The pleading note in her voice was near hysteria.

"Now," the woman on the bed said, as if she hadn't heard a word, "now I'm going to get rid of you once and for all." The eyes had a crazy, driven-over-the-edge glint in them. "Pack whatever you can carry. You and Ishmael. I've given orders that you're to be out of here by noon tomorrow. Noon tomorrow, do you hear? When my son is born, there'll be one heir and one heir only. You know that. It's our law. Any other claimant has to leave. If he's ever found in Abraham's domain again—"

"But . . . Sarah. We can't just . . . where will we go? Who will take us in? Who will . . . ?"

The sick woman raised her head, with its tangled locks, from the pallet. There was venom in her hoarse, half-strangled voice as she said, "That's your affair. You'll be taken a day's march into the Negeb and headed south. Go back to Egypt with that bastard of yours for all I care. *You!*" she bellowed at the guard who had brought her. "Take her away. Make her ready to leave. Her and her son. Just as I instructed you to."

"No," Hagar said as the guard led her away. "No, please, Sarah." But it was no use. The pains had begun again, and the only voice Sarah could hear now was her own, screaming incoherently at the advent of the greatest pain a woman suffers this side of death.

She sent a messenger to Abraham: a sympathetic slave who had taken pity on her plight and volunteered to try to get through. He was turned away by Abraham's private guard: the old man was going through his own private agony, a vision of more than common vividness, power, and duration.

When the moon was high, the old man emerged from the tent haggard and drawn, looking like a man who had fasted for days. He came out into the firelight and sat down cross-legged on the ground. The night was cool, the air dry. Below in the encampment he could hear, faintly, the sound of someone striking up an old love song—an Egyptian love song, sad even in its celebrations. *When will they forget Egypt?* he thought idly.

But then he looked up and saw the moon. Hours till morning! And in that time . . . what had the Stranger told him in his dream? *"Sarah will bear in the morning. A king will be born in Canaan. Your line, a line of kings, will live forever. And on the day the dynasty of Abraham begins, the life of the city of evil will be snuffed out forever. It will be as if it had not been, and people shall forever after seek for its ruins in vain. And you, Abraham, will live a new life. And in learning the new, you will lose the old. One life is given you, that of your son. For this you will lose all the old lives, and though there will be pain in their loss, all will be well with you, for you are blessed. . . ."*

Blessed. The word was empty, bitter as gall. He would lose all that he loved. Yes, and his wayward kin as well: Lot, whom he'd promised his brother to protect, would die in the fire on the morrow, in Sodom; and it was too late to do anything, anything at all, about it.

II

Abraham, looking over the heads of his guests, saw a familiar face—familiar, but a surprising visitor in the present company. Sarah had given birth to a small, struggling, ruddy baby boy in the dawn hours, and since then the chiefs from the outlying country, many of whom had come to the groves a day before when Sarah's labor pains had begun, had streamed past his tent in an unbroken procession, congratulating him on the birth of his firstborn, a young prince of his realm. But now, recognizing the ex-slave Rekhmira, he asked leave of an Amorite chief to go speak to the lame herdsman. "Rekhmira!" he said. "I'm glad to see you."

"Congratulations, my lord," the herdsman said. His face, however, remained grave as before. "It's a great day in Canaan. I was on my way to see the child and to congratulate the lady Sarah . . . but . . ."

"But?" Abraham was quick to catch the nuance. "Is something wrong, my friend?" Curious, a week before, feeling old, infirm, beaten, he'd have let the matter pass him by. But now he felt young and vigorous and sharp-eyed. He missed nothing. "Please, if there's something I should know, it would be a disservice not to share it with me."

"Well, sir . . . if you're sure . . ."

"You mean you might get in trouble if it's something I don't want to hear? Look," he beamed, "there need be no reticence between us, my friend. Not any more. Please. Tell me."

Rekhmira hesitated. As he did he looked Abraham up and down, and then looked him hard in the eye. Finally he seemed satisfied with what he saw. "I . . . it's good to see you looking so well, sir. This birth—it's taken twenty years off your age, if you don't mind me saying so."

"Thirty," Abraham said. "I feel like a stripling again. But enough of the small talk. Please, tell me whatever it is." He stood back, arms crossed over his still-broad chest. "Come, I'm at your disposal."

"Ah," Rekhmira said. "I wasn't sure whether you might have already heard. But I guess you haven't."

"Yes?"

"I have the flocks on the south slopes, sir. Along the road to Beersheba, leading into the Negeb."

"Yes?"

"Your . . . concubine, Hagar, passed through my fields this morning, sir. With her son . . . *your* son, sir."

"Hagar? Going away from here? On the morning of Isaac's birth? But I don't understand."

"You don't sir? She said . . . she'd been expelled from your camp, sir. Expelled because now Ishmael was only another counterclaimant, and had to be— well, she was feeling very hurt and bitter, sir. She used the term 'gotten rid of.' I didn't question her, sir . . . you see, there was one of your servants with her. She spoke of him as leading her out into the desert, where he was to abandon her and the boy to die."

"Abandon her to . . . ? I've never heard of anything in my whole . . . " Abraham, open-mouthed, stared at him. "But . . . what could have given her that idea? I gave no such order. I *could* give no such order. Abandon a good and faithful servant and friend? Abandon the son of my blood to die? How could she . . . "

He stopped then and thought about it for a moment. He did not say anything for a long time. Then he said, "This servant who was with her. Who was it?"

"A man named Elishama. I do not know him well."

"Ahhhh. . . . " The sound escaped him like a long and painful sigh. "A servant of Sarah's, my friend. And I can guess what happened. Ah, why did no one come to me? Why did . . . ?" But then he remembered his own isolation during the night, an isolation unbroken until the midwives had come to him with the news of Isaac's birth. "Look," he said. "We'll send someone after them right away. They can't have gone far."

"Very well, sir. I'll get to work on that immediately. And, sir . . . I'm glad you see it this way."

Abraham saluted him and watched him go. Poor Hagar! But then . . . poor Sarah as well. Imagine her feeling that insecure . . . he'd have to comfort her and reassure her. He'd . . .

But then the thought struck him: if Hagar and Ishmael *were* to leave just now, certain problems would be much abated. Certain complications *would* be made simple again.

He sighed and turned once again to his guests, the patriarch again, all lordly dignity and smiles. And not even the nagging guilt and self-doubt in the back of his mind could seriously diminish the powerful feeling of masculine pride that surged through him as he spoke to them. After years of being a dotard in his own eyes, it was splendid feeling himself a man again.

Along the high road Ahuni raised one long arm to call a halt. The three men pulled their horses up. The road to Beersheba in the north stretched away before them, winding its way across the barren hills in the baking heat of midday.

Ahuni shook his head impatiently. "This is too slow," he said. "I'm going to cut across the mountains into the plain of Arabah and strike north. The trade route takes too roundabout a road."

"But . . . there's no track, Ahuni," Belanum said.

"I don't need one. For heaven's sake, I know how to find Siddim. There's nothing else in the world that looks like it."

"Well . . . what do you think, Zakir?"

Zakir's face was dark and troubled. Then, firming his jaw, he said, "I agree with Ahuni. But . . . I'm not going with him. You go along. This business of picking a trail through the hills, that's a young man's game."

"Father?" Ahuni said. "You're not coming?"

"No," Zakir said. "Son, I'd only hold you back. And . . ." He took a deep breath. "I . . . I'm going back to Mamre's Grove."

"You're going back?"

"To Hagar." Zakir, half defensively, glared at them, almost daring them to disagree. "My place is with her. Now and . . . well, as long as she'll have me. She'll need me."

Ahuni let a slow look of understanding unfold over his young face. "Father," he said, reaching out to grasp Zakir's good left hand. "I'm happy. You're making the right choice. It *is* the best thing to do. Go with every blessing I can give you. But as for me . . ."

"Yes," Zakir said. "Yes, son. Go to her! Ride! What are you waiting for?"

Ahuni squeezed his arm. "You put heart in me, Father. As always. Belanum, are you coming with me?"

"Need you ask?" the scribe said. And lightly nudged his horse in the ribs, setting out to the east over the open country.

Ahuni struggled with the lump in his throat. "Brave and true as ever . . . both of you."

"For heaven's sake," Zakir said gruffly. "Go! Ride!"

"There she is," said a voice behind her. Shepset turned her head around as quickly as she could, caught in the crush as she was. She struggled to stand on tiptoe, to crane her neck to look above a crowd mostly half a head taller than she was. As she did she saw them: two rough-looking men as big as Ahuni, shaggy-haired, bearded. And . . . and it was her the larger one was pointing at! Her!

She pushed hard at the clot of people ahead of her. For a moment something gave; then the crowd closed about her again. Terrified, she looked back; the two men were pushing people aside—adults—as if they were children. They were getting closer! "You, girl!" the larger one said again in that distinctive, gravelly voice of his. "Yes, you!" His voice carried easily over the crowd noises. "You know who I'm talking to."

She pushed, squeezed . . . and managed to put another two people between her and her pursuers. Up ahead there appeared to be a break in the crowd. One of the men called out to her again, but now the music burst forth once more: joyful music, played on horns and lyres and high-pitched flutes. It, and the noises of the crowd, which did not diminish at all, drowned out his words. She pushed ahead.

What could they want with her? There were plenty of women as comely as she in the streets now—as comely, and certainly more willing. With the first day of festival, the great autumnal feast, under way now there would be two whole weeks of license in which anyone interested in the pleasures of the flesh would be encouraged to divert himself, and disport himself, in any way he pleased. Certainly there was no necessity under the circumstances to molest a young slave on her way home from an errand.

There! Up ahead there was a definite break in the crowd. She pushed forward but was swept back by a wave of force from the other side as more revelers joined the crowd in the little bazaar, pushing, shoving.

She looked back in a panic. They were closer! Her heart almost stopped. Closer! If she could not push her way through . . .

A hand grabbed hers. Gently. She whirled. A kind-looking middle-aged man looked into her eyes. "I've been watching, ma'am," he said. "Those men . . ." His words were drowned out by another furious burst of horn flourishes. Then he repeated his words, almost in a scream. "Those men . . . they're following you. Correct?" She bellowed yes, and could not even hear her own voice in the din; but he nodded understanding. He tugged on her arm and shoved the crowd. An opening! She felt him break free for a moment, stop, and push again. As he did, she squirmed into the opening he'd made. When she looked back, she saw the two wild-haired heads above the crowd. They were a little farther away, now, at least.

"This way!" the man ahead of her said at the top of his lungs. There was another burst of music, and she could smell the sudden pungent reek of incense released into the air. "Through here, now."

They exited the Bazaar of the Olive Tree at one and the same time. She looked at the man who'd pulled her free. He was gray-haired, humbly dressed; a slave like her. His face had a battered but honest look about it. "Quickly," he said. "Up this alley. I know a way of escaping from them."

"But . . . who are they?" she said. "And why should they want me?" The moment she'd said it she realized how stupid she must sound. Why, indeed? At festival time, why? "I . . . I'm sorry. But who are they?"

"Servants of Agbar," he said. "You don't want to fall into *their* hands. Believe me."

"Agbar!" She put one hand over her mouth. "But . . . you—"

"Look, ma'am. I'm just a friend. Trust me. This way." He beckoned again; this time she gave in. She followed him down the narrow passage into a cross-road where two additional, larger thoroughfares came together. "This way," he said again, and set out, still holding her by the hand. "Nobody will be able to follow."

She jogged across the street and down a side avenue, keeping pace with him as she pulled her hand loose.

"But where are we going?" she said. "You don't even know where I live."

"Yes I do," he said. "You belong to Lot, in the Street of Anath. I saw you coming out of the door there once. I asked a friend . . ."

She slowed down, stopped. "But . . . you. I thank you for helping me. It was kind of you. But . . ." She looked up and down the street; it was, for the moment, free of revelers. For now at least, they seemed to have congregated in the bazaars and squares. The infiltration of the city's alleys and side streets would come later. It was a good time to get home.

A noise in the street startled him. He ran to the corner and looked around it. "There are people in the entrance to your street," he said. "We'll have to go around." He looked at her, noted the skeptical look on her face. "Trust me," he said. "My name is Yamm. I'll get you home all right. I . . ."

But then he looked behind her and smiled. "Oh, here you are," he said. "What took you so long?"

Shepset whirled. The two big men from the bazaar stood within arm's reach. "Y-you!" she said. She stood for a moment, paralyzed with terror; then she tried to turn and run. But one long arm snaked out and the big hand at the end of it grabbed her wrist. "No!" she screamed. "Let me go! Please."

Yamm, behind her, chimed in now. "Not a chance," he said. They turned her around to face him. He stood before an open door, holding it mock-gallantly for her. "After you, my dear."

"Look," she said, struggling. "Stealing a slave is a serious offense. You'll all hang for this. You . . ."

Yamm smiled that gentle, utterly false smile of his. The bogus light of reassurance shone in his brown eye. "Stealing?" he said. "I think not. The documents were witnessed this morning. We're just making the delivery."

"Documents?" she said. They were trying to thrust her through the door. She managed to wedge herself in the narrow doorway for a moment. "What documents?"

"Oh," Yamm said mildly. "You were sold to Agbar today. And for what I'd call a quite substantial price, if it does you any good to know it."

"*Sold?*" she screamed. "No! No! He couldn't have! He promised! He'll never get away with this! No! I won't go! I won't."

"Won't go?" Yamm said, his expression unchanged. "But you don't *have* to go, my dear. You're already here." And, raising one broad foot, he kicked her gently free of the door, into the darkness inside.

The revels went on all day and well into the night. In the streets there were fights, killings, rapes. Things quieted down for a time when the moon was high; but in the dark period just before dawn three inebriated partygoers came away from a flagging feast and, once in the street, conceived the notion of mounting to the top of the building and looking out over the city. They carried a firebrand against the still-thick darkness, now that the moon, full a moment or two before, had plunged below cloud banks to the west.

Atop the roof one of their number, holding the brand high, walked the wall, teetering dizzily back and forth. Rounding a corner he staggered, spun, and fell —back onto the rooftop. "Hey, wasn't that something?" he laughed.

But then, seeing the glow in the air, he got up and walked unsteadily to the roof's edge. He looked down at the source of the glow. The torch had fallen on the wattled top of a shed; the shed's roof had caught fire. Now sparks leaped from this to a wagon full of kindling wood. The dry wood caught, sputtered, turned to leaping flames.

Inside the house below, the wagon's owner smelled smoke and jumped, still naked from his bed, into the alley. He pushed the wagon away from his inflammable house and set about putting out the fire on his shed roof. The wagon rolled a dozen paces and rammed against a wheelwright's timbered shop, deserted for the night. The high-piled faggots tumbled into the shop, still ablaze. The seasoned, dried wood stacked so neatly against the walls crackled in the brisk little blaze, and the brisk little blaze became, all too quickly, a large and formidable one. Next door to the wheelwright's shop was a carpenter's shed. . . .

High on the city wall the sentry post stood all but deserted. Someone had smuggled two wineskins of palm wine up to the guard, and he had had a private little party of his own. Now the wineskins lay flat and empty at his feet, and he slept the deep sleep of the inebriated.

III

Lot awoke on the floor in a mess of broken pottery and spilled wine. He had a splitting headache and his back ached in half a dozen places. After several tries he managed to sit up, his head spinning. Thus erect, he suddenly felt a rush of nausea; leaning forward, he vomited the night's ingestions onto the dirty tiles of his floor.

"Gods!" he said when he caught his breath again. The air was dank and close in the shut-tight room. Over in a corner a woman slept, her robe hiked up around her waist, snoring loudly; he idly tried to connect the gross naked body to a face, a name, and gave up in disgust. He wondered where Zillah was.

Ugh! The air was foul. Vile. The very smell of it sickened him totally. On unsteady hands and knees he crawled toward the door. Light poured from beneath it; it was morning, then. Holding onto the thrown bolt, he rose first to one knee, then to an uncertain standing position. And—the feeble act took all his strength now—he drew the bolt and opened the door to let sunshine and fresh air in.

The bright rays of the morning sun blinded him for a moment; but already he could smell the acrid reek of the smoke. And after half a dozen blinks he managed, shading his eyes, to make out the black column of smoke behind the building opposite. Gods! The city . . . it was on fire!

He stepped out into the street in his ruined robe, foul-smelling, unshaven, filthy from disheveled head to bare feet. As he did he was nearly bowled over by Balak the merchant, hurriedly wheeling his pushcart through the streets, still dressed in his nightclothes. "Balak!" Lot croaked. "What in hell's name is going on?"

"Fire, you damned fool! Can't you see it? It's wiped out a whole street over east of here! Houses, a whole bazaar! Zadok the carpenter lost his whole business! His whole supply of wood! Everything."

"But . . . is it contained? Have they stopped the spread?"

"Stopped it?" Balak's impatience was nearing the anger point. "Well, maybe they have, maybe they haven't. I'm taking no chances. I'm moving my goods to the warehouse on the other end of town. Thanks be to the gods, I don't live near enough to there for it to be much worry." He looked up at the column of smoke with a shiver. "The fire cut off a whole block of dwellings. Nobody could get out. And one of the first places cut off was the well. The well they would have been using for water to fight the fire." He shivered. "Thank heaven, my end of town has water from the mountains. While the aqueduct holds—"

But just then the first tremor hit.

As earthquakes go it was no more than a hint, a rumor, a prelude, a rehearsal of disaster. There was no sound, no sound at all; but the whole world seemed to move a handspan under their feet. Lot staggered but did not fall. He shook wildly as the aftertremor followed. Above them a jagged zigzag line appeared in a tall brick wall, and there was a place down the street where the surface of one side of the thoroughfare had sunk by the length of a man's thumb.

"Gods!" Lot said again. And went back inside in a panic, looking for Zillah and the girls.

All the wells in Sodom but one were poisoned by sulphur deposits; the water stank and could not be used for drinking or cooking purposes. To replace these the inhabitants of the city had set up an ugly but serviceable system of stone aqueducts to bring water from the hills. Once this system had been put in, the citizens capped the fouled wells. Why bother to keep a cistern clean when even the animals would no longer drink from it?

Now, with the first tremors of the great quake, cracks opened in the main aqueduct. Water poured through the holes onto the bare ground. The cracks widened. The flow of water, once lusty and full, became a trickle.

Then a second series of minor quakes shook the area. At a point where the aqueduct crossed a wadi on stone uprights, the tremors shook them to rubble; the structure collapsed. The remaining water poured out onto the parched sands of the wadi.

And, in the northeastern quarter of Sodom, the great fire raged—unchecked now, and well-nigh uncheckable. Fire had already gutted the bazaar where the one open well lay; now the aqueduct-fed wells had no water but the water previously stored. That didn't last long. Workmen, hastily roused, pounded open one of the capped wells whose artesian flow, if filtered through sulphur-bearing earth, could usually be depended upon—only to find that water levels in all the wells had fallen disastrously.

The cloud column was huge, dominating the entire valley. The fire in Sodom was a fire storm now; the spread of the flames followed none of the patterns of smaller fires. A wall of flame would be seen to leap upward, arch over a broad street, and pour down on the other side. Under the flaming arch all oxygen was quickly exhausted. Anyone under the arch died of asphyxiation.

Ahuni and Belanum had ridden all night. When dawn arose they were far down the vale of Arabah, the continuation of the great rift at the bottom of which lay the Great Salt Sea. And . . . once the morning fog had burned off . . . they could see the column of smoke.

The animals were lathered, half dead from the punishing ride. "Ahuni," Belanum said. "Can we make it? I mean, this horse—"

"He'll have to make it. Too bad, but we might have to ride him into the ground. By the gods! Look at that smoke, will you? It looks like the end of the world. . . . Ride, Belanum! And when your horse falls out from under you, man, run! At this rate there won't be much time! That's the way a city looks when it's going to be burned right down to the ground."

Agbar was huge, grossly fat, impotent. Sexual release came seldom to him, and when it did it was usually in his sleep. Always, the dreams were of giving and receiving some sort of pain, humiliation, degradation. In the morning after such a dream the not-quite-fulfilled desires still lay heavy on him, and, aided by a large and well-trained household, he restaged his dreams.

He awoke drenched with sweat. There was smoke in the room. The house—he rose, called about, flung doors ajar—the house was empty, abandoned. He drew the shutters over open windows, shutting out the smoke. Where was everyone? Where was . . . ?

Then he saw the Egyptian girl on the floor. Someone had taken pity on her and thrown over her collapsed body a rough coverlet. He lifted it, looked at her . . . and the desire began to arise in him again. The night's dreams slipped insidiously back into his mind: the night's dreams, in which he was young and slim again, and the woman begged him to do it to her, roughly, savagely, like a conqueror.

He looked at the little naked body. Someone else, mindful of his wrath if she were lost, had roped one of her slim ankles to a ring in the wall. Well, that was all right; she hadn't got away—and the restraint needn't interfere with any pleasurable activities.

He pouted briefly. There was no one to prepare her, to wash her, to sponge off the caked blood and filth.

Well, there was nothing for it. He'd have to do it himself. He tore a rag from the coverlet and went to the cistern to soak it in running water. But the trough was dry as a bone. How curious! He'd have to complain bitterly about this when the elders of the city met tomorrow. Someone's head would fall for this.

A brick wall fell and killed an ostler in the street. He had been on the way to his stable to set his animals free. Now, with no one to let them loose, the horses of the stable panicked. One of them kicked down a door. Six of the seven escaped; ran, frightened, through the city streets; a child, scampering in abject fear before them, fell and was trampled to death. At the end of the passageway a solid wall of flame glowed. The horses were cut off. They reared, pawed the air with their hoofs. One of them, panicked beyond endurance, raced madly into the flames. As the towering wall of fire climbed above them, there was less and less air to breathe. One of the horses fell in its tracks and lay there, pawing the air feebly.

Ahuni and Belanum dismounted while their horses were still moving and fought their way to the city gate. Armed guards tried to stop them; cursing, Ahuni drew the sword of his father and battered their shields aside. Belanum ducked under a spear-thrust and joined him. They fought their way through the frightened crowd to an open space. "Let's see," Belanum said. "Lot's place . . . where was it, now?"

"This way," Ahuni said. He set off at a trot, weaving his way through the narrow streets, Belanum at his heels. People pushed past, carrying children, valuables, the very old and ill. . . . Ahuni would have stopped to help them if his mission had been any other than this. But now? Now the main priority was Shepset, Shepset. . . .

One of the avenues was already blocked by flame. He reversed his field, ducked up an alley, cut through a close, climbed a wall. Atop the wall he reached down a hand and pulled Belanum up. "Now," he said. "Through there and around the corner."

But once around the corner he ran into a sight which stopped him dead . . . and almost stopped his heart. There was Lot, with his oldest daughter, holding a drugged, half-asleep Zillah erect as they tried to get her to walk. His younger daughter staggered along beside them, bowed under the weight of a small casket which she was obviously too little to carry. "Here," Ahuni said. "Give her a hand."

Belanum took the box from the child and shouldered it. Ahuni got one big shoulder under Zillah and stood up. As he did he looked up and saw Lot's house. Black smoke poured from the windows; as he stared open-mouthed, red flames licked out from the front door. The roof was already ablaze.

"Lot," Ahuni said. "Remember me? I'm Ahuni the armorer. Your servants . . . where are your servants?"

Lot stared at him wide-eyed. Silent. His mouth hung open stupidly. Ahuni, tight-lipped, reached out one hand and slapped the man's slack face. "Damn you, answer me! Where are your servants? What have you done with them?"

"Servants? Slaves? Oh, I . . . Zillah! Zillah, are you all right?"

The woman was stirring on Ahuni's shoulder. He set her gently down. "Here. Can you stand? There, now . . . take it easy."

She stood, one hand to her disordered hair. She looked about her. "Fire? Fire all around? Lot . . . what . . . what's happening? Where's our house?" She looked up and saw. "My house! My beautiful house!" She tried to rush forward; her daughters grabbed her by the arms.

"Just hold her," Ahuni told them. He turned to Lot again, shaking him by the shoulders. "Now! Damn you, answer me—or I'll kill you right here! The slaves, man! The slaves! What have you done with them?"

"Oh," Lot said. "They . . . they all ran away. While I was trying to rouse Zillah."

"All of them?" Ahuni's voice had a desperate edge on it. "What about Shepset? Was she with them? Where did they go?"

"Oh," said one of the daughters. "Shepset? *Her?*

She's no concern of ours now. Father sold her to Agbar yesterday."

"*Sold her?*" Ahuni cried out, in a rage. He raised the sword high; in a moment he would have beheaded Lot. But he lowered it, red rage in his eyes. "Where does Agbar live?" he said. "Quickly."

Lot shrank back, aware for the first time of his situation. "Live? He lives in . . . in the Street of the Dry Wells. Middle of the block. The house bears the sign of a crescent moon."

Ahuni turned to Belanum. "Get them to safety," he said. "It's for Abraham. I'm going after her. I only hope I'm not too late."

"My house!" Zillah screamed beside them. Startled, they turned to look at her—but, her mind turned incoherent by the great volume of drugs she'd taken, she dashed free of them and ran toward her own flaming stoop. As she did, the earth shook again, and the high brick wall of Lot's house slowly came apart brick by brick and slid down into the street. For a moment Zillah stopped, half aware; and it was then that the wall hit her, falling, driving her to the ground, crushing her and burying her under a peaked pile of broken bricks.

Ahuni stood, shocked; then Belanum hit him in the ribs with his closed fist. "Ahuni! Make haste! Find her while you can! Don't worry about us."

Prodded, Ahuni, sword drawn, sprinted to the end of the passage; then he stopped for a moment and turned around. Belanum and Lot had the two girls by the hand and were leading them toward safety. Belanum had dropped Zillah's little box on the ground in the middle of the street. It had spilled its contents— shining gold, jewels of various colors—into the gutter. No one turned around or took notice.

He turned. Up ahead oil from a broken jar had spilled across the street; flames leaped from the shadows and ignited the oil. A line of fire crossed his path. He took a harder grip on his father's sword and, breaking into a trot, vaulted over the line of flames and disappeared into the smoke-blackened streets of the dying city.

IV

"There!" Agbar said. "That's better." He rocked back on his heels to get a better look at his handiwork. Shepset's slim body, sponged clean of dirt and bloodstains alike by water from a pitcher, lay atop the coverlet. She had stirred once or twice from her sleep while he worked; but now she had settled once again into fitful dreams, groaning or wincing from time to time.

Agbar looked at her thoughtfully. At the moment the sight of her, trim and bare, did not stir his blood. He had come around to a solicitous, almost motherly feeling for her while cleaning her up in preparation for the little scenario that had begun to take shape in his mind. And now the discovery that she, too, dreamed, and presumably dreamed of the things that had happened to her during their first encounter . . . this put some interesting thoughts in motion in his mind.

Agbar's evolution into what he was had come by stages; the greater his finances and the greater the power he wielded in Sodom, the more latitude he had had to make his own sexual daydreams come true. And, irresistibly, his own nature had unfolded to him little by little, unaccompanied by much understanding of the thoughts or natural inclinations of others.

Now, looking at Shepset in her troubled sleep, an odd notion occurred to him. What if the girl's dreams, which spoke visibly of pain and fear, were also in some way pleasurable to her . . . as his own pain ultimately pleasured him on the odd occasions when he visited the whores, male and female, at the House of Pain?

Agbar wiped his sweaty brow—it was getting close in here!—and stood up, slowly and painfully. His knee joints complained bitterly; steadying himself as he rose, he reached out and put one hand against the wall . . .

and then recoiled in pain. It was hot to the touch, like the stones of a recently used oven!

He wiped his forehead again. Then it *wasn't* his imagination! And . . . there was the smoke in the room, a little earlier, before he'd closed the shutters tight against it.

He reached for the bolt on the nearby shutter. It burned his hand! He cried out in pain!

"Yamm!" he called for the supervisor of his slave staff. "Yamm, where are you? Come quickly! I need you!" And, unwilling to wait, he waddled to the front door of his house. The bolt on this door was cool to the touch; he opened it with ease.

The street was deserted. Across it, his neighbor's house stood, a blackened hulk, gutted by fire. He stepped out into the street; his next-door neighbor's house was ablaze! The roof was in flames! Fire licked out of the open window!

"Gods!" he said. He looked up and down the street. The twin thoroughfares that abutted on his one-block street were walls of fire. He was cut off from any avenue of escape.

"Yamm!" he bellowed again, fear clutching at his guts. "Yamm, where are you? Answer me!"

He rushed back inside. There was always the back way.

Behind him, Shepset groaned. He glanced at her quickly and forgot her. "Gods!" she said, her voice hoarse and husky. "We're on fire! Please! Let me loose! My ankle . . ."

He ignored her. "Yamm!" he bellowed. He made his way to the back door that led into the alley behind. In the little street the neighbor's fire raged on the one side; the other seemed, for now, unobstructed. He rushed back inside his house. No doubt about it, the whole street was going to go. He had little time, very little indeed. His valuables . . .

Shepset, with fevered fingers, tore at the knot that held her. Every moment or so she would glance at the open window, where she could see the windblown smoke drift past. The city! The city was on fire! And

Agbar's household had apparently deserted him, as everyone had—to judge from the empty street out the front door—deserted this quarter.

She kept quiet now. Now that she'd had time to think about it, her only chance seemed to lie in *not* being noticed by Agbar. If she could only loosen these knots, perhaps she could run for it. Perhaps there might be a chance for her to escape him. With no servants to run errands for him, she could easily outdistance him on foot, slow as he was.

There was a nearby noise; a sharp one, one that carried above the dull roar of the flames next door. She looked up, startled, to see Yamm standing before her, a stolen sword belt around his middle and a small box in one hand. The box glittered with gold trim and inset jewels. He put one finger over his lips. "Shhh!" he whispered. He patted the sword, pointed to the rope around her ankle. "I've been feeling bad about you. I hope he didn't hurt you too much."

"Please," she whispered back at him. "Cut me loose. We've got to get out of here."

"Yes," he said. "The old fool is in the back looking for his baubles. I've got them, and I'm going to take them with me. But . . . I got you into this, my dear, and . . . here." He put the box down and drew the sword to saw away at the rope restraining her. She let her eyes roam the room. There was a pile of cloth in one corner: perhaps rags, perhaps something she could find some clothing in.

"You're strange," she whispered. "I thought you looked like a good man. Then you betrayed me. Now—"

"Years of slavery don't make you good, my dear. They make you uncommonly self-centered. You do what lands you in the least trouble. But in the end, when you're up against it, well . . ."

"Up against it? You mean we're trapped?"

"We may well be. There's no way out up front. I've just established that. There may be a way out in back. If there is, we'll take it. But he . . . he'll never make it. He's too heavy. He can't move fast enough. Now's our chance to make it to freedom. And if I go, I go first class." He nodded at the stolen jewels.

He hacked at the rope. "Now," he whispered. "Pull! Pull loose."

"*Yamm!*" cried a voice behind him. "What are you doing? I've been calling for you." Then, as the two of them whirled to look at the fat man standing over them, Agbar spotted the sword, the little box of valuables. "So . . . you were going to . . . you ungrateful swine! You . . ."

Yamm tried to bring the sword up in time; but the fat man's heavy arm, with all his weight behind it, swung out and knocked the slave reeling. The sword clattered to the ground. Agbar, with surprising agility for his bulk, picked it up and made for the fallen slave. Yamm, his eyes full of fear, scuttled backward on hands and knees.

"You dog! You son of a whore!" Agbar said, his voice full of petulance and venom. "You'd steal from me, after all I've . . ." He swung the sword; it caught Yamm's arm a glancing blow, opening a wound. The gray-haired slave got his feet under him and dodged backward, trying to circle away from Agbar's sword arm. "Pig!" Agbar screamed. "You . . . you abortion. . . ."

A heavy, shuddering tremor shook the ground beneath their feet. It was the strongest tremor so far, and it knocked both men to the ground. A huge oblique crack appeared in the wall behind them; a section of the roof collapsed inward in a cloud of dust. Outside they could hear even louder crashes over the constant hum of the fire.

Agbar recovered first, picking up the sword and lunging, still on his knees, at Yamm. The slave, crying out, jumped backward. Agbar got to his feet. Yamm was cornered now; the fat man knew it, and smiled. He moved forward, the sword in his hand. . . .

Another aftershock hit. Shepset, still pulling on the rope, felt the last fibers part, freeing her, just as another section of the roof fell free. A giant timber, its moorings loosened, dropped like a stone, crushing the fat man to the ground in a heap of gross, bloody flesh. Shepset caught a quick sight of Agbar's head, smashed to pieces by the blow, and looked away. "Yamm!" she said. "Are you all right?"

"I . . . I think so. But . . . I have a terrible feeling. I've got to have a look." She watched as he scampered to the open back door. "Just as I thought," he said. "There's a wall fallen down the way. We've got some climbing to do. Get something on, quickly!" He headed back to where the box stood on the floor near the cut end of the rope; picking up the little container, he then walked over to the remains of his master and pried the sword from the dead fingers.

He sighed deeply and, for a moment, seemed to come apart. "I could scarcely bear to touch him," he said, weeping. "The . . . the bad things I've done in his service . . . how can I . . . ?"

"Come," she said, slipping a simple tunic over her head and stepping into a pair of slightly too large sandals. "Forget all that. The thing is to get out. The . . ."

There was another shake, and a violent crash outside. The doorway disappeared in a cloud of dust.

Out of the dust stepped a figure, tall and commanding. The figure stood silhouetted in the doorway for a moment, trying to brush away the dust and smoke. "Shepset?" it said.

"Ahuni!" the girl cried out, and rushed into his arms.

The embrace lasted no more than a moment; with a quick extra squeeze, Ahuni let her go. "Quickly," he said. "We may be cut off by now. I barely got through as it was. If the fire has reached . . ." Then he noticed Yamm. "Who—"

"This is Yamm," she said. "He helped me to escape from Agbar . . . who lies dead over there under the timber."

"Good," Ahuni said, nodding to the gray-haired man. "You're sure to know the streets of the city better than I do. I'll tell you what's closed off right now, and you can tell me what the alternatives may be."

"Fine," Yamm said. "But let's do it while walking. I gather the quarter's largely evacuated by now."

"Yes," Ahuni said, leading them into the street. "We may be the last people left alive in this section of the city. I ... oh, no. The wind's turning. So far we've escaped the smoke—but now it'll be blowing our way. Quickly...."

They passed through one gutted bazaar whose stones, underfoot, were hot to the touch; Shepset was thankful for the ill-fitting sandals she'd found. Now the smoke blew at them in gusts as the fire storm raged to the south and east; everywhere they looked they could see smoke and flames as a backdrop for the city. And now, as they looked across the rooftops that framed the ruined bazaar, they saw new columns of smoke rising above the northwestern quarter of the doomed city. "I could have told you," Ahuni said. "That was the way I came in. I hadn't made it a hundred strides into the area before a grain warehouse behind me collapsed, blocking the street. You can cross off the whole quarter. There's only one route left to safety— toward the southwest gate." He broke into a jog and the others followed suit.

"Southwest?" Yamm said. "Try that alley over there." Ahuni headed in the direction the slave pointed; but halfway down the block they had to reverse their direction, as a wall of rubble higher than a man's head blocked their way. They tried another street and found it already a holocaust, in which the blackened remains of dead bodies could be seen through the leaping flames.

Shepset, rounding a corner suddenly, ran into a faceful of smoke; she collapsed for a moment into Ahuni's arms, coughing. Ahuni looked at Yamm. "Well?" he said.

The gray-haired man shot him a perplexed look. "I ... I'm not sure. We may be blocked off. I mean ... well, there's another way, perhaps, but ... here, now. What's this?"

He stopped dead. They followed his gaze. In the middle of the wrecked, charred bazaar stood a boy, dirty, skinny, unkempt; he wore only a tattered rag about his loins, and the slave-mark stood out on his scrawny arm.

"There's a way out," the boy said. "But . . . it's full of looters. I tried it. I couldn't fight my way through. Maybe . . . maybe if you . . ." He looked nervously from face to face.

Another aftershock—was it the twentieth? the fiftieth?—jarred the ground underfoot; the boy fell to one knee, his face full of fear. Behind him a weakened wall fell to the ground in a jumble of bricks; high above the ruins of the house new flames leaped as yet another wooden roof caught fire. They could feel the heat on their faces.

Ahuni stepped forward to help the boy up—and his heart almost stopped. Looking into the child's twelve-year-old eyes and seeing the sudden flash of weary, forty-year-old wariness, he suddenly, for no more than a moment, felt the years fall away. He saw himself standing there, skinny, dirty, desperate.

He clapped the boy reassuringly on one shoulder. "You know a way, son? Show it to us. We're in your hands."

V

"Now," Belanum said, one hand on each of Lot's shoulders, looking him squarely in the eye. "You're sure you'll be all right—you and the girls? You're quite sure?"

Lot's pupils danced, avoiding his inquiring glare. "Yes," he said in a phlegmy voice. He looked back down the hill at the black flames that had all but engulfed the walled city, at the milling thousands around it. "I . . . I suppose I'm luckier than most. I've herdsmen on the slopes above. . . . I can stay with them for now."

"Is that the best idea?" Belanum said, pressing the matter. "I mean, you could go to Zoar, or . . ."

"Oh, yes," Lot said. "I . . . suppose I could. But look. You go on. Don't worry about us." He glanced at the girls; they were playing some leaping, athletic child's game, paying no attention at all to the fire. "Go back. Save your friends. And . . . tell them something for me, will you?"

"Yes?" Belanum stood back, still looking hard at him.

"About . . . about Enosh. Zillah bragged about having him . . . assassinated. I had no idea. It was done before I heard of it. I . . . I'm sorry. You see. Agbar was pressuring me. . . . We owed him money, a great deal of money. But . . . I'd never have done that."

"I'll tell them," Belanum said, thin-lipped, without sympathy. "Is that all? I've got to go. Ahuni . . ."

Lot put a hand on his arm; Belanum tried not to shrink away from his touch, but the loathing showed in his eyes. "Please," Lot said. "It's important. There was something Zillah didn't know. I . . . I registered the sale of Shepset—"

"Yes, I know about that," Belanum said coldly. "Now, will you please—"

"No. No, you don't. I mean—I registered the sale to Enosh. It was witnessed before the scribe. I was sending the documents over to Mamre's Grove when I heard of Enosh's . . . death." His face was full of self-loathing. "Please . . . tell them . . . the girl is Enosh's. And I suppose Ahuni's, if he was a partner in the purchase."

"I'll tell them," Belanum said. "If they're still alive. Farewell!" And he turned and began to jog down the hill, gathering speed little by little. Lot noticed the girls, now still, looking at him. An enigmatic smile played on Adah's features: half mocking, half . . . what? Almost carnal. . . .

The commercial quarter was the last one remaining in the all-but-gutted city. Within it, madness reigned. The merchants had fled first of all; they had been followed by the residents. But none of these had suc-

ceeded in getting all of their valuables to safety. Much
had had to be abandoned. Now, with the haves gone,
the have-nots came into their own, and a man was free
to take from the empty houses whatever he could carry
away. After that, it was a matter of keeping what you
had taken—and for that, a man had to carry a knife
and know how to use it. Evidence of this was to be
found every few steps in the cluttered streets; dead
bodies, gutted, throats cut, lay untended everywhere.
Some of these had once been women—and the bloody
corpses of these showed that sexual violence, too, had
attended their last struggles.

Climbing to the top of a wall, Ahuni looked down
into this madhouse. Then he stepped back to where his
companions awaited him on the far side. Briefly he
explained what he'd seen: a solid wall of knife-
wielding flesh through which they'd have to cut their
way—all the while protecting an almost-naked girl and
a child.

"No," Yamm said. "I've no fear of a fight, but . . . I
don't think we can keep these two safe through that.
No, Ahuni."

Surprisingly the big armorer agreed. "Well said. But
. . . with this avenue of escape gone, what is there?"

"Help me up," Yamm said. "I'll look around."
Ahuni boosted the gray-haired man to the top of the
wall and stood holding his legs. As he did he looked
back down the street they'd come in on: at the end of
the block the flames already licked into the cross
street. There was no place to go but forward. Shepset
caught his thought and, one arm still around the boy's
shoulders, reached out to touch Ahuni's bicep reassuringly. Her lips shaped silent words: *I love you.* . . .

"Well," Yamm said from the top of the wall.
"There's one chance. If we can get to shelter before
that crowd spots Shepset and the boy . . . there's a
warehouse that's backed up against the city wall. I've
been in it . . . it has an upstairs loft, and the loft has a
window. We could perhaps make it from the window
to the top of the city wall. I'm sure we could get down
from there—down, and outside the city." He sighed.
"But . . ." He jumped down and brushed himself off.

"But?" Ahuni said.

"Well, you'll have to see for yourself. The flames are getting close to the warehouse, too. The wind's shifted, and the fire is spreading rapidly down from the northwestern corner. And—"

"Look, the fire's spreading down this *street*," Ahuni said. "We'll try your warehouse. Shepset? Up the wall with you."

"No, no," Yamm said. "You go first. We'll want a man with a sword on the other side before Shepset and the boy go over. We don't want them landing unprotected—and the crowd seeing them. If you go over first, you're big enough that if they see you they may think twice about attacking."

"Good thought," Ahuni said. And, in one quick motion, he went to the top of the wall and over.

Stepping down into the street, he could see what Yamm had talked about. He stood at the end of a short alley, in a cross street; at the alley's other end he could see the rape of the commercial quarter in full swing. As he watched, he could see two men attacking a third, from front and rear; their deft knife strokes left him in ribbons as they ransacked the dying body for valuables: a purse, rings, anything.

Next over the wall was Shepset. He helped her down, keeping one wary eye on the scene at the end of the alley. Then the boy vaulted lightly down into his arms. Ahuni shooed them to cover and only then motioned to Yamm to come down. When all four were out of the looters' view, Ahuni whispered, "All right. That warehouse you were talking about."

Yamm's face was grave. "Ahuni, I had a good look at it again, coming over the top. It . . . it's going to be very dangerous. The fire is *very* close now; maybe too close."

"Never mind," Ahuni said. "We're already browned on one side now. If the building lasts long enough for us to make it to the roof—"

"But . . . there is a problem. The warehouse—"

"Yes? Yes, man! Out with it!"

"Damn it, it's full of oil. Dozens and dozens— maybe hundreds—they usually stock up at festival time—of tall jars of oil." He looked Ahuni in the eye, speaking the words carefully for emphasis. "*Lamp* oil, Ahuni. Do you know what's going to happen when the flames reach it? It'll be the end of the city, with only this quarter remaining."

Ahuni bit his lip; looked again at Shepset and the boy. "That means we haven't much time. Come on, all of you."

Things were worse than they'd thought. So far the warehouse hadn't been touched; but the winds were now driving the flames hard, from the inferno of the northwest corner of Sodom to the south. And, to make things even worse, in the first panic after the fire had broken out, someone had tried to pull a cart loaded high with lamp-oil jars out of the warehouse and down the street. The cart had proven too heavy and had been abandoned in the middle of the thoroughfare. Now, from the north, flames from a burning house licked out toward the vulnerable wood of the cart, with its explosive cargo. To gain the warehouse they'd have to pass within an arm's length of the wagon—and if and when the wagon's contents blew up, the warehouse itself would be quick to follow.

Nodding to his companions, Ahuni set out down the street at a trot, hearing their footsteps behind him.

And as he did, the flames reached the wagon. The softer wood of the driver's high seat was the first thing to catch fire. For a moment, breaking into a dead run, he thought of trying to move the cart farther from the warehouse; but then he saw how loosely the jars were packed in the back of the wagon. If one of them were to lose balance and fall . . .

He broke stride, looked behind him. He saw Shepset trip on the outsized sandals and fall; when she arose she kicked the cumbersome shoes off and broke into a boyish sprint. Yamm and the boy passed him. "Quickly," he told them. "Up into the loft, as fast as you can."

Shepset slipped past him into the open door of the warehouse. Only then did he follow her. Inside, the jars were packed tightly on one side, and sparsely arranged on the other. Access to the half-loft was by a knotted rope ladder. Yamm struggled up this. At the top the boy awaited them, holding a thin little hand down to Yamm.

Ahuni looked nervously back at the wagon in the doorway. The flames ate away at the front wheels. When the spokes gave way the wagon would tip forward; the jars would tip forward with it, spilling the oil directly into the path of the leaping flames. "Quick, Shepset," he said. "Up the rope."

Last of all, he himself climbed the rope hand over hand. Shepset bent over the edge, watching him. "Hurry, Ahuni!" she said. "The wagon's giving way."

From the window Yamm called out. "Ahuni!" he said. "The catwalk's old and rotten. You can't walk on it. But . . . there's a loading hoist here, and a rope . . . maybe we can swing across to the city wall."

Ahuni made it to the window, Shepset at his side. In the open air they could already feel the heat of the fire across the narrow street; down in the right-of-way the wheels of the wagon were blazing merrily; already the earthen sides of the lamp-oil pots in the wagon would be hot to the touch . . . yes! One of them had cracked from the heat, and a trickle of oil spilled down into the street. The flames caught this, and now a line of flickering flames connected the raging blaze across the street with the wagon, and with the warehouse itself. The trickle became a rivulet, the rivulet a . . .

"Oh, Ahuni," Shepset said. "I . . . I can't swing over there on that rope. I—"

"Yes you can!" Ahuni said in a hoarse, insistent whisper. He squeezed her arm. "Look, I'll go over first. Then, when one of you swings to me, I can grab him and pull him up onto the wall. I'm the only one of us strong enough to do that."

"Right!" Yamm said in a tense voice. "Do it! *Do it!* Don't talk about it."

Below, the street itself was aflame. Now the rear wheels of the wagon ignited, soaked with oil as they were.

Ahuni grasped the rope, took a deep breath, and swung—far out, over the blazing street, feeling the heat of the flames below. His heart almost stopped for a moment . . . but then his feet were on the parapet, and, wobbling crazily, he got his balance and wrapped one arm around an upright timber. He let out a deep breath. "Here," he said, and tossed the rope back with one mighty heave. Yamm caught it and handed it to Shepset.

Below there was a flash of flame from inside the warehouse. *Inside* the warehouse! "Quick, Shepset!" Ahuni bellowed. "Hold on tight . . . don't look down. I'll catch you when you get here."

The girl struggled with the binding sleeves of her tunic; then, in one rapid motion, she pulled it over her head and threw it into the street. Naked, she grasped the rope and swung, out, far out. . . .

Again his heart almost stopped beating . . . but in a moment she was in his arms. He gave her a quick hug and shoved her to the far side of the city wall, away from the blazing street below. "Here, Yamm!" he bellowed. "Now, the boy."

But as he threw the rope back, the front wheels of the cart gave way. The oil jars spilled forward, into the path of the advancing flames.

The fire leaped forward in one great rush—across the little street, into the open door of the warehouse.

"No! No!" screamed Shepset behind him.

A fierce tremor shook the city once again. Ahuni was almost shaken off the wall. Shepset fell at his feet, holding onto the wooden upright that projected from the wall.

Below, a huge crack appeared in the street. Vile-smelling steam issued forth. Half a dozen sulphurous fumaroles opened in the ground below them. And . . .

"No!" Ahuni said. His fists clenched spasmodically. Impotently.

The warehouse in whose upper window Yamm and the boy stood slowly collapsed beneath their feet. He watched them fall in slow motion, as if in a dream . . . and as they fell the flames at last reached the standing jars inside the building. Ahuni flattened himself beside Shepset on the top of the high city wall. There was a terrific flare of intense heat, and a sound louder than anything they could ever have imagined, and the wall beneath them shook as if another tremor had hit.

Ahuni sat up, watching the flames and black smoke. His eyes sought Shepset's. "Ahuni!" she screamed. "You're on fire!" He looked down: his robe was ablaze. He sat up, ripped at it, flung it away down into the smoke-filled street to stand beside her as naked as she.

They took one last look into the streets below them. Ten fumaroles had become a hundred. A huge geyser of stinking steam shot high into the air. Where the warehouse had been was now a wall of flame; the wind had changed and was blowing away from them now, and they could see no sign of life in the city anywhere. "Poor Yamm," Shepset said. "And the boy ... Ahuni, we never even learned his name."

"Don't think about them now," he said. "Let's get down from here—outside the walls—before the wind changes again. Here's a rope. I'll toss it down, and ..." He stopped short, a strange, pained look on his face. "Shepset," he said. "Father's sword. I must have left it in the warehouse. It's gone."

Shepset took the rope from his hands and looked at him with fierce pride. "It isn't gone," she said. She tapped his forehead gently with a soot-stained finger. "It's up here, Ahuni. You can't lose it any more. And you don't need it any more—it, or anything else. You're not a user, you're a maker. You can make everything you'll ever need." Her hand brushed his cheek. "Now ... let's get out of here."

Thus it was that Belanum, coming down the hill, saw them land on safe ground at last with nothing but each other, naked as First Man and First Woman. But of course she was right. They needed nothing, and could make everything they needed for themselves. Even a dynasty of armorers. ...

Dusk overtook the three of them, still far short of any city or settlement. As the evening wind changed directions, Hagar could feel a dank chill in it; she pulled the shawl closer about her and shivered. "Ishmael," she said. "Put something on. You'll catch your death of—"

But just then her eye caught Elishama's. There was a look on his face midway between deep sympathy and resentment, and for a brief moment she felt something like pity for him, her captor. After all, he was doing what he was doing under orders, and he didn't like it. And here she'd used the word *death,* and reminded him of his bitter and hateful errand.

Ishmael, up ahead, gave no sign he'd heard. She spoke again, this time to Elishama. "I suppose it's time for you to return, isn't it? I mean, if you're going to make it back by morning."

Elishama bit his lip. "How can I leave the two of you here?" he said. "I'll be abandoning you to your deaths."

"Well, that's what you were sent to do," she said. "Look. It's all right. I forgive you."

"I won't forgive myself," he said. "I know the Negeb at night, at this season. I can help you make camp . . . but there are scorpions, poisonous snakes, wild beasts. . . ."

"I know the Negeb better than you," she said. "I walked all the way from Egypt across it—yes, and across worse country than that, when you were a child. Nine parts naked, too, in worse weather than this."

Elishama's face contorted with self-loathing. "How can I leave you?" he said. "I've been asked to do some cruel things, but—"

"Help us make camp," she said. "You bear no blame in this." She turned, raised her voice. "Ishmael! Ishmael! We'll make camp here."

The boy turned now and came back to her. "All right, Mother." There was a sullen look of resentment on his face as he added, "Is *he* staying with us?"

"No," she said. She looked off to the west. "We've a few more moments' sun," she said. "The moon will rise three-quarters full. He'll help us set up for the night, then . . ."

But the boy stood, hands on hips, facing them. "Tell him to go away, Mother. I can make camp for the two of us. We don't need help from any—"

"Ishmael!" She turned to Elishama, embarrassed. "Don't mind him. But . . . he's right. We can make camp for ourselves, now that I think about it. And the less we're reminded of . . . well, back there . . ."

"I understand." His face was desolate. "Then I'll take my leave of you." And he turned to go. She watched him for a moment or two, then turned to her son. He was already tugging the sheepskins down from the donkey's back. As he threw the first one down, she could see the determination in his face, the strength in his untested young body. And, through the gloom that had settled on her, she felt a sudden thrill. Her son! Her own proud, lion-hearted, manly, son!

The wind stirred her hair again, and another chill ran through her body. She shivered . . . and happened to look up the road, to the point where the Beersheba road wound westward to the top of a low hill before turning back south again.

All the breath went out of her.

She put one hand to her heart. And when she got her breath again there flowed into her a feeling she had never experienced before, not even with Sneferu. A feeling of peace, contentment, unalloyed joy. She sighed, and the sigh was almost a sob. Somehow she'd known . . . somehow, in her heart . . .

The man on the horse stood looking down at them, silhouetted against the sunset, waving a ruined right arm. He was as solid, as broad as a stone statue, and he sat a horse as if he and the animal were one. She had never seen anything so strong, so manly, so powerful, in her life. Yes! Yes! Here was a rock to lean on, to shelter one against the wind and the cold. Here was sustenance sweet as honey in the comb. And somehow, somehow she'd known he'd come, and the thought had put heart into her all the way from Mamre's Grove.

Now, though, Ishmael looked up and saw him, and with a wild cry he ran up the hill in a mad sprint. The man on the horse dismounted and walked down to meet them, the reins in his left hand. When man and boy came together, Zakir's right arm swept him off the ground and hugged him to his bearlike chest—but his eyes were only for her.

"Z-Zakir!" the boy said. He hugged the burly man close. And Zakir's other arm reached out to beckon Hagar forward. "Hagar," he said. "Come. Come, my dear." She walked forward as if hypnotized, stifling the urge to break into a run as Ishmael had done. There was, after all, no need to run. That comforting arm beckoned not for now, but for always. She smiled, and threw the shawl off her long hair, knowing how he loved the sight of it. And now she could see his broad grin, open, loving, warm, accepting. "My darling," he said in that mellow voice of his. "We're going home. Wherever that turns out to be."

CHAPTER TWENTY-ONE

I

The great feast celebrating the circumcision of Abraham's infant son, and his consecration to Abraham's God, gave way to the wedding feast of Ahuni and Shepset; the chieftains from the surrounding country stayed over and put heavy burdens on Abraham's bounty for many days. Ahuni and Shepset, radiant in their own happiness, thought the old man had never seemed so young or so vigorous. He bore the immense cost of the feast with kingly largesse, gaining greatly in the respect of his neighbors; Ahuni noted with interest that intertribal disputes were now routinely referred to Abraham for arbitration.

There was a time for feasting, however, and there was a time for parting. When Belanum returned a second time from the Egyptian camp near Enmishpat, Abraham knew that the young couple would be leaving with him soon. He came to Ahuni's tents and found the armorer loading the pack asses while Shepset packed his small traveling forge.

Here he stood looking at them for a moment, a slow smile spreading over his old face. Ahuni turned to face him. "Speak," he said. "I'd like to hear what thoughts provoke so happy a smile."

"I was thinking," Abraham said, "of your father— of Belsunu. There was a great sadness in him, and all of us who knew him constantly wished that something would happen to drive the sadness away. Seeing things turn out well for you, Ahuni—it's like seeing a happy end come to Belsunu after all these years."

"My good friend," Ahuni said, embracing the old man. "Here I spent so many years with no father at all . . . and now I have three. It's indecent." He stood back, looking Abraham in the eye. "But let's have no talk of endings. It's a time of beginnings. For all of us." He made room inside the curve of his long arm for Shepset, who snuggled close to him. "Beginnings," he said. "You've a new son; Canaan has a new prince and a new nation and a new faith. Shepset and I have a new life, better and richer than the old could ever have been. Even Belanum, who has had little to do with women in all the time I've known him . . . well, he tells me there's an Amorite girl in Enmishpat who—"

"Ahuni," Belanum said, blushing like a girl. "Please."

"Don't be ashamed of it," Abraham said. "It's the greatest blessing of all." His face darkened for a moment. "I was going to ask, but I almost don't know how. Zakir and Hagar?"

"It's all right, sir. She wouldn't come back—the memories bother her, you understand, and she wants Ishmael to think of the future instead. But Zakir is warm and accepting and gentle with her, and I think there are few hurts she has ever suffered that will not in time heal at his hands."

"I see. I'm glad."

"Yes. Give Ishmael five years with Zakir and . . . Besides, the boy is a natural leader himself. The time will come when he will be the head of a tribe of his own." He stopped, blinked, looked nervously at Ahuni.

Abraham's eyes followed his. "Ahuni," he said. "Then you'll be going to Enmishpat too?"

"For a while. I have some work to finish for Nakht-minou, and then he wants to send me back to the garrison at Sile, to make arms for the outpost there. It appears that Sesostris, the Lord of Two Lands, is beginning to remember that he comes from a warlike line. The blood of Amenemhet is stirring in his veins. He plans personal inspection tours of all his border fortresses, and Nakhtminou wants me to put the arms of his own garrison in order."

"Then your work will be seen by the Great King," Abraham said. "Ah, when I think of how arrogantly I treated him when we left Egypt, and what could have come of that . . . well, of course the God was looking out for us, as always." He smiled wryly. "Then most likely you'll end up doing more work in the service of the king . . . perhaps up the Nile."

"I wouldn't be surprised, sir. It'll be a treat for Shepset: she'll get to be among her own people."

"Ahuni," she said. *"You're* my own people." She hugged him happily. "You and Hagar and Zakir and Ishmael and Belanum—"

"And me," Abraham said. "Although it saddens me to think I may never see you again."

"Thank you," Shepset said. "I was going to say . . . I've never had a family before. I feel that I have one now. I've had so little of anything in life . . . now I'm so rich, so . . ." She couldn't say any more in words. She finished the thought with another hug. Ahuni's big arm went around her in a quick, decisive motion.

"You gladden my heart," Abraham said. "All of you. I wish you were of my blood." A fleeting look of sadness passed over his face again. "I have heard news of Lot," he said in a flat voice. "I think he has not drawn a sober breath since the death of Sodom. A herdsman found him and his daughters, living in a cave above Zoar." The disgust in his voice was exquisite. "He was living with them . . . as a man might live with two wives."

Shepset put a hand on his arm. "Don't think about them," she said. "It's no longer your concern. It's a matter between them and—"

"Between them and the God," Abraham said. "I know that." He shook his head sadly. "But I'm not going to let such thoughts spoil our last moments together. Ahuni, will Shepset bear you a Child of the Lion, do you think? One who bears the birthmark?"

"At *least* one, sir," Shepset said enthusiastically. "And if I have my way, there'll be more."

"Well said! And if you do, raise them to know that in all times to come the Children of the Lion will be welcome among the people of Abraham. Five, ten, a hundred generations from now, we'll still be here—and your seed will always find friends among us. We've come to stay," he said with pride.

"Then you'll need us," Ahuni said gravely. "Me and my kind." He gripped Abraham's arm, feeling the strength that remained there even now, in his old age. "You've won this land—but you're going to have to fight to keep it. Stay strong." His arm around the old man's shoulders, he watched as Belanum formed their mounts and pack animals into a straight line. He called out, "Are we ready?"

"Whenever you are," Belanum sang out, helping Shepset up onto her mount.

Ahuni turned, gripped Abraham's hand, looked wordlessly into his eyes. Then he released his grip and sprang onto his horse. He waved once and then turned away. And, step by sure-footed step, the little caravan wound its way down the hill through the olive trees into the broad vale below Mount Hebron.

EPILOGUE

The last words of the Teller of Tales rang in the air. There was a hush upon the crowd, a hush so charged with emotion that the listeners avoided one another's eyes. In the profound quiet a single sound spoke volumes: there was a tiny sob from a woman in the front row, a woman who wept now, quietly, giving vent to an emotion that mixed sadness with joy. It was an emotion all shared.

The last rays of the setting sun picked out the strong features of the Teller of Tales as he stepped forward once again, one hand raised to compel their attention. He spoke in a voice that began softly, then grew in power:

"Attend me, O my beloved," he said. "I go now ... but I will come again. And when next you see me, you will hear how the seed of Abraham spread through the land; how his sons and grandsons became kings, lords of great wealth and power—only to risk all against the might of an invader so strong, so ruthless, that none could stand before it. You will hear of the Shepherd Kings, and how they came to the Lands of the Covenant, bringing death and slavery with them...."

There was a great sigh from the crowd. The Teller of Tales gestured them to silence with a sorcerer's hand. He continued in a strong voice:

"*You* will hear of how war came to the Lands of the Crescent, and of how the great strife called the seed of Abraham home from exile to defend the land of his fathers. *You* will hear how the conflict also called forth the seed of Ahuni, the Children of the Lion, to arm them against the merciless hordes from the northern lands. . . ."

He held their complete attention now, and seemed for a moment about to continue. Instead, he held those magician's hands high to erase, for now, for tonight, the outlines of the picture he had once again begun to create for them. His eyes swept over the crowd; silent, palms pressed together over his chest, he bowed his head slightly. Implied in the eloquent, almost reverent gesture was the promise of gifts to come: a rich and vivid tapestry full of thought and emotion, to be unrolled for their delight on some morrow. A tale that would weave the destinies of many men and women. A tale of love and hatred, of births and deaths, of jealousy and treachery and sacrifice and fear and exultation and passion. The magic had passed for now; but it would come again.

"Go with God," the Teller of Tales said. And night fell. . . .

Volume II in the
Children of the Lion saga

THE SHEPHERD KINGS

by Peter Danielson

It is a time of civil strife, a time of revolution, a time of change. Far across the Great Sea, on the sea-girt isle of Crete, a bloody rebellion threatens the mighty throne of Minos, greatest of the sea kings. To the south, the grandsons of the great leader Abraham have broken his kingdom in half, and Jacob, though heir to the kingdom and priest to the God of Abraham, has fled in mortal danger to the Plains of Aram, in the foothills far to the north of Damascus.

Worse—Haran, the city in which Jacob has taken refuge, is arming for war—too slowly, some say. Far to the northeast, a great migration of nomads, as numerous as stars in the desert sky, is moving south, fleeing a continent-wide drought in the European steppes. Settlements, towns, cities that lie in their bloody path are doomed, as the nomads cut a wide slash across the grasslands of the north country. And Haran, peaceful and powerless, lies directly within their deadly route to the sea.

But Haran has forgotten the way of war and is ill prepared to defend itself. Its garrison is captained by a brave and wise soldier—to whom no one listens. Its arms were once made by Kirta, son of Ahuni, one of the Children of the Lion; but Kirta is away on a ten-year quest for the secret of the smelting of iron, and cannot help arm the city.

His crippled, great-hearted son, Hadad, is the REAL Child of the Lion, an artist in metal or in any other medium. However, never having been able to afford an expensive apprenticeship, he is barred from the Guild of Artisans.

As pressure builds on the doomed city, the lives of our characters change. Hadad meets Jacob and the friendship between the exiled King of Canaan and the crippled artist, spiritual father and son, sets their feet on double paths of destiny. Jacob, whose years of exile have been years of bondage, takes his life in hand and decides to return to Canaan to claim his ancestral kingdom. He wants to save it from the wrath of the nomadic hordes with whom his enemy-brother, Esau, a hothead, cannot deal. But can he get away before the nomads arrive and the city falls? Hadad, comforted by Jacob's fatherly hand, falls in love with shy, beautiful Dana-taya, an orphan girl, who befriends him. Through the love of this remarkable young woman, a heroine in her own right, he finds courage to go on, and a clue to the greatness that is within him. It is their son who will pass on the precious gift of the Children of the Lion, the armorer caste who bear the legendary mark of Cain: the child will carry the seed of the family's immortal artistry to the next generation.

Now, however, Kirta discovers the secret he has been looking for: the secret of the making of iron. He barely escapes with his life from the bloody revolution which deposes and kills his patron, Minos of Crete, and heads east. In his hands is a priceless secret which could save Haran. But will he arrive in time?

One by one, Haran's defenses fall. Pacifists and adventurers infiltrate the city government, and weaken its armies and its strategy. Outright traitors sell her out to the enemy. Its only really valiant defender, the war-wise commander of the garrison, is jailed on trumped-up charges. And as the monster armies approach, bearing new and awesome weapons and invincible numbers, the odds against Haran's survival expand beyond all count.

With the enemy at the gates, Jacob and his beautiful wife, Rachel, prepare to face down his powerful, dictatorial employer, Laban, who will do virtually anything to keep him from leaving. And, as the last hopes die for Haran's future, only one man remains to save the city in its last hours—the weak and noble-hearted cripple, Hadad, who has never struck a blow in anger during his life, but who sets out on a quest, alone and unarmed, deep in enemy territory, hoping to save his city from certain death and destruction.

Fast moving, action packed, with flesh and blood characters of tragic and heroic stature, THE SHEPHERD KINGS builds to a tremendous shattering climax, carrying powerfully forward the magnificent legend begun with CHILDREN OF THE LION!

FROM THE PRODUCER OF WAGONS WEST
AND THE KENT FAMILY CHRONICLES COMES
A SWEEPING SAGA OF WAR AND HEROISM
AT THE BIRTH OF A NATION

THE WHITE INDIAN SERIES

THIS THRILLING SERIES TELLS THE COMPELLING
STORY OF AMERICA'S BIRTH AGAINST THE
EQUALLY EXCITING ADVENTURES OF AN
ENGLISH CHILD RAISED AS A SENECA.

☐	24650-X	White Indian	$4.50
☐	25020-5	The Renegade	$4.50
☐	24751-4	War Chief	$4.50
☐	24476-0	The Sachem	$4.50
☐	25154-6	Renno	$4.50
☐	25039-6	Tomahawk	$4.50
☐	25589-4	War Cry	$3.95
☐	25202-X	Ambush	$4.50
☐	23986-4	Seneca	$4.50
☐	24492-2	Cherokee	$4.50
☐	24950-9	Choctaw	$4.50
☐	25353-0	Seminole	$4.99
☐	25868-0	War Drums	$3.95
☐	26206-8	Apache	$4.99
☐	27161-X	Spirit Knife	$4.50
☐	27264-0	Manitou	$4.50
☐	27841-X	Seneca Warrior	$4.99
☐	28285-9	Father of Waters	$4.99
☐	28474-6	Fallen Timbers	$4.50
☐	28805-9	Sachem's Son	$4.50
☐	29028-2	Sachem's Daughter	$4.99
☐	29217-X	Seneca Patriots	$4.99

★ WAGONS WEST ★

This continuing, magnificent saga recounts the adventures of a brave band of settlers, all of different backgrounds, all sharing one dream—to find a new and better life.

- ☐ 26822-8   **INDEPENDENCE! #1** $4.95
- ☐ 26162-2   **NEBRASKA! #2** $4.95
- ☐ 26242-4   **WYOMING! #3** $4.95
- ☐ 26072-3   **OREGON! #4** $4.50
- ☐ 26070-7   **TEXAS! #5** $4.99
- ☐ 26377-3   **CALIFORNIA! #6** $4.99
- ☐ 26546-6   **COLORADO! #7** $4.95
- ☐ 26069-3   **NEVADA! #8** $4.99
- ☐ 26163-0   **WASHINGTON! #9** $4.50
- ☐ 26073-1   **MONTANA! #10** $4.95
- ☐ 26184-3   **DAKOTA! #11** $4.50
- ☐ 26521-0   **UTAH! #12** $4.50
- ☐ 26071-5   **IDAHO! #13** $4.50
- ☐ 26367-6   **MISSOURI! #14** $4.50
- ☐ 27141-5   **MISSISSIPPI! #15** $4.95
- ☐ 25247-X   **LOUISIANA! #16** $4.50
- ☐ 25622-X   **TENNESSEE! #17** $4.50
- ☐ 26022-7   **ILLINOIS! #18** $4.95
- ☐ 26533-4   **WISCONSIN! #19** $4.95
- ☐ 26849-X   **KENTUCKY! #20** $4.95
- ☐ 27065-6   **ARIZONA! #21** $4.99
- ☐ 27458-9   **NEW MEXICO! #22** $4.95
- ☐ 27703-0   **OKLAHOMA! #23** $4.95
- ☐ 28180-1   **CELEBRATION! #24** $4.50

Bantam Books, Dept. LE, 414 East Golf Road, Des Plaines, IL 60016

Please send me the items I have checked above. I am enclosing $_____
(please add $2.50 to cover postage and handling). Send check or money order, no cash or C.O.D.s please.

Mr/Ms _____

Address _____

City/State _____ Zip _____

Please allow four to six weeks for delivery.
Prices and availability subject to change without notice.   LE-9/91